ACCIDENTAL MAGE

JAMIE DAVIS
C.J. DAVIS

MEDICCAST PRODUCTIONS

 Created with Vellum

To the GameLit and LitRPG community. You all have been super supportive of this saga. Enjoy the final chapter in Hal's adventures.
— Jamie Davis

To Madison and my family.
— C.J. Davis

Get a free book and updates on new books.

Go to JamieDavisBooks.com/litrpg-list

—

Accidental Traveller LitRPG Series
Accidental Thief
Accidental Warrior
Accidental Mage

—

Accidental Champion Series
Accidental Duelist

—

Extreme Medical Services Books
Book 1 - *Extreme Medical Services*
Book 2 - *The Paramedic's Angel*
Book 3 - *The Paramedic's Choice*
Book 4 - *The Paramedic's Hunter*
Book 5 - *The Paramedic's Witch*
Book 6 - *The Paramedic's Nemesis*

—

Eldara Sister Series
The Nightingale's Angel
Blue and Gray Angel

—

The Broken Throne Series
The Charm Runner
Prophecy's Child
Queen of Avalon
Stolen Destiny
Mended Throne

PROLOGUE

THE IMPERIAL COURIER struggled to stay on his feet as he slid from
the saddle. Three long days he'd been on the road from Hyroth to the
Crystal City, capital of the Empire. The horse next to him, covered in
streaks of white lather from its extended exertion, was near collapse
as well. It was the sixth and final remount of the string with which
he'd started.

The order given had been clear: deliver the message of Baron
Norak's death and the defeat of the imperial army at the hands of the
rebels with all possible haste. The order was included in the message
he carried, and he knew his life depended on his carrying it out to the
best of his ability.

Two imperial guards stared at him as if he would turn into some
sort of assassin on the spot. Compared to his dust-covered and sweat-
streaked uniform, their gleaming, polished armor fairly blinded him,
reflecting the noonday sun high overhead.

A door opened at the far side of the courtyard. The courier struggled as he straightened to attention, pulling his shoulders back and
erect despite his exhaustion. A purple-robed man in gold slippers and
a polished silver skullcap emerged and strode across the yard until he

stood opposite the courier, scanning his dirty uniform and bedraggled appearance with apparent disgust.

"Well, out with it," the robed man ordered.

"I was told the message was for the Emperor's ears only, uh, sir, uh, my lord." The robed man wasn't an officer, and the courier struggled for an appropriate mode of address.

"If the message is bad news, you do not want to be present when it is delivered to His Imperial Majesty. Hand it over, and I will take it in with the afternoon dispatches."

The courier struggled to work up enough spit to moisten his lips and keep talking.

"By your leave, my lord, I have my orders. I was told to ride by the fastest route to deliver this message to the Emperor. I rode five mounts to death, and I fear this one will not carry a rider ever again. I must deliver this to the Emperor directly."

"Well, it's your funeral. You've been warned. The Emperor doesn't care for his luncheon to be interrupted. If the news you are carrying is sufficiently upsetting — let's just say, the Emperor has been known to literally kill the messenger."

The robed man turned and waved a hand over his shoulder, beckoning to the courier to follow behind him. Shifting the strap of the shoulder bag that carried the written message, the exhausted imperial courier quickstepped forward to catch up and fell in a few steps behind the robed functionary.

The courier tried not to stare wide-eyed at the palace as the man led him through the marble-floored halls, past rooms hung with brightly-colored tapestries and paintings. Every servant and petitioner he passed in his journey through the grand building stared at him. He felt self-conscious due to the unwanted attention and pulled at his wrinkled and stained uniform, trying to brush some of the dust away.

The robed man stopped at a pair of double doors, painted in bright colors of red and gold, the imperial seal prominently displayed in the panels of both doors.

"This is your last chance, soldier. Hand over the message, and I'll see you get a bath and ample reward for your service to His Majesty."

Gulping his doubts down, the courier shook his head without saying anything. He didn't trust his voice.

"Very well," the other man sighed. "When you approach the Emperor, keep your eyes on the floor and don't look him in the eye. As you reach the dais, bow and drop to one knee. Remain there until he acknowledges you. Only then may you stand and deliver your message. After you've handed it to him, step back to your original place and return to one knee while he reads it. If he dismisses you, remain facing him as you back away to the doors and into the hallway before turning around. Understood?"

The courier nodded.

The purple-robed man stepped forward and pushed open the double doors, revealing a room more massive than any the courier had ever seen before. The high ceilings rose upward to buttressed arches high above, and the walls stretched outward to either side before him in a broad square. The ornate floor featured marble slabs inlaid with mosaics of gold and silver, depicting scenes of people engaged in everything from sports to outright debauchery.

Wrenching himself back to the task at hand, he quickstepped to catch up again and followed the man in the robe to a raised dais at the center of the room. A large, round form reclined on a divan on top of the dais with several scantily clad women in diaphanous white and gold silks standing around him. One plucked grapes from a bunch held by another and placed them one at a time in the man's mouth.

Realizing he was staring at the Emperor himself as he approached, the courier wrenched his gaze down to the floor and raised his eyes only enough so he could see the heels of the man leading him up to the dais. When the robed man stopped, the courier halted and dropped to his knees, his eyes glued to the floor in front of him.

"What is it, Decimus? You know I do not like to be bothered this time of the day."

"I'm sorry, Your Majesty. This courier just arrived from the west and insisted his message is for you only. I tried to dissuade him and hold the missive for the afternoon affairs, but he was adamant."

"Adamant, was he? He's either a fool or a dedicated soldier. He's certainly dirty enough. You could've at least cleaned him up a little."

"He said it was urgent, Your Majesty."

"Well then, let's have it. Step forward, man. I will be the judge if this message is important enough to interrupt my lunch."

The courier stood, his knees shaking so bad, he was afraid he'd fall over as soon as he put weight on them. Trying to step with confidence, he advanced to the edge of the dais and mounted the first step, eyes on the floor while he pulled out the sealed message. He extended it toward the Emperor. A pasty white hand snatched the letter from him, and he retreated until he'd returned to his original position and dropped back to his knees.

The crackling of paper announced the breaking of the seal and the opening of the letter from the Warden of Hyroth.

"Courier, do you know what is in this message?"

"Yes, Your Majesty." Every imperial courier knew to commit messages to memory in case the original message was destroyed or damaged during delivery.

"Is it true? Has Baron Norak been killed and his army routed?"

"I'm afraid so, Your Majesty. I was likely the last courier to leave Hyroth before the city was fully besieged by the slave army marching on it."

"I told that fool Norak to be careful. The prophecies were clear that the Opponent would be formidable and not easy to defeat."

The robed man cleared his throat. "Sire, the Baron could be headstrong, that is certain. He must have underestimated the power of the Opponent. My council of mages and I have felt the power of his gateways once again. It is likely he's returned whence he came."

"You've put the plans we discussed in action then, Decimus, despite this setback with Baron Norak's unfortunate demise? You assured me your wizards are up to the challenge."

"All has been arranged according to your wishes, Sire."

"Then the Opponent will return to us. This time, he'll come to me on our terms, where he can be dealt with directly."

"Yes, Your Majesty." The robed man, who the courier now knew was Decimus, the leader of the Emperor's mage council, turned to leave. He stopped next to the courier.

"Uh, what should I do with the courier, Your Majesty?"

The courier stiffened. His fate was about to be decided.

"Reward him. He has served us well. Despite the bad news, we know the plan to deal with the Opponent once and for all is set in motion. Hal Dix will be my prisoner, and then I will show him what happens to those who defy me."

CHAPTER 1

THE LANDING GEAR of the airliner touched down with a jolt, jerking Hal's thoughts back to the present. He couldn't wait to share his news. The management leadership weekend had been a success after all. Hal's strategy for their paintball capture-the-flag games had won the day for his team over his nemesis Barry's team. It had even earned him a coveted invitation to sit at the table with Arrantis CEO Justin Thomas. Justin had personally congratulated Hal on his leadership skills and told him he was "a person to keep an eye on."

The dinner had ended with an offer to join the young executive track reserved for only a few select trainees. Hal had accepted immediately and been told they'd reassign him to the corporate headquarters downtown upon his return to Baltimore.

Hal couldn't wait to tell Mona about his good fortune on the weekend trip. His wife was a successful engineering executive, but she'd always told him she had faith in his abilities, too. She said she expected him to rise as high as she had. Now he could tell her he was on the way.

He pulled out his phone and turned it on, so he could text Mona and tell him he would be headed home soon. He sent the message then pocketed his phone without waiting for a reply. They'd reached the terminal already, and he was ready to leave the plane. He wanted to be home with Mona and their eighteen-month-old daughter, Cari.

It took him longer than usual to collect his suitcase and catch the shuttle to the long-term parking lot. He checked his phone several times. There'd been no reply from Mona.

She told him she was going to try and get home early from work tonight so they could have dinner as a family when he got back in town. Maybe she stopped at the grocery store on her way home after picking Cari up at daycare.

Hal shrugged and started driving home. Traffic was lighter than usual, and he made good time across town to his neighborhood. He pulled into his driveway and saw Mona's SUV parked in front of the garage. The rear passenger door was open, along with the rear lift-gate, and Hal saw grocery bags sitting in the back, waiting to be carried inside.

After parking, he opted to leave his suitcases for later and grabbed several grocery bags instead.

The kitchen door was open, and Hal called out as he walked inside.

"Mona, I'm home. Wait until I tell you about my trip."

There was no reply, and before he could call out again, Hal saw the spilled bags on the floor next to Mona's upended purse. Cari's empty sippy cup lay on its side next to the kitchen table.

Something was wrong, and Hal's heart sank in his chest. He dropped the grocery bags he carried and ran through the house. He searched every room, calling for both his wife and daughter.

There was no answer. The house was as still as death.

No one was home but him.

There were more signs of a struggle in the family room. The fight had overturned the coffee table, and one of the legs had been snapped off at the base. He picked up the broken table leg and noticed the sticky smear of blood and hair on the jagged end.

The hair was black, bringing him a moment's relief. Both Mona and Cari had blonde hair. Whoever had been whacked by the broken table leg, it hadn't been his wife or daughter.

Hal pulled his phone from his pocket and started to dial 911 to notify the police of the apparent home invasion and his missing wife and daughter. His thumb stopped before hitting *send*, hovering over the button. His eyes fell on a sheet of parchment with an old-fashioned wax seal affixed to the bottom. A steel dagger pinned the parchment note to the drywall.

Letting the hand holding the phone drop to his side without completing the call to the police, Hal crossed to the letter left for him on the wall. He already knew in his heart what it meant. He recognized the seal impressed into the wax. Hal dreaded reading the words he feared were written there, but he pulled it down from the wall, broke the seal, and unfolded the parchment.

Greetings to Hal Dix from His Imperial Majesty Emperor Kang, Warden of the Four Winds, Ruler of the Eastern Isles, etc. etc.

It is time we meet in person so that we might come to an arrangement agreeable to both of us. I have extended an invitation to your wife and child to join us in our palace in the Crystal City.

Your presence is requested at your earliest convenience so that we might put an end to our mutual enmity. Do not keep us waiting too long. I suspect your family would not like it if you disappoint us.

Sincerely,

Kang

Hal stared at the message, trying to understand how this had happened. Tildi had never let on that he or his family was ever in any danger.

The old wizard would have told him, wouldn't she?

He stood there for a long time, mulling over his options. It was dark out by the time he managed to spur himself to action. After folding the message and shoving it in his pocket, Hal went outside, closed the two cars, brought his luggage inside, and unzipped his checked bag.

Sitting on top of his clothes were his matched daggers. Tildi had managed to get them to him in his checked suitcase after using them to get him picked up by airport security before his trip to the leadership weekend.

He supposed he should be thankful he had them back. Now he needed to figure out how he was going to return to Fantasma and retrieve his family. Kang assumed he knew how to get there, but Tildi had always been instrumental in opening the portal in the past. Would the computer game portal he'd used the first time work again?

Hal strapped on his dagger belt so that one dagger rode on each hip, the black leather scabbards hanging down on either side of his blue jeans. He didn't know if they would be able to make the trip to the very real gaming world he'd just left behind, but Hal wanted to be ready if he managed to initiate the transfer.

He raced up to his office in the spare bedroom and powered up his desktop. While it booted up, he dug through a stack of game cases and DVD boxes until he found it. It was a plain, clear plastic jewel case with a DVD inside. The disc was labeled *Fantasma* in black permanent marker.

This was the original disc Tildi had sold him over six months ago. It seemed like longer to him. He'd spent more than that amount of time in Fantasma on his two forays there. Time passed differently between the two worlds, or so Tildi had told him. Months might unfurl in Fantasma while only a few days or even a few hours passed here on Earth.

It worried him because, if Mona had been taken a few hours ago, who knew how long it might have been once they'd arrived in the game world. He had to hurry. Every second could be hours or days of captivity for Mona and Cari.

Hal popped the disc from the case and placed it into the computer's optical drive. It slid inside as the mechanism grabbed it. He clicked the prompt that popped up to load the program contained inside. Soon, the familiar display of the *Fantasma* game screen loaded.

Do you wish to continue your game?

The prompt flashed in a window hovering above the main game menu. Hal wasn't sure this would work, but he sat in his chair and leaned back, making sure his body was comfortable before he clicked on the *continue* button. He wasn't sure if his body usually made the journey or not, but he didn't want to take the chance.

Once he settled in, Hal reached out and hovered his hand over the mouse. He hoped this worked. Clicking on the *continue* button, Hal was rewarded when the screen went black, followed by a series of familiar flashes of white strobing in the darkness of his office. Rather than blinking and trying to avoid the harsh pattern of strobing white and black, Hal forced himself to stare at the screen and absorb the flashing pattern as the pace sped up.

He felt himself start to fall despite being firmly planted in the chair, and he smiled. It had worked. The darkness closed about him, not a surprise this time. This time, Hal welcomed it with open arms. He just hoped he was not too late.

CHAPTER 2

"He's dead, I tell you. Look at him. He's not moving."

"He is too moving," a second child's voice said. "He's breathing, stupid. That means he ain't dead."

A third voice, higher-pitched than the other two, chimed in with a question. "Why's he here and what's with the strange clothing?"

"I think he's from the ships in the harbor," the first voice surmised. "Maybe he's a visitor from one of the ships, and he got drunk in the tavern around the corner last night."

"We should tell Mama about him," voice two said. "Maybe he's hurt."

Hal forced his eyes open and immediately noticed the familiar cobblestones and smells of the original alley he'd arrived in the first time he landed in Fantasma. Three children, two boys and a girl, leaned over him, staring down at his face.

"See," the girl said. "He's not dead. I told you so."

"You did not," one of the boys blurted out. "I was the one who noticed he was breathing."

"Wh-where?" Hal asked. His voice was raspy, as if he'd been asleep a long time.

"Where what, mister?" the girl asked.

Hal rolled to his side and winced when something hard dug into his hip. Reaching down, he felt his dagger there. A quick check confirmed the second blade, identical to the first, rested on his other hip.

"I'm in Tandon, right? Tell me I'm in Tandon."

"You're right," the first boy said. "Where else would you be?"

Pressing his hands down on the cobblestones of the alley, Hal pushed himself up to his feet and rose slowly to get his bearings. He was still a little woozy from the journey, and he didn't want to move too quickly and trip.

Something was different about the trip to Fantasma this time. He'd arrived in Fantasma with his regular clothes intact and managed to bring his daggers with him from home. On both previous trips, he'd showed up in basic Tandon garb of homespun pants and shirt. He wondered if it was because he'd traveled here without Tildi's help this time.

Concentrating on himself for a second, he managed to bring up the familiar menu screen that contained his game stats and inventory. Sure enough, he saw blue jeans and T-shirt listed there along with his daggers and the sneakers he wore. A switch of the screen brought up his ability and attribute stats.

Name: Hal Dix
   Class: Thief/Warrior
   Level: 11/11

Attributes:
   Brawn: 24 — +8 defense
   Wisdom: 10 — +1 defense
   Luck: 28 — +10 to all saving throws
   Speed: 12 — +2 defense
   Looks: 8

Health: 116/116

Character skills: Chakra regeneration — 3 (heal 18hp; 1/day).
    Warrior skills: Shield bash — 2, One-handed combat — 3, Combat misdirection — 1, Prescience — 2, Riposte — 2.
    Thief skills: Taunt — 2, Dark vision — 1, Acrobatic dodge — 5, Hide in shadows — 2, Sneak attack — 3, Open locks — 2, Find/remove traps — 1.
    Weapon proficiencies: Longsword — 4, Crossbow — 1
    Warrior experience: 140,800/250,000
    Rogue experience: 146,100/250,000

Hal remembered the hit from Baron Norak's cursed sword that had drained three levels of his thief abilities. He noticed that not only had he lost points from his brawn, luck, and speed, but he had also lost his master thief skills. It seemed that, while most of the stat changes could be fixed after he leveled up, he had permanently lost his master thief skills. It was the sole blemish on what he thought of as a pretty good game character sheet. He was going to need every bit of talent he had to get his wife and daughter back.

The three children all stood watching him, curiosity blazing in their eyes. Hal smiled down at them. He wished he had a few silver pieces to give them for watching over him as he woke up. He'd have to settle for his gratitude.

"Thank you, young lady and gentle masters," Hal said, adding a bow and a sweeping flourish of his hand. "I am a visitor to your land, and though I have been here before, I have never been greeted so kindly as you three have greeted me this fine day."

The little girl giggled, and the taller of the two boys nudged her with an elbow.

"What's your name, mister?" the girl asked.

"I am known here and beyond as Hal Dix. You and your families might know me better as the Hood, though."

"Nuh-uh," the shorter boy said, shaking his head. "The Hood is dead. He disappeared, dying during a great battle far to the east. Word came back weeks ago, and the Duke declared a day of mourning for the city."

"A day of mourning, huh? Well, I hate to tell you, but rumors of my demise are premature, to say the least."

Hal remembered why he'd returned and the urgency of what he had to do.

"Kids, I hate to leave you all so abruptly without proof of who I am, but you'll just have to take my word for it. I need to get to the palace and see the Duke. There's something important I must do."

All three kids shrugged. What did they care? Adults never asked their permission to do anything.

Hal smiled and headed out towards the mouth of the alley and the throngs of people passing by there. Judging by the angle of the sun over the rooftops, he had to move fast to get to the palace gates before they closed at sundown.

―――――

The streets were filled with crowds of people and freight wagons coming up from the wharves in the harbor below. Hal weaved his way through, trying not to jostle people. Soon, he managed to leave the Harbor District of Tandon and enter the even busier Merchant District with its market-places and streets lined with shops of all varieties. He'd missed the famil-iarity of Tandon after his foray to the dusty, eastern city of Hyroth.

While Tandon was considered provincial by most people in the larger imperial cities to the east, Hal found he liked it here. Maybe it was because this was his first home in Fantasma or perhaps because he'd come to know the people here while he liberated the city from the Emperor's rule.

Hal drank in the sights while he walked and started noticing small differences from the last time he was here. It hadn't been that long, even with the time differential. It should have only been six months or so. In that time, though, something had changed.

It took him a while to notice what it was, but once he did, it seemed obvious. There were soldiers everywhere. Not the typical city guard or even the Duke's personal retainers, no, there were also soldiers wearing strange livery he'd never seen before.

At first, Hal wondered if the Emperor had reclaimed the city during his absence. He slowed and started moving with more care as he passed through the streets. While he walked, Hal tried to figure out where the soldiers were from or to which faction they belonged. It wasn't until he saw a familiar crest on the tabard worn by one cavalry officer that he started to understand.

The crest was that of the House of Englewood, headed now by one Lord Anders Englewood, recently reunited with his childhood sweetheart, Hal's friend and fighting companion, Kay. He still didn't understand completely what her place in the nobility was here in Fantasma, but she had friends in high places.

If he were to guess, Hal figured she was some kind of princess. He knew the Emperor had deposed her family during his conquests, but he'd never been able to ask her outright. It pained her talking too much about her murdered parents or her younger brother and sister sold into slavery.

If one of Anders' officers was here, that meant that it was likely Anders and his contingent of knights and cavalry were here, too. It could indicate Kay was here as well. Hal could use their help in mounting a rescue.

After crossing the street to catch up with the officer and his companion, Hal reached out and tugged at the billowing sleeve of the man's shirt. Looking back, Hal realized it was the wrong thing to do on a busy street like this one. Soldiers were notoriously touchy about getting caught unawares.

The man spun around, drawing his sword in a single fluid motion. He brought the blade up to Hal's throat before Hal could react at all. That wasn't entirely true. Hal had to resist his own hard-earned instincts to draw steel and parry the blade coming at him. It had taken all his control to hold back on that reaction.

"I'll gut you, thief, if you've so much as removed a copper from my purse," the officer snarled.

"Easy, my friend," Hal said. He held his hands out away from his body to show he held no weapons. "I wanted to talk, that is all."

The man stared at Hal and seemed about to skewer him anyway when his eyes widened in surprise.

"You're — I know you! But it can't be. You're supposed to be dead."

"Yeah, that seems to be the consensus. I'm afraid conventional wisdom of my untimely demise is mistaken."

"Lord Hal, I mean, uh, General Dix, uh..." the man sputtered as he lowered his sword from Hal's throat and tried to speak coherently.

"Lord Hal will do, I suppose. I'm sorry, soldier, I don't remember your name?"

"Lieutenant Warren, my lord. I don't expect you to remember me. I remember you, though. That speech you gave before the Battle of Mountain Vale inspired my men and me as nothing we'd ever heard before."

"Well, thank you, I guess. Don't tell Sir Anders that, though. He might get jealous." Hal laughed a little now that he'd diffused the tension some.

"He would not be jealous at all. He had one of the scribes write down your words and had them spread to each of the free cities as an example of the leader you were before you — well, before you disappeared."

"Oh, he did, did he? I'll have to have a few words with him about that when I see him. That brings me to the reason I stopped you so unceremoniously, Lieutenant. Could you tell me where His Lordship is? Is he here in Tandon?"

"Yes, of course," Warren replied. "He is staying in the palace with the Duke and the Princess."

"Kay's here, too? Excellent. That means I won't have to track her down to get her help."

"If by 'Kay' you mean Princess Kareena, then yes, she is staying in the palace as well."

The lieutenant paused and looked Hal up and down, taking in his strange clothing.

"My lord, your dress is strange in cut and fashion. Might I inquire where you have been? Did you arrive on a ship just into the harbor?"

"Let's just say I've been home to my own land and only just returned here. There is something of the utmost importance that I must speak with Anders, Kay, and Duke Korran about immediately."

"Then let me and my companion escort you through this rabble so you may reach the palace forthwith. I know Lord Anders will want to speak with you himself to offer what aid he can."

"Thank you, Lieutenant," Hal said. "Lead on and I will follow you."

The lieutenant's companion, a younger officer, probably on his first deployment with the army, seemed a little star-struck after learning who Hal was. He made a brief, polite greeting and then fell silent as he brought up the rear of their small group. Lieutenant Warren, meanwhile, led Hal through the crowd, pushing people out of the way and calling for the road to clear ahead of them.

Hal didn't want to cause a fuss, but on the other hand, who knew what was going on with Mona and Cari at the hands of the Emperor? He needed to get to his friends and try and come up with a plan to rescue them as soon as possible.

Warren was true to his word. Within a few minutes of walking, he'd rounded up a squad of infantry from another unit and had the sergeant clear the way for them. The burly foot soldiers made quick work of opening a path, and soon Hal found himself jogging to keep up with the excited Warren and his impromptu command.

They made excellent time on the way to the palace, reaching the gates well before dark. Before Hal could stop him, Lieutenant Warren marched up to the guard sergeant at the gates and beckoned back at Hal, who was still walking up the hill, catching up with his escort.

"Make way, my good man. Do you know who this is? He has come with great news for the Duke and his royal visitors."

The sergeant started to resist the young officer's excited commands, but then he spotted Hal at the rear of the group.

Hal thought he recognized the grizzled sergeant at the gate. The man's eyes bulged. He remembered Hal, that was for sure. The sergeant turned and called something to the guards inside the gatehouse then whispered to his companion. The second gate guard shot a startled glance at Hal and then sprinted away onto the palace grounds. Hal suspected he was running ahead to announce his arrival to the Duke.

As Hal reached the gate, he noticed a hastily arranged honor guard forming up inside the gatehouse passageway, the men rigid at attention, their pikes all held in front in uniform precision at a slight angle away from them. Hal decided it was time to do the "Lordly" thing. It was expected at times like this, as he'd learned while running an army of his own.

Hal paused as he passed the assembled guards, letting his gaze linger on each man in turn before turning to their commander.

"They look very sharp, Sergeant. You've done well commanding them."

The sergeant's chest puffed up a little bit, and a hint of red crept across his face.

"Yes, sir. Thank you, sir. I trained them myself, I did."

Hal smiled and looked past the assembled soldiers to the end of the gatehouse passage.

"Well, Sergeant, don't let me keep you from your business.

Thank you for the honor guard, but they won't be necessary. I know the way from here."

A scowl flashed across the sergeant's face. It disappeared as soon as Hal noticed it.

"I wouldn't think of letting you proceed without an escort, sir. The Duke would have my head on a stick if I showed you any disrespect, what with you being back from the dead and all."

"Yeah, about that. It's all a bit of a misunderstanding, as you can see. I'm sure there was some confusion following the battle and all. Tildi should have told someone where I was. I just left to return to my homeland."

"From the stories I've heard, Your Lordship, there's been no sign of the arch mage since before the battle. Besides, however you got here, now that you're back, it means Tandon and the Duke must need you once more. If you do not wish the full honor guard, then my corporal and I will escort you to the throne room ourselves."

"Very well." Hal struggled not to roll his eyes. "Lead on, Sergeant. There is a matter of some urgency I must attend to."

"Yes, sir. If you'll follow me. My corporal will bring up the rear."

Hal turned and thanked Lieutenant Warren and the others who'd escorted him this far and then followed the royal guard sergeant up into the palace.

CHAPTER 3

KORRAN, Duke of Tandon, stood waiting at the door when Hal and his escort arrived in the Duke's private dining hall. Next to him was a striking woman in a blue silk dress with a tight-fitting bodice and a sheathed dagger at her waist. Beside her stood a man in knight's livery, his broad shoulders filling out the chainmail shirt he wore as if the links in the chain would burst from the muscles bulging beneath.

The Duke's face split into a broad grin when the doors opened and Hal stepped into the room. The woman rushed forward and pulled Hal into an embrace, holding him close for more seconds than Hal felt comfortable, seeing as how her betrothed stood watching.

"How are you Kay, or should I say Princess Kareena?"

She snorted a small laugh. "Kay will do."

A break in her voice told Hal she might be tearing up as she embraced him. He resisted the urge to push her away while she clutched him under Anders' watchful eyes. *Let her compose herself first.*

"Hal, you have no idea how hard it was to give Junica the order to loose that fire arrow at the wagons holding the fire sand while you stood so close," Kay whispered into his shoulder.

She was talking about the final moments of his last foray here.

He'd commanded them to blow up wagons full of gunpowder, what they called fire sand. They'd followed his orders even though he was standing nearby.

"She's not kidding, Hal," Anders said. "She was beside herself about it for weeks afterward, especially when we couldn't locate your body for a proper burial."

Kay released him and held Hal at arm's length, staring up at him with glistening eyes.

"I made them gather all the bodies we could find, no matter who they were. We created a barrow on the site to mark the place of your death."

Anders stepped forward, the big knight extending a calloused hand to clasp wrists with Hal in the way of warrior comrades in Fantasma.

"The speeches were epic, and I had my bard pen a new ballad to your supreme sacrifice. I can't wait to have him recite it for you."

Hal's shoulders slumped a little. It wasn't his fault Tildi decided to open the portal back to his world at that moment.

"There was a funeral?"

As Anders released Hal's wrist, Korran stepped forward and repeated the gesture with Hal.

"From everything I've heard, it was spectacular."

Hal groaned. While he occasionally dreamed of what people would say about him in the event of his death, this wasn't how he'd expected to learn about it.

Duke Korran took one look at Hal's sickened expression and let out a burst of loud guffaws that Hal thought were most un-Duke-like.

Anders and Kay joined in then, and the infectious noise spread until Hal couldn't avoid laughing along with them at his own expense. At least Kay was no longer crying.

As he got ahold of himself once again, Duke Korran wiped a tear from his eye and waggled a finger in Hal's direction.

"I must say, I needed that, Hal. It's been a long time since we've had reason to laugh about much of anything."

Anders nodded. "Things have been dire since you left, Hal. Though we pushed the Emperor's army back that day a few months ago and took the city of Hyroth, the tide has started to turn against us, and we are hard-pressed to hold back the Emperor's reinforcements streaming westward to try and retake Hyroth from us."

"That is why we're here, with Duke Korran," Kay said. "We are preparing to take a new force of recruits from Tandon and the other free western cities back east to bolster our defenses."

"Things are really that grim?" Hal asked. It wasn't idle curiosity about the war effort. He needed to know. He would have to penetrate those battle lines if he hoped to rescue his family.

"Perhaps not," Korran said, still smiling. "Now that you're here, it must be time for another epic quest for the mythical Opponent himself. I have to say, Hal, I never bought into that legend myself. But after hearing all you did in Hyroth, and then during the battle in the hills afterward, and now coming back from the dead like this, I suppose I have to give it some credence. Now that you're back to lead the troops in battle, I feel like there is nothing we can't do."

Hal coughed and looked away. The pause was not missed by his companions.

Kay was the first to speak. "You have returned to do what you do so well, right? You're going to tell us you have a clever plan, and I'm not going to believe you, and then you'll make it so we all see how you save the day."

It was Hal's turn to shake his head. His lips pressed together into a grim line as he tried to come up with words that would let them down easy while conveying the urgency of his family's kidnapping.

"What is it, Hal?" Kay asked. "It's not like you to be at a loss for words."

"It's Mona and Cari..." Hal's voice broke before he could finish.

"That's your wife and baby, right?" Kay asked.

Hal nodded, unable to bring himself to speak as he thought of what they must be enduring as captives under the Emperor's power.

"Did something happen to them back in your homeland?"

Anders asked. "I swear, Hal, upon my honor, as soon as this war is completed, I will accompany you myself and return with you to avenge them."

Struggling, Hal finally said, "They're not there. They are here, in Fantasma. He has them."

"He? You mean the Emperor took them?" Korran asked. "But how? You said yourself you come from a faraway land that requires great magic to transport you here."

"They should have been safe. I don't know what he did, but somehow, he found out where I was from and sent people to take them right from my home. They were gone by the time I returned. All I have is this."

From his pocket, Hal fished the folded parchment from the Emperor and held it out. Kay reached for it and read it before passing it to Anders and the Duke in turn.

"That is why I cannot help you with your cause. I must do everything I can to travel to the imperial capital, get inside the Crystal City, and rescue them. If not, then I have no choice but to turn myself in."

"He'll kill you, Hal," Kay said. "You know that. He will do to you what he did to my father and mother. Then he will either enslave your wife and daughter, as he did my siblings and me, or kill them while you watch before your own execution."

"Don't you think I know that? What choice do I have?"

"You have to meet power with power of your own, Hal Dix."

A new voice had sounded from behind them by the fireplace. All four spun in place, shock distracting them from the seriousness of their discussion.

The wizened and hunched form of Tildi the Elder stood by the fireplace, her back to them. She used the metal-shod base of her staff to prod the coals beneath the burning logs. She continued poking the fire without turning around.

"He wants your power for himself, Hal. If you turn yourself over to him without the proper training, he and his pet mages will leech the strength of the Opponent from your very soul, leaving you a husk of your former self."

"How long have you been standing there?" Korran asked.

Tildi looked up, the tiniest of smirks at the corners of her mouth. "Long enough to know I should have stuck around for the funeral feast after the explosion, instead of leaving after I sent Hal home."

"What do you mean by the Emperor taking my power for himself? What power do I have that he could want? He's the freaking Emperor for God's sake."

"Hal, you know you have something special that happens when you come here to Fantasma. It is why I created the game in your world to begin with. I discovered that, using magic from Fantasma, coupled with the science of your world, I could create a way for you to directly tap into magic that would enable you to become whatever you needed to be in the moment. You did that twice, first becoming a master thief, then transforming yourself into a blade master and great war leader. The Emperor has discovered what you can do, at least in part. He seeks that power for himself, and he will find a way to do just that. After that, none of us will be able to defeat him."

"So? All I have to do is stay away from him while I rescue my family. I can do that. I've got a few more tricks up my sleeve. I'll do whatever it takes."

"You don't understand, Hal. It's not just you that's at risk here," Tildi continued. "You're not the only one anymore."

Hal struggled to piece together what the mage was saying to him. It was all a lot to figure out, and it was clear he was missing something key.

Kay got to it first. "Your wife and daughter, Hal. They came through the portal the same way you did. That means they have the power, too, doesn't it, Tildi?"

Hal groaned aloud. "It's already too late, isn't it? He already has them."

"No, Hal," Tildi said. "I would have detected that kind of power transfer, and I have not sensed anything like it. It is likely the

Emperor and his mages are unaware of the particular mechanics of how the magic-game interface works. But it will not take them long to realize that Mona and Cari are empowered in much the same way you are, especially if the two of them start exhibiting special abilities of some sort before they learn to control them."

Hal let his shoulders slump in defeat. "What do I do, Tildi? You're telling me I can't rescue them. Then, in the same breath, you say the Emperor already has everything he needs to accomplish what he wants with my wife and daughter. He doesn't need me at all."

Tildi nodded. After leaning her staff against the wall beside the fireplace mantel, she took out her pipe and, with a fingertip, channeled a tiny jet of flame into the bowl while she puffed at the stem. She paused to blow a few smoke rings before continuing.

"That is why you have to train and learn to block his ability to siphon the magic from you and your family. Only you possess the ability from both worlds, Hal. You could harness both the magic and the game at once and defeat the Emperor and his mages before they figure out how to counter you."

"I don't know anything about magic or game programming. That's what you're talking about, isn't it? If I can somehow use magic and get inside the code of the *Fantasma* game at the same time, I could find a way to defeat them while keeping them from hurting Mona and Cari."

Tildi's eyes twinkled. She didn't say anything. She just kept puffing on her pipe.

Korran cleared his throat. "I don't suppose it matters that there hasn't been a new arch mage born in over a hundred years and the old academy has long been disbanded."

"He's right, Tildi," Anders said. "There are only four free arch mages left in the world. All the others are dead or work for the Emperor. How's Hal supposed to train if there's no academy to teach him anymore?"

"Not only that," Kay added. "I thought it took decades to train a wizard with any level of power?"

Hal discovered his knees quivered beneath him and a pit of quicksand swirled deep in his gut, churning his fear to higher levels. He wasn't afraid for himself. He was scared for Mona and Cari. His friends all made it sound impossible for him to accomplish what Tildi had suggested.

"What if I fail? You've all come up with good reasons this can't work."

"And yet, you've managed the impossible before, haven't you?" Tildi asked.

"Not like this. We don't have years to do this. My wife and daughter are being held in whatever horrible dungeon the Emperor has devised for them. I can't let them rot in there for decades."

"You have something no other mage-in-training has had, Hal. Certainly, I didn't have it all those long years ago."

"What's that?"

"You can access the game. That is what I discovered, and because of that, you should be able to shave years off the time it takes to train in magic. Most of that time is spent in the early stages, where a young wizard struggles to merely connect with the world's magic. You can bypass all of that by simply adopting a new class."

"Pardon me," Duke Korran interrupted. "What is all this talk about a game and adopting a new class? How does Hal's ability to play a game impact his strength in learning magic?"

Hal thought about how weird it must seem to the others to hear all this talk about science and games alongside magic and their world. It made him chuckle to himself. If they only knew. He turned back to Tildi.

"You can explain it to them if you want another time. If that is all I need to do to bypass those years of training, then I will do that. I have to do whatever it takes to free my family before Emperor Kang figures out what he's got in his grubby little hands."

Hal stared off into space and concentrated for a moment on his stats menu. When his character stats were up in his field of vision, he cleared his throat and spoke in a loud, clear voice.

"I wish to change my class to mage."

A message and a prompt replaced his stats screen.

Class changed to Mage. All experience as a rogue and warrior erased until Arch Mage status is reached.

Say "yes" to confirm this selection.

"Yes."

Hal's stats screen popped back in place, this time with all the fighter and thief abilities grayed out. A flashing message appeared at the bottom.

Choose your magical element. (Ice, Fire, Earth, Wind)

"Hey, Tildi. I'm supposed to choose my magical element. I have to pick between ice, fire, earth, and wind. What should I select?"

"Well, that is interesting," the mage said. Her eyes shifted up to the ceiling, and she stared for long seconds before she said anything more. She kept her eyes upward as if an invisible answer was displayed somewhere on the ornately carved wooden panels that stretched across the hall.

"I should have thought about this. Usually, the school of magic a wizard is attuned to is discovered while they learn to tap into the power centers within themselves. In this case, you must choose for yourself."

"Too bad he can't choose all of the above," Anders quipped. "That would come in handy."

Tildi snapped her fingers. "That is a wonderful, and terrifying, suggestion." She leveled her gaze at Hal. "Do it."

"Wait. What?" The hair on Hal's neck stood on end. "You just said it was a terrifying suggestion. That doesn't sound good."

"Good and bad are two sides of the same coin in this instance. It's how you spend it that decides the outcome. Usually, a mage only has enough power within to control a single source of magical energy. Once attuned to that source, trying to tap into one of the others can cause the mage to burn out their abilities completely, or worse."

"That definitely doesn't sound like what I want to do."

Tildi raised a finger and pointed it at Hal. "But, you're not from here. The same rules don't apply. At least, I don't think they do. You have the game, and that gives you something no one else has. It empowers you through the science of the code and not from the magic of our world alone. It might be what sets you apart from the rest of us. That could be the root of the prophecy's power."

"So, you want me to do it simply because you have a hunch? I can't take that kind of chance. My wife and daughter's lives depend on it."

"All the more reason you can't afford not to take the chance, my boy," Tildi scolded. "You said yourself it's the most urgent thing in the world to you. What other time would you take a chance like this?"

Korran, Kay, and Anders stood still. Their eyes shifted to each other, perhaps seeking answers there. Eventually, all eyes rested on him.

The silence closed around him like a lead blanket, smothering him while it threatened to crush his resolve. Hal swallowed hard and cleared his throat once more.

"I select all."

Confirm your decision to select specialization in all magical elements. Arch Mage status reached with mastery of all elements.

"Confirmed."

Tildi took her pipe from her mouth and pointed the stem at Hal. "That went better than I expected."

Hal opened his mouth to protest but stopped as the old mage held up her hand.

"I couldn't know what would happen, Hal. No one has ever tried what you just did before. Besides, it is done, and you survived."

"What's next, then? I need to do this fast before the Emperor discovers what he can do with Mona and Cari."

"I think ice is as good a place as any. You need to travel north to work with a friend of mine."

Korran grinned. "You're thinking of Ragnar? I have heard he is, uh, difficult, shall we say."

"He has his moments, as do we all. He is the best alive at manipulating ice magic. He will also be able to help Hal here adjust to what he needs to learn about casting and protecting himself as a mage. I'll open a portal once we get Hal some proper gear."

"I should go as well," Kay volunteered. "Hal can't keep himself out of trouble on a good day. Stumbling around amidst the barbarian tribes, he will need someone to watch his back."

"Then I shall accompany you both too," Anders added.

"No," Tildi said. "I can only open a portal wide enough for two."

"I cannot let Kareena accompany Hal alone. They both have need of my sword and shield."

"I can handle myself, Anders," Kay said. "Besides, one of us has to lead the new forces east, as well as tell Otto, Junica, Rune, and the others Hal has returned. I have been Hal's companion the longest. It should be I who accompanies him."

She laid a hand on Anders' arm. "Don't worry, my love; I'll be careful."

Anders grumbled under his breath. His teeth ground together and his hands formed fists at his sides. The knuckles of both hands blanched white as the knight clenched them.

Hal thought Anders was going to refuse, but the big knight

surprised Hal as he relaxed his grip and flexed his fingers before reaching out and stroking an errant strand of Kay's blonde hair away from her face.

"Kareena, I know you must do what you think is right. I will do as you wish because I would not risk losing you to my own pig-headedness. Hal, you will look after her?"

"As if she were my own flesh and blood, Anders."

Tildi grabbed her staff where it stood by the fireplace and tapped the steel-shod butt on the wooden floor.

"Good, that is settled, then. Your Grace, with your leave, I will take our young mage here so he might be equipped for his journey and trials to come."

Korran nodded.

With that, Hal began what would become his most challenging task in Fantasma yet.

He would become a mage.

CHAPTER 4

THE GREEN-CLOAKED IMAGE stared back at him from the mirror. From the black tailored breeches tucked into the tops of the polished black boots to the billowy white linen shirt, the laces at the V-neck collar left open and dangling, Hal saw the image of a dainty nobleman gazing back at him. Only the comforting weight of his twin daggers, one on each hip, gave him any sense of being ready to start on this quest to learn magic.

Hooking a finger inside the hammered gold broach holding the moss-green cloak firmly around his neck, Hal tried to shift the heavy cloak forward to take more of the weight on his shoulders. It sort of worked.

"I feel naked."

"You look dressed to me, thank the gods," Kay snorted.

"You can say whatever you want. You've got some armor on at least."

Kay brushed a hand down the shining shirt of chainmail hanging down to just above her knees. Her sword belt pulled it in over her hips, securing the armor in place above the chausses protecting her thighs and the greaves below that.

"You heard what Tildi said. No armor. Come to think of it, I never recall seeing any mage wear armor of any kind."

"Yeah, that's just what I want to hear when I'm headed out into the Northern Wastes, inhabited by tribes of barbarians and monsters of various sorts. Thanks."

"No problem." Kay chuckled. "Don't worry. I'll protect you from the bad men."

"Very funny."

A rap at the door interrupted them. It opened to reveal Tildi and several servants carrying bulging backpacks and pouches.

"Set them down over there and give us some privacy." Tildi gestured to the canopied bed in the corner.

The servants complied and pulled the door closed behind them as they left. Tildi held up a finger to her lips as she crept to the door and put an ear against it. She nodded once and muttered something under her breath, pointing her index finger at a spot on the wood at shoulder height. The mage's finger glowed then flashed with a bright white light.

A muffled yelp from the other side of the carved door drew a smile to Tildi's lips.

"There, now the eavesdropper is attended to. We can talk in private."

"How did you know one of the servants would linger behind to listen to our conversation?" Hal asked. "Is he alright?"

"He'll be hearing nothing but the ringing in his ears for a few days, but it will fade with time. I always assume the servants in these places are listening in on private conversations. Most palace servants I've known deal in information. It's a good way to supplement their income, and idle gossip spread around social circles is usually harmless enough. What we're planning is more important, however."

The mage turned from the door, seeming satisfied they wouldn't be overheard. She gave Hal an appraising stare from head to toe and back again.

"You'll do, I suppose. You're wearing better clothes than I remember having as an apprentice."

"I still feel exposed without some decent armor on me."

"No armor, not even leather. Feeling exposed and vulnerable is good for an apprentice mage. It'll keep you alive a little longer."

"But why?"

"Because magic is finicky and doesn't like things that get in the way of the casting. Bulky armor that constricts movement, iron and other metals, even jewelry can impact the ability of a new mage to cast spells successfully. You don't need distractions from what needs to be done right now, my boy. I get the feeling you're going to be a difficult enough pupil for me and my companions."

"I'm an excellent student. I've always gotten good grades. Not the best, mind you, but respectable. I'll learn what you have to teach."

"Really? You've already failed the first lesson, Hal. You must give up your preconceptions about how the world works. That starts with following instructions without complaint."

"You sound like you're about to say, 'There is no try, there is only do or do not.'"

"I wasn't but it's not a bad way to put things. I'll have to borrow that one. Who said it?"

Hal rolled his eyes. He was kidding but had to admit he felt a little like trainee Luke getting dressed down by Yoda for questioning the little green man's teachings.

"It was from a movie. Never mind."

"Hal, you're not going to be hacking your way through obstacles anymore for a while. You need to finesse your way around things now. That is the way mages and wizards solve challenges. Magic has strict rules, and often the solution requires the mage to think of ways the rules can be turned on their heads without breaking them. You can't afford to have anything distracting you from concentrating on the magic you're trying to cast."

"But I don't even know how to cast anything yet. Shouldn't I protect myself in the meantime? At least until I start learning."

"We'll start on the trip north. I can open a portal to get us close to Ragnar's tribal lands, but we'll have to travel several days in the wastes from there to his camp. I'll work with you while we ride. If I turn you over to him without any preparation at all, he'll never let me live it down."

"Fine, what's my first lesson?" Hal crossed his arms.

"Ho, ho? So, that's the way you're going to be? Very well. Hold this."

Tildi held out a translucent, polished white crystal the size of a grape. Hal took it and yelped in pain at the icy cold emanating from it.

"Why didn't you warn me it was so cold?"

"Why didn't you ask?" Tildi replied. "Don't put that away. You must hold it in your hand until you master its properties."

"What does it do?" Hal turned the crystal in his fingers, catching the light, and moved it from hand to hand to avoid the burning chill that permeated the object. It was going to be a pain to hold on to this with his bare hands.

"It's a northern scrying crystal. They're very rare since they're made of pure ice magic, held together by very strong spells of protection and warding. Ragnar's going to be annoyed when he finds out I've been holding out on him."

"How does it work?"

The milky depths of the translucent gemstone gathered the light from around him to glow in his fingers. Either that or it had light of its own emanating from within.

"I have no idea. It takes pure ice magic to activate it. Hopefully, Ragnar can tell you how to use it. Once you master its use, it should allow you to see your family and make sure they are still alive. That will be the first part of your quest to learn magic. Master enough ice magic under Ragnar's tutelage to operate the crystal. Once you've done that, you will be ready for the next test of your abilities."

Tildi raised her arms and stared just over Hal's shoulder, her eyes wide as she opened her hands in a pretty good rendition of jazz hands. A gust of cold wind blew past him, rustling the weighted hem of his cloak around his boots. A chill ran down Hal's spine, and he pulled the edges of his cloak close about him as he turned to see where Tildi was looking.

Hal's eyes widened in shock to see an opening in the palace wall through which flakes of swirling snow blew, settling to the finely woven carpet on the floor below. He was about to ask Tildi where they were looking when someone shoved him from behind, and he stumbled from the flat, stable stones of the palace's floor to the uneven, snow-covered ground of this northern plain.

Struggling to remain on his feet, Hal put a hand out to steady himself on a boulder nearby and almost dropped the crystal in the process. The wind gusted around him, whistling in his ears as if trying to teach him a strange, eerie tune.

From far away, a voice called out to him. It was Tildi, still standing back in the palace bedroom. She was the one who had pushed him through.

"Concentrate on the crystal. It can work the cold around you, drawing it in and channeling it outward as well. When you master the art of staying warm in a few days, Kay and I will catch up to you."

"Tildi, I'll freeze to death out here."

"That is a distinct possibility, my boy. But if you do, then who will save your wife and daughter from the Emperor's plans? Once he figures out what they represent, he'll use the magic all three of you hold to take over the world once and for all. He'll kill you in the process of extracting the magic. My suggestion is you take my advice and learn from your earlier mistakes. You can do it, or not — there is no try."

Tildi threw her head back and laughed at the joke she had made at his expense, using his own earlier reference. She waved her hand in front of her, and before Hal could call out to her, the portal snapped shut, leaving him standing in knee-deep snow, shivering hard enough to rattle his teeth in his head.

Quest offered: Access the magic of the crystal. Avoid freezing to death.
Do you accept the quest?

Hal blinked his eyes against the blast of icy wind threatening to turn his eyeballs into frozen globes in his skull. The quest prompt remained plastered across his vision even with his eyes closed.

"Y-y-yes, I accept the q-q-quest."

Quest accepted.
Cold damage: Health -18

Damn, this was starting to hurt. He had to work fast. Pulling up his stats, Hal looked at the magic user class abilities. There had to be something there to use to energize the crystal or whatever he was supposed to do.

He noticed right away the mage class abilities and levels were not set up like the rogue or warrior classes. Instead of levels, he had the four schools or elements of magic beneath his core attributes. There was also a blank space below the four elemental forms of magic with a question mark. Perhaps he was supposed to unlock that space at some point.

Name: Hal Dix
Class: Mage
Level: 1

Attributes:
Brawn: 24 — +8 defense
Wisdom: 10 — +1 defense

Luck: 28 — +10 to all saving throws
Speed: 12 — +2 defense
Looks: 8
Health: 98/116

Character skills: Chakra regeneration — 3 (heal 18hp; 1/day).
    Mage experience: 0/300
    Ice elemental school: locked
    Earth elemental school: locked
    Fire elemental school: locked
    Wind elemental school: locked
    Unknown elemental school: locked
    Warrior experience: 140,800/250,000
    Rogue experience: 146,100/250,000

The *locked* message next to the ice elemental magic school entry flashed, signaling it was active in some way. Maybe he could level up there to activate the crystal so Tildi and Kay would catch up with the winter clothes and supplies he'd need to stay alive out here in the middle of nowhere.

He couldn't believe they'd leave him out here alone like this. This was just a test. It had to be. Soon, Tildi would open the portal again, and he'd tell her he'd learned a valuable lesson. What good would it do anyone if he died out here because he froze to death before he could learn to use ice magic?

Cold damage: Health -14

He dropped the crystal then, as his shivering shook the small stone from his hands and into the snow at his feet. Hal's blue and trembling fingers worked in the air to catch it before it disappeared into the snow, tunneling a tiny hole down into the powdery frozen fluff at his feet.

Hal fell to his knees as the frigid wind blew against his exposed skin. Needles of air drove into his face and hands while he dug around the small hole the crystal had made as it fell from his grasp into the deep powdery snow.

It had to be in there somewhere.

The more he dug, however, the more he disturbed the fluffy snow. Before he knew it, he found himself packing it down, obscuring and covering the area where the crystal had fallen.

Cold damage: Health -21

Blinking away the searing pain, Hal tried to scoop away the snow, sift it between his shaking fingers, and locate the crystal. He saw the snow pass through his extended fingers. No longer pink or even reddened by the cold, they were now turning white as the blood flow left his hands.

Hal shook his head. Strange how he could see the snow in the bottom of the shallow hole as he dug, but the cold crystals left no trace of feeling in his fingertips anymore, just the biting sting of the cold down to his bones.

Hal blinked his eyes to clear away the tears. A combination of deep aching pain and the biting wind in his face brought the tears to his eyes. The tiny, salty drops froze to his cheeks in twin icy streams down his face.

He didn't know why he was even looking for the crystal anymore. It wasn't like he was going to be able to do anything with it once he found it. His fingers were stiffening now; the frozen white claws at the ends of his arms might as well have belonged to someone else. They no longer did his bidding.

Hal was pretty sure frostbite was setting in, meaning he was going to lose his fingers, if not his hands, from the exposure to the cold. He snorted a weak chuckle. He couldn't bring himself to care.

It was over.

Cold damage: Health -16

Just about to give up, Hal caught a glimpse of something glowing blue-white in the snow at the bottom of the shallow pit he'd dug.

Dropping to his knees, Hal reached in and scooped his crippled hands together. His fingers wouldn't move, so he tried to get his palms under the crystal he'd exposed.

Hope caught him once more. He had to live.

Cold damage: Health -18

Desperation drove him onward despite the pain. He must live to save Mona and Cari.

Leaning over, he managed to get his cupped hands under the crystal and lift it out of the hole in the snow. Relief flooded through him as he saw the crystal roll into his palms and lift upward. A final tear fell from his eyes as he leaned over the crystal. Freezing in mid-air, it dropped and then shattered against the round, milky crystal Hal had lifted from the ground.

Pale, muted blue light flared from his palm at the instant the frozen tear hit the crystal.

Quest completed: Crystal unlocked with the frozen fluid of one's greatest fear.

300 experience points awarded.
Spell learned — Resist cold.
Level Up!

Hal clutched the crystal between his frozen palms and rolled over onto his back, staring upward at the dark northern sky and the swirling snow dropping from the dark clouds above.

He started laughing and concentrated on the new glowing ability. He'd done it, but he wasn't in the clear yet.

Cold damage: Health -12

Concentrating, Hal focused on the ability to resist the crippling cold. He struggled to remain conscious, awake, as everything became still. Even his shivering stopped.

That was bad.

His life slipping from his frozen grasp, Hal renewed his attack against the frigid chill that threatened to overwhelm him once and for all.

Channeling his little remaining energy into the newly unlocked magic, he discerned a blossom of blue-white light opening at his core, and a strange sensation spread through him from his center outward.

It wasn't a feeling of warmth as he'd expected.

Instead, it was as if he pushed the cold away from himself. He wasn't controlling the heat. He wrestled against the intangible cold, pressing it out from his center until the biting chill of the frozen tundra around him no longer touched his body.

Hal's fingers moved again, though he cried out at the pain of returning circulation. It was a cry mixed with joy, alongside the dull ache of feeling seeping back into his frozen nerves.

Hal laughed aloud, his voice piercing the swirling wind and snow in the darkness.

He'd not die out here after all.

He was going to live.

He was going to be an ice mage.

CHAPTER 5

THE FIRST NIGHT was the worst.

Every time Hal drifted off to sleep, his control over the tiny glimmer of ice magic he could access would slip away. The cold instantly insinuated itself back into his exposed skin and threatened to overwhelm him once again.

He found a place beneath a scrub pine where the boughs formed a natural break against the wind and snow. He burrowed into the hollow beneath the branches, and it was a little better. At least the wind didn't reach him here.

Hal sat at the base of the tree throughout the long hours of the northern winter's night, rocking back and forth to remain awake. The black cloak, which had seemed so heavy when he first put it on, now seemed pitifully inadequate, even with his newfound resistance to the cold.

Knowing he had to stay awake at all costs, Hal tried to discern the source of the tiny ball of magical energy that he could now see in his mind's eye, centered in his chest. To him, it looked like a blue gas flame, flickering in the darkness at his core.

It took him a while to hold the cold flame in view. He found he could do it best with his eyes closed and his chin pressed down against his chest. From this position, the flame flickered and wavered as if touched by an invisible wind.

Drawing on some of the meditation techniques taught him by his monk friend, Rune, Hal tried to reach out with his mind and touch the cold fire at his core.

At first, it eluded him.

The harder he reached, the farther away the blue flame seemed.

Hal struggled and pushed for a long time before it occurred to him to try a different tack.

Relaxing, Hal stopped reaching toward the light and instead tried to invite the fire deeper into himself.

Right away, Hal was rewarded with a strengthening of the light. The flame grew brighter, stronger, and ceased flickering.

As the light of the sun brightened on the horizon, after hours of time alone with the ice magic within himself, Hal discovered a sort of semi-trance where he could remain in contact with the magic. He could now resist the cold and still rest enough to try some healing.

By meditating and engaging his chakra healing skill, Hal was able to begin the process of recovery from his near-death experience of last night.

18 health points regained.

It wasn't much, but he instantly felt a little strength returning. The southern sky brightened a bit more, and Hal remembered he only had a few short hours of what amounted to daylight in which to find some food and rig a better shelter.

Tildi had told him she and Kay would catch up to him in a few days. That meant he had at least one more miserable night ahead of him, unless he could come up with a way to get out of the elements.

His tiny pine bough cave might suffice again if he could reinforce it with more branches from other nearby trees and shrubs. He had his daggers. He could cut more and layer them in a lattice that would provide more protection from the wind and snow than the tree offered alone.

Climbing out of his shelter, Hal emerged into the snow-covered plain. There was no sign of civilization in any direction. Tildi had said the wizard named Ragnar lived up here somewhere, but Hal had no clue which direction to go.

It was better to remain here and wait for Tildi and Kay to reach him than to stumble about in search of someone he didn't know, especially when he had no clue where to begin looking.

Hal set to work on his meager shelter. He drew one of his daggers and saw the pale skin of his hands for the first time in the dim light of the northern sun. They looked almost white, blanched by the cold of any pink to signify warm blood beneath.

He wasn't cold anymore. The cold resistance spell he maintained still worked, and his fingers moved when directed as if they'd never been nearly frozen solid, despite their appearance.

Hal shrugged. Whatever was going on, he'd have to go with the flow.

After stumbling through the deep snow, Hal reached another of the scrub pines nearby, began cutting the branches with the thickest boughs of evergreen needles, and dragged them back to his shelter.

Hal brushed back the snow that had drifted up against the base of the tree, then layered cut branches over the limbs hanging down around the bottom of the tree until he'd formed a cone that surrounded the base of the tree's trunk.

Satisfied with his work, Hal used the last branch like a broom and brushed the snow back against the lattice of branches until he'd created an artificial drift of snow all around the tree, except for a narrow opening through which he could enter his makeshift shelter.

Standing back, Hal nodded to himself. He remembered those survival reality TV shows he and Mona used to watch back home. Hal thought the hosts of those programs would be proud of the work he'd done here.

With shelter taken care of, Hal decided his next task was to find some food.

He thought about digging for roots to eat but decided that would be futile. He didn't have the slightest idea of where to begin looking, and he wouldn't know an edible root from a poisonous one anyway.

That left hunting.

Hal had seen what looked like tracks atop the powdery snow while he dragged the cut pine branches back to his shelter. He retraced his steps and soon spotted the marks in the snow.

Following the animal tracks, Hal saw they led to a small hole in the rocks against a low hill nearby. Finding a hiding place about ten feet from the hole, Hal crouched down behind a small bush and waited for the creature, whatever it was, to emerge from its den.

Even with his cold resistance spell maintained, sitting still in the snow for an extended period started to sap at his strength. After what had to be two hours of waiting, and as the light began to dim with the coming night, Hal's patience was rewarded.

The first hint of movement at the edge of the burrow drew Hal's attention right away. A head emerged from the hole as the snow hare searched the surroundings for danger, its white fur blending into the snowy background. Hal tightened his grip on the dagger in his hand and froze in place. He'd only get one shot at this.

After sniffing at the air and scanning the surroundings, the rabbit emerged from the burrow and began hopping across the surface of the snow. It retraced its steps from before, taking it past Hal's hiding place.

It was now or never, Hal knew. In a fluid motion, Hal's hand drew back and then whipped forward, flinging the dagger at the snow hare as it approached its nearest intersection with his location.

The dagger turned end over end as it flew through the air. The rabbit jerked its head around at the sudden movement, but it was too late to run. The pommel of the dagger struck the creature in the head, knocking it to one side in the snow, stunning it.

Hal drew his other dagger and ran forward from his hiding place, pouncing on the downed rabbit, grabbing it with one hand and plunging the blade into the creature's neck. A rush of red poured forth, staining the white fur and the surrounding snow with a spray of warm blood.

25 experience points awarded.

The sudden warmth of the life-giving fluid on Hal's hand felt like it burned when compared to the cold to which he'd become accustomed. He put the rabbit down, scooped up a handful of clean snow, and scrubbed the blood from his hands.

The instant he applied the snow to his skin, he felt better. It was as if the cold had become his accustomed medium after his battle to reach the ice magic within himself last night.

After grabbing the rabbit and retrieving his thrown dagger, Hal returned to his shelter and set to skinning and cleaning the fresh kill. He was not an experienced hunter by any stretch, but he'd seen and assisted the hunting parties while working as a caravan guard on his last visit to Fantasma. He'd learned enough to work out how to get the job done. Soon, there was a freshly skinned rabbit hanging from a branch next to the entrance of his shelter.

The furry white pelt was too cut up by his awkward knife work to be useful, so he used it to scoop up the innards he'd removed from the rabbit and buried it all in the snow a few yards away from his shelter.

Hal returned from disposing of the remains of the snow hare just as the sky began to darken to night. The short winter day was nearly over. He'd accomplished a lot in a brief time, and Hal was pleased with his progress. This night would be much more comfortable than the last one, he knew. He had a better shelter and some food.

All he needed now was a fire to cook his dinner. Hal considered his options. He could try to rub two sticks together like a boy scout, but he had no clue how to do it and suspected he'd waste too much time and energy working at it without any return on his investment.

Tildi could start a fire with her magic. He'd seen her light her pipe with a jet of fire from her fingertip on more than one occasion. He didn't know how it worked, and that seemed to be the opposite of the ice magic he was just learning to master.

Hal stopped and thought for a moment. Ice magic was the opposite of fire magic, right? Perhaps there was something to that line of thought.

He knew he needed three things to start a fire: a heat source, fuel, and oxygen.

Fuel he had. The pine sticks and dead needles that lay at the base of all the trees were full of pine sap. It was highly flammable in its dried state.

He drew in a deep breath. Oxygen was no problem.

Now he just needed heat. He couldn't channel a jet of fire, but perhaps he could do something else. It was a crazy idea, but maybe he could remove cold to the point that what little heat remained would be enough to start a fire. He was sure the physics of it was impossible, but this was magic, right?

Hal knew he didn't want to eat raw rabbit, so he had to try.

Quest accepted: Start a fire with ice magic.

After gathering a pile of dried pine needles and stacking them in a cone shape on the bare earth of a cleared spot near the entrance to his shelter, Hal next took dead pine sticks and crisscrossed them over the cone of needles until he had a small stack of layered branches.

Now came the crazy part. Hal sat down in the snow next to the cleared area on the ground and closed his eyes. He focused on the cold, blue flame of the spark of ice magic within himself and invited it to work with him.

Next, he opened his eyes and stared at the stack of sticks and dried pine needles on the ground in front of him. Boring his attention to the center of the pile, Hal used his newfound ability to push the cold out from himself and apply it to the frigid collection of needles before him.

Grabbing ahold of the cold at the center of the pile, Hal focused on creating an area where there was no cold, no chill, and drew the cold outward away from the pile of ready fuel. It was like picking up handfuls of loose sand at first. He felt as if the cold slipped from his magical grasp as fast as he grabbed at it.

Soon, with work and practice, Hal managed to hold on to more and more of the icy cold with his mind and push it away from the pile of sticks in front of him.

Hal stared at the pile as he worked, the intense concentration beading sweat on his brow.

Wait.

Was that a wisp of smoke?

Hal redoubled his efforts, pulling at the cold with all his meager power, drawing as much as he could hold and still grabbing for more.

This time, he was sure. There was a small column of smoke, the merest tendril drifting upward from the pile of needles at the base of the cone of sticks surrounding it.

Continuing his magical efforts, Hal leaned forward and gently blew into the base of the cone, which lent fresh oxygen to the pile of pine needles. The tiny column of smoke thickened.

While blowing still more air into the center of his would-be campfire, Hal pulled at the last vestiges of cold in the center of the pile of needles.

With a small pop, a lick of yellow flame appeared within the dried pine needles and began to consume the tiny brown needles as the pine resin fueled the fire.

"Fire! Yes!"

Hal laughed aloud and started placing more sticks and small

branches around the growing flame while he pulled more cold from the surrounding air. He couldn't give up now.

With five more minutes of work and coaxing, the small fire grew to the point that Hal felt comfortable releasing his hold on the ice magic. He almost collapsed from the accumulated exertion.

There was no time to succumb to his weariness, though. Reaching out to the small pile of firewood and branches he'd gathered, Hal continued to feed the fire until a satisfying blaze burned there outside his shelter.

Hal smiled to himself. He wouldn't freeze this night and he'd have fire and hot food to eat. Things were looking up.

Quest completed: Start a fire with ice magic.

300 experience points awarded.

Level Up!

CHAPTER 6

"Ho, the camp."

Hal stopped plucking the quail he'd killed and peered into the gloomy darkness outside the circle of light from his fire. His free hand dropped to rest on the pommel of a sheathed dagger on his belt.

"Who's there?"

Three forms materialized out of the shadows, walking into the firelight thrown outward by his campfire. Two were familiar. One was not.

"You said two days, Tildi," Hal said, returning to plucking the game bird in his hands. "It's been four."

"It took us longer to locate Ragnar than expected."

"What can I say? We're nomads," the tall, gruff-voiced newcomer quipped. He towered over Tildi's short figure next to him. "You must be Hal, my new apprentice. Tildi said you'd be cowering in the cold, half-starved. It seems you're more resourceful than she let on."

"Oh, she was mostly right. I almost died that first night, no thanks to her."

Hal turned his gaze to the third visitor.

"Kay, why didn't you make Tildi come find me sooner?"

"I tried, Hal. She refused to open a new portal until she'd

contacted Ragnar directly. Something about protocol when visiting another mage's territory."

Tildi limped over and poked at the campfire with the butt of her staff. "Stop complaining, boy. You seem to have done pretty well without my help. I'm surprised you managed to get a fire burning. I expected to find you eating grubs and slugs dug from under logs. Here you are with a veritable feast."

"I figured out enough ice magic without your friend's teaching to stay warm and start a fire."

"Oh, really?" Tildi exclaimed. "You started a fire using only ice magic." She slid a glance sideways at Ragnar. "Can you do such a thing?"

"It's not easy, Tildi, but yes, it can be done." The ice mage crouched by the fire and warmed his hands while he concentrated on the center of the blazing logs.

"You used the absence of cold," he continued, "to generate increased molecular activity and enough friction to start a fire. That takes some talent. It's easier to learn a few simple fire magic spells for use around the camp or home, but that takes an experienced mage to shift elemental schools like that."

"Yeah, well, I didn't have that option, so I had to come up with my own version of what you call the hard way to do it. Same result, though."

Hal finished plucking the bird and added it to the makeshift spit he'd created with two other quail already plucked and dressed out on it. He leaned forward and suspended them over the flames, resting the ends of the spit on two stakes he'd carved and driven into the ground on either side of the campfire.

"Something told me to expect company either tonight or tomorrow morning, so I prepared extra food. You're all welcome to join me. I don't suppose you brought some bread or cheese with you, though. Some salt would be nice, too. I'm getting tired of just having plain meat."

Kay sat down, dug into her backpack, and pulled out a hard loaf of brown bread and a wedge of cheese. She grinned at Hal and tore off a piece from the bread before handing it across the fire to him.

He took it and tore off a piece for himself, then reached for the wedge of cheese. He sliced a slab as thick as his finger free with his dagger and slapped it on the chunk of bread he held.

"Mmmmm, that is just what the doctor ordered," Hal said, taking a bite of the bread-and-cheese combo. "You know, the one thing I missed most about Tandon was the artisanal cheese I could get from the farmer's market in the Harbor District. There's nothing like it in the grocery stores where I'm from."

"Someday, Hal, you're going to have to take me to your land," Kay said. "It seems both a strange and wonderful place."

"It has its pluses and minuses. Most people don't get left out in the wild to fend for themselves for days on end unless it's part of a contest on TV."

Tildi laughed at that statement. "At least you'll be ready if you ever want to become a contestant on *Survivor*, Hal."

"I'll pass if you don't mind. I'm not a fan of extreme camping, and this experience hasn't changed my mind. Besides, I've got more important things to do."

Hal reached into his pocket and pulled out the milky white crystal Tildi had given him that first night.

"Here's your magic stone, Tildi. I kept it safe for you."

"What's this?" Ragnar asked. "You have a scrying crystal, Tildi?"

"It turned up while I was searching through an abandoned tower a few years back. I never needed it until our friend, Hal, turned up. I figure he can use it to locate his family and home in on them when the time comes to initiate a rescue."

"You think he's got the power to activate it?" the northern mage growled. "I could have used it on several occasions trying to avoid the Emperor's mage hunters. You should have given it to me for safekeeping. I'm the ice mage, after all."

"I think not, Ragnar. You know the stones can become attuned to a particular user. I think it was best to hold it for Hal here. Now that he's used it to unlock his access to ice magic, it'll give him access to its full powers once you school him in the use of ice magic's potential."

"It takes a spirit mage to use all the powers of a scrying stone, Tildi. There hasn't been a user of the spirit school for hundreds of years." Ragnar scowled at Hal. "I suppose our mythical Opponent here is supposed to not only be an ice mage-in-training but a potential spirit mage, too?"

"I think Hal will be able to use all the schools equally well. Ice, earth, fire, wind, and spirit."

"I don't have time to learn all of that, Tildi. You told me that Ragnar could teach me to use the scrying crystal to see if my wife and daughter were alright. That's what I aim to do. Then I can use it to home in on them for the rescue mission."

"The Emperor is surrounded by powerful wards at all times, boy. Did you think you'd just learn a few parlor tricks, open a portal, and waltz in there with your magical guns blazing?"

"Something like that."

"Then you're a fool. The Crystal City's wards are created by mages from each of the four primary schools. There's no way to open a portal within a hundred miles of the Emperor's palace without the wards engaging and frying you before you take one step. The only way is to master the magic of the spirit and that requires you to become schooled in all of the elements. Only then can you hope to rescue your wife and child."

"So, I'm stuck jumping through hoops you set up for me until I learn what I need to learn? That's what you're saying."

"Stop acting like a spoiled child, Hal." Tildi leveled a stern gaze at him. "I didn't steal your family, but I will help you get them back because the alternative is allowing the Emperor to become so powerful no one will be able to defeat him. We can either work together or die independently. There is no longer any other alternative."

"Unfortunately, my boy, Tildi is right," Ragnar added. "We tried working against Kang and his pet mages on our own, and it hasn't worked. All our friends have been killed off one at a time until there are only four of us left. Tildi is the only one who had the vision to find you. Since you've been coming to Fantasma, the Emperor has been suffering defeat after defeat. I don't like it but you're the key, and that means you've got some more work to do."

Hal started to say something in return, but Ragnar held up a hand, forestalling his response.

"I'll take you on as an apprentice, teaching you what you need to use the crystal to scry your family and watch over them from afar. It'll take the combined magic of the other three schools to unlock the other attributes of the stone, though. If you can learn to do that, then you might have a chance to access the spirit element. That's your only way of reaching the Emperor's palace and getting your wife and child free."

Hal turned the stick acting as a spit for the quail roasting over the fire. He took another bite of the bread and cheese and considered everything Tildi and Ragnar had said. In the end, he turned to his only real friend present for advice.

"Kay, what do you say? You and the rest are fighting the Emperor on the front lines. You know more about what's going on here than I do. What do you think?"

"I hate to say it, Hal, but I don't think you have a choice. This isn't the place for one of your 'clever plans.' They're the mages and I trust their assessment of the magic needed to get to the Emperor and your family. If this is the path they've laid out for you, then I figure it's the best option you have. Whatever you decide, though, I'll have your back."

Hal nodded and returned Kay's smile. Through all his adventures here in Fantasma, she'd been right there, making sure he got to where he needed to be.

"Fine, I'll be your apprentice, Ragnar, and I'll follow the rules to learn what I need to learn from you and the others, but only until I have the skills needed to get my family back. Once that happens, I'll expect you all to back me up. If I really am the mythical Opponent of prophecy, then that means you have to follow my lead in the end. Fair?"

Ragnar and Tildi exchanged glances, and Ragnar extended a hand to Hal. The two clasped forearms to seal their agreement. Tildi just met Hal's eyes and nodded before she pulled out her pipe and started puffing away while she waited for the dinner to be ready to eat.

Hal settled back and finished cooking the game birds over the fire. He was tired and more than ready to get started learning how to do more than just survive using magic. He needed to dig into the depths of each mage's knowledge until he could do everything they knew how to do. Only then could he confront the Emperor directly.

Hal Dix was ready to get his magic on.

CHAPTER 7

Hal, Ragnar, and Kay set off the next morning, heading northwest into the deeper reaches of the Northern Wastes. They left Tildi seated by the campfire, puffing on her pipe and blowing rings of smoke into the early morning air.

"She always has to be mysterious, it seems," Hal remarked.

"Oh, you have no idea." Ragnar laughed. "She has been that way since we started our training together years ago. She once told me it behooved us to live up to all the expectations people had for wizards and mages. That's why she is always seen puffing away on that pipe. She knows it's strange. Honestly, I don't think she enjoys it very much. It's just for effect."

Hal turned to see if she was still blowing smoke rings at the campsite. He blinked in surprise, noting she had already disappeared. He looked forward to the day when he could just open a portal and vanish into thin air. It would be a much more efficient way of traveling.

"Ragnar, why don't we travel by portal, too?" Hal asked. "We could move faster that way."

"It's not as easy as all that, boy. I can travel that way by myself, but it is difficult to bring anyone with me. Each elemental school has strengths and weaknesses. Wind elemental mages are much better at opening portals from one place to another and are more able than the rest of us to transport more than just themselves from place to place."

"So, what do ice mages specialize in, then, besides being cold all the time?"

"Ice is a crystal; it is rigid because it is hard and cold, yet flexible because ice is just frozen water. Ice magic offers great protection spells and other abilities to obscure us from detection."

"What about offensive capabilities? Will I be able to fight back if attacked? I'm not wearing any armor, and I don't look forward to getting up close and personal with my daggers if I don't have to."

"There are some things we can do that enable offensive capabilities, but nothing like the fire mages can do. Fire is inherently destructive, so most of their spells are focused on attack and devastation."

"Sounds like fire is stronger than the others in some ways, if it is the elemental school offering the greatest forms of attacking others."

"You'd think so, but then you'd be a fool," Ragnar said with a snort. "There must be a balance to all things. This is especially true with magic. Fire is a great offensive tool, but how would you use it to protect yourself? You can't wrap yourself in fire without burning yourself, even with a protection spell in place. Just as with resistance to cold, fire resistance isn't absolute. There are limits to what a fire mage can do without injuring themselves. But you can surround yourself with ice if need be and force others to batter their way through the ice to get to you."

"So, you have to carry water with you to freeze wherever you go?"

"Of course not. There's water all around us. Even in the most remote desert, water is present in small quantities. Not enough to do anything major, but enough to use simple spells to protect oneself."

"Teach me a protection spell."

Ragnar stopped and turned around to face Hal.

"Very well. Enable your resist cold ability. Then reach out and search the air around you with your mind. Do you sense the water vapor present all around? It will seem as if there is mist everywhere when you finally see it in your mind's eye."

Hal closed his eyes and selected his resist cold skill from the menu. Then he tried searching around him for the water vapor in the air nearby. While it wasn't particularly humid in the frozen north like it would be farther south along the coasts, he started to sense a... dampness to the air, a quality to it that seemed just like Ragnar said it would. Like a mist suspended all around him.

"Now pull at the mist and draw it to you like a cloak until you feel it touching your skin and clothes all around."

Hal did as he was told, and soon enough, his shirt had a clammy property to it as if he'd put it on wet from the clothes washer without drying it first.

"Good, now for the fun part. Push the cold from the air together around the cloak of mist until you've super-chilled it and it freezes. Make sure you don't drop your cold resistance, or it's going to hurt, a lot."

Hal knew how to do this. This manipulation was how he'd started the fire two nights ago, and he'd practiced it more since. He grabbed at the chilly air around him and drew it in tight against the misty cloak he'd created. The mist froze instantly, forming a hard shell all around him.

And now he couldn't move. Not an inch. He was frozen solid inside an inch-thick block of ice all over.

"Nice." Kay chortled from behind him. "You could do that at a party sometime and be the ice sculpture in the center of the food table. It would save the host dozens of gold pieces if they didn't have to hire a sculptor or have the ice carted in from the ice house."

"Laugh if you must, woman, but before you put it up as a cheap party trick, try your sword against the ice he created."

"You're not serious."

"Oh, I most definitely am serious. Do it now and you'll see what I mean."

Hal tried to protest, but he couldn't even speak from his place encased in the ice. In fact, he was starting to panic. He couldn't breathe either.

A jarring clang hit him from behind, and he realized Kay had just taken a swipe at him with her sword. Judging from the force behind the second and third blows, he assumed she had little effect on him with her blade.

"That water crystalized in a near-perfect lattice of ice surrounding him and is nearly impervious to simple blows by weapons, at least until you manage to chip your way through it."

Hal's vision was starting to tunnel, with blackness encroaching from all around his field of view as the available oxygen in his lungs was used up. He managed to groan from within the ice encasing him.

"You fool!" Ragnar exclaimed. "Didn't you leave an opening for your mouth and nose?"

The wizard moved around into Hal's field of view again and placed two fingers against Hal's face. The ice melted, and water flowed down his cheeks and chin until his face was free and he could breathe again.

Gasping as best he could with his chest encased in ice the way it was, it took him a few seconds to regain his composure. Ragnar shook his head in exasperation.

"You've got to think ahead, boy. Even the dumbest simpleton I've ever worked with knew enough to leave their head and face free the first time they did that. Idiot!"

"How do I dispel it? Or do I have to wait until spring to thaw me?"

"Push the cold away from the water, and it will liquify again. I should warn you..."

Hal didn't wait to hear the warning. He pushed the cold away from himself, returning the inch-thick layer of ice to water in an instant. And then he was soaked to the skin, as if he'd jumped in a swimming pool in his clothes.

"As I was saying... If you're not careful, and you don't let the water vaporize again as you push the cold away, you'll get very wet."

Ragnar turned away and shook his head. "What kind of dolt has Tildi saddled me with?"

Even with the cold resistance spell in place, Hal felt every inch of his soaked clothes, and he began shivering in the frigid northern air uncontrollably.

"Th-th-that's a n-n-nice trick, but w-w-what good is it in battle if I can't move?"

Ragnar turned and pointed to his dripping sleeve. "Do it again, but this time focus on just your forearm, from your elbow to your wrist."

Hal closed his eyes again, and when he opened them seconds later, his right forearm was encased in a cast of ice from the elbow to his hand. He could bend his arm and twist his hand and fingers. Focusing his energy again, he was able to encase his upper arm in a similar tube of ice from the shoulder to the elbow.

Ragnar drew his hand axe from his belt and tapped it on the ice encasing Hal's right arm from shoulder to wrist. Hal could see the ice chip a little, but the frozen armor held.

"Well done. Now you see how it could work for you in battle. Of course, it will be some time until you've practiced enough to bring it all together fast enough to save you in a sudden fight. The same can be done to create a shield of sorts between you and missile weapons if needed."

"It's a shame it's so clunky-looking."

"It doesn't have to be."

Ragnar stood straight with his arms outstretched from his shoulders, and within seconds, he was encased in a clear crystalline armor of overlapping plates covering his entire body. The ice armor was etched in runes and animal shapes. It was beautiful.

Kay clapped and cheered. "Now that's a useful spell. How wonderful."

Ragnar drew his axe and went through a few practice swings while calling a circular shield into being on his arm. The round panel of ice had the shape of a wolf's head molded into it.

After a few more moves to demonstrate how flexible the armor could be, Ragnar stood still and concentrated. The armor dissolved into mist and dissipated from around him into the air whence it came.

The northern mage glanced at Hal with an eyebrow raised in question.

Hal nodded. "Fair enough. I have a lot of practice to do and a lot more to learn."

"That's the first intelligent thing you've said all morning. Now come on, we've got a long walk ahead of us if we're going to catch up with my tribe before the caribou move on to better feeding grounds."

Hal and Kay fell into step behind Ragnar, Hal's boots squishing with each advance as the remaining icy cold water sloshed beneath his feet.

He had a lot to learn indeed.

CHAPTER 8

They trekked for four days, and they still didn't catch up to Ragnar's tribe following the caribou herds across the tundra from feeding ground to feeding ground. Hal tried to make the most of it. He spent the time practicing the few ice magic spells he'd learned so far. He wanted to work on them until he could cast them in his sleep.

Resist cold was easiest. It had become second nature since that first difficult night in the wilderness, but he still had to concentrate for a few seconds to cast ice shield and ice armor, and even longer to start a fire. The shield spell was the easiest of the latter three so far. Hal could now summon a disc of magically hardened ice three feet in diameter, centered on his forearm.

He convinced Kay to test her sword on it. After a few tentative taps on the ice to make sure she didn't accidentally cut Hal's arm off, she hammered on his magical shield with gusto. Eventually, she chipped away at the barrier, though if Hal concentrated on it, he could repair the damage as fast as she caused it.

The armor presented another challenge altogether. Hal remembered the complexity of Ragnar's ice armor. During one of the breaks in their trek, he tried to create something similar to Ragnar's articulated armor.

It was a complete failure. Hal ended up with a series of paper-thin layers of frost all over his body. The ice cracked and flaked away as soon as he moved.

Ragnar grunted a laugh at his pupil's first attempt at real armor made of ice.

"You can't start at the top, boy. You must work up to it. I've been perfecting my armor for decades. Start with something simple and practical first, like a single breastplate to protect your vitals. See it in your mind's eye and make it happen."

"I'll try."

Quest accepted: Create an ice breastplate.

Hal considered the advice and focused his mind on encasing his torso in a layer of ice. This time, he was able to visualize what he wanted. He closed his eyes and drew in the moisture around them while he formed the armor.

When he opened his eyes and looked down, his chest and back were encased in a simple breastplate of opaque light blue ice. He twisted his body and bent down to see how mobile he was. Unlike his previous attempts, he could move, and the ice didn't crack or fall away.

Hal rapped on the armor with his knuckles and smiled. It seemed sturdy enough.

"Kay, try out your sword on this."

"I'm happy to, but this chipping away at magically hardened ice is ruining my blade. You have to agree to repair my edge with a whetstone tonight if you want me to keep testing it on your armor."

"Agreed. Go ahead. Give it a try."

Hal thumped a fist on his armored chest and then stood still, with his arms raised, to give her a clear shot at his chest and back. By this point, Kay was more confident in Hal's abilities, and she took a full swing at Hal's chest, following it with a return blow to his back.

He felt the contact, and the force nearly knocked him down with each hit, but the armor held.

Quest completed: Create an ice breastplate.
600 experience points awarded.
Level Up!

He was pleased with what he'd created but it wasn't practical yet. Any opponent would slice him in half by the time he'd concentrated long enough to build his armor, and it only protected his torso. A glance at his magical level status menu showed he'd gained some skills but still needed more practice to level up to the point it would be practical in battle.

Mage experience: 1,225/2,400
Ice elemental school:
Resist cold; Ice shield; Ice armor.
Attribute points: 6

He allocated four of his attribute points to his wisdom attribute, deciding he needed to bolster his spellcasting abilities if he was going to be successful as a mage. He split the remaining points between his luck and speed. Hal didn't see himself needing his brawn attribute anytime soon. He noticed that, unlike the other classes, it seemed the mage class didn't reward the player with new skill points at every level. It looked like he would have to learn new skills the old-fashioned way.

Hal spent the next day creating and then dispelling his breastplate until he managed to don the ice armor on his torso in a few seconds. His practice came in handy sooner than he expected.

The first signs of trouble appeared when they spotted the circling vultures in the sky ahead. It could have been anything, including a dead animal on the trail. It wasn't. The five people, two women and three men, had been dead for at least a day, their bodies stripped of clothing and armor and staked out with arms and legs extended on either side of the trail.

Hal wanted to look away and vomit, but he swallowed the bile in his throat and forced himself to examine the corpses. Though the vultures and other animals had picked at the bodies, it was clear they'd been tortured and cut up before they died.

He recognized flaying when he saw it, having experienced that particular torture in person at the hands of one of the Emperor's henchmen on his previous visit to Fantasma. Ragnar had stopped to examine one of the women, and Kay walked in a wide circle around the bodies, searching the ground for something.

"What are you looking for?"

"Tracks, Hal. Whoever or whatever did this had to move on when they were finished. It would be nice to know which direction they were headed."

"It was grendlings," Ragnar growled. "I recognize their rituals in the way they mutilated the bodies. What I don't understand is what would drive them to do this. Our tribes lived in peace alongside them for decades."

Hal turned and scanned the scrub brush on either side of them for signs of those who'd done this. He realized he didn't know what he was looking for.

"What's a grendling?"

Kay completed her circle of the bodies and stopped next to Hal. She had her sword out.

"They're a northern variety of goblin. They mostly roam the edge of the ice floes of the far north, hunting and fishing, though they come south from time to time to trade with human tribes and settlements."

"That's why this doesn't make sense to me," Ragnar said as he stood and scanned the horizon. "This time of year, the grendling bands should be in the north, following the sea lion migration along the coast to their breeding grounds. There shouldn't be any this far south at all."

"What do you want to do with the bodies, Ragnar?" Kay asked. "We can't leave them out here like this."

"Leave them. The ground's too frozen to allow us to dig any graves, and we need to pick up our pace and catch up with my tribe. They have to be warned there's a grendling war band around."

"These people deserve some sort of burial or something," Hal protested. "You may not care about them, Ragnar, but someone does, somewhere. It's the right thing to do."

"I do care about them. They are from my tribe, a hunting party probably, and they stay where they are. We cannot let the grendlings know we were here if they pass by this way again. They'd expect someone to move the bodies, and that will be their alert to track us. We have to leave, now, before they return."

"Kay and I can fight. We will stand against them. They have to pay for what they've done to these people."

"Our priority is to the living, not the dead. We move onward and warn the rest of the tribe. That's final. Now, come on. We've got to move."

Ragnar took off at a jog, his hand axe in one hand, a short sword in the other. Hal and Kay exchanged glances, he spared one last look at the scattered bodies, then the two of them ran to catch up with their guide.

The ice mage set a grueling pace, and Hal's lungs soon burned from inhaling the cold, dry air as they ran along the trail. Judging by the wheezes coming from Kay, he figured she was doing little better. After the end of the second hour at the pace Ragnar had set, Hal had had enough.

"Ragnar, we have to rest. Kay and I can go no further until we catch our breath."

The mage stopped and came back down the trail to where Hal and Kay were hunched over, struggling to regain their breath.

"We cannot stop here, boy. There've been signs of the grendling war band for the last mile. They are close but spread out. If we stop, they'll be able to gather their group and attack us. We have to keep moving."

Hal straightened and scanned the scrub trees in the small hollow where they'd stopped. It was lucky he did. He spotted the gray-green skin of the creature as it stepped out from behind a tree and drew back its bow to take a shot at the trio.

Hal didn't have time to think; he acted on instinct.

Shoving Ragnar to the ground, Hal brought up his round ice shield just as the grendling released the arrow.

Hal made the shield as broad as he dared while keeping the ice a sufficient thickness to hopefully stop the incoming missile.

It worked.

The arrow snapped and broke apart when it impacted Hal's shield. Two more arrows shattered and fell to the ground next to the first.

Two other grendlings had emerged next to the initial one. After dropping their bows, the three creatures, their gray-green bodies wrapped in thick furs, pulled out wicked barbed war axes and charged at the trio of humans on the trail.

Hal barely had time to materialize his ice armor before the lead grendling set upon him. The leader's war axe descended and took a chunk out of the edge of the ice shield.

That was the problem with making it too thin, Hal thought, shaking his head. The lighter, broader shield could stop an arrow but not those heavy iron axes.

Kay had her triangular kite shield in place and met the second grendling with her sword in hand. Hal drew one of his daggers and tried to reconfigure his shield to a more useful size on the fly, while the lead creature continued to hammer at it.

Ragnar was on his feet now and had donned his ornate armor,

suddenly covered in gleaming, reflective plates of translucent ice. The third attacker, the largest of the three, focused on Ragnar.

The ice mage had sheathed his short sword and extended his hand with fingers spread and pointing at the incoming grendling.

The creature's eyes widened, and a frightened yelp escaped as six-inch shards of ice darted from the mage's hand, heading straight at its face.

Hal didn't have time to see if the ice shards impacted or not. His grendling had finally hacked his way through Hal's shield, and he couldn't manage to reform it in time to stop the next attack.

Rather than just stand there, Hal chose to charge the creature, trying to get inside the arc of the bigger weapon borne by the grendling.

Hal's ice-encased torso slammed into the lighter creature, and the two of them fell to the ground before the sweep of the war axe completed its swing.

The axe skittered away as the grendling let go of the larger weapon and fumbled for a knife on its belt. Hal's free hand scrabbled to get a grip on the hand reaching for the knife while he tried to stab downward with his dagger, evading the grendling's other outstretched hand attempting to stop him.

The grendling missed with its grab at his dagger hand, and Hal was able to bring his blade down and strike at the creature's shoulder. A snarling grunt told him he'd managed a hit on his opponent.

Hal brought the dagger up to strike again when a roundhouse punch caught him on the right cheek and sent him sprawling to the side.

He shook his head to recover from the blow and rolled over on his back to meet the attack he knew was coming. The grendling had regained his feet and picked up his weapon from the ground. He lifted the axe to strike down at Hal, lying on the ground.

There was one chance and Hal took it. The familiar, rumbling slot machine of Hal's luck sounded in his mind as he extended his hand, just as he'd seen Ragnar do seconds ago. He thought he had the theory of what the mage had done to create the flying ice shards. It was time to see if he'd guessed right.

Hal grabbed at all the moisture he could draw toward himself and froze it as fast as he could, driving it outward at the same instant.

His effort worked better than he'd planned. Instead of a series of dart-like shards, a single, giant shard formed and drove forward, hitting the grendling standing over him in the chest and knocking him backward onto the ground.

Shocked at the power of his impromptu spell, Hal sat up to see his opponent pinned to the ground by the four-foot-long ice shard, eyes glazing over as it stared unseeing at the blue sky above. The slot machine pinged with success as his luck played out in his favor once more.

500 experience points awarded.

Kay had finished off her attacker, and Ragnar sat atop his foe, belt knife pressed to the creature's throat. The mage spoke to the grendling in what must be the creature's native tongue. Hal couldn't understand a word of what they said.

Whatever was uttered, the grendling snarled and launched spittle into Ragnar's face. His beard dripped with the creature's spit, and Ragnar howled with rage. He drove the knife up under the grendling's chin, through its throat and into its brain. It spasmed once then lay still.

Kay stood over the mage looking down at the dead grendling.

"I hope you managed to learn what they were up to before you let him goad you into killing him."

"I did. They were offered a great bounty from the Emperor himself for my head, delivered to the mage hunters who are currently on a ship anchored off the northern coast. It seems they grew tired of trying to track me down themselves and decided to enlist the grendlings to hunt me down. That was why they tortured the hunting party. They were trying to extract my whereabouts from them before killing them."

Hal climbed to his feet, brushed himself off, and retrieved his dagger from the ground. Ragnar stood as well and gestured to the grendling still pinned to the ground by the long shard of ice.

"Nice ice lance. How'd you figure that out?"

"I saw you shoot the darts from your hands. I tried to do the same thing and overcompensated a bit."

Ragnar shrugged. "It did the trick. When in doubt, go for overkill. You may not get a second chance. Good work, though. Looks like you are processing the use of your magic faster than I thought. That's good because things are likely to get dicey fast with the Emperor's lackeys roaming about up here, stirring up the grendling bands."

"We should get moving again," Kay suggested. "There have to be more of these things around. Like you said... If we stay still too long, they'll be able to gang up on us."

"The girl's right," Ragnar agreed. "Come on. With luck, we'll catch up with the tribal camp by nightfall. Hopefully, the grendlings won't attack before then."

After a final scout around to make sure they weren't advancing into a trap, the trio set off at an increased pace once more. Urgency overcame exhaustion, and Hal dug deep into his reserves to keep going. They had to warn Ragnar's tribe of the impending attack.

CHAPTER 9

THE THREE OF them took a little longer than expected to catch up to the roving tribe. It was near midnight, by Hal's reckoning, when they encountered the first sentries outside the camp.

"Hold!" a voice called out of the darkness. "Identify yourselves."

"Alfric, stand down. We are friends, not foes."

"That you, Rags?"

A shadow detached from a boulder outside the camp, outlined by the campfires beyond. The figure was massive, standing well over six and a half feet tall. Ragnar stepped forward and approached the sentry.

"Where's Tripp? I have to speak to him right away."

"He's in the camp. Who's that with you?"

Ragnar gestured to Hal and Kay to step closer.

"These are some friends of mine. They're traveling with me for the time being. Hal, Kay, this is Alfric."

Hal and Kay both nodded a greeting before Ragnar continued his explanation.

"Look, we have to rouse the camp. There's a grendling war band out there. They killed Karn and the others in her hunting party a day's travel east of here."

As Hal got closer, the shadow solidified into a broad-shouldered northern tribesman in chainmail and thick furs. He wore a square steel helm atop his chainmail coif.

"grendlings? There hasn't been a dispute with them for generations. You're mistaken, surely."

"I wish I were. We were attacked this afternoon by an advance party on the trail between here and where I found Karn and the others."

"Tripp is in the central yurt. You know how to find it."

Ragnar nodded. "Spread the word among the sentries to be watchful for signs of the grendling approach. Unless I miss my guess, they'll likely be here in eight hours, if not sooner."

Alfric gave Ragnar a sharp nod and started around the camp's perimeter, spreading the word of the impending attack.

The three travelers passed through and made their way into the camp. Despite the late hour, there were several men and women up and about inside the campsite. All seemed to know Ragnar and called out greetings to him as they passed.

Soon they made their way to the large central yurt. It consisted of caribou-felt canvas stretched over a portable wooden frame. There were many like it in the camp, but this one was significantly larger than the others scattered around it and could probably hold up to twenty-five or thirty people inside.

"Wait here," Ragnar told them. "I must talk with the chieftain before I introduce you. He's distrustful of strangers."

The mage pulled aside a felt curtain draped over the entrance and disappeared inside. Hal and Kay waited outside. Voices, muffled by the distance and the thick felt walls, drifted out from inside. Judging by what he could pick up of the tone, Hal noted someone was more than a little upset.

The entry curtain was pulled aside, and Ragnar's face appeared from the interior. Golden light emanating from inside backlit the mage's face.

"Come in but stay silent and let me do the talking. Tripp is a little angry about me bringing you both here when the mage hunters are so close by. I told him they were hunting me and not you, but he doesn't want to take the chance."

"You're the boss," Hal said. He pulled the curtain aside to hold it for Kay, then followed close behind.

Inside the yurt were several sleeping platforms created by stacks of furs on the tarp-covered ground. People were waking and getting dressed in armor or buckling on weapons.

"Are these the two new mages you told me about?" The big chieftain wore his blond beard braided into two thick ropes of hair hanging down to his chest. He scowled at Hal and Kay. "I'm still more than a little pissed you brought them here."

"Only one of them is a mage, Tripp. The other's just good to have around in a fight. We'll be able to lend a hand."

"You're sure these grendlings are going to attack?"

"The one I questioned before he died told me all I needed to hear. They have been whipped up into a bit of a frenzy by the imperials anchored in the North Sea off the coast of their central village. I don't think they had much choice to come and find me."

"How many are there? Maybe we can hold them off long enough to parlay and broker a peace."

Ragnar shook his head. "I was told three full war bands. That's nearly two hundred warriors. You are going to want to run. Standing and fighting will be suicide. Think of the women and children, Tripp."

Hal couldn't hold his tongue any longer. "Ragnar, if they're looking for us, why don't we let them see us and lead them on a chase away from the camp?"

"Way ahead of you, boy. That's exactly what we're going to do, but I fear they won't settle for leaving Tripp and the tribe behind them to harass their supply lines. They might opt not to attack the camp, but I don't think we can afford to take that chance."

"I agree," Tripp replied. "We need to get everyone ready to travel before dawn. If we can move on before they arrive, it might let them know we mean them no harm."

"What can we do to help?" Kay offered. "I don't want to get in the way, but I'm keen to help somehow."

Tripp thought for a few seconds and nodded.

"You two can relieve some of the sentries from the perimeter if you're willing. They'll be needed to dismantle the yurts. That would be a huge help."

Kay smiled. "We can certainly do that. Ragnar, we will go speak to that big sentry we passed on the way in."

"Good, go and do that," Ragnar agreed. "Have Alfric send those he can spare to me, and I'll assign them tasks when they get here."

Hal and Kay left the central yurt and made their way back to the edge of the camp. They found Alfric by the big boulder along the trail into the campsite. After telling him what they were there to do, he found a pair of guards who could be spared to go help in the camp and settled the two visitors to cover the approach to a steep hillside on the southern boundary of the tribe's camp.

After sending the tribesmen back with Alfric to help with breaking down the camp and packing everything to move, Hal and Kay prepped their position in case they encountered any approaching grendlings. While he'd demonstrated he could create a larger missile made of ice, he had not mastered small precision darts like he'd seen Ragnar cast.

Kay made a round of the perimeter in their area, and Hal practiced creating smaller and smaller ice missiles until he was able to craft a pair of six-inch-long ice daggers he could direct to fly straight in whatever direction he faced. It still wasn't the six missiles he'd watched Ragnar create, but he suspected that came with practice and increased level.

After walking the perimeter twice and scouting out about fifty yards away from the hilltop, Kay returned and sat on a low, flat stone.

"What's the plan if they do come at the camp from this direction?" she asked.

Hal stopped and looked down the slight rise to the rolling plain extending away from them.

"We only have to stop them for a short time until the tribe's rear guard arrives to help hold them back."

"Too bad we can't slow them down, so they don't reach us on the hilltop before help arrives," Kay said while she scanned the horizon. "There's no time to build any fortifications."

"Maybe we can do something to disperse and confuse them." Hal stopped and snapped his fingers. "I wonder."

Hal stood up and walked to the edge of the hilltop. "This should work if what Ragnar told me about ice magic in the beginning was true."

Kay joined him but didn't say anything.

Hal closed his eyes and imagined what it would look like if a fog bank rolled down the hill from his position.

Kay gasped, and Hal opened his eyes to see a fine mist extending outward from his hands and flowing down the hillside, thickening into dense fog as it spread out. He held onto the spell as long as he could, about thirty seconds, before he had to release it. It was kind of like holding your breath. At some point, you had to let go and breathe again. Creating the fog bank had the same sensation.

Spell learned — Wall of fog.
  700 experience points awarded.
  Level Up!

Hal knew he could increase the size and duration of the fog with practice, but for a first try, it wasn't half-bad. Anyone trying to approach their position would enter the small fog bank and hopefully become disoriented, giving him and Kay the chance to pick them off one at a time as they exited the thick mist.

"Uh-oh!" Kay pointed beyond the wall of fog he'd created. They could see over the top of it to the far side. Gray-green figures advanced across the plain in their direction.

The grendlings had arrived. They were here much sooner than expected. As he watched the enemy approach, he picked out something else in the distance. Squinting, Hal spotted a line of six horsemen riding behind the advancing grendling force.

"Kay, I think the mage hunters have joined the battle. They're here for either Ragnar or me. Go and tell him they're here. I'll do something else to slow them down while you're gone."

"Hal, we're sentries. We're not supposed to fight the battle on our own."

"Don't worry; I only want to slow them down. The fog is a good start, but once they find their way through, all they have is this hill to climb and they'll be storming into a camp full of families on the run. Every second I can buy is more time for them all to head east, away from the attack."

Kay spared a single glance in the enemy's direction then started down the far side of the hill towards the camp. She called out to Hal as she hurried off.

"Don't be a hero, Hal. If they break through, run for it."

Hal waved his hand in reply. His attention was already on the leading slope down to the fog bank. He had a hint of a plan, but his thoughts came slowly as if they had to move through jelly to get to his brain. Creating that fog bank had spent him, depleting a reserve of power deep inside he hadn't known he could tap. He needed rest but there was no time.

The grendlings were now closer than before. He could hear their growling yips and yowls, alien war cries carried on the wind to his position. The first of them entered the fog bank and disappeared inside it. It would slow them, but eventually, they'd find their way to the other side.

Shaking off the cobwebs in his mind, Hal had one more idea to try. He spread out his fingers horizontal to the hillside with his thumbs touching and his palms down. He closed his eyes and drew upon as much of the hidden reserve of energy as he could bear. Opening his eyes, Hal directed the vapor in the fog bank at the base of the hill to chill, until it began to freeze onto whatever surface it contacted.

Shouts of alarm inside the fog signaled his success. The coating of ice on the ground inside the fog and on the lower slopes of the hillside below would be hard to cross with any speed now.

The exertion didn't come without a penalty. Hal swooned then clutched at his chest as crushing, squeezing pain tore at something inside him.

As the darkness closed in, he had a final wry thought. Pushing himself beyond his limited magical abilities wasn't a good idea apparently.

Health damage: Health -55

Hal fell to his knees and tried not to cry out in pain. He needn't have worried. He lost consciousness before he had a chance to give voice to his agony.

CHAPTER 10

"THE BOY'S A DAMN FOOL," Ragnar growled. "What was he thinking?"

"What's wrong with him?" Kay asked. "He looks dead, worse than dead." Hal heard worry flooding her tone.

"I don't have Bronwynn's abilities at healing, but I could delve him well enough to know he broke something important inside. His magical spark is dimmed, almost missing entirely."

"Is he going to live?"

"Probably, though he'll not be casting any magic for a while."

Hal tried opening his eyes but squeezed them shut again when the light from the blue sky overhead flooded in. The brightness sent a stab of pain into his brain. At the same instant, the wagon or cart he lay in rolled through a rut and slammed him rapidly up and down. He let out an involuntary groan.

"He's awake," Kay said. She placed a hand on Hal's arm. "Hal, what were you thinking? You could have died before anyone got back to you. As it was, we nearly didn't. Whatever you did to the grendlings forced them to circle around and try to approach the camp from a different direction. That was the only reason we had time to go back and search for you."

"It worked? I wasn't sure."

Ragnar let out a brief chuckle. "It worked, though I've never seen anyone as new to magic as you harness that kind of power. You probably took a year off your life force, drawing on your internal reserves that way."

Hal realized he was shivering, despite being under a pile of blankets. He accessed his menu and tried activating his resist cold ability. It was grayed out and wouldn't allow him to turn it on. In fact, all his spells were grayed in the menu rather than sporting their usual glowing golden hue.

"I can't cast anything. My magic is gray."

"Boy, I don't know what that means, but you're right about not casting anything anytime soon. You damn near burned yourself out yesterday. I'm surprised it didn't kill you outright."

"But I have to have magic. My family..."

"Will have to wait, Hal," Kay told him. "Ragnar thinks your damage can be repaired but not by him."

"Who? Tildi?"

Ragnar laughed. "Tildi is able to do a lot of things the rest of us cannot, but she's not up to healing this. Bronwynn is the only one who can help you, if anyone can."

"That's where we're taking you," Kay explained. "Ragnar thinks, if we can get you to the High Forest and Bronwynn's stronghold in time, she can restore your magical power. Now lie still and rest. It'll take us two days to reach the place where Ragnar can reach out and contact Bronwynn for help."

Hal nodded and let sleep overtake him again. It brought a welcome respite from the sensation of a hammer trying to drive a spike into his skull. Anything was better than the constant throbbing pain.

———

Hal woke as Kay and Ragnar moved him from the cart to a blanket spread on the turf at the foot of a tall rounded stone, which stood within a circle of smaller square blocks carved of the same light gray rock. Beneath the lichen and moss covering much of the stone, Hal could make out weathered patterns of runes and etchings in the surface.

His hand drifted to his head. The pain was still present but much less than it had been.

"How long did I sleep?"

Kay turned and pulled the edge of the blanket back over him to keep him warm against the chill of the northern wind blowing through the stones.

"You've been in and out of sleep for the better part of two days. Ragnar kept having to stop and cast more healing spells on you."

The ice mage leaned over him, scowling.

"I hope it's not a waste of time, boy. I'm not much at healing, and it took a great deal more of my energy to keep you alive than I'd like to spend when we're being pursued like this."

"Pursued? Who?"

"Those mage hunters are likely still on our trail." Ragnar paused to spit on the ground at the mention of the Emperor's thugs. "I think I managed to throw them off the scent for a while. The problem is, the way they followed us to the camp makes me think they are tuned in to my magic use somehow. If I'm right, then they're going to know exactly where I am when I activate the stones to send you to Bronwynn."

"Why couldn't you open a portal where we were and send us to her then?" Hal asked.

"Like I told you, boy, not all of us are as good at teleporting as Tildi is. Most of us need to use natural centers of power like these stones to enable magic outside our chosen elemental school. We were lucky this place was as close as it was to us."

"Will Bronwynn be able to help me recover my magic? I have to get it back, Ragnar."

"If anyone can help you, she will do the trick. Healing's her central ability. She knows more about the life force that runs through all of us than anyone alive. Once you're fixed up, she can also teach you about earth magic, which is the next task Tildi has for you. I have one piece of advice for you. Bronwynn can be, uh — prickly — yes, that's the best word for it. She is big on courtesy and knowing one's place in the world. I suspect it comes from being an elf princess, but whatever the reason, you need to keep that in mind and stay on her good side. If she decides you're not worthy of teaching, not even Tildi and all her stubbornness will change Bronwynn's mind."

"I'll keep that in mind. So, what's next?"

"I'm going to contact Bronwynn using the stones to focus my power. Once I reach her, you and Kay must place a hand on the central stone and keep them there while the two of us transport you to the High Forest. After that, it's up to Bronwynn."

A shout in the distance interrupted their conversation.

"Damn, that's got to be the mage hunters. They've found us. Quick, put your hands on the stone."

Hal rolled to his side, gritting his teeth as the sudden movement set his head to throbbing again. He reached out and pressed his hands against the smooth base of the stone where it met the turf.

Kay reached over him and did the same.

Nearby, Ragnar muttered something under his breath Hal couldn't make out, and then a bright light flared overhead, the glare blinding Hal for a moment until his eyes could adjust.

A woman's voice filtered down from the light source.

"Ragnar, you startled me. What are you doing opening the stone portal without the proper preparations?"

"No choice, Bronwynn, I've got the one Tildi sent me. He's injured beyond my ability to heal. I need to send him and his companion through to you. The hunters are almost here, and I didn't have time to follow the normal procedure."

"You know what that does to the inherent power of the stones,

Ragnar. Once I bring the two of them through, the portal will close for a fortnight. You'll be trapped there on your side without a way to escape."

"Don't worry about me. I'll find a way to slip past their wards. I've done so before."

More shouts reached them from outside the circle of stones. The voices were much closer now.

"We're out of time, Bronwynn. You've got to pull them through. I can't do it from this side without letting go of the doorway."

"Be careful, you old fool. I expect to see you again, soon."

Ragnar didn't say anything. He gave a half-snarl, half-grin and nodded.

The light above flared once more, and this time Hal felt something shift, like when an object outside a moving car went in the opposite direction, disorienting you for a moment about which way you were going. When the light subsided, and Hal's eyes adjusted to the dim light, he and Kay were somewhere else entirely.

It was no longer cold, the chill of the northern wind replaced with a gentle forest breeze, carrying scents of wildflowers and freshly mown grass within its gentle caress. They had arrived in a forest clearing, surrounded by a ring of enormous trees stretching high into the sky. At the center was an even larger tree, taller than the others around it.

Hal struggled to a sitting position to look around. Kay stood nearby, her hands raised. She faced four archers clad in muted greens and browns. All had their bows drawn with arrows nocked. When Hal moved, two shifted their aim to him.

"Don't move."

Hal didn't need the shouted order from the closest archer. He got the message and raised his hands over his head.

Studying his captors, he noticed the slightly pointed tips of their ears, which had slipped out from beneath the braided strands of their straight blonde hair. *Wow, real elves.* He'd known they existed in

Fantasma, but they usually kept to themselves and were rarely seen outside of their forest strongholds.

Behind the four elves, a figure in white robes stepped from behind a tree into the clearing.

"Stand down," Bronwynn ordered.

Hal recognized her voice from the light shining over the stones back in the Northland.

The elves lowered their bows but stood ready to intervene. Judging by their discipline and the way they carried themselves, Hal assumed these men were hardened warriors. They were ready to act, even with their weapons at rest.

The elven princess approached. A silver circlet lay across her brow, disappearing into the long strands of blonde hair that draped her white-clad shoulders. She was probably the most beautiful woman he'd ever seen and totally out of his class. Heck, she was in a class all by herself.

"Greetings to you, Hal Dix, and to you, Princess Kareena. Welcome to the High Forest. I'm sorry for the stern nature of my guardians. They take their responsibilities seriously and don't like it when I receive visitors unannounced."

Hal needed to say something. But what? He was at a loss for words. Luckily Kay was not. She executed a perfect curtsy, even in her armor.

"We thank you for your hospitality, Princess Bronwynn, though we expect no less from one such as yourself. Your reputation precedes you and does not begin to live up to the reality of your presence."

Hal thought Kay had laid it on a little thick, even after getting Ragnar's warning of how to act. Bronwynn, however, welcomed the compliment with literal open arms, wrapping Kay in a warm embrace.

"We are cousins in nobility, Princess Kareena. How could I not extend the hospitality of my ancestral home to you and your companion? Please call me Bronwynn. Between we princesses, there must be some familiarity, yes?"

"Then you must call me Kay, Bronwynn. It is how I'm known now, since my family's downfall."

"A most unfortunate turn of events and one that will hopefully be remedied someday."

"That is why we are here, Bronwynn. Hal has certain abilities, according to the mage, Tildi the Elder. She believes he could be..."

Bronwynn raised a hand, interrupting Kay's explanation.

"I'm well aware of who and what Hal Dix represents to Fantasma. I did not agree with Tildi's initial decision to involve him in this world's conflicts, but I have to admit, he's demonstrated a certain ability to insert himself in places where he will most disrupt the status quo."

Kay chuckled. "That is an apt representation of him, Bronwynn."

"You both know I'm right here and can hear you talking about me, right?"

"Ah, the man can speak for himself, I see." Bronwynn smiled down at Hal then pointed in his direction. "Guards, place him under house arrest until I decide what to do with him. The princess and I will discuss his disposition in private."

The elf princess gestured to the edge of the circle and nodded to Kay. She returned the nod and, with a brief glance back at Hal, followed Bronwynn from the forest clearing, leaving Hal and the four elven guards alone.

"Well, it's just the five of us now. So where to?"

The leader pointed to Hal, and two of the guards shouldered their bows and lifted Hal to his feet. They pulled his daggers from their sheaths on his belt and led him to a separate path in the opposite direction Bronwynn and Kay had taken. As they entered the trees and started down a winding path into the lush green of the High Forest, Hal tried to keep track of the twists and turns his captors took. He hoped he could get away from them and return to the clearing to find Kay. It was no use, though. Within a hundred steps, he was hopelessly lost.

Hal shook his head. This wasn't good. His interaction with Bronwynn, the second mage he needed to learn wizardry from, had not started off on the best of terms.

CHAPTER 11

HAL HAD TO ADMIT, this was the most comfortable jail cell he'd ever been in. It was more of a jail apartment than a cell. There were several rooms in the small stone building, including a bedroom, a privy chamber, and what could only be called a parlor.

The furniture featured ornate wooden carvings and designs, along with embroidered cushions in tones of greens and tan. The bed, though a tad small for Hal's size, had a feather mattress and a thick comforter, useful against the chill of the forest at night. He didn't need it, though. After staying in the frozen north, Hal thought the night here was practically balmy by comparison.

Despite the presence of all the creature comforts, it was still a prison. There were bars in the windows with a wrought-iron lattice resembling living vines. His guards remained outside the single door and only opened it to bring him a tray bearing bowls of fruits and nuts that must be what elves called dinner.

Hal tried talking to his captors on several occasions, but the elves either didn't understand him or refused to talk with the prisoner in their custody. After the third time the guards refused to answer him, Hal gave up trying. Eventually, they'd tell him what was up, though he wasn't sure what he'd done to deserve getting locked up in the first place. Bronwynn was supposed to be one of Tildi's mage friends.

Hal winced when he turned too fast away from the window. He was still recovering from the injury he'd done to himself stopping the grendlings. Perhaps some chakra healing would help. Hal started the meditative trance taught to him by his friend Rune and went through the motions of the Tai Chi-like chakra exercise. After several minutes, he was rewarded with a chime and a notification.

18 health points restored.
   Health: 93/130

He noticed a difference right away. The dull ache in his bones had lessened, and he felt mentally refreshed though physically tired at the same time. Hal decided he wasn't going to learn anything useful from his silent guards, so he might as well turn in early for the night. It was hard to judge the time this deep in the forest canopy, but it was definitely getting darker.

Hal took the lamp, already lit on the table in the parlor, and carried it to the nightstand in the bedroom. On the way, he scooped up a handful of nuts and munched on them while he got ready for bed.

Maybe Kay would talk some sense into Bronwynn, and she'd let him out of here. In the meantime, there was nothing to do but get some sleep.

It was morning when Kay's voice jolted him awake.

"Hal get up and get presentable. Bronwynn's agreed to take a look at you and see if she can heal your injury."

"Great, so she's decided to train me after all? I was beginning to think I'd done something wrong."

Hal rolled out of bed, pulled on his boots, and reached for his cloak hanging on the post at the foot of the bed.

Kay lowered her voice. "I don't know that she's ready to teach you her magic. Look, all elves are prickly, like Ragnar said. Bronwynn is worse than most. You'd do well to keep that in mind and pay attention to your manners while here among them."

"Why? I didn't do anything wrong."

"Stop whining. It's bad enough you're here in the first place. They don't like unannounced visitors or humans in general."

"They treated you well enough."

Hal leaned forward and sniffed in Kay's direction.

"You've had a bath at least. That's not the way I was treated."

"I'm considered visiting royalty of a sort, even though my family is deposed. It's a formality, but it's that formality which makes it important to them. Just remember manners and rules."

"Manners and rules, got it. It still would have been nice to have a bath, too."

"Oh, my goodness, Hal, stop complaining. You were extended hospitality, even if you were confined to this cottage. Be gracious Bronwynn took us in when Ragnar sent us here. She could have refused. We would have been captured by the Emperor's mage hunters for sure. Remember that."

"I'll be good. I'm just saying it would be nice to know what was going on for a change."

"That's a luxury we don't often get in life. Come on. Bronwynn is waiting."

Hal followed Kay from his forest cottage prison. The guards waited for them, then formed up in front and behind them, and led them down the path into the forest. Hal resisted the urge to make a snarky comment. He'd promised Kay he'd be good.

Once again, the path they traveled wound and twisted through the trees until Hal was thoroughly lost. He thought maybe they'd take him back to the original clearing. Instead, they ended up walking up to a tall, thin spire, rising above the surrounding trees. The guards led them to the base of the spire, where an iron-bound double door offered the only entry he could see.

The guards took positions beside the door, and Kay reached up and pushed it open.

"We are going upstairs to Bronwynn's private rooms. Remember to let me do most of the talking. I think I can convince her to take you on as a student, but first, we need her to fix whatever you did to break your magic."

Hal pretended to zip his mouth shut and throw away the key. Kay rolled her eyes and led him inside. One of the guards reached around and pulled the door closed once the two of them had entered the base of the spire.

A spiral staircase led upward from the entry room. There was also a single wooden bench along the wall, above which were several mounted pegs and a few hanging cloaks.

Kay sat down and pulled off her boots. "Take off your boots. It's rude to wear shoes indoors here."

"Ah, Japanese rules, then."

"What are you talking about?"

"Nothing," Hal replied as he pulled off his boots. "Lead on. Let's get this over with."

Kay started up the spiral stairs and Hal followed.

They passed through several rooms on their way up the inside of the spire. One of them looked like an alchemy or potion lab, complete with liquids of different colors bubbling within glass beakers and tubes on the tables around the room. Hal, intrigued by the setup, wanted to inspect the room some more, but Kay shot him a glance when he started to say something to the two silent elven attendants working in the lab.

They finally reached the audience chamber where Bronwynn sat on a silver throne, equipped with a green, cushioned backrest and seat. The elf princess wore a similar white robe to what she'd worn yesterday when Hal arrived. The delicate silver tiara still encircled her brow.

Kay led him across the room to stand a few feet from the raised throne. Hal followed Kay's lead, even when she offered a deep curtsy to their hostess. Hal tried to deliver a formal bow, bending at the waist and sweeping a hand in a broad arc to the floor.

He wasn't sure if he pulled it off successfully or not. Bronwynn's expression did not change when she addressed him.

"I did not agree with Tildi's decision to bring you here the first time, Hal Dix. She bullied us into assisting her with her plan, something she often tries to do."

"If it's any comfort to you, the first time I came, I didn't give permission to be sent here, either."

"Indeed. Yet here you are on what, your third trip to Fantasma? Why did you return twice more to a place where you did not want to be?"

Judging from Kay's expression, he was treading on thin ice here. Hal decided to be concise and honest in his response to the question.

"The first time I returned to your world, I came because of a friend. Kay needed rescue."

"And the reason for this journey?" Bronwynn's face remained impassive and unreadable as she asked the question.

"The Emperor sent his minions to my home and took my family."

Silence.

Hal watched the elf's eyes for some sign of a response. It was as if a master sculptor had carved her face from unyielding ivory.

He opened his mouth to explain more but stopped himself. This was a test to see if he would volunteer information she could use against him in some way. He wasn't sure why she wanted to trip him up, but he was sure his assessment was correct.

Hal closed his mouth and adopted an impassive glare of his own, remaining silent. He was unsure how long he and Kay stood facing Bronwynn without speaking. After what seemed like interminable minutes passed, it was the elf princess who spoke first.

"The message from Tildi did not relay this information about your family. She only said you had returned and I would be required to teach you the ways of earth magic. Tildi is — well, that old woman can be — shall we say, caustic?"

"That is a good way to put it," Hal agreed.

"You realize your family is likely already sold into slavery. That is the way Kang handles the families of his adversaries."

"It is my hope to use a scrying stone, given to me by Tildi, to see my family and verify they are well. I am unable to cast that particular spell with my current abilities."

"You are unable to cast any spells at all after your foolish actions in the Northland. Princess Kareena informed me about what you did. I must admit, it was an admirable effort to save the escaping tribe from the threat."

"I couldn't stand by and do nothing."

"No, I do not suppose you could."

Bronwynn slid forward on her throne, her back held ramrod straight as she moved. Pushing her sleeves up her arms, she exposed the alabaster skin underneath, only a shade darker than her pure white garments.

"Approach so I may delve you and determine what you have done to yourself."

Hal shuffled forward, uncertain if he should kneel or wait for her to stand. When Bronwynn didn't rise, Hal went down to one knee and leaned towards the elven princess. She placed her delicate finger-tips on either side of his head. The power of her grip on his head surprised him.

He heard her breathing become deeper and more even, and he sensed a tickle in the back of his mind. It was something he couldn't touch, but it was there, just out of reach inside his brain.

The tickle became a vibration, increasing in intensity over time until he could no longer remain silent. Letting out a gasp, Hal tried to pull away, but Bronwynn pressed inward, increasing the pressure of her grip on his head. She released a gasp of her own when he tried to move and then hissed at Hal.

"Hold still. I'm almost finished. If you break the connection now, it will destroy your mind."

The vibration inside his head had reached the point it was rattling his teeth. A low, guttural groan rose up from his chest.

Health damage: Health -12

"Stop it, Bronwynn," Kay shouted. "You're hurting him."

"Almost there."

"Ahhhhhhrrrggg." Hal couldn't respond in coherent words anymore, no matter how he tried.

Health damage: Health -16

"Almost there."

"Bronwynn, there's blood coming from his ears." Kay's voice sounded distant to Hal, echoing as if at the end of a tunnel.

"Almost th— Yes!" Bronwynn released Hal's head, and he collapsed to the floor, his breath coming in heaving gasps.

"It is done, though I'm not sure how you managed to damage yourself in that way."

Hal rolled over and stared at the ceiling of the audience chamber. He was drained. He'd never run a marathon, but he imagined this would be how one felt at the end.

"Wh-what did you do?" Hal croaked through a parched throat.

"There is a place inside each of us that allows a connection to the power coursing through the whole universe. Some are more attuned to it than others, and those may become a mage in one of the elemental schools, according to their talents. Your magical center is more...open, I would say the best word is. It seems able to allow more flow from the power centers of Fantasma than would ordinarily be allowed. Somehow you forced one of the channels, the one for ice magic, open to an extent I've never seen before."

"I needed more power, and I pulled at a flow I could sense inside me to do what needed to be done."

"That makes some sense, then. It acted like a drain in the bottom of a tub and siphoned all your magical reserves away when you did that. In time, you might have refilled on your own, but in all likelihood, it would have drained away before you could use it."

"Were you able to fix what was broken? I must train. I need to save my family."

"I have repaired the broken portal inside you. You seem to have broadened the size of the reservoir for magic within you to a size I've never seen before. With time, your reserves will return and may become even larger than before."

"When will I be able to train and learn again?"

The pleasant laugh cascading from Bronwynn's smiling face surprised Hal.

"Be patient. I fear you will not be ready for anything resembling training in magic for several days now. We will revisit your request at the end of the week, once you've regained some strength and healed what was broken."

"But..."

"Hal, Bronwynn is right. We've done enough for today. She is tired from her exertion on your behalf. Let's give her some peace to rest."

For the first time, Hal noticed the tightness around the elf's eyes and what looked like crow's feet on the ageless face. She had leaned to the side in her seat, supporting her body with one elbow on the padded arm of the silver throne.

"My pardon, milady. I did not see what should have been clear to me." Hal bowed again as he had when he arrived. "We shall take our leave and look forward to our next meeting."

"Thank you, Hal Dix. I believe we both will need time to recover. Farewell."

After his bow, Hal tried to spin in place to execute a graceful exit. He stumbled and caught himself on Kay's shoulder. He realized how unsteady he was after Bronwynn's healing treatment. His companion reached out to steady him, and together they walked back to the spiral stairs to return to the ground floor.

A new determination filled him. He'd wait, but he wouldn't be patient. Too much hinged on getting his abilities back.

CHAPTER 12

EVEN WITH HIS IMPATIENCE, the next four days passed by in a rush for Hal. No longer under house arrest, he found exploring the elven city deep inside the High Forest fascinating. Though most of the elves he encountered were aloof and deigned not to talk with him, they would answer direct questions if he needed to find his way back to his apartment or was seeking someplace to get food.

On the fourth day, as he wandered through the trails that made up the city's thoroughfares, Hal found his way back to the great tree at the city's center. This was where he and Kay had first arrived.

The enormous tree, dozens of feet across at the base, was situated in a broad grassy clearing. Thirteen other trees surrounded the central trunk, spaced at even intervals around the clearing's edges.

Upon discovering the location, Hal slowed and drank in the aura of the peaceful forest glade. He felt a reverence for the place he hadn't appreciated when he was here the last time. After taking a step forward, he moved onto the grass inside the ring of trees. A chime sounded, and it took a moment to realize it was a game notification in his head. Hal pulled up the source of the sound.

Do you accept the quest to help the great tree bud and flower?

Hal stopped. He didn't know what he was supposed to do. Was this a trick? Bronwynn might be furious with him if he broke something on the great tree. It was apparent this was a holy place to the elves.

The golden letters of the menu hovered in his field of view while he considered the offered quest.

It was only a flower. What could it hurt?

"Yes, I accept the quest."

The chime sounded again, followed by the quest notification.

Hal wondered what he was supposed to do now that he'd accepted the quest. Moving forward until he stood next to the central tree, Hal looked up. The first branches started high above, around twenty feet up. He wasn't going to climb up there anytime soon.

Unsure what to do next, Hal circled the base of the huge trunk, his right hand outstretched, his fingertips brushing against the smooth white bark of the tree. Now and then, a spark of static electricity stung his fingers. He didn't pull away, though, instead seeking out the next spark as he strolled around the tree.

A pattern emerged on his third circuit around the trunk. At the four cardinal directions — north, south, east, and west — the tree sparked against his touch. Realizing he could predict the next spark, Hal continued for a fourth circuit around the tree, this time ready for the tiny electrical jolt to signal him again.

At the next tiny zap to his fingertips, Hal stopped and examined the tree at that location. At first, he didn't see anything. Leaning forward, Hal ran the fingers of both hands over the smooth surface that resembled white birch bark from back home, though it didn't peel from the trunk as birch bark did.

Hal stopped running his hands over the trunk when he discovered a small raised area under the surface. It signaled something different from the otherwise smooth, rounded surface of the tree.

This time, instead of a static spark, Hal felt the tingle of a continuous charge flowing into the palm pressed against the bump on the tree's surface. Not sure what else he was supposed to do, he closed his eyes and tried to visualize the flow from the tree into his hand.

Hal found himself inside a darkened place, blackness all around him except for a pinprick of light directly ahead. As he noticed it, the light drew him closer, growing brighter the closer he got.

The light's source was a small wooden pod the size of a golf ball. It was egg-shaped with smooth ridges of raised wood grain across the surface. Hal couldn't resist the urge to reach out and touch the glowing pod.

Do you wish to share life force with a seed of the Tree of Life?

Hal shrugged. It seemed like the right thing to do.

"I will."

A tiny jab against his index finger made him draw back his hand. A single drop of bright red blood rested on the surface of the pod. Hal stuck his finger in his mouth by reflex and watched as the droplet of blood vanished into the wood.

The glow flared white, brighter than the light of the sun, and Hal shielded his eyes from the glare. When the light faded away, Hal was once again in the forest glade, standing before the great tree. Everything was as it was before.

Well, not everything.

A flower bud, the size of his fist, now grew out from the side of the tree where the bump under the bark had been moments ago. Chills ran down Hal's spine as the bud opened and a flower emerged, individual petals of yellow, purple, and blue unfolding in front of him.

It was the most beautiful thing he'd ever seen in his life. He felt something on his cheeks and raised his hands up to his face to find tears. It was a strange reaction, but in some way, it was totally perfect for the moment.

Quest completed: Help the great tree bud and flower.
    2,500 experience points awarded.
    Level Up!
    Earth magic elemental school unlocked.

"Hal Dix, what have you done?"

Hal turned to see Bronwynn and a squad of guards standing behind him.

"I touched the tree and it grew this flower."

He knew the answer was simplistic, but he was still overcome by the emotion of the connection to the tree and the new life the magic had sprouted because of him.

"That tree has not flowered in a thousand years. What did you do? Tell me. Now!"

"Bronwynn, I did not mean to do anything wrong. I came here as I wandered the city this morning and walked around the tree. When I touched it, it sort of talked to me and asked me to share life force with it. I didn't know what that meant until now."

The guard captain started forward to seize Hal, but Bronwynn raised a hand, forestalling his advance.

"How did you do this? You did not possess any earth magic abilities when I delved you, yet I sense in you a new awareness blossoming even as the flower of the Forest's Heart grows behind you."

"What is the Forest's Heart?"

"Every one of the great elven forests began when a seed from this tree was carried to a new grove and planted at its center. There hasn't been a new seed produced in a thousand years. You arrive in our midst and, after only a few days, cause the tree to produce something no living person has seen."

"So, it's a good thing?"

Relief flooded over Hal. He'd thought he'd screwed up somehow.

"It is a very good thing indeed, Hal Dix. You have been given a great gift and handed an even greater responsibility. Turn and accept your destiny."

Bronwynn pointed behind him. Hal turned and saw the small wooden pod of his vision revealed at the center of the flower, now in full bloom.

Reaching out with one hand, Hal touched the pod with his fingertips. It surprised him when it fell from the flower at his touch. He snatched it from the air before it fell to the ground. Its strange internal warmth flowed into him through his hand until it reached his core.

Spell learned — Plant growth.

Quest accepted: Plant the seed of the great tree.

Hal glanced back over his shoulder at the elf princess. "I think I'm supposed to plant this somewhere."

"You are. That is your quest and responsibility now that the tree has chosen you to be the bearer of its seed."

"Great, lead me to the garden or wherever you plant baby trees, and I'll dig a hole for it."

"That is not my task, Hal Dix. It falls to you to journey to the Fallen Forest to the east and plant the seed there. Once you accomplish the task, the forest will be cleansed, and our people may return to it after many years in exile."

"But I don't have time to travel to your lost forest and plant this seed. I grew it for you. Your elves can plant it."

Hal held out his hand, trying to give the seed pod to Bronwynn. She stepped backward, her hands remaining at her sides.

"I may not take the seed from you. No one may plant the seed but the bearer entrusted to the task by the tree. You must make this journey and cleanse the forest of the evil that drove us from it centuries ago."

"But I have to learn earth magic. You're supposed to teach me. That was what Tildi wanted."

"You have two great talismans now, Hal. You possess the scrying crystal, and now you have a seed pod from the Tree of Life itself. Go and plant the seed. Use the magic you now possess to grow the new tree. The magic of the earth will reveal itself to you in the completion of your quest."

"Sounds like a bunch of mumbo jumbo," Hal muttered under his breath.

"What was that?" Bronwynn asked.

Damned elf ears.

"Nothing, Your Highness. I don't suppose you can give me directions to this Fallen Forest of yours?"

Bronwynn smiled and gestured for Hal to follow her. She turned and strode back into the forest, taking the path leading to her spire. Hal was going on another journey, and he'd only just gotten here.

Hal pulled up his stats as he walked behind her. He had four more attribute points to allocate. He dropped two in wisdom, hoping to improve his spellcasting abilities even further, and then used the remaining two to bring his luck and speed back to their original values lost to Norak's cursed sword.

Name: Hal Dix
    Class: Mage
    Level: 6

Attributes:
    Brawn: 24 — +8 defense
    Wisdom: 16 — +4 defense

Luck: 30 — +11 *to all saving throws* (*Max*)
Speed: 14 — +3
Looks: 8
Health: 130/130

Character skills: Chakra regeneration — 3 (*heal 18hp; 1/day*)

Mage experience: 4,925/9,600
  Ice elemental school:
  Resist cold, Ice shield, Ice armor, Ice darts, Ice lance, Wall of fog.
  Earth elemental school:
  Plant growth.
  Fire elemental school: locked
  Wind elemental school: locked
  Unknown elemental school: locked
  Warrior experience: 140,800/250,000
  Rogue experience: 146,100/250,000

CHAPTER 13

HAL KICKED at his horse's flanks with the heels of his boots, increasing the mount's pace to keep up with Kay and the two elven guardsmen accompanying him on their journey. Bronwynn had provided them everything they needed to make the trek to the Fallen Forest, including the captain of her guard and his sergeant.

The four of them had been on the road four days, and the two elves had said less than ten words to him. They spoke to each other in their elvish tongue, but neither he nor Kay could understand what they said.

"Kay, tell Gareth to slow down."

"I think he wants to reach the edge of the hills ahead before sundown, Hal. That seems to be where we're heading. According to the map Bronwynn gave us, the Fallen Forest is just on the other side. If we camp there, we can reach the forest by midmorning tomorrow."

"Well, at least there's that good news. I'm not used to riding a horse, and I will be happy to get out of the saddle for a few days."

"Hal, what kind of hero can't ride a horse?" Kay chided him.

"What kind of princess can't drive a car?"

"What's a car?"

Hal sighed. "Never mind."

He kicked his horse to catch up and found his hand once again resting on the smooth leather of the pouch at his waist. Inside, he felt the bulge of the seed pod.

A few days ago, he'd taken the pouch off to go and wash up in a stream. Two steps away from the pile of clothes he'd left on the stream's bank, nausea and dizziness overcame him and knocked him to his knees.

It took Hal only a moment to realize he had to remain close to the seed pod or it made him very ill. Since then, he'd checked for its presence by reflex. Stranger still, he wasn't bothered by the need to keep the pod with him always. It made him happy when he held it close, like it was feeding him with its presence.

Kay was right. As soon as they reached the foothills of the ridgeline ahead of them, Gareth dismounted and signaled to his sergeant to begin gathering firewood. Hal and Kay caught up to the two elves, and the four of them set to getting their camp ready.

They had fallen into a routine whereby Kay helped the sergeant with gathering firewood while Hal set up the small camp stove they carried on their pack mule. The device consisted of a metal grate with four tall, metal legs to hold it suspended over a campfire or hot coals, which made it easy to cook a meal using their small collection of pots and pans.

Earlier in the day, Gareth had shot a small wild pig with his bow, and now the captain started working on the carcass to cut some chops for them to roast over the fire. Hal took their largest cook pot and walked to the brook running past their camp a few hundred yards away to retrieve some water.

He returned to see Kay and Chance, the sergeant, had started a small fire. Kay was placing the camp stove over the burning logs as Hal approached with the pot.

"I'm thinking polenta since we have the cornmeal."

"Is that all you know how to cook, Hal? There must be something else you can make with the supplies Bronwynn gave us."

"Do you want to cook dinner?"

Kay held up her hands in surrender. "No, you know I cannot cook. No one wants to eat anything I manage to create over a campfire."

"I think you burned those griddle cakes on purpose, so you wouldn't have to cook any more meals on this trip," Hal said.

Kay shot him a smile as she walked away to gather more wood. "A woman never reveals her secrets."

The comment drew an actual snort of laughter from Gareth on the other side of the camp. He was tending to the horses and their pack mule, picketing them at the edge of the clearing so they could graze but not wander away in the night.

"You want to share some of your elven wisdom for handling women, Gareth?"

The elf shook his head and returned to his work with the animals.

"Chicken," Hal said.

He picked up the large cast-iron skillet and placed it on the stove grate over the fire to preheat while he drew one of his daggers to trim some of the fat from the chops Gareth had cut from the pig for dinner. He dropped the pork fat in the skillet to render it before he added the chops to sear.

Hal enjoyed cooking dinner, even though he didn't like to let the others know. It reminded him of home. He did most of the cooking in his house. It had to do with his schedule being more amenable to getting home in time to start the evening meal. Mona often worked late at her job, and it fell to Hal to do a lot of the meal preparation for the three of them.

His thoughts drifted to his wife and daughter while he tended the fire and prepared the meal. He'd tried every night of this journey, once he settled into his bedroll, to get the scrying crystal to show him his family. No matter how he tried to manipulate the translucent stone with his hands or his magic, it remained inert and silent regarding the secret powers it possessed.

Hal would try again this evening, but he was losing hope of ever completing his training and reaching his family. The futility of doing the same thing repeatedly, with no change in the result, weighed on him.

"You've got that look on your face again, Hal."

Kay sat down on a saddle on the opposite side of the fire from him.

"I don't want to talk about it."

"This is a journey with many stops along the way. At each stage, we are closer to getting your family back. You have to keep that in your mind. If you lose hope, then you've already failed."

Hal used the point of his dagger to stab one of the chops in the skillet and turn it over. He shook his head at Kay's point.

"It's easier said than done, Kay. You know that, right?"

"You know I do. I've been searching for my brother and sister since we were sold as slaves years ago. I haven't given up and you can't either."

"I'm not giving up, Kay. I want to push harder and get to the end faster. I feel like I'm stuck in the mud here, going off on this random quest to plant a tree somewhere."

"But you have to learn to use the earth magic, and this is a way to do that. It's all connected. The fastest route between two places is rarely a straight line on a map. There are mountains and rivers and oceans in the way that dictate a different path. That is the case here, too. Stay the course, Hal. Every day brings us closer, even if it seems like we're going in the opposite direction."

Gareth and Chance, sitting cross-legged on the ground nearby, used whetstones to hone the edges of their sword blades. Gareth must have been listening to their conversation, and he nodded and made a harrumphing sound that bothered Hal.

"Gareth, you sound like you have an opinion."

Kay raised a hand to stop him. "Hal, leave it be."

"No, I won't leave it be." He pointed his dagger in the captain's direction. "You don't like to talk with us for some reason. Maybe it's because you're just rude, maybe it's because you don't like me. I don't know. But if you want to say something about my quest to find my family, let's have it. What am I doing wrong?"

Gareth's eyes remained locked on his sword blade as the whetstone scraped along the sharpened steel for a long time before he spoke. He didn't look up, but Hal had no doubt the elf was talking to him.

"You are a mere visitor to our land, Hal Dix. I have questioned Princess Bronwynn about who and what you are. She said you come here to play some sort of game. She said we are all just story characters to you who go away when you return home. You think none of this is real. Now reality has caught up with you and you complain. Many have lost their families in the Emperor's conquests. What makes you think your quest is more special than anyone else's?"

Gareth looked up at the end and fixed Hal with a baleful stare. It was as if he'd sharpened those eyes on the whetstone, too. They pierced right to Hal's soul along with Gareth's words.

Hal's grip on his dagger tightened as the fury washed over him in a wave, leaving his whole body rigid with tension. He jumped to his feet, pointing his blade at the elf.

"I never said my family was special to anyone but me, Captain. But they are more important to everyone here than you know, so you'd better do your best to help me get where I'm going, or I'll take you out myself."

The elf dropped his whetstone and jumped forward with his sword blade extended over the fire towards Hal.

He opened his mouth to say something but was interrupted by a snarling yowl to his left. Another just like it answered from the right.

"Damn, skitterlings," Gareth said. "I was afraid of this."

Hal turned and put his back toward the fire, facing outward. He cast a spell, and a breastplate of ice wrapped his torso. He had a dagger in one hand and the other outstretched, readying an ice dart spell. Hal searched the darkness outside the firelight.

"What the hell is a skitterling?"

A third yowling snarl sounded from a different direction. They were surrounded by whatever was making those sounds.

Kay moved to stand next to Hal with her sword and shield ready. "Skitterlings are humanoids distantly related to spiders. They have poisonous bites that can paralyze, so be wary of their attacks."

Gareth nodded in agreement. "The spider-kin will attack in a pack. It is their way. Watch for one to distract while another attacks."

The elf captain and his sergeant now stood side by side on the opposite side of the fire. Hal searched the darkness outside the ring of light. He thought he picked up movement on several occasions, but he couldn't be sure if it was his mind playing tricks on him or not. The yips and yowls from the creatures surrounding them continued.

The attack launched from the darkness with such sudden violence, Hal almost lost hold of his magic energy. He had the spell ready to go, though, and released it at once, launching a pair of ice shards outward from his hands. Hal was able to aim each shard at a different target as a group of four black and tan beasts ran at them from the darkness.

They had small round bodies with spindly arms and legs, all covered with coarse black spiky hair. Their faces contained six black eyes and a broad opening for a mouth with opposing mandibles on either side, each with an oozing black fang. Hal suspected the ooze dripping from the fangs was poison.

The dual ice shards each hit their mark. One pierced the leading skitterling in one of its bulbous black eyes. The shard must have struck straight to the brain because the creature's legs and arms folded in and it fell quivering to the ground.

600 experience points awarded.

The second shard hit another skitterling in the shoulder. The wounded arm dropped and hung limply at the beast's side, but it still charged onward.

Hal had a bare instant to cast another spell, and he used it to bring up his ice shield. He managed it just in time. The wounded skitterling launched at Hal from six feet away, catching him by surprise with the length of its leaping bound.

Hal raised his shield, taking the creature's weight on his right arm. It was shorter than a man and weighed less than he expected. Hal pushed the thing away from him to send it crashing back to the ground. He forgot Gareth's warning, though.

Pain lanced through his calf. Hal stared in horror at his leg. Another skitterling had latched on to his flesh and was working its mouth parts on his lower leg, stabbing him repeatedly with its poison-covered fangs.

Health damage: Health -4
   Health damage: Health -4
   Health damage: Health -4
   Health damage: Health -4
   Save vs. poison successful.

Hal shoved the point of his dagger down at the beast, stabbing into its exposed back again and again.

On the third strike, he managed to get it to let go of his leg. As it tried to run away, Hal stabbed down one more time and shouted in triumph when his blade sunk home into the creature's back.

600 experience points awarded.

Checking on Kay, Hal realized she had already dispatched her attacker, along with the wounded skitterling he had pushed off with his shield.

She pointed towards their mounts. "The horses, they're attacking the horses."

Ignoring the pain in his wounded leg, Hal raced after her. He could hear the screams of the horses over the noise of the attacking pack now.

One of the horses was down. Two others had pulled their lines up from the pickets and bolted into the darkness. The mule had two skitterlings attached to its back, and it bucked and kicked into the air with its hind legs, attempting to dislodge the attackers.

Hal got an idea. He sheathed his dagger and placed both hands together, with his thumbs touching and palms facing away from him. Channeling his ice magic while he envisioned what he wanted, he shot a stream of frost and ice crystals out from his palms and coated the mule in a blanket of ice.

The shocked look in the mule's eyes would have been comical if the situation weren't so deathly dangerous. The good news was the spell worked. Their target suddenly too slippery to hold on to, the two skitterlings fell to the ground and struggled to rise. Kay jumped into their midst and finished them with her sword before they could get back on their feet.

Another skitterling, still feeding on the first downed horse, saw its companions die, turned, and started loping away. Hal drew on his last shred of magic and sent a single shard of ice into its back. The creature's arms flew outward and it fell forward in a heap, twitching on the ground for a second before it stilled.

600 experience points awarded.

Out of the corner of his eye, he spotted another of the beasts running at Kay's back.

"Kay, watch out!"

She tried to turn to meet the new attack, but the surprise, coupled with twisting to face her attacker, caused her to fall backward, losing her balance.

Hal let loose a guttural war cry and charged to her rescue.

The skitterling had her down on the ground in an awkward position. Her body weight trapped her shield arm underneath her, and she couldn't get an angle with her sword due to the close quarters. It was all she could do to fend off the snapping mandibles inches from her face.

Hal raced in and kicked at the round abdomen of the skitterling, bowling it over onto its back and off Kay. He continued his advance, not giving the beast a chance to rise. Hal stomped downward with his boot on one of its spindly legs, pinning it to the ground.

Holding it in place with his foot, Hal drew both daggers and stabbed downward in a simultaneous attack. The skitterling spasmed once and died.

600 experience points awarded.

Hal searched the darkness outside the campfire's perimeter. The yowling sounds had stopped, and it seemed they'd broken the attack. It wasn't without consequence. One of the horses was dead, another wounded, and two others had run off into the night. The mule seemed fine and had taken to grazing again, though it seemed more than a little skittish. After the attack they'd just fought off, Hal couldn't blame the beast.

A groan from the camp's center drew his attention back to his companions. Chance collapsed toward the ground. Only Gareth's quick action prevented him from fainting into the campfire. The elf captain lowered the sergeant to the ground.

"He's been bitten. Damn, it must be the poison." Gareth cursed.

"There's nothing we can do for him. We're too far from help to get him anything to counteract the effects."

Hal ran over and checked the fallen elf. Chance's body was limp. The paralyzing effects of the skitterling bite had hit him with full force. When he examined the wound on the sergeant's arm, Hal saw something odd.

It took him a few seconds to realize he could see something in the magical spectrum around the bite. This was the first time since he'd awakened his earth magic Hal had seen any kind of injury or wound on a person.

As he examined the ragged edges of the bite where it had torn open the skin, he could see a sort of glow, like the purple ultraviolet gleam of a black light. It was just outside of the ordinary, visible light spectrum.

In addition to the strange glow at the edges of the wound, there was a sort of putrid stench coming from it, corresponding to a greenish cast to the torn flesh. After more scrutiny, Hal realized it must be the poison he was sensing and smelling deep inside the wound. It was entering the body through the blood.

If Hal could see the wound in this way, could he do something about it, too? He focused his will on the sickly green cast at the base of the ragged hole in the elf's arm, trying to touch the poison, to draw it out.

At first, nothing happened. Then, Hal's magic started working and the greenish glow began to turn to dust. The motes of sickly green powder floated up and out of the wound to dissipate into the air, fading away as the magic consumed it. When he could detect no more poison in the injury, Hal sat up and examined the injured area once more. The edges of the wound seemed healthier somehow.

Healing complete — Poison neutralized.
  Spell learned — Neutralize poison.
  1,500 experience points awarded.

"Bind his wound," Hal instructed. "I've done what I can for him."

"What did you do?" Gareth asked.

"I was able to neutralize the poison, but I'm not skilled enough to knit the edges of the wound together again. He'll have to heal that the old-fashioned way."

Hal stood and stumbled as a wave of dizziness washed over him.

Kay rushed over to steady him.

"I think I need to lie down and rest. I used a lot of magic tonight."

"You do that. Gareth and I will take turns on watch in case those things return."

Hal tried to smile at Kay. He wasn't sure it was successful. He was so tired he didn't care.

After stumbling to his bedroll by the campfire, Hal lowered himself to the ground and fell asleep almost as soon as his head hit the side of his backpack he used as a pillow.

CHAPTER 14

HAL WOKE to the sounds of the camp being struck by his companions. Kay was tying the bedrolls to the mule's pack harness. The mule seemed none the worse for wear after the night's attack.

Standing, Hal saw the previously wounded horse lying on the ground beside the dead one. Its throat had been slashed. The wound looked even and clean.

"Did you have to put the other horse down?"

Gareth nodded. "It was succumbing to the poison, and its wounds were severe. We couldn't ride it, and if we left it here alone, predators would have finished it off as soon as we moved on."

Chance walked into camp carrying the canteens, refilled with water from the nearby stream.

"Sergeant, how's the arm?" Hal pointed to the white bandage wrapping the wounded area on his forearm.

"Better now that there's no poison lurking inside it. Thank you for what you did."

"Not a problem. If you were able, you would do the same for me, right?"

"All the same, thank you," Chance repeated. "I don't know what my wife and kids would have done if I hadn't come home."

"I know the feeling."

Hal wondered what Mona and Cari were up to this morning. Were they scared and cold in some dungeon cell? Hal pulled the scrying crystal from his pouch and stared into its translucent depths again, trying to will the stone to work.

Nothing.

Kay placed her hand on his shoulder. "Come on Hal. Maybe once we plant that seed you're carrying, the crystal will start to work."

"You sound sure of yourself, Kay."

"I only know standing here, wishing things were different, won't change anything."

Hal nodded and pocketed the crystal next to the seed pod in his belt pouch again.

It only took him a few minutes to gather up his bedroll and shoulder his backpack. They wouldn't be riding anymore unless the other two horses who'd run off turned up. That meant they'd walk the rest of the way into the Fallen Forest. A thought occurred to Hal as they started walking east toward the nearby forest.

"Gareth, why is this called the Fallen Forest?"

The captain shrugged. "It is mostly told as children's stories to scare younglings into minding their parents. I don't know how much is true. Legend says that this was once the grandest of elven forests, but something killed the great tree at its center, and soon, all variety of evil denizens started encroaching on the elves who lived here."

"What sort of creatures are we talking about?" Kay asked.

"It would be helpful to know what we're up against," Hal added.

Gareth hooked a thumb over his shoulder back to their old campsite. "Mostly small humanoids like the skitterlings back there. There are rumors of other things, but who knows."

"You said the skitterlings were related to spiders in some way. We aren't talking about some sort of giant arachnid, are we?"

"It's possible," the captain agreed. "As I said, most of what I know is a legend based on children's tales. One does talk of a great black spider dwelling deep in the forest that comes out and drags off children who wander away from their parents."

"Great, I've had the heebie-jeebies for spiders since we fought that thing down in the sewers of Tandon, Kay."

"We defeated that one, Hal. We can kill another one if we have to."

Hal shivered as a chill crept down his spine. He really didn't care for spiders.

The foursome trekked over the hills on the outskirts of the forest ahead of them. They reached the first scattered trees around noon. They were sickly, deformed shadows of the magnificent, tall versions Hal had seen in Bronwynn's High Forest. Something had changed the soul of this forest.

Hal wasn't sure how a single seed could set things right again. He supposed he'd find out. Gareth had them pause for a brief rest before pushing forward into the darker depths of the forest core.

The gloom of the surrounding trees and undergrowth was accented by the complete lack of sound. It took Hal a while to realize he couldn't hear a single bird, insect, or other animal sound of any kind amidst the dark and rotting trunks and branches.

The leaves of the canopy overhead were spotted with blotches of brown and yellow. Instead of moss and lichen growing on the north side of the trunks, there was a tan slime coating the lower portion of the trees. Hal struggled not to touch the nasty stuff, but soon their clothes and cloaks were all stained by the foul-smelling goo.

After two hours, Gareth stopped searching the ground in front of him. Turning around, he walked back to the rear of the group and checked the ground behind Chance.

"What's wrong?" Hal asked.

"The trail we were on disappeared as we were walking. One minute it was there, stretching out ahead of us, and then next it was gone. It's been erased behind us, too."

Hal didn't like the thought of getting lost and wandering around this place in the dark once night fell.

"You can find your way without it, can't you?"

Gareth shrugged. "Possibly. It's like the forest itself decided it didn't want us going any farther."

"We have to get to the clearing Bronwynn said was at the center of the wood. Only there can we plant the pod and learn what to do next on our quest."

Gareth walked back to the front of the group and scanned the trees ahead, then looked back behind them again.

"It's likely I can figure out the way back. I'm not sure where I'm going if we proceed forward. It's your call."

Hal looked around but found nothing but the same sickly trees in every direction. There was nothing to indicate a direction of travel. He knew from what Bronwynn had relayed to him that the clearing where they were to plant the tree lay at the center of the forest. They had to find that to complete the quest.

If Gareth couldn't track their way to the center, perhaps Hal could discern it using his newfound magic skills.

"Let me try something," Hal said, moving to the front, past the captain.

The earth magic inside him had a golden quality to it, like sunlight warming your face when you tilted it upward on a bright summer's day. Perhaps he could use this to sense the magical core of the forest, even as corrupted as it was.

Hal closed his eyes and tried to expand his awareness outward. He had no idea what he was doing, so he tried several things at once, including taking a deep breath through his nose to see if he could smell anything new over the surrounding rot.

When that didn't work, Hal extended a hand and placed it on the trunk of a nearby tree. The bark squished under his hand. The tan slime dissolved the outer covering of the trees close to the ground here. He resisted the urge to pull his hand away and kept it in place, trying to reach the core of the tree, the part that might still retain some of its health and remember the old ways of this forest.

The skin on his hand began to itch and burn as the gelatinous ooze started to digest his skin.

Health damage: Health -6

Hal ignored the building pain and drove his senses deeper into the tree. Then he broke through and entered the tree's center with his extended mind.

It was wonderful.

He experienced the forest in all its former glory. The clean breeze blew through the rustling, lush, green leaves of the canopy. Below, various sorts of wildlife lived and died in the natural process of all things.

And then he saw it.

The great tree at the center of the forest, situated in its holy glade, surrounded by thirteen trees set in a circle around it.

He knew where to go.

Hal opened his eyes and pointed off to the right. "There. That way."

"Are you sure, Hal?" Kay asked. "It all looks the same to me."

"I'm sure. The heart of the forest lies in that direction, or at least it used to."

"You're the boss, I guess." Kay fell in behind him, followed by Gareth and finally Chance leading their pack mule.

Hal kept his senses tuned to the trees while he walked along. He could feel the old heart of the forest getting closer with every step. He could also sense the corruption there, too.

Something horrible was waiting for them, expecting them to come and to fail in their quest.

He thought about telling the others what he sensed but decided not to say anything. What would it change? They were ready for a fight. Nothing he could tell them would change any of that or the way they prepared.

Hal cast his ice armor spell. He noticed right away his armor had upgraded with his increased level and practice. He now had full leg and arm ice coverings, too. It wasn't ornately carved the way Ragnar's had been, but it was an upgrade. Hal was glad to see it.

"Expecting trouble, Hal?" Kay asked when she saw the armor appear.

"I figure we're going to face something up here. There's no way to know for sure, but this forest didn't end up like this on its own. Something is at the center of all this corruption."

"Maybe it's a big hairy spider," she quipped, trying to make a joke.

"Lord, I hope not."

Hal pushed the thought aside and pressed onward. Judging by the sense of impending doom he now felt through his magical connection to the trees, he assumed they were very close.

"We're almost there. Be ready for anything."

A glance behind him showed the others nodding back at him. All three of his companions had their weapons drawn. Even Chance had his bow strung and an arrow nocked, ready to fly.

Hal drew upon his magic reserves and readied his sole offensive spell, though he upgraded it to the larger and more powerful ice lance instead of the darts he'd used against the skitterlings last night.

He pressed forward, pushing through the undergrowth until he reached the circle of trees at the center of the forest. There in the center of the clearing was a rotted stump of what had once been an enormous tree. The middle of the stump was sunken, forming a hole in the ground that disappeared deep into the earth below.

Hal paused outside the ring of trees for only a second before he stepped into the clearing. Once he was standing on the yellow, stunted grass, Hal stared around, expecting an attack at any moment.

Nothing came.

Kay moved up to his left, and the two elves entered the clearing to his right.

"Well, Hal, we found it. Now what?" Kay asked.

"I think I have to plant the seed pod in the center of the old stump. That is where I'm drawn when I concentrate."

"Good, then plant the damned thing and let's get out of here."

Hal nodded and took a hesitant step forward, followed by another and another until he stood next to the stump. It wasn't the smooth flat stump of a tree cut down by the saw of a lumberjack. This tree had been ripped from its base and thrown aside, probably by a significant storm. Hal could see the remains of the colossal trunk lodged between two of the surrounding trees and extending into the darkness beyond.

He returned his mind to the task at hand, climbing up onto the stump and over the rough and rotten wood towards the center. Just next to the middle of the old trunk, a hole extended into the blackness below.

Hal couldn't see the bottom of the hole in the dim forest light. He decided to ignore it for the time being. He wasn't going down there, and he had no light strong enough to penetrate the thick darkness below. Best to get to work and finish his task.

Kneeling in the center of the stump, Hal pulled one of his daggers from his belt and started digging at the rotted wood and dirt of the sunken stump. He didn't know how deep a hole he should make, only that he needed to plant the seed pod here. He decided to follow his instincts and stop when there was enough room to deposit the pod all the way in the hole he'd made, with enough other material here to cover it back up again.

Hal pulled the seed pod free from his pouch and reached out to place it in the hole he'd dug.

A screeching roar from his left froze him in place, and he turned just in time to see a monstrous spider heaving itself out of the hole beside him.

Hal fell over backward and crab-walked in reverse to the edge of the stump to get away from the creature.

A strand of web shot out from the spider and wrapped around the hand holding the seed pod. As soon as the sticky tendrils grabbed him, it started pulling Hal back towards the enormous thing. It was the size of a small car.

Hal reacted on instinct and swiped with his dagger, cutting the two-inch-thick rope of spider web attached to his other hand.

After several slashing cuts, he managed to sever the tough spider silk and pull away from the spider's advance.

It wasn't fast enough.

One long, segmented leg stabbed down. Hal didn't see it in time to roll out of the way.

The chitin-encased tip of the foreleg pierced his ice armor as if it were cracking open a peanut shell and stabbed through Hal's thigh.

The spider leg pinned Hal to the rotted wood of the stump.

Health damage: Health -22

Hal screamed in pain. His leg felt like the creature had ripped it off his body. He dropped his dagger and tried to pull the thick spider limb out of his thigh so he could slide it free.

He realized the spider had decided to ignore him for the time being, choosing to pay attention to the other three intruders.

Chance was off to one side, launching arrow after arrow at the massive creature. Most ricocheted off the armored sides of the spider's body, but a few managed to find gaps. It wasn't enough to stop the beast, though.

Gareth and Kay leapt into action, both drawing their swords and charging at the spider that pinned Hal down.

Their weapons had little to no effect, unable to get through the body armor of the spider. They did, though, serve to distract the beast from attacking Hal, other than the leg pinning him in place.

Gritting his teeth against the agony tearing at his right leg, Hal worked to gather his concentration. He couldn't get ahold of his magic, and there was no way he could cut through the leg with his daggers.

Hal hummed one of the chakra tones Rune had taught him and found his focus returning, and his tenuous grip on magic strengthened.

Clenching his fists, Hal drew on his power and concentrated on the place between the spider's bulbous abdomen and the thinner thorax where the eight legs attached to the body.

Locating a spot that appeared to be a segmentation between two armored body plates, Hal pointed his right hand at the target and stabbed outward with his palm.

A clear pole of hard ice lanced outward, spearing straight into the spider's side, right where Hal had aimed.

A deafening, screeching howl cut loose from the spider. The ice lance had impaled the creature, with half the length buried inside the giant bug.

"Payback's a bitch," Hal shouted through his haze of pain.

The leg pinning Hal to the ground went limp after the ice lance struck. As the spider rocked back and forth in its attacks on Kay and Gareth, the tip of the leg worked free of the stump under Hal and he was able to liberate his thigh.

He slapped his hand down over the open wound in his leg. Blood flowed in a rapid stream from the hole, and Hal knew that wasn't good. He pressed down, trying to staunch the blood flow.

Health damage: Health -18

He had to stop the blood loss, or he was going to bleed to death.

Remembering what he'd done for Chance yesterday, Hal focused on his wound and once again saw the black glow at the edges.

Grabbing at the glowing areas with his mind, Hal tried to pull the edges of his wounded leg together.

To his shock, it actually worked. As he watched and directed the magic, his skin stretched back together, pulling the sides of the gaping wound closed and staunching the flow of blood coming out of the torn flesh.

After mentally tying off the magical tabs he'd used to pull the wound's edges together, Hal ground his teeth against the pain and forced himself to stand.

Spell learned — Heal wounds.

The spider had Gareth down, and the elf rolled back and forth underneath the spider, avoiding the jabbing mandibles that dripped with venom. Kay hammered at the body with her sword, trying to distract the beast from its attacks.

Chance jumped into the fray, his arrows spent. He had pulled out a long knife and hand axe and was chopping at the joints of one leg, trying to unbalance the spider.

"Keep distracting it," Hal called out to his companions. "I'm going to try another spell."

"Hurry up, Hal," Kay yelled. "Gareth's almost done."

Hal drew in all the power he had, ignoring the pain in his leg, and channeled every ounce into his hand. His plan relied on being able to create a double ice lance and take down both the abdomen and the central thorax at the same time.

"Yeaaaahhhhhhh!" Hal let loose with his spell, gratified to see duplicate ice lances spearing outward from him into the giant creature.

The giant spikes of magically hardened ice slammed into the

spider, pinning it down to the base of the stump. A final, weak shriek sounded from the beast, and then it went still.

6,000 experience points awarded.
    Level Up!

Hal limped over to where Gareth struggled to drag himself out from under the bulk of the spider. Blood seeped from several puncture wounds across his body.

Chance and Kay raced over to help Hal pull the captain free. Just as they got him out from under the spider, his eyes rolled up in his head and he went limp.

Hal knew what to look for this time, and he saw the sickly green tint of the spider's venom within Gareth's body.

Knowing he only had one shot at this because his magical strength was about tapped out from his exertions, Hal delved down with his mind into Gareth's wounds and applied his limited remaining spell ability to the envenomed areas.

Poison slowed.

Hal sighed and sat back on the ground, shaking his head.

"Were you able to help him?" Kay asked.

Gareth groaned but didn't wake up.

"I think so. I was only able to slow the progression of the poison. Provided I can get some rest, I should be able to neutralize it fully tomorrow once I regain my strength."

Chance nodded. "Then we'll have to stay here for the night. There's no way Kay and I are going to carry you both out of here back to our original camp."

"Is it safe?" Kay asked.

"I doubt there are more than one of those things around. We didn't hear a single animal on the way here. Likely it's hunted this place bare for a few miles in every direction. I'll scout around to be sure, but I think remaining here is our best bet."

The sergeant left the two humans to care for Gareth while he started checking for any more danger nearby.

Kay glanced at Hal's belt pouch. "What about planting the seed pod?"

"Oh, yeah." He dug in his pouch then remembered where he'd seen the pod last. He scrambled over to where he'd been pinned to the ground. After a frantic search, Hal found the seed pod under some dry leaves.

"Keep an eye on him while I finish this. Maybe planting the tree will do something positive here for a change."

Hal pulled his dagger out and began digging at the center of the stump again. Once he'd cleared the hole of debris, he dropped the pod in, scooped the dirt from the pile back into the hole, and lightly tamped it around the seed until he'd covered it completely. Hal searched his mind for what to do next.

"Kay, bring me some water."

"Got it."

She went to fetch their canteens from the pack mule tied nearby. When she returned, Hal pulled the cork on his and upended it over the place where he'd buried the pod, soaking the earth with water.

Quest completed: Plant the seed of the great tree.
   5,000 experience points awarded.
   Level Up!

Hal sat back and stared at the damp earth before him. He wasn't sure what he expected but nothing happened. Disappointed, Hal crawled back over to where Kay sat with Gareth. His color looked a little better, though Hal knew he wasn't healed yet.

"We'll stay here tonight; then tomorrow we'll start the trek back to Bronwynn and see what the reward for our efforts is. I can't help but have the feeling something big is happening here."

Kay nodded. "I'll go help Chance check the perimeter. You stay here and keep an eye on Gareth."

Hal smiled as she went to scout the camp. She was a terrific companion. Someday, he hoped he could introduce her to Mona. He thought the two would get along great.

After gathering his gear from where it had scattered during the battle, Hal pulled strips of cloth bandages from his pack and used them to bind the captain's wounds. He planned to heal them in the morning when he'd regained his magical strength again.

While he worked, he allocated two more attribute points to wisdom and two to his speed. Hopefully, that would keep him from getting stabbed by any more giant spiders.

Name: Hal Dix
   Class: Mage
   Level: 8

Attributes:
   Brawn: 24 — +8 defense
   Wisdom: 18 — +5 defense
   Luck: 30 — +11 to all saving throws (Max)
   Speed: 16 — +4 defense
   Looks: 8
   Health: 68/140

Character skills: Chakra regeneration — 3 (heal 18hp; 1/day).

Mage experience: 19,825/38,000
Ice elemental school:
Resist cold, Ice shield, Ice armor, Ice darts, Ice lance, Wall of fog.
Earth elemental school:
Plant growth, Neutralize poison, Heal wounds.
Fire elemental school: locked
Wind elemental school: locked
Unknown elemental school: locked
Warrior experience: 140,800/250,000
Rogue experience: 146,100/250,000

CHAPTER 15

HAL AWOKE the next morning to a changed landscape in the central glade of the Fallen Forest. As he rubbed the sleep from his eyes and looked around, he reconsidered the name for this place. It should be called the Forest Formerly Known as the Fallen Forest.

Overhead, the sun shined down, beams of light filtering through the leaves of the trees. Those leaves were now lush and green, as they should be, not the sickly yellow with blotches of brown seen last night.

That wasn't the most notable change in the clearing, though.

A forty-foot-tall tree had sprouted from the center of the old stump in the middle of the clearing. Looking up to the top, Hal marveled at the display of nature's magic as the branches continued to grow and shoot upward, as if accelerated by a time-lapse video as he watched.

"Pretty spectacular, huh?" Kay noted from his left.

"I wouldn't believe it if I didn't see it for myself."

"It started growing soon after the moon became visible overhead last night. I had just taken sentry duty from Chance when it began shooting upward."

Hal searched the camp. Gareth still slept nearby but Chance was nowhere in sight.

"Where is the sergeant?"

"He went to scout around and see how far the transformation of the forest extends. He hasn't been gone for long."

Hal started to rise and groaned as a sharp stabbing pain radiated out from his injured thigh. He'd forgotten he was injured for a second. His leg, however, had not.

The bandage had a red spot of blood on it where some had soaked through from underneath overnight, but it wasn't dripping, so the wound hadn't opened up again, which was good.

"Don't get up, Hal," Kay cautioned. "I'll bring you some water, and I made the last of our cornmeal into griddle cakes for breakfast. There's a few for you when you're ready."

"Thanks. I should unwrap this bandage and check the wound anyway."

Hal removed the bandage and examined the injured area underneath. His attempts to close the edges of the puncture wound yesterday had held up overnight, but the wound was far from healed. Hal pulled up his magic menu and selected the heal wounds spell then focused his will on the ragged hole in his thigh.

At first, nothing happened, then a tickling itch started deep inside his leg. It became so strong, Hal had to clench his fists to resist trying to dig his fingers into the wound to scratch at the source of the sensation.

Just when he thought he could stand no more, he watched the skin fill in from beneath the open wound in his leg and grow upward until it stitched together with the jagged skin at the edges. Within seconds, there was nothing to show for the place where the spider's leg had pierced his own leg but a puckered pink scar the size of his palm.

Placing his hand atop the scar, Hal felt a residual warmth. It was probably a side effect of the spell's rapid regeneration of the tissue inside the wound.

Hal took his time climbing to his feet, under Kay's watchful gaze. He took a few tentative steps around his bedroll on the springy green turf that had grown up overnight in the clearing.

"It seems like it's good as new," Hal told Kay while he tested his leg out.

"Do you have any of that magic left? Gareth could probably use it, too."

Hal blushed with embarrassment and crossed over to where the elf captain lay on the grass, covered with a blanket pulled up to his chin.

"I should have tended to him first. I wasn't sure if the new spell worked or not, but I should have used the fresh energy of the morning to heal him."

"Don't beat yourself up, Hal. You can't be at your best with a hole in your leg. Use what you have left to fix him up now that you're healed."

Hal knelt at Gareth's side and looked over the numerous puncture wounds in his chest and abdomen. With his magical sight, he could see the faint green glow of poisoning at each location. While he'd been able to slow the progression of the poison last night, he hadn't been able to remove it. He set to remedy that now.

Hovering his hands over the sleeping elf, Hal spent a few seconds over each wound and cast a neutralize poison spell while he concentrated on removing the source of the sickly green tint at each location.

As soon as he dissipated the final bit of poison, Gareth's breathing became more relaxed and less labored. A few seconds later, his eyes fluttered open, and he looked around the clearing.

To Hal's surprise, the usually taciturn captain turned and smiled up at him. "Good morning, Hal. It looks like you managed to complete the quest my lady set before you."

"It worked out." Hal shrugged and tried to downplay the results with his humble response.

"The elves owe you a great debt for restoring this forest for us."

"If Bronwynn will help me get my family back, I will call it even."

"I'm sure she will do that. She gave me something to give to you should you succeed in your quest to plant the seed here."

Gareth dug a hand under his cloak and handed Hal a folded parchment. Hal noted the wax seal impressed with Bronwynn's crest. He broke the seal and unfolded the note to read what the elf princess had written there.

Hal Dix,

If you succeed in this dire mission, I have no choice but to acknowledge you as the Opponent of Tildi's vaunted prophecy. Congratulations. In payment for the services you have rendered to the elven people in restoring the great forest that was our ancestral home, I offer you a boon.

There is a little-known tale that, when a seed is planted and becomes one of the great central trees of our sacred groves, the spirit of the forest will grant an answer to the planter's greatest wish. This I share with you because I believe the tree you have started there will help you in your ultimate quest to rescue your family.

I wish you well. My work is complete, as you have learned what you must to grow your skills with earth magic. Now you must seek out Theran, the next mage with whom you must train. He will teach you the magic of fire.

Perhaps we shall meet again. Until that day, Godspeed.

Bronwynn

Hal folded the message and considered what he'd read. Bronwynn said the forest spirit would answer his greatest wish if he asked. How was he supposed to ask the question, though? He saw no evidence of any forest spirit floating around the clearing.

The message frustrated him, and he nearly crumpled it and threw it away in the campfire. Instead, he tucked it into his belt pouch next to the scrying stone.

That was when he noticed the stone's soft white glow in the shadows at the bottom of his pouch. Hal reached inside, removed the stone, and held it out in front of him. As soon as the crystal emerged into the sunlight, the internal light grew brighter still.

The light in the stone pulsed now, almost like a heartbeat.

"Hal, are you doing that?" Kay asked.

"No, I don't think so. It's coming from within the stone itself. I think it has something to do with the message Bronwynn sent me."

Hal handed the message to Kay as he stood and looked around the clearing, with his hand outstretched before him. The pulsing of the light quickened as his hand passed by the center of the clearing and subsided when he turned away.

Bringing the stone back around, he faced the still-expanding trunk of the great tree growing at the center of the glade. The stone's pulsing light became rapid and regular; it was accompanied now by a gentle vibration, in time with the flashing light.

Hal took a step closer to the tree. The light in the stone grew brighter and the vibration increased in intensity. Realizing what the stone wanted him to do, Hal strode up to the tree trunk, now grown to a much more massive size. He held the stone up to the tree, pressing the smooth, translucent crystal against the smooth bark of the great central Tree of Life he'd planted last night. Both the tree and the crystal responded as soon as they touched. The scrying crystal flared with a bright, blinding light while the trunk and its smooth bark parted along a vertical seam nearly six feet tall directly in front of him.

To Hal's amazement, the seam in the side of the tree opened and revealed a cavity inside. Hal held the crystal against the tree with one hand and reached inside the cavity, unsure what he would find. His fingers brushed against a smooth round surface, and when he wrapped his hand around it, the object in the side of the tree came free and he pulled it out from the cavity.

In his hand, Hal held a five-and-a-half-foot staff of smooth, light brown wood covered with faint silver runes etched into the surface. At the upper end of the staff was a small, concave socket which, upon examination, seemed intended to hold the scrying crystal.

Without hesitation, Hal placed the crystal from his other hand into the socket of the staff. The crystal flared brightly one last time and then it fused in place as the socket molded around its base.

Following a hint of an idea at the back of his mind, Hal held the staff upright in both hands and pressed the base into the ground while staring into the crystal. As the glowing translucence seemed to envelop him, Hal's vision blurred until all he could see was the light coming from the center of the stone.

For a moment, he felt himself falling, then the sensation passed, and he was standing inside a room he'd never seen before. Rich tapestries covered the walls, and the floors were inlaid with intricate mosaics. The room was lightly furnished with a finely carved table and black and gold lacquered chairs with red velvet cushions.

Unsure how he had come to be in this place, Hal took a few tentative steps toward an open doorway on the far side of the room. He froze when he heard a familiar voice. It sounded just like Mona.

"Please tell His Majesty that, despite him being the Emperor of this land, I am my daughter's mother and I say it is time for her to go to bed. She has had enough play time today."

A second, heavily accented voice replied, "I will, of course, pass along your message, Mistress Mona, but I fear His Majesty will be most displeased with your refusal."

"He may take that up with me when we next dine together tomorrow evening."

"As you wish, mistress."

Hal heard footsteps retreating in the opposite direction, and then a door closed. Realizing Mona was alone, he raced across the remaining distance to the doorway and into the next room, where he saw his wife. She was wearing expensive silk robes, the kind worn by imperial nobility. Her hair was drawn back in double braids, and it appeared that silver and golden wires were woven into the braids alongside the strands of her beautiful blonde hair.

"Mona, thank God you're alright. Look, we don't have much time. I'm not sure how I got here, but we need to find a way out now that I have found you. Where's Cari?"

As he spoke, Hal scanned the room, looking for his daughter. Then he realized Mona was paying no attention to him at all.

"Mona, can't you hear me?"

Hal waved his arms and ran across the room to stand in front of his wife. She looked right past him then turned away, her eyes never connecting with his. It was then Hal realized he wasn't really here. He was only watching from afar, a mere spirit observing inside the room.

Hal looked around the room, frantic in his desire to leave a message for Mona that he'd been here. At that instant, the falling sensation returned, and a few seconds later, he found himself once again standing in the glade in the middle of the forest.

He collapsed to the ground, sobbing.

Kay was at his side in an instant. "Hal, are you alright? You pulled that staff from the tree and then you froze. When I called to you, you didn't answer. Before I could reach you, you collapsed."

"I saw her, Kay. She's alive. She's well."

"Who's alive? You mean your wife? Your daughter? Who?"

"It was Mona. She's somewhere with the Emperor. I overheard her talking to someone, telling them to relay a message to His Majesty that she couldn't bring the baby to him right then."

"What about your daughter? Did you see her?"

Hal turned to Kay. Tears streamed down his face, but he didn't care.

"I didn't see Cari, but I know she was there. Mona told the messenger she was sleeping."

"Hal, that's great news. Don't you see? This means they're alive. Describe to me what you saw. Describe the room she was in."

Hal related every detail he could remember about the room and its contents. He described the scenes displayed on the various tapestries and the pattern on the mosaic floor.

Kay nodded. "I know that place. It is in the east wing of the imperial palace. It used to be reserved for the royal family's chambers when in residence in the palace."

"How could you possibly know that, Kay, from just my description? You act like you used to live there."

She stared back at him, not saying a word, and Hal didn't know why there was suddenly this silence between them.

From across the clearing, Gareth answered the question hanging between the two companions. "She knows those rooms, Hal Dix, because she used to call those rooms her home. Did you not know Princess Kareena was the eldest daughter of our former Emperor?"

Hal realized his mouth was hanging open, but he didn't care right then. His gaze shifted back and forth between Gareth and Kay. Finally, his eyes settled on Kay.

"You were the Imperial Crown Princess? I mean, I knew you were of the nobility, but I had no idea you were part of the imperial family."

"That's because I didn't tell you. You would've treated me differently, and I enjoyed having a friend who only knew me as a simple traveling companion and a comrade in arms. I told the others who knew to keep it from you. I'm sorry."

"So many things make more sense now," Hal said. "That's why everyone important knows who you are. That's why everyone defers to you."

"But not you, Hal. You treat me like Kay, a thief and sometimes warrior. That is important to me."

"So, all this fighting is to put you and your family back on the throne? But won't that give everyone just another Emperor or Empress? How does that make this world a better place?"

"It makes it better, Hal, because, unlike Emperor Kang, my family has always seen our place as servants of the people. We took our role being members of the royal family as a sacred duty."

Hal's thoughts spun in circles. He tried to wrap his mind around the new information about Kay. All that time the two of them had spent running around Tandon, Hal wondered how many people knew who she really was. As he looked back at it, he recognized the signs that there was more to Kay than met the eye. He'd chosen not to see them.

A hopeful thought occurred to him.

"Kay, if you grew up in the palace, then you must know a secret way to where my family is being kept. You know, like the courtesan's entrance we used to sneak into the Duke's palace in Tandon."

Kay shook her head. "There are two secret passages I know of into the imperial palace. However, neither of them lead to the east wing, and they both will be guarded against intruders."

"But..."

"No, Hal, we must stick to Tildi's plan. Only when you are strong enough to breach the palace's magical defenses, will you be able to rescue your family from a position of strength and safety."

Hal stood, gripping the staff with both hands to help lever himself to his feet. "If that is what we must do, then I will use the staff and crystal to find the mage Theran's location. Bronwynn seems to think he's in hiding somewhere. Let's see if I can fire this thing up and find the missing mage."

Hal took the staff in both hands and pushed the base into the earth at his feet. Leaning forward, he stared into the milky depths of the crystal and tried to replicate the magic that had shown him his wife on the other side of the continent. This time, however, he focused on the name Theran, trying to impress the strength of his need on whatever magic the crystal used to show a location.

The crystal was dark. No matter how hard he tried, he could not get the internal spark to light within the center of the translucent stone. He attempted everything he could think of, including shouted commands to summon the magic. He even tried pressing his head painfully against the side of the crystal. None of it worked.

After many minutes of attempting to open the magic within the staff and stone, Kay placed a hand on Hal's shoulder.

"Give it a rest, Hal. Maybe this stone needs to recharge. I have heard of magic that can only be used every so often. Perhaps the crystal must wait a day, or even a few days, before its magic can be used again."

"But that doesn't help us find the fire mage, does it? Just because Mona and Cari are alright now doesn't mean they will remain that way."

Kay opened her mouth to continue arguing with Hal but was interrupted when Chance came running into the clearing. The elf sergeant was out of breath, pointing behind himself into the forest beyond.

"Men are coming. Many men on horseback. I spotted them searching the forest a mile away from here. I think they are imperial mage hunters."

Gareth got up, his arm pressing against the wounds across his abdomen. "We have to go, now. If they find you, Hal, all will be lost. Everything Mistress Bronwynn has done to train you will be for nothing."

Kay and Hal ran to their bedrolls. As Kay shouldered her backpack, she looked at Chance.

"Can we outrun them? We have no mounts."

"They slowed when they reached the edge of the forest. I believe they're having trouble navigating the thick brush that has grown up overnight as the forest comes to life again. If we slip away now, we should be able to evade them and exit the forest to the south."

"How did they find us?" Hal asked. "They are supposed to be chasing after the final four great mages, not me."

"Don't you see, Hal?" Kay said. "Now that you have begun your training, you are one of the great mages, too. Somehow, they have detected the use of your magic. That is the only way I can think of that they could be tracking you."

"Great, now I have to fight off mage hunters while I try to train and learn new magic. Maybe it makes sense for us to stand and fight rather than run away."

Kay shook her head. "Now is not the time to try and be a hero, Hal. Mage hunters are trained from a very young age to capture and kill magic users. It is better if we run."

Hal pulled on his backpack. "Fine, which way is south? The sooner we get away, the sooner I can try and find Theran again."

"This way," Chance called, setting out across the clearing to the far side of the ring of trees.

Gareth untied the pack mule and followed. Hal and Kay brought up the rear. Hal hated running away from a fight, but he had a lot to live for now that he knew his family was alive and well.

With a last glance over his shoulder, he hefted the staff and followed the others into the depths of the forest beyond.

CHAPTER 16

CHANCE WAS RIGHT: by slipping away to the south, the four of them were able to evade the mage hunters. It took them just over two days to travel to the southern edge of the Fallen Forest. Each night, Hal held the staff and attempted to locate the fire mage, Theran. The crystal refused to glow even a little bit.

It was midday on the third day after they'd left the central grove of the forest when they emerged onto a grassy plain of rolling hills. Gareth suggested they stop to rest.

Hal sat down on the grass with the staff atop his knees and stared off across the hills lying between them and their return to Bronwynn and the High Forest. Kay walked over and handed him a slice of jerky she'd carved from the slab in her pack.

"Here, try this. It'll help you feel better."

"How is chewing on this shoe leather going to make me feel better, Kay?"

"It will make you feel better because we all have to keep our strength up to do the things we are destined to do. I am not giving up on you, and you better not give up on yourself, either."

"I'm not giving up, Kay. I'm frustrated. How am I supposed to be some sort of great mage or wizard when I can't even get my staff to work?"

"I don't know, Hal. I only know that you will figure it out, just like you've figured out everything you had to accomplish since we've known each other. What happened to the guy who always had a clever plan? That guy wouldn't give up. That guy would keep going no matter what happened, until he figured out how to make that stupid staff work."

Hal thought about what she'd said. During his time in Fantasma, he'd always been able to remain positive by focusing on what he needed to do to beat the game. But this wasn't a game anymore. This was his family. This was real life. He shook his head.

"It was different back then, Kay. I didn't have so much riding on whether I succeeded or failed."

"That's ridiculous. There was just as much riding on our success fighting against the Wardens of Tandon. There was even more riding on our success when we built an army of escaped slaves and fought off Baron Norak outside of Hyroth. Both times you found a way to beat everything, no matter what the odds were. I don't know why you doubt yourself, but now is the time to dig deep and find strength where you thought you had none because you have to."

"Those times were different, Kay. All I had to do was hack and slash my way through the game, or what I thought was a game. Using magic is different. It's like solving a new and more difficult puzzle all the time without a break. I don't think my mind works that way."

"Nonsense! When Tildi kicked you through that portal into the snow with nothing but the clothes on your back, you found a way to unlock your magical abilities, despite the odds against you. If your mind didn't work that way, we would've found you frozen and dead when we finally caught up with you."

Kay sat down across from him and ducked her head so she could meet his downcast eyes.

"We are out of the forest now. We couldn't go chasing off after Theran before anyway, until we escaped the mage hunters. But now we can think about locating him. So, think Hal. What haven't you tried to get that crystal to fire up again? Now's the time to step up and be the Opponent we all know you have the ability to be."

"I've done everything but bleed on the damned crystal, Kay. What do you..."

Hal stopped. He thought back to when he had used the crystal before. Gareth's blood had covered his hands after tending the elf's wounds. Could it be that simple?

There was only one way to find out. Hal pulled out one of his daggers and pricked his thumb with the tip. A drop of blood welled up at the end of his thumb.

Standing, Hal held the staff in front of him and pressed the base down into the thick grass at his feet. Then, he smeared his bloody thumb across the top of the translucent crystal. Instantly, the glow returned to the center of the stone.

Kay cleared her throat. Hal looked down and gave her half a smile. He felt more than a little embarrassed at the way he'd been acting over the last several days. She didn't seem to care, though. She nodded, smiling back.

Closing his eyes, Hal held the staff out away from himself, with both hands pressing the base down into the grass to ground it. He cleared his mind of all additional thoughts and focused his energy on everything he knew about the fire mage and where he might be hiding. The magic worked the instant he concentrated on Theran. Once again, he fell forward into the crystal.

Hal didn't fight the sensation. Instead, he went with it. When he "landed," he opened his eyes. Hal stood in a small room. There were wooden slat walls, with a rickety table and two wooden chairs situated in the center of the wood floor. Netting and rope hung from the walls. In the distance outside, he heard seagulls crying out their piercing calls as they fought and argued over food and position. A man dressed in a dirty, red robe stood on the other side of the room, staring out the single cracked window.

This had to be the fire mage, Theran, the man for whom he was looking. His magic had worked. Now, all he had to do was figure out where *here* was. From its contents, there was no way to tell which city or town this room was in. He only knew he was along the coast somewhere.

After crossing the room, Hal tried to open the door, but his hand passed right through the door's latch. Thinking about his ethereal nature, Hal theorized he could just walk through walls. He took a step forward to go through the closed door. He smacked his face up against something hard and unyielding, only a half-inch from the wood panel of the door.

That wasn't going to work.

Not knowing how much time he had before the scrying spell wore off, Hal walked toward the man in the red robe and stood behind him. Peering over the other man's shoulder, Hal saw a harbor filled with tall-masted ships. Across the harbor, on the point of land opposite their position, there was a tall castle atop a cliff overlooking the harbor below. Above the battlements, Hal saw a banner flapping in the sea breeze with a crest he did not recognize. It was light, sky blue with some sort of fish emblazoned across it.

Hal was still trying to gather more details about his location when the man in the red robe turned around and stared directly into his eyes. To Hal's surprise, the man's eyes widened, and he screamed in alarm, throwing up his hands in Hal's face. The next thing Hal knew, flames shot out of those hands and fire burned all around him.

Screaming and beating at his head to put out the flames, Hal let go of his staff and fell backward. In an instant, he returned to the grassy plain outside the forest and landed on the grass at Kay's feet. His head was not burning. He didn't have any injuries at all from the fire spell.

Kay wore an amused look on her face, likely due to his antics to put out the fire that was no longer there.

"He could see me. Theran tried to burn me with a spell. Mona couldn't see me when I traveled to where she was, but Theran could."

"Maybe he could see you because he's a mage, too," Kay surmised. "Were you able to see where he was?"

"All I could see was the limited view out a window. He's in a harbor town with a castle opposite the village on a cliff overlooking the harbor."

"That could be anywhere," Gareth said. "Every harbor of any size has a castle overlooking it."

"This one was flying a banner I've never seen before. It had a blue background. Light blue, like the sky on a summer's day. And there was a fish across the banner."

"What kind of fish?" Kay asked.

"How do I know what kind of fish? It was a fish. It was big, and it had a pointy nose, kind of like a spear sticking out of its face."

"You mean a marlin?" Gareth asked.

"What's a marlin?" Hal replied.

Kay rolled her eyes. "A marlin is sometimes called a swordfish or spearfish because of the long spike extending from its upper jaw."

"Oh, then maybe it was a marlin fish."

"I know that banner," Gareth said. "It belongs to the Baron of Morton Creek."

"Morton Creek has got to be more than two weeks away from here, and we don't have mounts. Are you sure?" Kay asked.

"I'm sure, and it is more like three weeks from here, if my reckoning of where we are is correct."

"If we know where this place is, we need to get there as soon as possible," Hal said. "Are you with us, Gareth?"

"I'm afraid this is where we must part ways, Hal Dix," Gareth said. "Morton Creek is in the opposite direction of my lady Bronwynn's High Forest. Chance and I must return there and tell her of the success of your quest to restore the Fallen Forest."

"I understand," Hal said, trying not to let his disappointment show. The elf captain and sergeant had grown on him. "You have to do what your mistress would want. Do me a favor, though. Tell no one of where we are going except Bronwynn, and do that in private. Do you understand?"

"I will do as you say, Hal Dix. Your secret is safe with me. One more thing you should know. Theran the fire mage is difficult at times. I have witnessed his disagreements with my mistress on several occasions. I do not think it will be easy to convince him to take you on as a pupil."

"Good. According to Kay, I love a good challenge. Don't worry. I'll find a way to bring him over to my side."

Quest accepted: Convince Theran to teach fire magic.

Hal clasped wrists with the elven captain. "Until we meet again."

"Until then."

Chance and Gareth shouldered their packs again and turned west towards the High Forest and Lady Bronwynn. They waved once and set off at a quick pace. Hal watched them go until they disappeared over a nearby hill. He turned to Kay.

"I guess we're off to Morton Creek."

"I guess so, Hal. It lies along the coast southeast from here. Ready for another exciting adventure learning magic?"

"I am. This time, I'm not letting anything get in my way or distract me from what I need to do."

Hal spared a final glance to see if he could spot the two elves one last time as they returned home to Bronwynn. Failing to locate them, he turned and followed Kay southeast. They had several weeks of hard travel ahead, and he wanted to hurry. There was no telling how long Theran would remain there in his hiding place in Morton Creek.

CHAPTER 17

THE NEXT TWO and a half weeks were a blur for Hal. He and Kay traveled as fast as they could, but they only had a little money between them, and they were holding on to what they had because they knew they would need the few gold and silver coins when they reached Morton Creek.

That meant they spent many nights outdoors, sleeping under the stars, or at least they would've been sleeping under the stars. Unfortunately, it seemed like it was the rainy season in this part of Fantasma.

By the time they got to Morton Creek, Hal felt like he'd never be dry again. While Kay didn't complain much, he was sure she felt the same way. It was near dark when they passed through the city gates. There was no time to begin their search for Theran tonight, so they started to look for an inn.

"How much money do we have, Kay?"

"We have about fifteen silver pieces left. I think, if we shop around, we might be able to stretch that to last a week, and that's if we share a room."

Hal shrugged. "We've shared a room before."

"Morton Creek is in a very conservative district of the Empire.

The people here will frown upon a man and woman staying together in the same room if they are not married."

"I suppose we could pretend to be married as long as it doesn't go too far."

"Believe me, Hal, there's no danger of that."

"Let's look for an inn, then."

They checked in at several locations near the main gate. All of them were full and had no rooms to rent. The last innkeeper suggested they try closer to the harbor, though he seemed to think very little of the inns in that part of town.

Hal and Kay started to walk down the hill towards the harbor as the sun dropped below the walls. If he weren't distracted, Hal would have thought the view beautiful. Instead, he was just tired. All he wanted to do was find a place to sleep for the night.

The innkeeper by the gate was right. There was an opening at the first inn they found near the harbor. It was a run-down place, and judging from some of the clientele, Hal was sure he'd be scratching at fleas for weeks to come.

There was a single room available to rent, and the innkeeper didn't seem to be overly concerned about checking whether he and Kay were a married couple. That was one advantage to staying in a seedier part of town.

Hal threw his backpack down on the first bed in the room they were going to share and flopped down next to it. Compared to sleeping on the hard ground under the stars, this mattress felt like sleeping on air.

"I'm going to sleep like a baby tonight," Hal told Kay.

"One of us should try to stay awake and keep watch." Kay lowered her voice then and whispered, "Those mage hunters could be right behind us and we'd never know it."

Hal groaned. They hadn't seen any sign of the mage hunters since leaving the forest weeks ago.

"I think we're safe for now. Any hunters are going to have to search the whole town for us. We're far more likely to spot them before they spot us."

Kay shrugged. "You're probably right. I guess we can get by for one night. I'm as exhausted as you are."

"The innkeeper said the room came with dinner," Hal reminded her. "Why don't we head back down to the taproom and see what they've cooked up for tonight? We can also try and pick up some of the local gossip. It might help us in our search tomorrow."

"You think there's news of our missing mage somewhere in town?"

"I think it can't hurt to check. If we buy a few drinks for the locals, maybe we'll turn up a lead on where to start looking."

Kay nodded and opened the door. There was a startled boy crouched outside, as if he had been listening to their conversation. Before he could run away, Kay reached out and snagged him by the arm, then pulled him into the room and closed the door.

Hal stood and grabbed the boy from Kay, tossing him onto the other bed.

"Why were you listening at our door, boy? Did someone put you up to this?"

"N-n-no, sir, but the Guild Master pays for information on anybody new who comes to stay in the Harbor District. It's not much but it fills me up. Perhaps you'd like to offer to pay me instead; then I could tell him that you are just traveling merchants, instead of bounty hunters looking for someone."

Hal liked the kid's gumption. He had a lot of sass for someone caught in the act of spying.

"Or, maybe we just slit your throat and leave you to die in the alley," Kay said, drawing her dagger.

"Either way, the Guild Master will come looking for you. No one leaves a body in the Harbor District without paying for the privilege."

Hal and Kay exchanged glances. He knew she had no intention of killing the boy. The kid must be a good judge of character, too, because he didn't think she'd kill him either, based on his flippant response.

"So, how much does it cost to pay you off?" Hal asked. He held up a hand as he changed his mind. "We don't have that much to spend anyway. Maybe it makes more sense just to go see the Guild Master in person and pay the toll."

"I could take you to him. I wouldn't even charge you that much."

"Really." Hal laughed. "And how much would that be?"

The boy studied their faces for a few seconds before he answered. "One silver piece, each."

"One silver piece, for the both of us, and you fill us in on what the Guild Master is like before we get there."

The boy hesitated for just a second, then he smiled and nodded. "One silver piece it is."

He spat into his hand and held it out towards Hal. Smiling, Hal spat into his own hand and shook it with the boy.

"Well, now that's done, let's go down and get that dinner we were talking about."

"Oh, you don't want to eat here," the boy cautioned them. "It'll make you sick. I know a place that's much better and it's on the way to where we have to meet the Guild Master."

"Alright, tell us your name, and you can lead the way," Hal said.

"Tobias Shroot, but you can call me Toby. Everyone else does."

"Greetings, Toby. I'm Hal and this is my partner, Kay. We might have some additional work for you after we pay our respects to the local authorities. Are you interested?"

"Sure." He looked back and forth between them before he continued. "It isn't anything weird, is it?"

Hal laughed out loud. "Believe, me, Toby. It's nothing weird. Now lead on, my stomach is growling something fierce."

He and Kay followed the boy down the back stairs out of the inn. It was very dark on the street, though there were a few gas lamps here and there, as Toby led them down the hill closer to the harbor. He stopped below a sign showing a fisherman holding a net full of fish.

"This is the Daily Catch and it's got the best food in the Harbor District. Come inside; my mother is the cook."

"It smells delicious," Kay said. "What's good here?"

"Pretty much anything, but the chowder is my favorite."

"Chowder sounds great after nothing but trail biscuits and venison jerky for weeks," Hal said, sitting down at a table near the door.

He propped his staff against the wall and sat so he could see the entrance and anyone who came inside. Kay sat opposite him so she could watch the door to the kitchen. Old habits died hard.

An attractive girl of about sixteen came out of the kitchen and smiled at them. She resembled Toby a little around the eyes. Hal guessed she was probably his sister.

"Hey, Hannah, these are my friends. I'm taking them to see the Guild Master later, but they wanted dinner first. What's Mama making tonight?"

"Good evening, folks. As he said, my name is Hannah. It's a little late, but we still have a pot of chowder on, and there are a few fillets left we could fry up if that's more to your liking."

"I heard the chowder was excellent," Hal said. "I'll have that."

Kay nodded. "Make that two. And two ales, if you have them."

"Sure thing. I'll be right back with your drinks."

"Alright, Toby," Hal said as he turned back to the boy. "Tell us about the Guild Master."

"Well, he runs this town. Nothing happens without him knowing about it. Even the Baron is afraid to cross him, which is why His Lordship stays up in his castle all the time."

"Sounds like a scary guy. I suppose, if we are looking for someone in town, that would be the place where we would have to start."

"Yes, unless, of course, the person you are looking for has already paid the Guild Master to stay in hiding," Toby added.

"Oh, of course," Hal agreed. "Hopefully, that's not the case. I get the feeling, from the way you describe him, we don't want to cross the local authorities and step on any toes."

Toby nodded.

Hal liked the boy. If he managed to keep from getting killed while listening at doors, he might grow up to make something of himself someday.

Suddenly, Toby stopped smiling. Hal followed his gaze and noticed he was watching a group of boys a little older than himself walk up to the restaurant and come inside.

"Well, well, it looks like our friend Toby here has been trying to do a little business on the side. You wouldn't do that to us, would you, Toby?"

"No, I'm just sitting here with some fine patrons of my mother's restaurant. Go ahead and ask them."

Hal took an instant dislike to the leader of the group of boys. He had dark, greasy hair and what looked like a permanent sneer on his face. He reminded Hal of his work nemesis, Barry. He decided to teach this kid a lesson.

"Well, mister, is what Toby here says true? Because it sure looks to me that you hired him to show you around the town. That is something only I'm allowed to do in this part of the district."

"I'm afraid you are mistaken. My companion and I merely stopped in here to get a bite to eat. Toby was kind enough to tell us what was good on the menu, though I have to say he seems like a fine lad and I may well hire him to show me around later. You don't have a problem with that, do you?"

Hal leaned back in his chair and let his hand drop down beside him, where he could reach his staff quickly if needed.

The greasy-haired kid leaned forward until he was close to Hal's face. His breath was foul.

"You're gonna have a problem with it, mister. I make the rules here, and I say that I'm going to show you around town later, not Toby."

"I don't think so," Hal said. "It's going to be pretty hard to walk with that bad knee."

"What are you talking about? I don't have a bad..."

The boy never finished what he was saying. In one fluid motion, Hal tipped forward in his chair, grabbed his staff, and swept the boy's legs out from under him. Then, doing something he'd considered trying with his earth magic, Hal channeled the reverse of a regeneration spell at the boy's knee. There was an audible crack, and the boy on the floor groaned in pain, clutching at his leg.

Spell learned – Deal wounds.

"Now that's a shame," Kay said. "He should be more careful and not slip and fall like that. Don't you other boys agree?" She pulled the long knife from her belt and tested the edge with her thumb while she spoke.

After sharing glances with each other, the three boys still standing nodded but didn't say a word. Two of them grabbed the first boy under his arms and lifted him up while backing towards the door.

"Don't let me find out you came back here later to cause trouble," Hal called after them. "It would be a shame to fall and break the other knee."

At that last statement, the group of boys picked up their pace and soon disappeared.

"You probably shouldn't have done that, mister. That was the Guild Master's son, Gary."

"Gary? Really?" Kay said.

Toby nodded.

"Well, Gary needed to learn some lessons," Hal noted. "It's never too soon to pick up some manners. Maybe next time he'll show some respect to his elders."

"Maybe you and Kay should leave town for a while and come back later to find your guy. Gary's gonna tell his dad what happened. This is going to complicate things if you stay in town and go to meet the Guild Master tonight."

Hal shook his head. "We will enjoy the fine dinner your mother is preparing for us, and then we will go and meet with the Guild Master as planned. I have an idea that should cover us when it comes time to deal with anything Gary has told his dad about us."

"Meaning you have a clever plan? Careful, you sound like your old self again," Kay noted.

Hal laughed and pointed to Hannah approaching with their dinner. "Here comes the food. Eat first; then we go let this Guild Master know who we really are."

Quest accepted: Impress the Guild Master.

Hal put on an air of confidence as the slot machine started rattling in his head. He hadn't been using his luck as much on this trip to Fantasma. It seemed that magic use was not as prone to chance as the other abilities he'd used before. Hal wasn't sure what was going to happen, but he knew it was going to be a fun evening.

CHAPTER 18

THE DINNER WAS every bit as good as Toby had said it would be. Hal found himself sopping up the last of the chowder's broth with a piece of fresh sourdough bread. He shoved the final piece in his mouth and pushed back from the table, his hand falling across his full stomach.

"That was delicious, Toby." Hal smiled up at Hannah as she came to collect their dishes. "Tell your mother we will be back to try some of the other things on her menu."

"I'm sure she will like that."

Hal stood, grabbed his staff, and nodded at Toby. "Lead the way, my friend. Time's a-wastin' and we've got important things to do."

Toby got up and they followed him out into the street. The boy led them across the Harbor District until they reached an area filled with warehouses used to hold the various goods coming ashore from the ships in the harbor.

The last warehouse in the row had two burly men standing beside the double doors leading inside. As Hal, Kay, and Toby approached, the two guards hefted heavy truncheons, and one of them pointed at Toby.

"You're in big trouble, kid. Gary is inside, telling his father all about how you got his knee messed up."

Hal strode up to the man who had spoken, stepping in front of Toby to draw the guard's attention to him.

"Actually, it was I who had to teach young Gary a lesson in manners. He needed a refresher on how to treat a visiting Guild Master. Please advise your leader that an important visitor from Tandon is in town."

The lead guard looked at his partner, and the second man turned and ducked inside the double doors, presumably to deliver the message.

"What'd you do to the kid's leg, anyway? The boss had to send for a healing mage."

"Just a little trick I learned along my travels. I'm sure he'll be fine with some time to heal up and consider the repercussions of his actions."

The guard chuckled. "The kid's a punk, that's for sure, but his daddy is looking for blood on this one. You guys better talk fast if you want to get through the night without a beating or a hefty fine for hurtin' the kid."

"We'll take our chances," Hal said.

The whirring of the slots in his head picked up speed, and Hal suspected he was pressing his luck harder than usual on this one. Still, he had to confront this head-on. It was the only way to gain some respect in this town quickly. There was a lot he and Kay needed to do. Having a friend in the leader of the local thieves' guild would come in handy.

The second guard returned and whispered in the first guard's ear. He nodded at Hal with an evil grin.

"Don't say I didn't warn you. The boss wants to see you right away. Follow me."

Hal and Kay followed, with Toby bringing up the rear. Once inside the warehouse, they wove through stacks of crates and boxes until they reached another door. Hal could hear shouting from the other side, followed by cheers from what sounded like a large group of people.

His luck was spinning away in the back of his mind, so Hal knew he could still work this all out. The guard opened the door and gestured for Hal and the others to go inside.

There was a boxing match happening inside the large room. It was a bare-knuckled brawl between two men stripped to the waist. They were surrounded by about thirty cheering men and women. Hal saw money changing hands when one of the men got knocked down.

He wondered if he was going to have to take a turn in the ring. Hopefully, with his luck in play, they could avoid all of that mess.

Scanning the crowd, Hal found the Guild Master seated in a rocking chair atop a large crate. He was a portly man, wearing the clothes of a wealthy merchant. When their eyes met, Hal knew the Guild Master spotted him, too. Gary, leaning on a makeshift crutch, stood next to the crate, glaring at them and pointing in their direction.

"Enough!" the large man bellowed. "I have new business to attend to. Take the rest of the fight outside if you must keep brawling."

About half the crowd followed as the two fighters left the room out another door. The other half of the spectators backed up and lined the walls, waiting to see what happened next. Hal could tell a few of them were appraising him. Some even made bets. He smiled. He wished he could take some of that action. He didn't think they'd guess right. If they knew him, they might not bet against him.

The Guild Master pointed at them. "You three, come here."

Hal, Kay, and Toby walked up to stand in front of the crate, staring up at the man who held the key to finding Theran in Morton Creek and continuing Hal's training as a mage. With a grand flourish, Hal stepped forward, bowed low, then stood and addressed their host.

"Greetings, sir. We were traveling through your fine town while trying to locate a friend and decided we must pay our respects."

"Paying respects? What are you talking about?" the Guild Master growled. "Gary here tells me you're the one who messed up his knee."

"I am sorry about that, but he disrespected me and my companions. I simply cannot stand for that kind of treatment. I have appearances to maintain after all."

The big man stood up from his rocking chair and pointed a thick, calloused finger down at Hal. "Who the hell do you think you are?"

The room was quiet enough to hear a pin drop. Hal waited a few seconds before answering.

"I'm the Hood, traveling through from Tandon. I'd hoped to enjoy some mutual respect from the local guild, but I suppose such things are for more civilized places."

"You're the famous Hood, the thief who took down the Wardens in Tandon one by one all by himself?"

Hal snuck a sideways glance at Kay. She let out a huff and rolled her eyes. She hated it when his plans came together like this. He smiled at her and turned back to the man on the crate.

"I had some help along the way, but that is essentially what happened."

"We heard you were dead, killed in some slave revolt way off in the east."

"I was there, dealing with another rude gentleman, but as you can see, I didn't die. I simply freed another city from its oppressive and disrespectful leadership."

One of the onlookers peeled away from the crowd and approached the crate from one side. The Guild Master held up a finger, pausing the conversation with Hal while he leaned over to the other man. The newcomer glanced at Hal and then whispered something in the bossman's ear.

The Guild Master's eyes widened, and his eyes shot to Hal and then to Kay. He sat up. He appeared a little flustered and tried to regain his composure before continuing.

"It seems one of my crew was traveling through Tandon during that series of unfortunate incidents. He recognizes both you and your companion. That doesn't change the fact you injured my son, though. What am I supposed to do about that?"

"Heal him and tell him to do a better job assessing a situation before picking a fight he can't win. He was rude to me and my companions while we were eating our evening meal. I really had no choice but to put him in his place."

"Dad, you aren't gonna take this guy's word on it over me, are you?"

"Shut up, Gary. This wouldn't be the first time I had to bail you out of trouble your big mouth got you into. This time, you've managed to drag me into one of your messes."

Hal fought to hold back a smile. That was just the reaction he'd wanted to hear. Things were going very well indeed. Now, he had to seal the deal with the man in charge.

"I am willing to arrange some concessions with the Duke of Tandon that would be mutually beneficial to all to help smooth over some of this difficulty. Will that suffice?"

The Guild Master considered what Hal had said, then he jumped down from the crate and extended a hand to him. Hal reached out and the two men clasped wrists.

A chime sounded in Hal's head as the slots stopped rolling. A notification popped up.

Quest completed: Impress the Guild Master.
2,000 experience points awarded.

The Guild Master grinned at Hal and clapped him on the back. "The name's Tarak, but my friends call me Tracker."

"Good to meet you, Tracker. I'm Hal Dix, and this is my partner, Kay."

"Pleased to meet you, Kay. I can't believe I have the chance to meet the two of you in person. We've heard a great deal about your exploits, even here in this sleepy little town."

"I'm sure only half of it is true," Hal professed. "You know how these things can get out of hand."

"I do indeed," Tracker said. "What brings you to Morton Creek anyway? I would think you'd be doing business in one of the bigger cities, where your margins could be larger."

"Normally, you'd be right, but we got sidetracked looking for someone who has a particular set of skills we need, and I heard through the grapevine he was here in Morton Creek."

"If there's someone hiding out here in this town, I'll be able to find them. There's not anything happening here without me having a piece of it."

Hal smiled. "That's what I've heard and why I came directly to you. I wanted to show you the respect due to someone in our mutual positions."

"So, who is it? Who do you need me to find?"

Hal looked around at the room full of thieves and informants. "I think I'd like to share that information in a more private setting. I don't suppose there's a more intimate place we could chat and get more acquainted?"

"Of course, come with me." Tracker turned to his son as they passed him. "Gary, bring us a tray of drinks. The good wine, mind you. Nothing but the best for our new friends."

Hal smiled at the boy, who stood with his fists clenched as they passed him, fuming in silence.

"Thank you, Gary," Hal said. He couldn't resist.

The group walked to the far side of the room. Tracker pressed a panel on the wall, and a section swiveled aside smoothly, revealing a hidden room beyond. There was a table with six chairs. The table held stacks of documents, invoices, and orders for various goods.

Tracker gestured to the chairs, and Hal and Kay sat down. Their host gathered the scattered papers and placed them to one side.

"Do you want the boy here? If you have something sensitive to talk about, he should probably stay outside," Tracker suggested when he noticed Toby tagging along.

Hal pointed to a chair next to him, and Toby came and sat down.

"He's with us. I'll vouch for him. I hope you don't mind if I use him as a sort of assistant while I'm in town?"

"No, not at all. I'm all for the young folks showing some initiative. I only wish Gary had the same drive. Unfortunately, he takes after his mother and prefers to spend my money rather than help bring more in."

"A common problem everywhere," Hal said.

Tracker sat at the head of the table and folded his hands in front of him. "So, who are we looking for?"

"It's a mage named Theran. Do you know him?" Hal asked.

"I've heard of him. I didn't know he was in town."

"I have reason to believe he's in hiding here. Imperial mage hunters are tracking him."

"Those are some bad characters. I'd rather not cross them. Are you planning on picking him up and leaving, or turning him over for the bounty?"

Tracker rubbed his hands together in anticipation of a payout.

"Not exactly. I need to talk with him. If we can find him, we'll take him off your hands, and that should keep the hunters from coming into your town and causing a whole lot of trouble trying to capture or kill Theran."

Hal leaned back in his chair before continuing. He needed to make it seem more profitable to Tracker to let Hal take Theran rather than turn him in for the bounty.

"You heard about what happened with the mage hunters up north, right?"

"No, what?" Tracker's voice rose in pitch, worry creeping into his tone.

Good. Hal continued. "They caught up to Theran in a town about this size up there. He's a fire mage, you know. In the ensuing battle, both sides managed to burn three-quarters of the town down around them before Theran escaped. The hunters took off after him without so much as a by-your-leave, let alone paying for the damages."

"That's, uh, alarming, to say the least."

Hal watched as the Guild Master calculated his options. He hoped the local thief was the type to give more weight to long-term business opportunities over short-term payouts.

"If we can get to Theran first, the plan will be to get him on a ship out of town as fast as possible and take the pressure off Morton Creek, from an imperial perspective."

"That would be good," Tracker agreed. "We're a small town compared to the big ports like Tandon. Even a small fire could be devastating to the local business concerns."

"That's what Kay and I thought as well, which was why we came to you as soon as we arrived in town. We don't want a repeat of what happened up north."

"Can you describe him for me? Perhaps I can make a few discreet inquiries."

Hal thought back to the man he'd seen in his vision, describing Theran as he'd appeared in the storeroom. "He is a thin man. He has a goatee and black hair. When I saw him, he was wearing torn red robes and hiding in some sort of storage shed, where fishnets and rope were stored."

"You saw him?"

"I have some abilities that enable me to see people over long distances when I am looking for them. In this case, I was able to isolate Theran here in Morton Creek. But I only saw the inside of the room he was using to hide. He had a view of the harbor from a cracked window, but other than that, I have no idea where in the city he is hiding."

Tracker considered Hal's description, then waved his hands in the air.

"Honestly, Hal, what you describe could be half of the buildings in and around the Harbor District. It will be tough to narrow them down to just one, based on what you've told me."

Toby squirmed in his seat next to Hal and cleared his throat.

"Do you have some idea that might help us find this man, Toby?" Hal asked.

"Maybe. I think I may have seen a man like that around where my mother's restaurant is. If it's the same guy, then I might know where he is hiding."

Tracker smiled and slapped the table with his hand. "There you go. You don't even need my help at all. I still hope we can find a way to work together and perhaps get involved in some business ventures between Tandon and here."

"I would like that very much. In the meantime, we still need to charter that ship to take us away from here. Can you help us with that?"

"That I can definitely do. It might take me a day or two to line up a discreet sea captain to carry you and this mage to safety. Where can I find you when it is all set up?"

"I think Kay and I will base ourselves out of Toby's mother's restaurant. The food is excellent, and if our quarry is nearby, all the better."

Tracker stood, and Kay and Hal followed his lead.

"Excellent. When I find out where and when the ship will be leaving, I will send word to you there."

Quest accepted: Escape Morton Creek.

The door opened at that moment, showing Gary standing there holding a tray of wine and goblets. Hal wondered how long he'd been standing at the door, listening to their conversation. He didn't trust the boy.

Gary set the tray down, and Tracker poured drinks for each of them before holding up his goblet and offering a toast.

"To new friends and profitable business ventures."

"Indeed," Hal replied, and they all raised their drinks to success.

It was time for Hal to find his next teacher and learn fire magic.

CHAPTER 19

THE NEXT MORNING AFTER BREAKFAST, Hal, Kay, and Toby stood on the street, staring at a house that looked much like all the others next to it.

"That's the place," Toby said. "If it is the same guy, then he is hiding in the shed to the rear of that fisherman's cottage."

"How do you want to handle this, Hal?" Kay asked.

"I think I should go in there alone. If Theran saw me when I was there in my vision, perhaps he will recognize me, and I can tell him I don't mean him any harm. It's the best plan I have. The last thing I want is for him to start lobbing fireballs at me."

"Nobody wants that, Hal," Kay agreed. "A fire in this part of town would spread quickly to every house in the neighborhood."

"You and Toby, stay here. With luck, I'll be right back."

Hal grabbed his staff and crossed the street to the cottage. He considered knocking on the front door but changed his mind and headed around to the back of the house. When he turned the corner into the backyard, Hal bumped into Theran coming out from the rear of the cottage.

Theran looked even worse this time than he had before. His face was drawn and gaunt, and he seemed even thinner, his clothes hanging off his rail-thin figure. Hal raised his hand in greeting. The other man flinched, mistaking the gesture for an attack. He fired off a jet of flame from his fingertips at Hal's head.

Hal ducked under the attack, but not before the flames singed his eyebrows. He threw up his ice shield, catching the remainder of the flame attack on the disc of ice he held in front of him.

"Easy does it, pal. I'm just here to talk."

"Who are you? You're working for the Emperor. There aren't any free ice mages left since they captured Ragnar."

Hal hadn't heard about Ragnar's capture, but now wasn't the time to ask for details or find out how Theran knew about it.

"I'm Hal Dix. Tildi sent me. I'm the guy she brought here to fight the Emperor. I need your help."

The other man relaxed and put his hand down, so Hal released the ice shield, too, letting the disc of ice dissipate into the air between them.

"Don't tell me you believe all of that crap Tildi has been feeding you about the prophecy and everything? You aren't destined to save the world. There's nothing you or anyone else can do at this point to stop the Emperor from taking everything for himself. It's over."

"Then why don't you just turn yourself in? I think you're hiding because you hope there's a way out."

"So what if I am hiding? If I turn myself in to Emperor Kang's hunters, I'll end up in a prison cell, a dungeon, or worse. Hiding out in this backward fishing town is better than any of those options."

"I don't know about that. Have you seen yourself lately? Frankly, you look horrible."

Theran ran his fingers through his hair and straightened his robe, trying to press out the wrinkles with his palm.

"Look, come with me. I have a few friends here. We can sit and have a good meal and talk about what I need you to do. How does that sound?"

Hal could tell the thought of food sounded good to Theran. The fire mage's stomach rumbled loud enough for both to hear.

"I suppose I could come and talk with you, but I am done with Tildi and her crazy plans to overthrow the Emperor."

"We can talk about that and anything else you want to talk about over a hot breakfast. Come on. I have just the place for us to go and eat. Trust me, the food is amazing."

Hal and Theran walked around the cottage back to the street. They were about to cross and meet up with Kay and Toby when a shout came from their left.

"There he is! Don't let him get off a spell."

Five men in black leather armor all raised their crossbows as one and fired at Hal and Theran. Without thinking, Hal pushed Theran to the ground while casting his ice shield spell, spreading the ice disc as wide as it would go. Four of the crossbow bolts pinged off the ice shield and fell harmlessly to the ground. The fifth one broke through the ice, shattering the shield and striking Hal in the shoulder.

Health damage: Health -8

All five men dropped their bows, drew their swords, and charged at Hal and Theran. Hal fired off a pair of ice darts at the man in the lead. Both dagger-sized darts took the black-clad mage hunter in the chest and dropped him to the cobblestones.

1,000 experience points awarded.

The other swordsmen jumped over their fallen comrade and charged in, hacking at the two mages with their blades. Hal had just enough time to cast his armor spell. The first of the sword attacks slid off the ice encasing his chest. He caught the next sword on the shaft of his staff. The wood, produced from the magical glade, slapped the blade aside as if it were made of steel itself.

Hal knew, if he could hold out against his two attackers for ten or fifteen seconds, Kay would come from across the street and attack them from behind. Unfortunately, ten or fifteen seconds in a fight like this was an eternity.

Next to him, Theran fired off jets of flame from both his hands at the two hunters charging at him. The first hunter ducked under the fire attack, but the second was not so lucky. His hair and cloak caught fire. The unlucky hunter dropped to the ground, screeching in agony and rolling around in vain to put out the flames.

Hal lost track of Theran after that. The next part of the fight was a blur of sword blades coming at him from all directions. Hal focused on his desperate attempts to fend them off. There was no opportunity for Hal to get in any sort of attack or cast any spells. All he could do was bat some of the thrusting blades aside with his staff while hoping the rest of them didn't find a weakness in his armor.

Of course, he was not so lucky. An attack from the side broke through his defenses. The sword cut deep into his arm and he nearly let go of his staff due to the pain.

Health damage: Health -12

Sticky wetness ran down his arm from the fresh slash. Out of the corner of his eye, he saw Theran take a sword thrust to his shoulder and fall to the cobblestones beside him. He searched his mind for a desperation move that might get him out of trouble. Rescue came as Kay let out a war cry, hitting the attackers from behind.

Her attack came at the perfect moment. They never saw her coming. She dropped one of the hunters with the thrust of her sword into his back. Then, after kicking the dead man off her blade, she began a furious series of attacks on the remaining two mage hunters, forcing them to turn and face her.

This gave Hal the opportunity he needed. Casting his ice shield in a horizontal position on the ground under their feet, he was able to make both of them slip, fall, and crash to the ground. He dove on top of the closest hunter and stabbed downward with the butt of his staff, bashing his face multiple times until the man stopped moving.

1,000 experience points awarded.

When Hal rose from the body of the dead hunter, Kay had already finished off the final attacker. A groan from his left came from Theran. The fire mage was down on the cobblestones, his hand pressed to his shoulder, trying to staunch the flow of blood from the sword wound.

Hal knelt beside Theran and pulled his bloody hand away to look at the injury. He was tired from casting all the ice magic, but he had to try and do something, or his new teacher was going to die before he could learn anything at all.

"I need to look at that wound. Hold still."

"You led them right to me. Now I'm going to die here in the street because of your incompetence."

"They weren't after you. They were after me," Hal said. "Now hold still. I've got to close up this wound, or you're going to bleed to death."

"After you? Wow, aren't we a little full of ourselves. I am the arch fire mage after all."

"Yeah, and I am the mythical Opponent. Now shut up and let me do my work."

Closing his eyes and concentrating, Hal channeled his earth magic into the wound in Theran's shoulder and cast a heal wounds spell to knit the flesh back together.

The other mage let out a sigh, as the pain from his wound lessened.

Hal opened his eyes. The wound closed, leaving only a puckered, pink scar in its place.

"You've been to Bronwynn, haven't you?"

"Yes, and to Ragnar before her. Now I need you. You all have to teach me what you know. That, apparently, is my special ability. I can use all the elemental schools of magic."

Toby darted from the alley across the street and ran up to them. "That was amazing. I can't believe you killed all of them."

"What do we do about all these bodies?" Kay asked. "If we leave them here in the street, someone is going to get annoyed with us, or worse."

"Tracker can take care of it," Toby said. "He can have a wagon come through and pick up the bodies within an hour. We should get off the street, though, before too many people see us. Come on."

"Let's go to your mom's place," Hal said. "I need food to replenish my energy after that fight. Theran's going to need some, too, to help with his healing."

"You promised me a hot meal, anyway," Theran added.

"Have you changed your mind about me? Will you teach me fire magic?"

"What choice do I have? It looks like the two of us need each other right now until we get away from the mage hunters. There will be more around; you know that, right? These are just the common thugs they use to track us down. The real mage hunters use magic to counter us."

"Yeah, I figured as much. Don't worry, I've got plans to get us both out of here by boat, but it might take another day to line up the right captain for the job. Maybe you can teach me some fire magic spells while we wait for our ride."

"There are worse ways to pass the time. Mark me, though. I have little patience for sloppiness when learning magic. Use of any magic can be dangerous. Fire spells are especially risky."

"That's fine by me," Hal said. "You'll find me a motivated pupil. I have too much riding on this to not pay attention to my lessons."

"Then your studies begin as soon as we finish breakfast. Lead on."

Toby took the lead, guiding them all into the alley across the street, helping them escape the scene of the fighting.

Hal had won Theran to his cause. He would learn fire magic after all.

Quest completed: Convince Theran to teach fire magic.

    3,500 experience points awarded.

CHAPTER 20

THERAN WAS A STRICT TASKMASTER. He had Hal working on exercises to connect with his fire magic ability again and again for nearly twenty hours straight. It was some of the most laborious effort he had ever performed in his life, and even after hours of work, he still was not successful at connecting with the fire magic he knew existed somewhere inside him.

One of the exercises was particularly frustrating to Hal. Theran had him close his eyes while reaching out with his hand over a short, stubby candle. The goal had Hal trying to capture the flame on his fingertips. All he managed to do was burn his fingers, again and again and again.

On what had to be the one-hundredth attempt at capturing the flame, Hal yanked his hand back and stuck his burnt finger in his mouth. He cursed aloud.

Theran chuckled at Hal's frustration. "Did you think learning to cast spells and use magic would be easy, lad?"

"Believe me, Theran, none of it has been easy."

"And yet, you give up so easily."

"I'm not giving up. I just need to take a break."

"No breaks! There is no telling when those mage hunters will catch up with us again. Having another fire mage alongside me will go a long way to put those bastards in their place."

"I'm not without skills of my own. You saw me casting ice and earth magic."

"I did. I also know both are virtually useless in a battle. Fire magic is the god of the battlefield. There's nothing like it. The rest pales by comparison. But, it takes control, and control starts with you being able to capture that single, tiny little flame. Now, back to work. You've had enough rest."

Hal returned his attention to the candle burning in the center of the table. They were sitting in the back room at Toby's mother's restaurant. She had offered it to them while they waited to hear from Tracker about a ship to take them from Morton Creek and back to Tandon, where they'd have some protection from the mage hunters for a while.

Closing his eyes, Hal reached out with his mind once again and tried to see the flame with his inner vision while he sought it out with his hand. He was exhausted, both mentally and physically, but he pressed onward.

This time, perhaps because he was so tired, something different happened. When he tried to visualize the flame on the candle, instead of seeing the flickering yellow tongue of fire he usually envisioned, he saw a circular gradient of brightness against a black background. At the center of the circle of light, it was bright white. As the circle of illumination moved out from the center, it changed color from bright white to a deep violet at the outer edge of the circle, where it blended into the blackness beyond.

At first, Hal thought he might have dozed off. Maybe he was dreaming. But when he reached his hand towards the circle of light, the image of his hand had a gradient of color to it, ranging from an orange-red glow along his arm and hand out to blue at his fingertips.

Then, it hit him.

He was seeing the light in the infrared spectrum. He observed the flame and his arm as a thermal camera back home might, with different shades of brightness relating to the strength of the heat radiating off it.

Could he be imagining all of this?

No, Hal was sure it had to be significant. Moving his fingers carefully towards the circle of bright light that was the candle, Hal tried to imagine the heat from his hand connecting with the heat of the flame.

It worked. He touched his fingers to the circle of white-hot light that was the burning candle and lifted it on his fingertip while maintaining a separation between the heat gradient of his hand and the searing heat of the flame.

When he pulled his hand away, slowly this time, the circle of bright light came away with it and yet his fingers didn't burn. Hardly able to believe he'd managed to make it work, Hal cracked open one eye to peer at his hand extended before him.

There, right before him, was his extended hand. A tongue of yellow flame hovered over his index finger. Next to it, the candle sat, the wick still sending up a wisp of smoke after Hal had extinguished it by taking over the flame.

Understanding now how the heat from his body connected to the heat of the flame in some way, Hal tried to make the yellow flame grow larger by feeding it heat from his own body.

As if he turned up the wick of an oil lamp, the tongue of fire hovering over his finger grew larger and larger until it extended three or four inches above his hand.

Quest completed: Learn to use fire magic.
  6,000 experience points awarded.

"And to think you almost gave up."

Holding the image of the flame in his mind to maintain it over his finger, Hal turned and looked at his teacher.

"I didn't give up. Why didn't you tell me to imagine seeing this as if I was using an infrared camera?"

"What the hell is an infrared camera?"

Hal shook his head. "Never mind. I guess I figured it out. That's all that matters."

"You haven't figured anything out," Theran snapped. "All you have learned is the most basic of fire spells. If you think you know everything, go ahead and put the fire out."

Hal smirked and returned his full attention to the four-inch flame hovering over his finger. With his mind, he commanded the fire to extinguish.

Nothing happened.

He tried using a spoken command. "Off."

Theran laughed. "You think you can just ask fire to go away? Fire is destruction. All fire wants to do is destroy and consume everything around it. It will never just go away as long as there is fuel, air, and energy to power it. Think, lad. Use that brain for something other than making clever comments."

Hal scowled and stared at the flame hovering over his finger. Unable to come up with anything else to do, he closed his eyes so he could see the heat gradient again. The first thing he noticed was a line of white-hot power flowing up his arm and into the flame like a wick of energy. It was as if he'd become the source of the fire after he removed it from the candle.

Maybe he could give it back.

Moving his finger back over the candle, Hal touched the tip of the wick and tried to return the flame to its original position. When he pulled his hand away, he was disappointed to see there were now two flames. One hovered over the candle, and the other remained over his finger.

That didn't work.

Hal thought back and remembered something he'd learned in middle school science class. Fire required three things: oxygen, fuel, and heat. If you removed any of those three things, fire could not exist.

He thought about the flame hovering over his finger. He couldn't take the oxygen away, not without suffocating himself and everyone else in the room. He wouldn't know how to do it anyway.

He wasn't sure what fuel the fire was consuming. It wasn't burning his finger, and he couldn't see anything else fueling the fire. He couldn't take that away.

That left heat.

He could see the heat. There was heat coming from the flame. There was also heat coming from his body.

Then he realized what he was seeing. That line of white energy traveling up his arm to the tip of his finger was the heat energy traveling to the flame.

Focusing his mind on the tip of his finger, Hal willed the white heat extending through his index finger to the flame to return to the same blue heat level of his other fingers. It took him several tries to find the right combination of mental commands. Slowly, the flame grew smaller and then winked out entirely.

"Very well done," Theran remarked. "I am impressed. It took me nearly three days to figure out how to shut the flame off. I set fire to my clothes and even my beard several times before I figured it out."

"I'm glad that didn't happen to me. So, what's next?"

"For now, you practice starting the flame without using the candle. Once you can do that, you will be able to summon fire whenever you want. I'm going to bed. You can go to sleep once you've successfully summoned fire ten times in a row without failure. I'll see you in the morning, provided you don't kill us all in our sleep."

Quest accepted: Create fire.

Theran left Hal alone in the back room and headed upstairs to the bedrooms provided to them. Despite being exhausted, Hal continued to practice. It took him more than an hour to successfully summon the flame over his index finger ten times in a row.

Quest completed: Create fire.
    Spells learned — Summon fire, Control fire.
    10,000 experience points awarded.
    Level Up!

He was proud of his accomplishment and wanted to tell someone, but everyone was asleep. Instead, Hal called up his stats menu and looked over his new abilities with fire magic. He immediately placed two attribute points in his wisdom score, increasing his spell success rating.

Satisfied with how things looked, Hal dragged himself upstairs and crawled into bed. He was asleep within seconds.

CHAPTER 21

A MESSENGER ARRIVED from Tracker during breakfast the next morning. He handed Hal a sealed envelope and hurried off. After breaking the wax seal with his thumb, Hal unfolded the letter and scanned its contents.

I hope this message finds you in good health. I have secured you and your friends passage on a ship leaving with the evening tide. The Sea Sprite's captain is expecting you. His name is Josiah Barnes.

I have arranged payment in advance of the profits I anticipate from our future joint ventures. Fare thee well.

Tracker

Hal passed the letter to Kay. She could read it while he idly snapped his fingers several times, summoning a flame above his hand with each snap, then extinguishing it.

Theran came down the stairs and noticed his pupil practicing.

"Good, you seem to have mastered that skill well enough. With a few more months' work, you will be ready to progress to some real spells."

"I don't have a few months. I'm ready to progress to more advanced spells now."

Theran started to say something, then stopped and seemed to reconsider what he was going to say.

"If you are who Tildi thinks you are, then perhaps you can progress faster than I did at your age."

"I'm glad you have such faith in me." Hal tried not to roll his eyes as he said it, but he was sure Theran got the gist of what he meant.

The mage sighed and sat down across from Hal and Kay.

"You don't know what it's been like over this last year. The Emperor's thugs have hounded me from place to place relentlessly. They destroyed my tower, my country house, and every place I've stayed in since. I'm tired of running."

"Good. Stop running and start fighting. Ever since I came to Fantasma the first time, it hasn't been just me fighting back. I had lots of help from ordinary people who just want a better life. None of them had the skills you have, yet they still found the strength to stand up to the Emperor and his minions."

"I'm not sure my skills matter that much anymore. I've heard about the Emperor's new invention, fire sand. With power like that at his disposal, he won't need fire mages at all anymore, and neither will anyone else."

"Fire sand, or gunpowder as we call it in my world, is very potent. It's not just a weapon; it's a history-changing innovation," Hal explained. "Warfare as we knew it changed once gunpowder was invented and began to see widespread use. Swords and arrows were insignificant compared to bullets and cannonballs."

Kay jumped into the conversation. "You've said this before with regards to fire sand. I have a hard time believing that swords will cease to be useful anymore simply because some people learn to utilize this new weapon."

"It won't happen overnight, Kay. Where I come from, swords

remained in use for centuries after gunpowder reached the battle-field. Eventually, though, gunpowder weapons developed to the point that swords and arrows were obsolete, except in ceremonial uses."

Hal shrugged. "I honestly have no idea what those changes will do to your world. It will probably take decades or longer to play out. It doesn't matter much to us in the here and now. First, we have to stop the Emperor. That starts tonight when we board the ship Tracker found to take us back to Tandon. I think we'll be safe there with Duke Korran long enough to figure out our next steps."

Theran laughed, though it sounded forced. "We may not have until tonight. Those scouts for the mage hunters we killed will surely be missed. Someone will come and investigate why they haven't returned from Morton Creek. I'm surprised they haven't attacked us already."

"All the more reason for you and me to continue my lessons. Let's return to the back room for some privacy. You can try and teach me the next level of fire magic skills."

"Very well." Theran sighed, then grabbed a plate with a stack of pancakes and followed Hal back to their study room.

Hal shut the door and prepared to work through the day until it was time to leave. It would serve dual purposes. He'd get more training and practice with fire magic, and it would keep both him and Theran out of sight until they had to go out in public again. With some luck, they'd escape the city without confrontation.

———

By the end of the day, Hal had mastered the ability to control five jets of fire on each hand, one for each finger. He could raise and lower the intensity and once nearly set the curtains on fire when he was a tad overzealous in his application of energy to the flames. With the mastery of this skill, Hal had seen another pop-up, this one showing him that he'd learned the fire spray and fire resistance spells and gained three thousand experience points. He was progressing his mage abilities, but he needed to move faster.

There was a tap at the door, and Kay poked her head inside the room.

"Toby says we should probably go. The tide will go out in an hour or two, and he fears the ship will leave without us."

She looked around the room and spotted several scorch marks on the drapes.

"How's it going? I see you didn't manage to burn the place down, though it looks like you tried at least once. Did you pick up anything new?"

"A few things," Hal said. "I'll show you once we get to sea. I'll be happy to be heading back to Tandon and a place I can relax in relative safety for a change."

"Fair enough. I've got all our packs already loaded up on a cart Toby found for us. All we have to do is walk down to the harbor."

"Excellent. Then I suppose we should be on our way."

Kay led the way to the front of the restaurant and out to the street, where Toby waited with a small, two-wheeled cart. It held their backpacks, as well as a bundle of belongings Toby had fetched for Theran from his nearby hiding place in the shack.

Together, the four of them started down the cobblestone street towards the harbor. People crowded the route, and they had to stop several times to let wagons loaded with cargo pass.

Each time they stopped, the hair on the back of Hal's neck stood on end, and a chill went down his spine. He felt like someone was watching them. But as soon as they started moving again, the feeling went away.

After the third time it happened, Hal decided it must be his imagination.

He was wrong.

The attack hit them as they arrived at the wharf where the *Sea Sprite* was docked. Hal's lucky slots started spinning for no reason. It gave him a split second's warning. He shouted for everyone to duck, spotting the man casting a fireball in their direction.

A flaming missile the size of a basketball sizzled past them, struck the side of a warehouse, and set it ablaze with a violent explosion.

Hal jumped to his feet and started to use his fire spray spell when he realized the mage would not only be expecting that but would be able to resist it, too. Instead, Hal cast his plant growth spell — focusing on some seaweed he saw at the water's edge.

A few seconds later, the mage hunter was staggering around with a long strand of seaweed choking the air from his neck as it pulled him towards the edge of the seawall. He toppled over the stone wall into the water, the choking seaweed pulling him down to the depths of the harbor.

2,500 experience points awarded.

Hal pointed to their vessel.

"Toby, get the bags to the ship and tell the captain to cast off. We'll be right behind you."

"I'm going with you?"

"You can't go back home now. The hunters know you helped us. Now go!"

The boy pushed the cart down the wharf while Theran and Hal fired spell after spell back at their attackers. Kay crouched behind a stone wall, trying to stay out of the line of fire. This wasn't a fight she could do much about. They didn't have a crossbow or other missile weapon for her to use.

Hal cut loose an ice lance that skewered a mage leveling a wand at Theran. The four-foot shaft of ice hit him in the chest, killing him instantly.

2,500 experience points awarded.

"Kay, you can't do anything here," Hal called out. "Go with Toby and help him load our gear onto the ship."

"You don't have to tell me twice. Don't be long; no captain is going to want to stick around with all this random magic flying around his ship."

Theran pointed to a dozen armed men with crossbows coming towards the end of the wharf as they retreated to the ship.

Hal was about to try another ice lance when his staff's crystal blinked with a white light. It seemed to be trying to tell him something. He got an idea and leveled the staff and crystal towards the end of the wharf at the oncoming hunters.

Softball-sized hunks of ice launched from the end of the staff in rapid succession while Hal channeled his ice magic down the shaft into the crystal.

He sprayed the chunks back and forth for about ten seconds. When he was finished, all the hunters were down. Judging from his experience notifications, he assumed his attack had killed several of them.

2,500 experience points awarded.
   2,500 experience points awarded.
   2,500 experience points awarded.
   Spell learned — Hail.

"That won't stop them for long," Theran yelled. He pointed to another group of mages gathering on a pier parallel to theirs.

The fire mage launched a fireball at the clustered enemies. It blasted the group apart, flinging several into the waters of the harbor.

If they didn't drown, the water probably saved their lives by dousing the flames on their clothing.

Hal shook his head. He was already exhausted from his energy expenditures during practice. He knew it was only a matter of time before one of the hunter's spells broke through their defenses.

"We have to get to the ship and hold them off long enough for the captain to get us out of range."

"Agreed, lad. I have an idea that should hold them long enough for us to reach the ship."

Theran took two steps forward and raised his arms over his head. A massive wall of flames burst from the cobblestones at the end of the pier, creating a barrier of fire to hold their enemies at bay.

Taking advantage of the barrier, Hal and Theran bolted from their shelter to the ship and ran up the gangplank as the captain was preparing to pull it in.

"You made it just in time," Captain Barnes snarled. "I wasn't going to wait for them to set my ship ablaze. I don't know what you all have gotten yourselves into, but I'm going to charge Tracker double what he offered me to take you on this voyage."

"Never mind that, Captain," Hal offered. "I'll make up the difference with a bonus when we get to Tandon."

The captain nodded and started bellowing orders to his crew while Hal, Kay, Theran, and Toby watched the fires burning along the harbor's edge.

Theran pointed at Hal's staff. "Nice work with that. I noticed the scrying crystal mounted on it, but I didn't know you could use it to magnify spells that way. No one I know of has ever tried such a thing."

"It was news to me, too. I figured it was worth a try, though. I was getting so tired and didn't have much energy left to cast."

"Neither did I, to be honest. That wall of fire was the last trick I had up my sleeve. If any of the bastards had made it through before I cast it, we'd have been fighting up close and personal. I've never been much use in that kind of fight. I prefer to keep my enemies at a comfortable distance."

Toby leaned out over the rail, watching the city recede into the distance. The glow of the fires lit the horizon.

Hal hoped the city's inhabitants managed to quench the flames before too much damage was done. It was a nice place and didn't deserve to get caught up in the affairs of the rest of the world.

"Sorry we had to bring you with us, Toby. I was afraid to leave you behind to fall into the clutches of the Emperor's people."

The boy wiped a tear from his eye and puffed up his chest. "I always wanted an adventure like in the stories. I guess this is my chance."

Hal tousled Toby's hair and laughed. "You'll be alright, kid. As long as you keep that attitude, the world is yours to conquer."

Toby brightened at the praise, and together the two of them stood at the rail as the *Sea Sprite* sailed into the night.

Quest completed: Escape Morton Creek.

7,500 experience points awarded.

CHAPTER 22

AFTER TWO DAYS AT SEA, the four companions settled into a routine. Each day, Kay spent time teaching Toby basic sword work, and Hal and Theran headed to the forecastle, where Hal would continue his work on mastering fire magic. At the end of their session on day two, Theran pointed to Hal's staff.

"Ever since you used that thing to magnify your spellcasting back in Morton Creek, I've been thinking there might be a way to infuse magic inside it permanently."

"What do you mean?"

"It obviously has magic qualities related to earth and ice magic, and you were able to channel ice magic to cast a spell through it. It stands to reason that there might be the possibility of storing certain spells in the staff for use at a time when your energy was depleted."

Hal considered what Theran had said. It made sense, but he had a concern.

"Wouldn't tinkering with the inherent magic of the staff risk destroying it?"

"That is possible. I think, however, the wood and the crystal are stronger than just about anything we could throw at it. You said the staff came from the heart of one of the great elven trees. The crystal itself is a legendary relic of the past. Together, the two are far stronger than they are apart."

"How would we go about infusing them with permanent magic?"

"I know how I would do it if I were to infuse fire magic," Theran said. "I'd find an active volcano and dip the crystal in molten lava while casting the spells I want to store directly at the staff. The extreme temperature of the lava, coupled with the magical nature of the crystal and the spells cast, would combine to fuse the magic inside the staff. At least, that's the theory I have."

"It seems like a bit of a longshot."

Theran shrugged. "If it were me, I'd give it a try. There is a lot on the line in our battle against the Emperor."

Hal thought about it. Making the staff even more powerful would result in a nice addition to his arsenal.

"Where would we even find an active volcano close by?"

"If we detour out to sea, away from the coast, there is an island well known for its smoking mountain. That has to be a volcano, and an active one at that."

Hal gripped his staff in both hands and considered the idea Theran had posed. After staring out over the waves for several minutes, he turned back to his instructor.

"I agree, I think it's worth the risk, too. Let's go talk to the captain."

Captain Barnes was in his cabin, as was his custom this time of day. Hal knocked on the door and waited for a reply.

"Come in."

Entering the captain's cabin at the stern of the ship, Hal marveled at the spectacular view of the sea and horizon the man had from the windows across the rear wall of his cabin.

The captain sat behind his desk, charts laid out before him, as he made notations and measurements. He looked up as they entered.

"Ah, Masters Dix and Theran, what may I do for you this fine morning?"

"We have a request about a detour. We were wondering if you

knew anything about an island in these waters said to have a smoking mountain."

The captain leaned back in his chair and stared at his ceiling.

"I seem to remember tales of such a place. It lies to the south of our current position. Let me see if I have a chart that shows it."

The captain opened a drawer in his desk and pulled out several rolled-up maps, looking at each one until he found the one he sought.

"Here it is."

The captain stabbed a finger down on a small dot in the middle of a large ocean.

"It doesn't look very big," Hal said.

"Oh, it's not. But I do have it on the chart, so it's there. Do you want me to change course and make way to the island? There would, of course, be an additional fee involved."

"Of course," Hal agreed. "My companion here seems to think going to this island is important for our quest."

The captain nodded.

"That's up to you two. I can get you there; the quest will be yours to accomplish. It should take us about five days out of our way and will deplete the supplies I'd stocked for the shorter voyage to Tandon. We should be able to forage for provisions once we get there, however."

"Make way to the island, then. Theran and I have preparations to make."

Quest accepted: Energize the crystal and staff in the volcano.

"I'll pass along the new orders and course changes to the helmsman. Good day, gentlemen."

Hal and Theran left the captain's cabin to make their preparations as well. They had to decide what spells to prepare and how they would protect themselves from the volcano's extreme heat.

Favorable trade winds shaved a day off their travel time, and Hal awoke on the morning of the fifth day and went up on deck to see the island off the starboard side of the *Sea Sprite*. That was the first thing he noticed. The second thing he noticed was the cluster of small outrigger canoes carrying groups of natives paddling out to their ship.

The captain came up next to Hal with the spyglass, scanning the oncoming canoes.

"Do you think they mean us harm?" Hal asked.

"Not sure. I can't see evidence they are armed. They might be just coming out to greet us. I'm sure they don't get many ships out this way. They probably just want to trade with us."

"I'll go below and gather my companions. If the natives prove friendly, we can go ashore with them instead of bothering you for a lift."

The captain grunted in agreement and Hal left to go below decks. He knocked on the cabin door where Kay and Toby stayed. Toby pulled the door open with a big grin on his face.

"Did you see the island? We could see it out the porthole. There's a bunch of people coming out to the ship, too."

"Yes, Toby, that is why I came down to get you. Gather your things. We are going ashore."

Kay was already dressed in her armor.

"I'm going to get Theran, so I'll meet you and Toby up on deck," Hal said.

"We will be ready when you are."

Hal smiled and turned to the other side of the hall to knock on Theran's door. He never got the chance, because Theran was already coming out. He, too, was dressed and ready to go. Together, Hal and Theran headed up the stairs.

When Hal got back up on deck, the captain was entertaining a group of four natives. There was a lot of bowing and head-bobbing going on while the captain struggled to understand what they were saying.

"What are they trying to say, Captain Barnes?" Hal asked.

The captain took off his hat and scratched his forehead.

"Either they are trying to invite us to the island or they want us to go away. I am not sure which."

"There's a big difference between the two, Captain. You know that, right?"

"Of course, I do. Now hush so I can try to understand what they are saying. The language is similar to other islanders in the region, and I'm trying to get a handle on this particular dialect."

After ten more minutes of back-and-forth wrangling and hand gestures, the captain announced the natives were inviting guests to come ashore with them. Kay seemed to be apprehensive at the idea, but Hal overruled her. If they could make friends with the natives, one of the islanders could guide them to the volcano.

Kay shook her head.

"I hope you know what you're getting into, Hal. This is just the kind of thing that can go from good to bad in a heartbeat."

"Have a little faith, Kay. All we need is a little luck, and luck is right up my alley."

She didn't reply. All she did was check her weapons one more time, then she headed to the side of the ship, ready to climb down into one of the canoes.

Kay and Toby rode in one canoe while Hal and Theran settled into another. Soon they were paddling along with the natives. Others paddled to shore in the boats alongside them. Their new friends were smiling and jabbering amongst themselves in an excited tone. Their smiles were infectious. Hal found himself smiling and nodding along with them even though he couldn't understand a word they said.

When they reached the beach, the fellow in the front of their canoe jumped out and pulled at the bow until it was beached on the soft white sand. Hal and Theran climbed out and jumped down into the ankle-deep water of the lagoon. There were palm trees and other lush tropical vegetation not too far from the edge of the beach.

More natives came rushing out of the jungle, and for a moment, Hal prepared to defend himself. It proved unnecessary, though. These folks were just as friendly as the ones who'd come out to the ship.

The four companions followed a procession of the islanders as they streamed back up the trail that led to their village. Looking up, Hal could see the cone of the volcano ascending in the distance. Smoke rose in a dark pillar from the center of the peak.

When they arrived in the village, a feast was already laid out with roasted pig, chicken, fresh tropical fruit, and coconut mugs full of some mysterious beverage. It was as if the islanders were expecting guests, or they had arrived during some sort of planned celebration.

Hal leaned over to Theran and whispered, "Too bad there isn't some sort of magic that can translate languages."

"Oh, there is. That, however, falls under the school of wind magic. I'm sure Tildi would know exactly what these people are saying."

A man in an elaborate headdress approached them with a big grin. He held up his coconut mug and drank from it. Realizing it might be some sort of custom, Hal held up his coconut mug along with his companions, and they all took swigs as well.

He expected it to taste like coconut milk, but it was more like some sort of fruit wine. It also had a strange aftertaste. He didn't want to be rude, though, so he took a drink whenever the headman lifted his cup. The others followed suit.

It wasn't the first mistake they made with the islanders, but it was a big one. Hal realized they'd miscalculated their hosts' intentions as soon as the dizziness began. It was already too late at that point. The drugged wine took effect and soon all four companions slumped over into unconsciousness.

CHAPTER 23

HAL AWOKE to the sound of drums. First, he thought it was just the pounding in his head. But he was wrong. As the fog lifted from his drugged mind, Hal realized they were actual drumbeats coming from the villagers somewhere nearby.

He tried to rise to his feet but stopped when he realized his hands and feet were tied up. The harder he pulled, the tighter the ropes wrapped around his hands and feet got. A groan nearby alerted Hal he wasn't alone.

Craning his neck so he could see all around the hut, Hal spotted the source of the groaning. It was Kay. She was tied up just as he was. She lay on the dirt floor only a few feet away from him. Other than Kay, he was alone. He wondered where Toby and Theran were.

"Kay, wake up," Hal hissed.

Hal watched as Kay slowly opened her eyes. When she realized she was tied up, she started to struggle against the bonds.

"What's going on, Hal? The last thing I remember was drinking that coconut wine with the chief of the village."

"It must've been drugged. I guess these natives weren't as friendly as we thought."

"You think?"

"There's no time for snark, Kay. We've got to figure out where Toby and Theran are. I wonder why they weren't put in here with us. It has me worried."

Hal heard Kay grunting as she struggled with her bonds. She soon gave up.

"I can't get free, Hal. Is there anything you can do? Maybe a spell?"

"I'm not sure. Let me think of something."

Hal closed his eyes. He was still groggy from whatever the villagers had used to drug them. If he concentrated, though, he was able to reach his magic. The question was which spell he should cast.

"Alright, I'm going to try something. It'll either break us free or set the hut on fire."

"I hope you're joking, Hal."

"Sure, let's go with that."

Hal called up his fire spray spell and tried directing it into a single jet of flame from his index finger. He simultaneously cast a resist fire spell on himself. Twisting his hands in their bonds, Hal tried to direct the fire from his finger at the ropes securing him. It took a few attempts, but eventually, he managed to burn away part of the bonds securing him and free his hands.

Hal rubbed his wrists, trying to return circulation to his hands, then reached down and untied his feet before freeing Kay.

The drums were still playing their complex rhythm somewhere in the village. After crawling over to the doorway, Hal pulled aside the colorful fabric covering the opening and peered outside.

There was no sign of anyone. The drums were loud enough that they couldn't be that far away, but that could be deceiving.

The native leader's hut sat opposite the one where he and Kay were. Ducking back inside, he turned to Kay.

"There's nobody out there, Kay. All the villagers must be celebrating with those drums. We need to find our weapons and Toby and Theran before we can escape. They must be in one of the other huts nearby."

"I vote for weapons first," Kay suggested. "We're going to need them. These villagers aren't as friendly as we thought."

"Agreed. I spotted the chief's hut just across from ours. I'm willing to bet our weapons and gear are in there."

"It's as good a place as any to start looking," Kay agreed.

Hal nodded and turned back to the entrance. There was still no sign of any of the villagers, so he decided to take a chance. After sweeping the curtain to one side, Hal sprinted for the village chieftain's hut. Kay followed.

Diving inside the other hut, Hal rolled and came to his feet ready for a fight. There was no one there. This structure was empty, too. Hal's choice to search this place first was rewarded when they recovered their weapons and packs from a pile in the corner.

Hal and Kay returned to the entrance and looked around. There was still no sign of anyone.

"The drums sound like they're coming from that direction." Hal pointed to the right. "Let's head that direction and search the huts along the way."

Kay nodded in agreement, and the two of them started towards the sound of drums. They passed through the entire village, encountering no one. All the huts were empty, and there was no sign of Toby and Theran.

Crouching at the edge of the village, they finally saw the villagers as well as Toby and Theran. Their two companions were tied up on a two-wheeled cart. The islanders were wheeling them up a path toward the volcano with a procession of villagers carrying drums right behind them. The rest of the people marched behind the drummers.

Hal shook his head. "I might be wrong, but I think our friends are about to be sacrificed to the island's volcano god."

"If that's the case, Hal, we don't have much time to rescue them."

"None of the villagers appear to be armed," Hal remarked. "In fact, I haven't seen a single weapon in any of the huts. We can probably break through to our friends if we attack them by surprise."

"Maybe we can circle around them through the jungle and get in front of them on the path. They're going pretty slow in that procession, and it looks like they're heading to the volcano. All we have to do is get there ahead of them."

"You take the lead, Kay. I'm right behind you."

Both of them started into the thick jungle growth. It was slow going at first, but eventually they discovered a parallel path and managed to get ahead of the procession of islanders.

"Let's keep going all the way to the volcano," Hal suggested. "We can set up our ambush there."

Kay nodded and the two of them, now on the central path, ran ahead of the procession up toward the smoking cone of the volcano. As they got closer, the jungle undergrowth became sparse and the hard rock of recent lava flows appeared.

The path led to a place where two stone pillars stood on a ledge, overlooking an active lava flow. From where they stood, the heat started burning through their armor.

Hal cast resist fire on himself. He told Kay to hold still while he did the same for her. Relief showed in her eyes as soon as the spell took effect.

She pointed to the stone pillars.

"My guess is they tie up their victims here and let them slowly roast to death."

"Well, we are not going to let that happen."

Hal pointed to a row of boulders nearby.

"We can hide behind those. We will wait until they tie Toby and Theran to the pillars. When the villagers retreat away from the heat, we can jump out and free them."

The drums got closer and closer, so they darted behind the boulders and crouched down to wait. Soon the procession from the village appeared on the path.

Hal and Kay watched as four villagers dragged Toby and Theran from the cart and tied them to the pillars.

"Kay, you go and cut Toby and Theran down. I'll hold back the villagers with a display of magic. That should scare them off."

"What are you going to do?"

"This is a tropical island. I'll bet they've never seen ice or snow before. What do you think they'll do when they get stuck in an ice storm?"

"It'll probably freak them out."

"Agreed. You ready?"

Kay nodded, and Hal ran from behind the boulder while preparing a spell in his mind and channeling it through his staff. He was going to need its help to pull this off.

The village chief shouted and pointed at them as soon Hal and Kay ran into view. A few of the villagers started toward them but stopped as hail and sleet started pelting them from the cloudless sky.

Spell learned — Blizzard.

There were shrieks of fear from the islanders as the ice fell all about them. Most of them turned and ran down the path back to the village. The chief and a few of the men struggled to find cover from the blizzard as they worked their way toward Hal.

Hal started firing ice darts at the oncoming villagers. The staff magnified his spell power, but he still had limited reserves and felt his energy waning. He managed to drop four of the oncoming islanders despite the increasing exhaustion.

1,000 experience points awarded.
   1,000 experience points awarded.
   1,000 experience points awarded.
   1,000 experience points awarded.

Only the chief and two others remained on their feet. They skidded to a stop, pointing at something behind Hal. All three men screamed in terror, turned, and bolted back to the village.

"What the hell?" Hal said as he turned around.

Then he saw the fire demon.

The creature stood twenty feet tall and looked like it had been molded from glowing, molten rock. It waded through the lava flow toward the stone pillars, and judging from the bellowing roar, Hal figured it was angry someone had freed its sacrifices.

Theran extended both hands and launched a fireball directly at the demon's head. The spell impacted and exploded just as expected, but when the flames cleared, the demon let loose a horrible, guttural laugh.

Hal ran up to his friends. "Fire magic is useless against that thing. We have to try something else."

"What have you got in mind?" Kay asked.

"I wonder if we can draw the heat away from it. That might deplete its energy. Theran, what do you think?"

Toby's eyes widened. "Duck!" the boy yelled.

Hal and the others dove to the ground just in time to avoid a massive ball of lava thrown by the demon.

The molten rock impacted a pair of trees behind them, setting the palms and surrounding vegetation ablaze.

"We have to act fast. It's getting closer," Kay noted.

"Maybe I can use the staff," Hal said. "It's got to be drawing its power from somewhere."

Theran pointed to the lava flow. "There, that has got to be its source of energy. It connects directly back to the volcano. If we can stop it, we can sap the creature's strength, maybe enough to allow us to escape."

Hal shrugged. "It's worth a try."

Crawling like a commando on his belly, Hal made his way toward the edge of the stone ledge looking over the river of lava. Even with his resist fire spell in place, he started to feel the extreme heat coming from the molten stone.

Health damage: Health -16

Ignoring the burning pain, Hal extended his arms with the staff and touched the crystal at the end to the lava flow. Instead of bursting into flames, the scrying stone glowed crimson, and pulses of red energy began to flow up the shaft and into Hal's hands.

If he thought the pain from the heat was bad, the agony of the burning pulses of the lava energy nearly drove him mad.

Health damage: Health -28

Struggling to hold on to the staff despite the pain, Hal focused all his remaining magical energy on reinforcing his resist fire spell. It helped some with the pain, but it didn't lessen the damage much.

Health damage: Health -20

A glance at his health status told him he couldn't keep this up for too much longer.

Health: 81/145

"Hal, it's working," Kay yelled. "The lava flow is slowing down and hardening."

She was right. The lava at the end of the staff had started to harden, and the area of cooling was spreading outward.

The lava demon bellowed in pain as its advance toward the companions slowed even more. Hal realized, if he could hold out for a bit longer, he would be able to freeze the demon in place.

Health damage: Health -18

Of course, he might not hold out that long. It was all a matter of whether Hal's health reached zero or the demon lost its source of energy first.

The thought of dying here, like this, enraged him. He was not going to let this stop him from rescuing his wife and daughter.

Summoning up his last reserves of power, Hal channeled a flow of ice magic down the staff and into the hardening lava. Just like the last time he drew upon the last vestiges of his energy, Hal's health rapidly drained.

Health damage: Health -30
Health damage: Health -30

The pulse of blue ice magic spread outward from the end of the staff. The new infusion of magic sped the rate at which the lava hardened into rock. The demon let out a final roar of defiance. It howled and sank back into the cooling lava flow just before it froze over.

8,000 experience points awarded.
Level Up!

Pulling the staff back, Hal rolled onto his back and stared at the blue sky above. Exhaustion washed over him in a wave that went beyond mere health damage. He locked his eyes on the crystal. He had to see if the spell and everything else he'd done had worked.

The darkness threatened to close over him, but he fought it back. The crystal glowed with its typical white light, but now there was a pulsing red core at its center.

Quest completed: Energize the crystal and staff in the volcano.
    10,000 experience points awarded.

Hal smiled at the completed mission. Now they could find Tildi and work on the rest of his training. Calling his name, his friends pulled him back from the edge of the rock shelf. They seemed so far away even though he knew they were close.

Theran leaned over into view and held something up to his lips. Hal smelled peppermint and he drank the cool liquid from the flask. The potion restored his strength and energy instantly.

Major health potion — 50 health points recovered.

Hal sat up. "Wow, that feels a lot better. Thanks."

The fire mage accepted his thanks with a nod.

"Sorry I couldn't do anything else to help you fight the demon. There wasn't a lot I could do against a fire-based creature like that."

"Don't sweat it. The staff helped me channel the heat out of the lava flow. You probably could have done the same thing if you had it."

"Maybe. Seriously, Hal, that was impressive. Seeing you in action gives me a new appreciation for what your capabilities might be. I think you're ready to learn a few new tricks before you move on to Tildi."

"I'll take you up on that, Theran. First, we need to get back to the ship. I hope the *Sea Sprite* didn't decide to leave without us."

Kay handed Hal a canteen, which he drained. All that extreme heat had dehydrated him, leaving him feeling like a piece of beef jerky.

She hooked a thumb over her shoulder, pointing back to the jungle's edge.

"I think we should go around the village on our way back to the lagoon. Something tells me they may not be happy that we killed their lava god."

"Good idea, Kay. You lead the way."

CHAPTER 24

CAPTAIN BARNES WAITED on deck as Hal climbed over the bulkhead.

"I wasn't sure I was ever going to see you all again. When I sent a party of men ashore to fill up our water casks, the islanders chased us off."

"They definitely weren't as friendly as we thought," Hal said. "They weren't inviting us to dinner; they were inviting us to become sacrifices to a demon living in their volcano."

"That sounds like an amazing story. Perhaps you can tell me the details over dinner after we get the ship underway again."

"I think we would all like to put some miles between us and this island, Captain. Then I'd be happy to tell you the whole sordid tale."

"We all would," Kay agreed.

As the crew unfurled the sails, Hal and the others retired to the galley, where they continued the process of recovering from their ordeal.

The ship's cook prepared sandwiches for them with sliced beef and cheese.

As Hal ate and savored the delicious meal, he waited for his magical strength to return so he could heal his burns further.

Chewing on his sandwich, he noticed the crystal at the end of his staff. It was flashing red and white. Wondering what it meant, he reached up and touched the flashing stone with his fingertip.

In an instant, he once again experienced the sensation of falling. Hal closed his eyes and rode with the wave of movement until it stopped. When he opened his eyes, he stood in the chamber at the imperial palace again. This was where he had last seen Mona.

Hal was relieved to see her here again. She wore the same type of fashionable silk robes she'd been wearing the last time.

A portly man in purple and gold robes sat across from her at a table set up in the center of the room. Between them lay a chessboard. The man reached out and moved one of the pieces, exchanging it for one of hers.

"Ooh, I didn't see that coming." Mona chuckled. "You know, Kang, when I taught you how to play this game, I didn't expect you to become such an accomplished chess master so quickly."

"It is not all that surprising, my dear. This game is very similar to one my tutors taught me as a child. It is all about planning your moves well ahead of your opponent while anticipating what they will do to counter you."

Mona laughed again as she reached out to move one of her pieces, countering the Emperor's advances.

Hal stared at the man with his wife. This was Emperor Kang himself. What was worse to Hal, he was flirting with his wife. Even worse was she seemed to be enjoying it. While Hal was glad Mona wasn't in some dank dungeon, he didn't expect to see her acting so cordially towards her captor.

He shouted her name until he was hoarse, trying to get her attention. Just as before, though, she could not hear him or see him.

Upset with the futility of standing here, watching the scene play out, Hal let go of the crystal in his mind and felt himself falling back once more. He opened his eyes in the galley of the *Sea Sprite*.

Kay stood beside him where he sat on the bench. She was bent over, staring into his face.

"I think he's back again," she said. "Hal, you blanked out on us again. Were you having another one of your visions?"

"Yes, I was back at the Emperor's palace. I saw Mona again. She was sitting at a table with Emperor Kang, playing a game of chess. It was odd. She seemed to be enjoying herself, but how could that be? She's his prisoner."

"Maybe she's making the best of a bad situation. If he's willing to treat her well, why should she misbehave and incur his ire?"

"That makes sense, I suppose. Still, it irks me how easily she seemed to adapt to the situation."

Kay rested her hand on his shoulder. "Remember, Hal, she's been in captivity for some time, maybe several months. She only knows what the Emperor is telling her. She may not even realize you're looking for her."

"That is all the more reason why I need to hurry. This is all taking too long, dammit. The longer Mona stays there, the more chance he has of turning her and Cari against me. Maybe I'm already strong enough to face him."

"Don't make that mistake, lad," Theran said. "You have shown remarkable abilities. Certainly, they are far beyond what I expected of you, but you are not ready to confront the Emperor in his stronghold with all its magical defenses, his pet battle mages, and his personal bodyguards."

"Then when? When will I have enough power at my disposal to do what needs doing? There must be a point when the additional time spent training leads to diminishing returns. At some point, we have to decide it is time to attack."

"If you're so set on going on this fool mission now, what's your plan to keep the Emperor from killing your family outright?" Theran asked. "Ask Kay about how mercurial his temper is. Ask her how he has no compunction against killing women or children."

"Theran is telling you the truth, Hal." Kay shook her head. "Now is not the time. It doesn't feel right to me, and I want a shot at killing that monster more than you do. If you search your heart and mind, I think you'll decide it's not time, too."

Hal's mind raced as he considered all the things Kay and Theran had said. He wanted to rail against the unfairness of it all, but he knew there was no use in doing that. He wasn't strong enough to take on the Emperor yet. There was so much to learn, and Hal still didn't have anything approaching a plan to get into the palace, rescue his family, and get out again safely.

"I'm going to get some rest," Hal said, getting up from the table. "Maybe if I get some sleep and heal my wounds more, I'll reason all this through. I know I'm not strong enough yet, but I'm getting closer. That means I need a plan. It's time to work on one. We'll start when I wake up."

Kay handed him his staff. "That's a good idea, Hal. We can figure out a way to get into the imperial city at least. That will get us more than halfway to our target. I'll start thinking about some ideas on how to do that as well. Have a good nap."

Hal returned to his cabin and settled into his bunk. He closed his eyes but found it difficult falling asleep at first. His mind kept returning to the images of Mona and the Emperor, acting like long-time friends. Then the exhaustion from his injuries overcame him. Hal rolled over and drifted off into fitful sleep.

———

It only took a day for Hal to recover enough of his magical strength to heal his wounds. The emotional toll of seeing his wife again still pulled his attention away from his studies.

Hal knew his distraction frustrated Theran, but the fire mage never brought it up. Instead, when training over the next week at sea, he redirected Hal's attention to the lesson at hand until Hal managed to accomplish the magical task set before him.

In this way, Hal continued to advance with his skills at fire magic. On the third day after leaving the island, he cast his first fireball, sending the missile launching out to sea where it exploded in a burst of steam over the ocean swells. This was followed shortly by the wall of fire spell he had seen Theran use as they escaped the port.

The ship's crew applauded every time he tested another spell as if it were a fireworks display. Hal began trying new variables when casting to alter the magic for different effects.

At first, Theran chastised him for straying from the traditional way of learning magic. But as Hal displayed his ability to improvise with magic, Theran changed his mind and began asking his student how he accomplished the various outcomes.

The first time Hal taught Theran a new spell, a notification appeared in Hal's mind, announcing the completion of what must've been a hidden quest.

Quest completed: The student becomes the teacher.
    Spell learned — Lava flow.
    10,000 experience points awarded.

Through the new spell, Hal discovered that, if he mixed a little bit of his earth magic into a fire spell, he created lava.

Theran was surprised by this combination of magic schools.

"You've progressed two stages beyond what I know. Those two spells seem to have melded fire magic with earth magic to create a hybrid spell I didn't know existed. I have to say, I am impressed."

"Does that mean you no longer have anything you can teach me?"

Theran laughed. "I'm sure there are a few things here and there I can add to what you've learned. We'll keep working at it until we get to Tandon. Once there, we can contact Tildi and see if she is ready to take you on for tutoring in wind magic. I think you'll be ready by the time we arrive."

Hal grinned. His thoughts charged ahead to the tentative plans he'd started forming on how he was going to assault the Emperor's stronghold. Kay had given him a few ideas based on her knowledge from growing up in the palace.

A minor storm blew the *Sea Sprite* slightly off its planned course and added three extra days to their trip. Hal used the time to soak up every last bit of knowledge he could get from his lessons with Theran. He wanted to have every opportunity, every scrap of knowledge possible, because he knew the outcome of his rescue plan might hinge on some obscure tidbit he'd picked up along the way.

Several weeks after they'd left Morton Creek, they sailed into the harbor at Tandon. Hal noticed right away something had changed. He couldn't put his finger on what it was until Kay pointed out the warships docked in the harbor and the many soldiers clustered around the docks.

"Do you recognize the colors, Kay? Are they friend or foe?"

She shaded her eyes from the noonday sun and peered at the ships as they headed to their berth.

"I recognize several of the flags flying from the masts. They are all from the free cities up and down the coast. I think the Duke has begun to amass an army to bolster the fight against the Emperor."

"That's good news," Theran surmised. "It must mean the war is going in our favor. Perhaps we won't need some elaborate plan to get to the palace after all if the troops have pushed far enough toward the Crystal City."

"Maybe," Kay added. "It could also mean things are going poorly and they need reinforcements at the front."

Hal refused to let her suggestion change his overall good mood. He forced a smile onto his face. It was time to employ some of those leadership skills he'd learned when serving as a general for the army outside Hyroth. Hal put on a positive outlook for the others while he puzzled out the final solution to the plan he'd been working in his head.

Hal smiled at his companions. "No need to worry about things we don't know. We'll be dining with the Duke soon enough and he can answer all our questions. Let's gather our things and prepare to go ashore."

Toby tugged at Hal's shirt sleeve.

"Will I be able to dine with the Duke, too?"

"Of course. You're with us. After all the help you've given, what kind of friend would I be if I left you behind to wander around a strange city where you knew no one? Go get your things and meet us on deck."

CHAPTER 25

THE DUKE WELCOMED them back with open arms. He had rooms prepared for them, and Hal enjoyed a relaxing bath while servants laid out fresh clothes for him. Much of what he had been wearing since the island was charred and burned in many places. He was tired of smelling like a barbecue.

The Duke and Duchess held a private dinner for the four of them later in the evening. Hal looked forward to news from the army engaged with imperial forces east of Hyroth. After a traditional toast to good health, the Duke took a moment to fill them in.

"Honestly, Hal, the information I'm getting back from the current campaign tells me the results are mixed. We've been winning most of the battles, but the casualties from the fire sand weapons are taking a heavy toll. That is why we've brought in more reinforcements to send to the front. That's the good news."

"Good lord, what's the bad news?" Hal asked.

"The bad news is, Hal, this is it. These are the last available levies from the free cities in this part of the Empire. From here on out, we have to make do with the troops we already have."

"Wait," Kay said. "If they've been winning as many battles as you say, surely they have pushed much farther into the Emperor's territory. He can't have many reserves to put on the field either."

The Duke nodded.

"That's true. But if you remember the things I'm sure your father taught you about war and logistics, the army with the shorter supply line doesn't need as many men to hold the territory. The harder we press the Emperor's army, the easier it is for them to resist."

"Have you heard from Otto and the others recently?" Hal asked.

"The last dispatch I have was dated over a month ago," the Duke said. "It detailed a victory in a major battle just fifty miles west of the Crystal City."

"That's great news. In fact, it's the first really good news I've heard in a long time. If we can rejoin the army, I'll only be fifty miles from Mona and Cari."

The Duke shook his head.

"You didn't let me finish. The rest of the dispatch goes on to say they've reached the outer edges of the Emperor's magical wards. Otto thinks they will be unable to penetrate them on their own. He's sending scouts ahead to try to find a way through, but so far, all have been run off, killed, or captured. I was hoping you, and our guest Theran, might be able to offer a solution to penetrate the barrier magically."

Hal looked at Theran. The fire mage shrugged.

"I'm not sure there's anything I can do. The thing that makes those wards so hard to penetrate is that they are created by a team of mages using all four schools of magic. Were I to team up with the other three remaining free mages, we might be able to break through, but the Emperor and his wizards hold all the cards. They could just as easily seal it up right behind us, trapping everyone inside where they could finish us off in small groups."

Hal frowned and shook his head.

"I'm not giving up. There must be a way to break through. Maybe after I complete my training with Tildi, I'll be able to figure something out. After all, I'm supposed to be the solution to all of this, right? That means I'm the one who needs to break through the shield and lead the army against the Emperor."

The Duke reached into his robes and pulled out an envelope.

"That reminds me. Tildi sent this message just a few days ago. She said you'd be arriving soon and to make sure to give it to you once you have recovered from your journey. I guess she knew you ran into trouble on the way here."

"Some," Hal said, taking the envelope. He broke the seal and opened it.

Hal,

By now, you should have completed training in ice, earth, and fire magic. I suspect you are anxious to complete the final task that lies before you. Before then, you must learn how to control wind magic.

Travel to the village of Garth, located in the mountains northeast of Hyroth. I will contact you there after you get a room at the inn. Don't worry; it's a small town. There's only one inn.

I'll know when you check in and send you word where to go next.

Tildi

"Well, it looks like we are heading east. Duke Korran, are there any units ready to move out and head to the front?"

"I'll have to check, Hal, but I believe there is a unit of dragoons headed out within the next few days. It might be as long as a week, but that is probably the best I can do."

"Any way you can hurry them up? I think it's important, even beyond my personal needs, to get to Tildi as fast as possible. Everything you told us about the progress of the war leads me to believe our armies are about to stall in their progress forward."

Duke Korran nodded.

"I can send for their commander and find out if there is anything I can do to speed up their preparations for departure. I'll do what I can."

"I know that. I'm just anxious to get on the road."

"Understandable," the Duchess said. "One of these days, I'm hoping we can convince you to stay with us more than a few hours."

"I'd like that very much, believe me. Perhaps when this is all finished, and I have my family with me, we can stay here for a while and enjoy our time in Tandon for a change."

Kay held out her hand for the letter. "Where is she sending us now?"

"It's a place called Garth. It doesn't sound like it's very big, probably just a farming village. I'm sure her tower is located in a very remote place, considering how long she's evaded the mage hunters."

"Oh, it's remote alright," Theran agreed. "I have the pass to be able to teleport in, and it still takes longer than it should because of all of her defenses. She is a paranoid old thing."

Hal laughed. "And you're not? I seem to remember finding you hiding out in a fisherman's shack, or was that someone else?"

"No, it was me. But, I've been chased halfway around this continent by the mage hunters, while Tildi has been able to stay out of their way entirely. My excuse is I've earned the right to become paranoid. What's her excuse?"

Hal held up his hands in surrender.

"I'm not one to judge, Theran. I'm just glad we found you before they did."

"Me, too." Theran paused, looking a little uncomfortable for a second. "Uh, you don't need me to come along with you to Garth, do you?"

"Not if you don't want to come," Kay said.

Hal nodded in agreement.

"She's right. You've been on the run long enough, and you should be safe here in the palace with the Duke and Duchess. Stay here and gather your strength. I'm going to need your services before long."

Theran's whole demeanor changed. He relaxed his shoulders, and a smile crept onto his face. Hal was happy to see his teacher realize he was in a safe place for the first time in a long while.

The Duchess leaned over and refilled Hal's wine.

"I don't suppose we can convince you to stay at least one night with us?"

Hal smiled and held up his wine glass before taking a sip.

"Until your husband figures out when that unit of dragoons is heading east, I suppose you're stuck with me."

"Well, if you're going to put it that way..." The Duchess feigned indignation, which made everyone at the table laugh.

"Honestly, I'm looking forward to having a comfortable place to stay. I know once I get back on the road, it will be long days on horse-back and sleeping under the stars."

"Ah, the adventurer's life," the Duchess said. "It must be so exciting."

Theran shook his head.

"Not when you're almost sacrificed to a lava demon. Then, the excitement of being an adventurer wears off rather quickly."

Duke Korran leaned forward. "That sounds like there's a story to tell."

"There is," Kay said. "Perhaps, though, we can wait until dessert?"

The Duchess rang a small silver bell sitting on the table beside her. It was the signal to bring the next course of the meal.

"We can wait. But I expect you to remember to tell the story when dessert arrives."

"I won't forget," Kay said. "It's a perfect example of one of Hal's epic plans not going the way he expected."

"Hey," Hal protested. "I have great plans. We all survived, didn't we?"

That response got a giggle out of Toby. The boy had been eating his dinner in silence, and Hal had almost forgotten he was here.

"That reminds me. I was hoping I could ask Your Grace to take in young Toby here as a ward. His assistance was instrumental in helping us find Theran and escape Morton Creek."

The Duke smiled at the boy and nodded.

"Of course, we can. We can raise him here as part of the household. After all, our only children are my wife's daughters from her previous marriage. They're fine young ladies, but it would be nice to have a young lad around to spend some time with."

"Perfect," Hal said. He was about to say more when Toby interrupted him.

"I was hoping I might be able to accompany you on the rest of your quest, Hal."

"I'm afraid it's too dangerous, Toby. I'd never forgive myself if anything happened to you. Stay here with the Duke and Duchess. They will make sure you go to school and learn all the things a young man should learn to get ahead in the world."

"But I don't want to go to school. There's nothing I can learn there that I couldn't learn out adventuring with you, Hal."

"I'm sorry, Toby. My mind is made up. You're staying here. Don't worry; I'll be back soon."

The boy sat back in his chair and crossed his arms, staring at his plate. He didn't object any further. That surprised Hal. He would have expected the young lad to put up more of a fight.

The dessert was brought in by two servants carrying silver trays. One held small casseroles, each filled with an apple tart, while the other held port wine along with other after-dinner drinks.

True to her word, Kay began telling the details of their ill-fated journey to the island and the volcano.

Hal relaxed and let her tell the tale, adding only an occasional detail. It was good to spend time with such excellent company, but it didn't take the place of the hole left by his missing family. He was more than ready to be on the road again.

CHAPTER 26

IT TURNED out the Duke was able to shave a few days off the planned departure date for the troop of dragoons. Three days after Hal had arrived in Tandon, the cavalry unit formed up in the square outside the palace, waiting for Hal and Kay to come out and join them.

Hal had met the captain in charge of the troop two days ago. He was the son of a baronet from a region to the northwest of Tandon and he was more than a little full of himself. The young officer seemed to think he knew everything there was to know about campaigning and war. Hal knew he'd find out how wrong he was all too soon.

Hal slid his staff into specially added loops on the saddle and mounted his horse. Kay had already mounted hers and sat waiting for him. Together, they rode through the palace gates to join the troop of thirty cavalry soldiers, both men and women, formed up for the trip east.

"Good morning, Captain Whitlock," Hal called as they approached the cavalry officer. "It looks to be a fine day."

"Every day's a fine day to be off to war, don't you think, Your Highness?" the captain asked Kay.

Hal winced. He knew Kay didn't like having attention drawn to her royal status. He waited to see if she snapped at the captain and set him straight.

To his surprise, she smiled and said nothing. Hal shot her a quizzical glance. This might be the first time he'd ever seen her hold back on correcting someone.

The captain signaled the bugler, and the young man with the horn played a peppy bugle call. The troop began to move forward at a walk, the captain riding down the double column, reviewing his soldiers as they passed.

As soon as the young officer moved away, Hal leaned over to Kay.

"Why didn't you say something when he called you 'Your Highness'? I expected you to tear his head off."

"It wouldn't do to belittle him in front of his command," Kay said. "I will sit him down when we make camp tonight. Don't worry; he will not make that mistake again."

"Hmm, sounds like fun. I can't wait to hear what you say."

"I'm glad I am here to amuse you, Hal. Now be quiet. He's coming back."

The captain returned from the rear of the column and took his place at its front. He sat ramrod straight in his saddle, his chest puffed out as he led his troops out of the city.

As they passed through the gates of Tandon, heading east, Hal gave the city one last glance before facing front and focusing on the journey ahead.

Captain Whitlock planned to travel east on the usual caravan trail. Hal knew that would take too long. That route added two weeks to the time it took to reach Hyroth. His previous trip there had been much shorter, because the caravan master had had an arrangement with the goblin tribes, allowing them to travel through their tribal valley and cut the trip in half.

It took more than a little convincing to talk the young officer into the shorter route through the mountains. Only Hal's reputation and stories of his prior exploits convinced Whitlock to venture through the goblin territories.

Hal hoped he wasn't wrong in his assumption that he could vouch for safe passage through the goblin valley. This was going to be one of those instances where he relied on his luck to succeed. All he knew was he wasn't going to waste any time getting east and completing this last leg of his training.

The new route did take them through some rough bandit-filled country, but Hal was pretty sure no one this close to Tandon would attack thirty armed cavalry troopers, no matter how green they were. Their journey should pass without incident.

Hal should have known better.

––––––––

The imperial raiders hit them at dawn on the sixth day.

Looking back, Hal, Kay, and the dragoon captain should have been more prepared. Duke Korran had told them there were small units of imperial troops working behind the lines, attacking caravans and supply trains. He'd said they were few and far between, and it had been difficult to track any of them down and stop them. It was as if they appeared out of thin air, the Duke had said.

The dragoons were starting to break camp, the morning fog still clinging to the ground, when the sentries sounded the alarm.

Hal heard the shouts from the far side of the camp and turned to see what the fuss was about. He felt a tingling sensation running down the back of his neck, but he wasn't sure what it was. It wasn't until much later Hal realized he'd sensed someone using powerful magic, like opening a gateway nearby.

Kay jumped up, her sword already drawn, as the first of the imperial raiders charged into the camp. Hal grabbed his staff and stood beside her. There were too many enemies to count, but it was clear the dragoons were outnumbered.

Hal cast his ice armor spell. The armor now covered most of his body, including his head. While practicing on the way to Tandon, he'd found he could add more intricate details that enhanced the armor's functionality.

"Hal, we've got to get out of here," Kay said.

"We don't have time to saddle all the horses. With this mist all around us, we might be able to save some of the troops and slip away into the forest."

"Sounds like a plan. We'll rally what troops we can and take them with us."

Nodding, Hal pointed his staff to the sky. A fist-sized ball of fire launched upward and burst in the air, lighting up the darkness of the early morning sky.

He waved his hands over his head, calling out to the nearby troopers. "To me, to me. Rally here."

The closest of the dragoons, about six in all, came over to join them. The rest were cut down in the confusion or rallied to join Captain Whitlock in trying to form a defensive line to stop the onrushing raiders.

Hal fired off a volley of ice darts at a cluster of five raiders who'd broken through the captain's line. All five imperials resembled dart-filled pincushions before falling to the ground.

1,800 experience points awarded.

1,800 experience points awarded.

1,800 experience points awarded.

1,800 experience points awarded.

1,800 experience points awarded.

Others busted through all along the hastily formed defensive line around Captain Whitlock. This fight was lost before it had begun. Hal knew it was time to salvage what they could and get as many away as possible.

"We're retreating to the east," Hal called to the nearby troopers. "Follow Kay and me. We'll break away from the attack in the forest."

"What about the captain and the others?" a sergeant standing next to Hal asked.

"If we stay and fight, we'll die or be captured along with them. Our mission is of paramount importance. I'll do what I can to give the others a fighting chance, but we have to get away. Are you coming with us, Sergeant?"

One more glance at the desperate fighting around the captain, and the man nodded. Hal nodded back. It was time to go.

Quest accepted: Escape the ambush.

Hal conjured up the same ice mist spell he'd used against the grendlings in the north country and filled the air around them with a dense cloud of icy water vapor. It magnified the early morning mist already present. Once he summoned it, he sent it out across the whole camp to obscure anything more than a few feet away in every direction.

"Come on. Let's get out of here," Hal called out. "Kay, lead the way. I'll bring up the rear."

Kay nodded and waved her sword overhead, calling out to the troopers within earshot. Then she headed east into the forest next to the caravan trail.

Hal followed at the rear, his head and eyes tracking back and forth in the mist, locking in on any shape coming out of the fog and trying to identify it as friend or foe.

Two more troopers joined the retreating force, but after that, all Hal saw were enemies. Realizing he had to leave the rest to make their own escape, he cast a horizontal sheet of ice over the ground back toward the camp. It would slow any pursuit.

Satisfied, Hal turned and ran after the others. He could just make out the tail end of the small column Kay had led away into the tree line.

The tingling at the back of his neck intensified suddenly. He spun around just in time to dodge out of the way of an ice lance aimed at his head.

The four-foot-long spear of ice shattered against a nearby tree, shaking the trunk so hard, several large branches crashed down from overhead.

Hal summoned an ice shield and launched a fireball back through the mist at a pair of shadowy figures emerging from the edge of the camp. The explosion threw both to the ground. One climbed back to his feet; the other didn't.

3,600 experience points awarded.

Hal turned and bolted after Kay and the others. He didn't know who the spellcasters were, but they were apparently worth a lot more experience points than the mages he had encountered before. That meant they were powerful enough to be avoided in a losing fight like this one.

The tingling in his neck started again. Realizing he was sensing magic, Hal dove to one side on instinct. This time, the fireball missed by about fifty feet.

Judging by their aim, Hal assumed the caster was firing blind. He decided not to fire back and signal his location. Instead, he ran to catch up to Kay and the others. They still raced through the woods, striving to put as much distance between themselves and the camp as possible before they stopped.

Hal caught up with them as another random fireball exploded

behind them. He had an idea who the pair of spellcasters were: mage hunters.

"Is that another spell going off back there?" Kay asked.

Hal nodded. "I think more mage hunters are on our trail. This wasn't a random attack by raiders. That means they've got trackers and we need to get out of here before they locate where we went."

There were seven dragoons with Kay, including the sergeant. That was a lot of people to move through the forest without a trace. Hal knew it wouldn't be hard to track them even using conventional means, and he suspected the hunters utilized some form of magical tracking, too.

"Let's keep moving, Kay. We're not too far from the pass into the Vale of the Morning Sun. Maybe we can enlist some aid from the goblin clans there."

"I hope they don't kill us first before they know we're friendly," the sergeant remarked.

"Don't worry. I know a guy. I've got this covered," Hal said with a tone of bravado he wasn't sure he felt inside.

Not fooled by Hal's tone, Kay shot him a grim smile before turning to the troops gathered around them.

"We've got to move fast and pass without a trace if we can. Try to keep up; we'll find a way out of here. Sergeant, you bring up the rear and keep any stragglers from falling behind. Hal and I will take the lead. He knows where we're headed. He's been through here before."

"Yes, ma'am."

The sergeant snapped a half-hearted salute and got the rest of the dragoons on their feet.

"What's your name, Sergeant?" Hal asked the man.

"I am Sergeant Matthew Madry of the Ironian Dragoons," replied the sergeant, still in a little shock from the ambush.

"Don't worry, Sergeant Madry; she's a princess. Play your cards right, and you and the rest of these troopers could become her royal guard someday."

"I'm not a princess anymore, Hal. Don't fill the sergeant's head with any of your grandiose stories and ideas."

Kay moved away, preparing to head up the trail. She didn't see the way the sergeant looked after her, his expression showing a new devotion. She also couldn't see the pop-up message in Hal's view.

Quest accepted: Establish the Imperial Dragoons.

Hal saw no additional information about the quest he had just received, but he could tell from the determined look and devotion on Sergeant Madry's face who might be involved.

Another distant explosion sounded behind them, spurring the men to move a little quicker. Hal picked up his pace to catch up to Kay and take the lead. She gave him a sideways glance when he fell in beside her on the trail.

"You shouldn't say things like that. I know things are different where you come from, but people here, especially house troops like these dragoons, take things like personal attachments to nobility very seriously."

Hal decided not to tell her what he'd seen. It'd probably just piss her off. It was better he stay focused on the trail ahead. It was time to test his luck again, along with the memory of the goblin rangers guarding the Vale of the Morning Sun.

Quest completed: Escape the ambush.
6,000 experience points awarded.

CHAPTER 27

IT TOOK ALL DAY, and long into the night, to cross the pass through the mountains. Hal and Kay trudged along, and the dragoons shuffled behind, trying to keep up. Sergeant Madry brought up the rear, keeping them moving. The most important thing to Hal was there was no sign of pursuit.

Wherever the raiders and the mage hunters were, either they hadn't found the trail of Hal and the others, or they had opted not to follow them into what must be certain death within hostile goblin lands. Either way, Hal was happy to have at least one problem off his plate.

That didn't remove the primary issue. He still had to figure out a way to contact the goblin rangers guarding the tribal lands and let them know he was a friend, not an invader.

Hal hoped they remembered the help he and the other caravan guards had provided the rangers when a group of trolls had invaded the goblin lands and taken some families hostage. His contact with the goblin guardians had been fleeting, but he'd learned some of their language and customs. He hoped it was enough.

Kay stopped beside a bend in the trail. A flat shelf of rock overhung the path, giving a bit of shelter from the winds blowing frigid air around them. Hal had forgotten the others didn't possess his ability to resist the effects of the cold.

One glance at the others told him he'd been a selfish idiot.

"We've got to stop, Hal. Do you think we've gotten far enough ahead of any pursuers to rest for a while?"

"I think so." He stared at the rock ledge hanging over the trail from the mountain wall beside them, and he got an idea.

"Stand back; I'm going to provide us some heat. I saw them do this on an old *Star Trek* episode once."

"Star what?" Kay asked.

"Never mind. Just watch. Setting phasers to kill."

Hal pushed up his sleeves and stepped toward the rock wall leading up to the overhang. Summoning his fire magic and the power infused into his staff by the lava demon, he shot jets of what amounted to white-hot plasma at the rock face until it glowed red in a patch about four feet in diameter. Hal stopped when it started to sag a little. He didn't want to start a lava flow.

The heat coming off the wall filled the whole area with warmth, and the overhang above reflected the radiant heat back down on the path. This should warm the party for several hours if Hal had calculated correctly. If they needed more, he could always fire off a booster shot or two.

The appreciative troopers came over and warmed themselves by the makeshift heater. Kay smiled at him as she returned to the cozy little nook Hal had created for them.

"Nicely done, Hal. I don't know that I would have thought of that if I had your powers."

"Not sure I would have either. Thank Gene Roddenberry for that life-saving idea."

"You'd think I'd get used to your unusual references and phrases, but you still surprise me with how odd you are, Hal."

"I like to keep myself mysterious as well as charming. It's how I keep my wife from leaving me."

He fell silent as the mention of Mona turned his thoughts to her and Cari. He stroked the crystal atop his staff with a few fingers, hoping for another vision, but nothing happened. He'd tried several times since his last vision to scry some knowledge of Mona and Cari again, but it felt like something was blocking his attempts. He feared that something had happened to them. He sighed and sat down at the edge of the glow coming off the rocks.

"Don't worry, Hal. We'll get them back."

"It's just that we've had one setback after another since this journey began, and now I can't even see her through the crystal anymore, no matter what I do."

"Yes, but you've still managed great things." She pointed to the hot, glowing rocks nearby. "That just happened because of the power you now have. Don't discount that ability. You're going to need every ounce of it before we get to the end of this quest to free your family. I promise you. We will free them."

"How can you be so sure?"

"Because you're Hal Dix, weaver of clever plans, and even more outrageous stories. You'll find a way to get it done because that is what you do. And I and the rest of our friends will be right there beside you."

The sergeant, overhearing their conversation, chimed in from nearby.

"And if Her Highness is there, we'll be there to protect her."

Kay leveled Hal with a baleful stare. He managed a half-grin in return and replied to the sergeant.

"Yes, you will, Sergeant. Yes, you will."

Kay balled up her fist and took a half-hearted swing at his head. He ducked away with ease.

"Don't fight it, Kay. It's about time you started having a retinue befitting your high rank. You are the Empress in exile after all."

"Stop that, Hal. I'm just Kay. My only task left in the world is to kill the Emperor. That is everything I need. Once that's accomplished, I'll fall back and settle somewhere in the countryside. Another person can lead this sorry excuse for a continent afterward."

Hal overheard murmurs from the dragoons on the other side of the ledge. He picked up several of them repeating the words "Empress" and "dragoons" in the same sentence. Kay heard it, too. She rolled her eyes, exasperated all over again, and stalked away to the far side of the outcropping.

Hal worried that he'd overdone it this time. Kay was his closest friend in this world. He didn't want to do anything to mess that up.

"Don't worry, sir. I'll have a few of the troopers move over and stay close to her. They'll keep her safe until she calms down."

Hal nodded and turned away to get some rest of his own.

The sergeant barked out orders, and a pair of dragoons, a man and a woman, shifted over until they were only about ten feet away from Kay. They settled in nearby, watching over her and the surroundings.

Hal chuckled, balling up his cloak for use as a pillow, and settled in to get some rest.

———

Shouting and the threat of armed conflict awakened Hal for the second day in a row. His eyes popped open to focus on the steel arrowhead leveled at his face from a few feet away. Following the shaft to the archer behind it, he noted the gray-green skin and brown leather armor of a goblin warrior, probably one of the border rangers.

Holding up his hands to show he was unarmed, Hal called out to Kay and the dragoons, who'd all stood and bared steel of their own.

"Put down your weapons. Show we mean no harm."

Some of the men complied but others hesitated.

"Do it. Now! That's an order."

Hal wasn't sure he could legally issue such an order, but he figured he was the officer in charge now.

It intrigued him that they all looked to Kay and not him at that moment. She nodded and set her sword down on the ground, then put her hands over her head.

Hal, still lying on his back, smiled up at the goblin ranger standing over him.

"Shalush, I'm a friend of Shalush, your chief. Do you understand me?"

He hoped, even if the goblins didn't speak the common tongue, they'd recognize his pronunciation of the chief's name.

The ranger standing over him lowered his bow, pointing the nocked arrow at the ground rather than Hal's head. A few words in the goblin tongue, and the other goblins lowered their weapons but remained on guard.

It was a start.

Hal sat up, moving with slow precision so as not to startle the goblins.

"Do any of you speak the common tongue?"

One of the rangers on the other side of the ledge stepped forward.

"Speak I — little."

Hal touched his chest. "I'm Hal Dix. Your name?"

"Tarront is name."

The goblin looked familiar to Hal, but he wasn't one of the rangers Hal had assisted with the troll raid.

"Do you know Gand, Zeth, or Plank?"

"Plank is brother."

"I helped Plank with a troll raid a year ago. With Shalush. Do you remember?"

"Caravan? Bilham Gary?"

"Yes, yes," Hal agreed. Thank God, they knew the name of the caravan guard captain, Bilham Gary. They remembered the caravan coming through. "I was one of the guards, Hal Dix."

One of the other goblins spoke up in their language. Hal recognized two things in what he said. He heard his name and the word "Hyroth." Maybe the other goblin knew of his befriending of the goblins in the gladiator pens and the slave army he'd raised afterward.

"Yes, I'm Hal Dix from Hyroth and the slave revolt."

There was a great deal of discussion he couldn't follow for a few minutes while he, Kay, and the disarmed dragoons waited for some sign the standoff was resolved. The debate ended and Tarront offered Hal a hand.

The goblin grinned, baring his teeth in an alarming display of filed points. "Come, Hal Dix. We go Shalush."

Trying not to let his relief show, Hal smiled back at the ranger and took the offered hand to help him stand. He called out to the others.

"They're taking us to their chief. He is known to me and I to him. We'll be fine, but no one do anything to provoke a response. No sudden moves, alright?"

He tried to make eye contact with all the dragoons. They nodded, picked up their weapons, and sheathed their swords. Once everyone was ready to move, Hal turned to Tarront.

"We are ready. We will follow you."

Tarront issued several commands. A few of the goblins jogged off down the trail ahead of them. Hal was sure they were sent on to alert the tribe they were coming.

Once all the humans had lined up, Tarront took the lead with Hal and Kay behind him. The other rangers formed up around them, and they followed the trail down from the pass and into the lush valley below.

Hal and the others followed the goblins without stopping for a long time. It was mid-afternoon when they arrived at the village serving as the central meeting place for the tribe living in the valley.

Shalush waited for them as they arrived at the edge of the small community. He and Hal clasped wrists in the traditional greeting Hal had learned on his last journey through the valley.

"Greetings, my friend," the goblin chieftain said.

"Greetings to you as well, Shalush. I want to thank your rangers for allowing us passage through the valley."

"You are known to us, Hal Dix. We know that you are a man of honor and you have helped us in the past. I'm sorry, however, we cannot offer you a place to stay in our village. It is not safe here. We have many of our number who've come down with a strange illness. Our healers are unable to help those afflicted. Many have died, and I believe many more will die before this disease has played out its course."

The news of the disease outbreak concerned Hal. He had helped these people in the past and he wanted to help them now.

"I will have my party camp here on the outskirts of your village to keep them and you safe. I, however, would like to come into your village and see if I could help in some way. I have gained some additional skills since I last passed through."

"Unless you have become a magician of great skill and healing ability, I do not see how you can help us."

"Actually, my friend, that is exactly what has happened. Take me to the place where you are tending to your sick. I will see if there's anything I can do."

Shalush took Hal to the center of the village. There was a large round structure that must have served as a central meeting place and home to the chieftain. Inside, rows of sleeping pallets lined the floor, all of them occupied by sick and emaciated goblins. There were children, adults, and the elderly among the ill.

"How long has this been going on?"

"For several weeks. We had just fought off an imperial raiding party, and one of our rangers came down with the strange illness a few days later. Several of our healers think the illness came because of contact with the human soldiers."

"That is possible. Is it alright if I examine a few of the people here?"

"Yes, of course, we will accept any aid you might be able to provide."

A goblin in robes standing nearby stepped forward.

"Excuse me, my chief. Do you think that is wise? After all, if it was contact with humans which caused this disease, wouldn't contact with more humans make more people sick?"

Before Shalush could answer, Hal confronted the robed goblin. "And you are?"

"I am Garand, chief healer and high priest of this clan. I believe your people are responsible for this illness, and I will not let you harm any others."

Hal knew he needed to defuse the situation if he was going to find a way to help these people. First, he needed to get on the right side of the goblin healers.

"Garand, even if humans are responsible for this illness, I am not currently ill and do not carry any illness with me. I am a healer of sorts myself and may be able to lend my magical abilities to help you and your people. May I examine some of your patients?"

"Let him look at a few of them, Garand," Shalush said. "It will hurt nothing; he is a friend."

The healer scowled but acquiesced, gesturing at the row of sick people next to him.

Hal approached the closest pallet and knelt down. The patient, a goblin who couldn't have been much older than his own two-year-old daughter, lay on the pile of blankets. The child's chest heaved as the patient gasped for breath.

Hal opened himself up to earth magic and delved into the child with his mind. Placing his hands with care, he touched either side of the baby's head with his fingertips and tried to sense the source of the illness.

The goblin child stirred but did not wake up as Hal continued his search. There was something strange about the child's sickness. When Hal tried to cast heal wounds, the spell found nothing to which it could attach. It was as if there was no illness at all.

After several tries and fighting down his frustration at being unable to do anything, Hal attempted a different approach. An idea occurred to him. If he couldn't cure the disease, maybe it was because there was no disease there. Perhaps these people weren't sick but poisoned or affected by some other external source.

He tried casting neutralize poison, but again, nothing happened.

Something else was at work here.

Recalling the tingling he had felt during the ambush, Hal wondered if he could intentionally detect magic in other ways. He reached out with his magical senses, feeling for any magical energy around him. Hal cast his awareness outward to draw in as much information about any nearby magic at work as he could. He discerned several sources of magic inside the large room. It was a blackness, leaving a vile aftertaste when he touched it with his mind. Each instance was associated with one of the sick individuals.

Spell learned — Detect magic.

Hal continued to draw from this new magical ability, focusing on one of the specific locations, the one closest to the child next to him. He saw a nexus of magic beneath the kid's pallet, and a thin black line of connecting magic leading off to the wall of the building on the north side. It was barely detectable, even with his advanced magical vision.

Walking to the next pallet, Hal found a similar magical source leading to the north wall. It was a variation of earth magic, but it had a taint to it. Instead of healing the individuals, this magic drew energy away from them.

Hal looked down at the thin line connecting the patient to the point on the wall and attempted to sever it. When he applied force to the connection, the patient began to thrash about in some sort of seizure. He stopped trying to sever the line as soon as the seizure began.

Garand pointed at Hal. "What did you do? See, my chief, he is injuring our people."

Shalush waved off the comment. "Hal, what happened?"

"This isn't a disease at all, or at least not in the traditional sense. This is all caused by a variation of earth magic. Their life force is being pulled away by a spell I've never seen before. It all leads to the north side of the building. I'm going outside to see what is there."

Hal left the building and headed around to the north wall. Shalush and Garand followed. Focusing his magic on the ground, Hal saw the thin line of magic coming from the building. It continued to the north before it disappeared.

Shalush and the goblin healer caught up to him where he knelt by the north wall, staring into the distance.

"What did you find, Hal?" Shalush asked.

"The source of your problem is coming from that direction. Is there anything out there to the north that might be causing a magical disruption?"

Shalush looked at the healer who shrugged.

"Nothing I know of, my chief."

"Well, something or someone is using a perverted form of earth magic to drain the life from your people. I'm not sure why or even how they're doing it, but I think we need to follow the magic north until we find out where it is coming from."

"I do not have many men left to spare, Hal. So many are ill. I could lend you one or two warriors but no more. Do you think that will be enough?"

I suppose it will have to be. I'll bring a few of the dragoons along as well. It is getting dark. Given how sick those people are, I hate to lose a whole night. More could die. Are your rangers able to lead us north in the dark?"

"If you can track the magic, they can help you travel safely through the forest and hills."

"Good, then we leave immediately."

Quest accepted: Locate and destroy the source of the evil earth magic.

"Godspeed, Hal," Shalush said. "We'll wait for your return. Two of my rangers will meet you where your soldiers camp outside the village."

Hal ran back to the camp and told Kay what was happening in the village. She began preparing her gear for the trek north. Hal turned to Sergeant Madry.

"I need two of your best men to accompany us. We shouldn't be gone long. The goblins will treat you well and bring you food while we're gone."

"I'll tell Jenkins and Williams to gather their kit and prepare to leave with you and Her Highness."

The sergeant turned and began calling out orders, leaving Hal to wait and ponder what sort of evil magic was at play here. Jenkins and Williams arrived at the same time the goblin rangers jogged into the camp. Hal recognized one of them as Tarront.

Tarront introduced his colleague as Bellen. Hal introduced the two dragoons who were accompanying them, as well as Kay.

"Is everyone ready to go?" He waited for nods all around. "Excellent, then let's hurry. This sort of magic is powerful but does not have a very long range. Wherever it's coming from, it has to be close by."

As dusk fell, the six of them headed out into the forest to the north.

CHAPTER 28

HAL LED THE WAY, focusing on the faint magical trail snaking away from the village. Tarront and Bellen walked on either side of Hal, helping him avoid tripping in the increasing darkness. Hal was grateful for the help. He was so intent on tracking the source of the magic, he had little attention to spare to keep from tripping over tree roots and branches on the ground.

The terrain through which they traveled grew increasingly damp until they found themselves inside a swampy area, thick with brush, trees, and a boot-sucking muck that made it hard to take each step.

"Tarront, how long has this swamp been here?" Hal asked.

"I was here a year ago; there was no swamp."

"Let's be extra careful, then, and be on our guard. I expect we are going to run into some trouble soon. Bellen, go back and join Kay at the rear and watch our backs. Make sure no one sneaks up on us. Jenkins and Williams will stay in the middle and be ready to jump and attack in either direction. Got it?"

Hal could barely make out the nodding heads in the darkness amidst the trees. Very little light filtered down from the full moon above, but there was enough to gather that the others understood their orders.

Turning his attention back to tracing the magic trail, Hal started searching for traps or pitfalls in addition to keeping his eyes on the thin line of magic still heading northward. They traveled for about an hour longer when they arrived at a strange hill sticking up from the center of the swamp. Its rounded, grass-covered surface formed a perfect dome in the midst of the marshy ground.

The trail ended here.

"This is it," Hal said. "This is where the magic is coming from. Search the base of this hill for an entrance of some kind."

Hal should have realized splitting up the group to search for an entrance was a bad idea. It was too late to change his mind, though, before the trolls attacked.

Shuffling out of the darkness, the enormous eight-foot-tall creatures snarled their war cries at the intruders. One picked Jenkins off the ground and flung him against a nearby tree. Hal heard a sickening crack as the impact broke Jenkins' back and he fell to the ground, limp and lifeless.

Williams was a little luckier. He managed to draw his sword and slash at the beast closest to him, drawing blood and causing the troll to howl in pain.

Kay darted in to help Williams and slashed her blade at the back of the troll's knees, cutting its hamstrings, bringing it crashing to the ground.

Hal drew upon his fire magic. He had to be ready to burn any troll as soon as it was taken down. Only fire would stop the creatures from regenerating. One of the trolls jumped in his way and tried to pull him close to bite his shoulder.

Firing multiple jets of flame from his fingertips, Hal set the creature ablaze. The troll's hairy hide went up like a matchstick and it fell to the ground.

1,000 experience points awarded.

Hal ran up to where Kay and Williams hacked at the troll on the ground next to them. Every time they thought they'd killed it, the creature would start to get back up again. That ended with a quick dose of fire spray as Hal finished the job.

1,000 experience points awarded.

Tarront and Bellen each fought a troll and were hard-pressed to gain an advantage. Both bled from multiple wounds when Hal arrived to assist them.

He launched a fist-sized ball of fire at the troll fighting Tarront. It hit the creature in the chest, burning a hole all the way through.

In obvious shock, the troll stared at the gaping hole for a moment before collapsing in a heap on the ground.

1,000 experience points awarded.

Bellen already had his troll on the ground and was hacking at it, striving to remove its head. He was tiring, and the troll would soon rise again unless he managed to cut all the way through.

Hal ran over, extended two fingers, and fired twin jets of flame into the wounded creature's neck while the goblin ranger hacked away with his sword. Together, they managed to destroy it.

1,000 experience points awarded.

With all four trolls killed, Hal rushed over to check on Jenkins, though he feared the worst. He was right. Jenkins' lifeless eyes stared up in the moonlight, his crumpled body lying next to the tree that had helped kill him.

Hal reached out with two fingers and brushed the dragoon's eyelids closed, then he turned and stood. They had a job to do and he couldn't worry about one dead companion right now. His corpse would have to wait until they returned.

"Keep searching. These trolls guarded something. Let's find out what it was."

Hal and the others fanned out around the base of the small hill. A shout from the far side drew them all together again. Bellen had found an entrance hidden behind a mass of thorny brush.

They pulled the branches back and cut some away until they exposed a cave entrance sloping downward, deeper into the hillside. A soft yellow glow came from somewhere below.

"Whoever it is, it looks like they're home," Kay remarked. "Shall we crash the party?"

"It would be rude not to," Hal agreed. "I'll go first, followed by Kay, Tarront, Williams, and Bellen in the rear."

The others nodded. They were ready.

Hal avoided the remaining thorns and entered the cave. He paused a few steps inside, waiting for the others to come through, then continued down the sloping passage.

He moved downward, trying to remain silent to avoid detection by whomever was down below. The hair on the back of his neck was up again, indicating strong magic at use. He drew on all his remaining magical energy, casting his ice armor spell and preparing several offensive spells for rapid use. They had to catch whomever was down there by surprise.

The glow ahead grew, and Hal started to make out voices. It sounded like there were several people down there. They were likely human or about the same size, based on the size of the passage dug into the hillside.

The five companions almost made it all the way down to the chamber at the bottom of the passageway without being detected, but one of the occupants below started up the passage and spotted them. Hal almost ran into a balding man wearing red robes. The robed man yelped and fired off a six-inch-thick stream of fire in their direction, causing them all to dive to the dirt floor of the passage.

The robed mage turned and darted back into the room, calling out the alarm. The shout choked off short as Hal's ice lance took him in the back of the neck, killing him instantly.

3,500 experience points awarded.

"Don't let them have time to react. Charge in there and get them!" Hal called, leading the rush into the room below.

The bottom of the passage opened into a high-ceilinged chamber about forty feet across. In the center was a huge glass globe, suspended from the ceiling by a great iron chain. A glowing green light filled the glass ball.

Seven robed mages surrounded the contraption, taking turns casting a spell into it. Five of them turned to face the attackers while the others remained in place, maintaining the magical force pouring into the globe.

Thorny vines grew up from the dirt in front of Hal, reaching towards him and twining about his ankles, tripping him up before he could counter them. Williams and Bellen succumbed to the vine attack as well, hitting the dirt floor under the assault. The vines tightened, driving inch-long thorns into Hal's legs.

Health damage: Health -12

Kay and Tarront managed to leap over the vines and charge forward at the closest of the mages. Darts of ice and jets of fire flew past them as they ran, but all the spells missed and the two of them fell on the hapless mage, their swords cutting him down.

Hal cursed and focused his earth magic on the spell that bound him. He overcame the vine spell, and the thorny plants released him.

Rolling to his feet, Hal threw up an ice shield on instinct and absorbed the impact of a fireball. The shield shattered but managed to dissipate the blast enough to protect himself, along with Williams and Bellen. The three of them ran through the residual heat of the explosion and joined Kay and Tarront attacking the rest of the mages.

Kay yelped in pain and fell under a hail of ice darts from one of the mages. Hal ran to her defense, launching a series of baseball-sized ice chunks from the end of his staff at the two mages she faced. The ice missiles hammered the two mages until they went down. He continued the attack spell until they both lay lifeless on the ground.

3,500 experience points awarded.

5,500 experience points awarded.

Level Up!

A massive blow struck Hal in the back, knocking him to the ground painfully cracking his ribs, and snatching the wind from him despite his ice armor.

Health damage: Health -20

After rolling over and levering himself up to a sitting position, Hal searched for the source of the new attack. He spotted one of the mages crouched by a crate in the corner. The man appeared to be readying another spell.

Hal didn't wait for it to materialize.

Focusing his energy through his staff, Hal tried something new. He decided to call it ice boulder.

The mage only had time for one scream before the giant ice ball crashed down from above, crushing both the mage and the wooden crate beside him.

Spell learned — Ice boulder.

3,500 experience points awarded.

"Stop them. For the Emperor, stop them!"

A man in blue robes, with silver cuffs and a silver collar, pointed at Hal and his companions from an opening in the far wall. Five trolls lumbered past him into the room.

The mages around the globe were all down, giving Hal and his comrades the opportunity to direct their attention to the new attackers.

Hal knew he was almost magically tapped out. His only option was to draw from the magical reserves that had nearly killed him before.

Kay, Williams, Tarront, and Bellen all charged in to meet the trolls head-on. Hal took a few seconds to tap into his life energy, the way he'd done against the grendlings and the fire demon. Maybe if he was more careful about how much he used, he'd be able to avoid burning himself out completely.

Health damage: Health -32

When Hal tried to join the others, a stabbing pain in his chest stopped him in his tracks. Damn, that hurt more than he'd expected. He shook off the damage and started forward again while readying a series of fire spells, careful to keep within his available energy reserves.

Kay already had the lead troll down, but her left arm hung limply at her side, blood streaming from a gash in her shoulder. Hal veered in her direction and fired off a burst of flame from both hands, spraying fire up and down the creature as it struggled to rise. The dry skin and coarse hair caught fire and spread the flames over the rest of the troll's body until it was immolated.

2,500 experience points awarded.

"How's your arm? Let me heal you," Hal told Kay.

"No. Help the others. I'll be fine. I can still hold a sword."

Hal didn't want to leave her but knew she was right. If he took the time and energy to heal her wounds, they'd lose this fight.

Spinning around to the side, Hal ran to help the nearest of his companions.

Bellen, the goblin ranger, took a hit on his shield from the massive clawed hand of his opponent. It knocked him backward, bowling him to the ground.

The troll stepped forward and stood over the goblin, ready to deliver the death blow.

Hal barreled into the troll from behind, ducking low and hitting the beast behind its knees. The troll toppled over backward and fell to the floor. Hal jumped on its chest and stabbed downward with his daggers, plunging the blades into the troll's chest again and again.

An idea occurred to him and he directed fire magic into his daggers, heating the blades until they sizzled and sent wisps of smoke up when they sank into the troll's chest. With the daggers cauterizing the wounds, the troll couldn't regenerate, and with a few more strokes, it lay still, dead.

Spell learned — Heat metal.

    2,500 experience points awarded.

Bellen had climbed back to his feet and charged off to help Kay with another troll. Hal rolled off the troll's chest to the floor, landing on his hands and knees. Exhaustion swept over him and he gasped for breath. The exertion of using his life force to fuel his magic was starting to take its toll.

His other companions had matters in hand. Tarront had found a torch somewhere and had managed to set fire to the other three trolls once they were hacked down.

Hal climbed to his feet and bolted towards the opening in the far wall. He had to reach the man in charge.

The man in the blue robes stood there, his eyes wide as the intruders dispatched his pet trolls with ease. He saw Hal coming his way, and he let out a yelp and dashed through the doorway, disappearing from view.

Hal stopped at the edge of the doorway and peeked around the edge to see where the man had gone. It wouldn't do to charge into a fireball or some other trap.

The passage went another twenty feet before opening into a different room. Hal heard a voice calling for help.

"Tell His Imperial Majesty I need assistance, my magic is depleted, my forces are all dead."

"I'm sorry, Jaden, there is no one else to send right now."

"Then open a portal and let me come back to the palace."

"I don't think I want to be the one who lets the latest failure of the Emperor's pet project back into the palace. Your stink might end up on me, too.

"But, you can't..."

"Farewell, my friend."

Hal had heard enough. He entered the passage and strode down it until he reached the chamber. A mirror attached to a wooden stand stood across the room. The blue-robed man named Jaden cowered in front of it. The mirror shifted with a foggy haze. Hal thought he caught the reflection of somewhere else in the mirror, then it went back to reflecting the room they occupied.

"Seems like they've abandoned you, Jaden," Hal sneered. "That's the problem with opportunists. You're only worth the value of your latest success or failure."

Jaden turned, pulled a dagger from his belt, and held it out in front of him.

"Don't come any closer or I'll cut you."

"No, you won't." Hal directed heat into the dagger the other man held until the blade glowed white-hot.

Jaden yelped in pain and dropped the dagger on the floor, staring in shock at his burned palm.

"How do you use both fire and ice magic so proficiently? It's impossible. No one can do that."

"I use earth magic, too."

Vines grew up out of the dirt floor, entwining about the mage's legs, holding him in place.

"Wait! You're him. You're Hal Dix."

"You've heard of me? Good, then it will be easier for you to understand why I'm going to stab the life out of you for what you've done to the goblins in that village."

"It was important to test the power of the new experiment somewhere to see if it worked before we deployed it against the rebellious cities."

"You killed children back there," Hal hissed through gritted teeth as he stepped toward the immobilized man, holding his daggers ready for the death stroke. "They never harmed you or anyone else."

"They were just goblins. Why are you so upset about them? You're human. You should understand."

"That's not the way we do things where I come from. I'm finished with this conversation."

Hal raised his daggers over his head, preparing to strike downward into Jaden's chest.

"Stop! I know about your wife. I've seen her with the Emperor. I can help you."

The daggers quivered in his hands. He wanted to kill this monster, but if he had information about Mona and Cari, he had to keep him alive. Damn, this guy didn't deserve to live, but he couldn't let Jaden die without telling Hal everything he knew.

Hal shifted his grip and slammed the pommel of his dagger into the mage's temple.

Jaden's eyes rolled up into his head, and he slumped partway to the ground, held up by the vines wrapped around his legs.

In the main chamber behind him, a crash of breaking glass signaled the destruction of the infernal machine.

Quest completed: Locate and destroy the source of the evil earth magic. 11,500 experience points awarded.

Hal let himself relax for the first time since they'd arrived at the mound outside. As the adrenaline flowed out of his bloodstream, crushing exhaustion replaced it. Hal sank to his knees and leaned over, supporting his upper body with one arm. He needed rest and food, a lot of both.

Kay ran in from the outer chamber. She must've seen him fall.

"Hal, what's wrong? Are you alright?"

"I just overextended myself a bit. Tie this guy up and make sure you gag and blindfold him so he can't use any magic. I think I need a little sleep.

That was as far as he got with his instructions before the darkness overwhelmed him. He sank to the cool earthen floor and passed out.

CHAPTER 29

HAL GROANED and pressed his hand to his face. Kay placed a cold compress on his head.

"You really have to stop this habit of using so much of your magic that you pass out, Hal. It's becoming a pain."

"I didn't lose my ability in its entirety this time. That's a plus. How are the others?"

"Tarront and Bellen left to help Williams bury Jenkins in the clearing just beyond the entrance. They should be back soon. While you were—"

"Resting. I was resting, that's all."

"Fine. While you were resting, I searched through the belongings of our dead mages. The Emperor was testing a new spell based on a twisted variety of earth magic that can mimic the plague when used against a village or town. They were trying to see how big they could make the effect by steadily expanding its scope against the goblins living in this valley. I have letters from the Emperor's chief mage and councilor, Decimus, giving them explicit instructions for how to conduct the test against these specific goblin tribes."

"The Emperor must know how instrumental the goblin and orc tribes were in the defeat of Baron Norak and his army, as well as our initial escape from the slave pens beneath the coliseum. We have to keep them from starting this project again somewhere else."

"I'm not sure, Hal. I think we have to focus on our original task. Everything we want hinges on getting you to Tildi so she can finish your training. Only then can we do what is needed to defeat the Emperor. That includes this and all his plans. I don't believe this is the only place he's testing the plague magic."

"First, we return to the village and Shalush. I want to make sure we have done everything we can for those suffering from this magical plague. Once that's finished, I'll go and search out Tildi and the next steps she has in mind for me."

Kay nodded and set to gathering all the documents she'd found and stuffing them into a spare leather satchel. Hal knew she'd want to send them back to Tandon for the Duke and others to review. There might be some small piece of information that could be pivotal in the war to win back the Empire.

While she went about completing her task, Hal focused on his internal energy reserves. Though this time he had not burned out his ability, he still felt every ounce of his body, especially in his legs and arms. Moving them at all caused him to breathe heavily, as if he had no fitness or stamina left.

Thinking about how he had drained himself to charge his spells, Hal wondered if there was some way to reverse that process and restore his magical energy. Energy flow couldn't just be a one-way process. It was something he'd have to ponder.

For now, he took a second to look at his stats. He spent his new attribute points on his brawn, hoping that the increase would help in his recovery. It did lessen some of his fatigue, but Hal still wasn't anywhere near his usual energy level. Hal glanced at his character sheet one last time before climbing to his feet and helping Kay gather up the documents she'd found.

Name: Hal Dix

Class: Mage
Level: 11

Attributes:
Brawn: 26 — +9 defense
Wisdom: 20 — +6 defense
Luck: 30 — +11 to all saving throws (Max)
Speed: 16 — +4 defense
Looks: 8
Health: 86/155

Character skills: Chakra regeneration – 3 (heal 18hp; 1/day)

Mage experience: 153,425/250,000
Ice elemental school:
Resist cold, Ice shield, Ice armor, Ice darts, Ice lance, Wall of fog,
Hail, Blizzard.
Earth elemental school:
Plant growth, Neutralize poison, Heal wounds, Deal wounds,
Detect magic.
Fire elemental school:
Summon fire, Control fire, Fire spray, Fire resistance, Fireball,
Wall of fire, Heat metal.
Wind elemental school: locked
Unknown elemental school: locked
Multi-elemental school:
Lava flow, Ice boulder.
Warrior experience: 140,800/250,000
Rogue experience: 146,100/250,000

Once they had all the documents loaded in the satchel, the two of them headed out of the underground chambers and back to the surface. Williams and the two goblin rangers were just finishing up their burial of the dragoon private, Jenkins.

Hal bowed his head while Kay said a few words over the grave. She nudged him with an elbow when she finished, and he realized she expected him to say something.

"Uh, well, while I didn't know the private very well, during our short time on this quest, I got the sense he took his role as a dragoon very seriously. I know I cannot expect more from any soldier I serve beside. That is the highest praise I know to give. He did his duty to the very end. Uh, yeah, amen."

It was awkward from Hal's perspective, but based on the looks he received from Williams and the goblins, the words struck home and rang true. He'd take it as a win.

After gathering everything they planned on taking back to the village, Hal and the others set out. It took them the rest of the night, but they arrived back at the goblin settlement just as the sun was rising.

Shalush rushed out to greet them on their return.

"Hal, our people, the villagers, they are recovering. Some seem as if they'd never been sick at all. Were you able to find the source of the illness?"

"We found a plot by the Emperor to try and kill your entire village, maybe every goblin in the valley. Kay uncovered the details."

Kay nodded and explained what they'd found inside the underground lair in the forest.

Shalush growled deep in his throat.

"We have tried to stay out of the affairs of men. Only those of my kindred to the north and east who fought in the slave pens have taken sides, and that was justified. We of the Vale of the Morning Sun have not joined them, striving to remain neutral. Clearly, that is no longer an option."

"I know our forces could use your rangers to bolster their scouts,"

Hal pointed out. "I've seen how good your people are in the wilderness, Shalush. Our army will welcome you with open arms."

Kay agreed. "I have to get these recovered documents and plans to the Duke in Tandon. If you send your rangers there, I'll write a letter of introduction that will serve to get them past the guards at the city gates. Give the Duke these papers and tell him what happened here. He must prepare in case the Emperor tries to implement his plot in Tandon or another of the free cities."

"I'll do that, mistress." Shalush nodded. "What will you and Hal do if not return with the news yourselves?"

"We are on a quest to stop the Emperor in a different way, but we will join the army when we complete our task, don't worry."

"Given how the Emperor's forces chased you here, I must offer you some aid in completing your task," Shalush insisted. "Perhaps we can offer some of our goblin rangers to join your dragoons. Your sergeant seems impressed with the swordplay some of my more promising recruits have demonstrated while sparring with his men."

Hal smiled and replied, "I'll talk with the sergeant and see what he wants to do. If he has a few he'd like to bring along, I'll take them with us to the east as we travel."

"Good, then it is done," the goblin chief declared. "We will have a feast in your honor this afternoon, and you and your newly reinforced party can depart first thing in the morning."

Hal shrugged and looked at Kay. He knew they both wanted to get on the trail sooner rather than later, but they were both tired from the fighting in the forest. A day's rest and some good food would serve them well.

"We can do that. I think we could all use a break to recover from the rigors of the last few days. I want to check on your sick people for myself in case there's anything I can do to help out with speeding their recovery."

The three of them went to work on their tasks. Kay ventured off to see how the dragoons were doing and to talk with the sergeant. Hal sought out Garand, the goblins' chief priest and healer, to check on the sick affected by the magical plague, and Shalush saw to the preparations for the night's feast. For each of them, it was a time to reset and realign their priorities.

The next morning, Hal, Kay, and the remaining dragoons, reinforced by a quartet of the most promising of the goblin swordsmen, set out east for the rest of their journey to the village called Garth. They had an escort of goblin rangers until they crossed out of the valley and into the eastern reaches, a desert of scrub brush and rolling, barren hills.

Instead of heading due east for the week-long journey to Hyroth, the group veered to the north, leaving the standard caravan trail to strike out cross-country. According to the map Hal had, the trip to Garth would lead them to the northeast, approximately five days' travel away.

It was during this time Hal noticed the dragoons' increasing deference towards Kay. Sergeant Madry seemed to take Hal's suggestion to heart and assigned at least two dragoons to accompany Kay anytime she left their camp in the evening.

When she asked them to stop, the sergeant shook his head.

"No ma'am, you should have a proper guard. While we may not look all that proper right now, we can still guard you. It's the right thing to do for a person of your station. Should you ever return to the throne, you will have an entire regiment of bodyguards. For now, you have us."

Kay threw her hands in the air and stomped off. The sergeant nodded to two of the female dragoons, one human and one goblin. The pair promptly gathered their weapons and raced after her. Hal smiled to himself. He had fun playing this little practical joke on his friend, even if it was no joke to the dragoons.

The rest of their journey to Garth passed without incident. They seemed to have shaken off the pursuit of any imperial forces or mage hunters that might be following them. Hal was happy to have a few days where they didn't get caught up in a fight or some quest. He needed the rest.

———

The sleepy farming village called Garth lay in a fertile valley on the western edge of the Great Northern Forest. Hal knew the forest extended east for hundreds of miles to where he and his slave army had fought their great battle and defeated Baron Norak's imperial forces.

On this side of the forest, people seemed to have carved out a quiet and peaceful existence far away from the ravages of the war gripping the rest of the continent. They passed several farms on the way to the village. The farmers were friendly, waving to them as they passed by.

It was near dark when they arrived. Tildi was right. It wasn't hard to find the inn. In fact, it almost seemed as if that establishment made up the bulk of the village. In addition to the inn and attached tavern, which was the only two-story building in the small community, there was a blacksmith, a trading post, and a stable.

Hal pointed at the stable.

"Sergeant, Kay and I have business in the inn, and we will be staying here for a while, perhaps a few weeks. When we move on, however, we may need to purchase horses so we can travel onward at a faster pace. Why don't you check in at the stable and see if they have enough horses to equip us? You can also inquire about long-term accommodations other than the inn."

"I'll see to it, sir."

He separated two of the dragoons from the group to follow Hal and Kay to the inn at the end of the street, then he and the others headed to the stable to check on the rest of Hal's orders.

Inside the inn, Hal approached a tiny man sitting in the common room at a roll-top desk. He looked up as they approached and scowled.

"I suppose you four want rooms?"

"Just two rooms actually," Hal said. "One for myself and one for the lady. The soldiers will be seeking other accommodations."

"Suit yourself. It's not like anyone else is staying here. I've got plenty of room. Just sign the guestbook and I'll get your keys."

The innkeeper disappeared through the nearby doorway while Hal leaned over the desk and signed his name in the guestbook. He handed the quill pen to Kay and she did the same. The innkeeper returned with their keys and glanced at the guestbook.

As soon as he read the names, he shot Hal a glance.

"You supposed to be meeting someone here?"

"Yes, I believe I am."

"I thought that name looked familiar. You can settle yourself in. I'll send word you've arrived."

Hal and Kay exchanged looks. Tildi said in her note she'd know when they arrived. Hal assumed she'd have used some sort of magical alert to his presence. It seemed the mage's solution was more mundane.

The innkeeper led the two of them upstairs to their rooms, with the two dragoons following along behind. When the innkeeper pointed to the room Kay was to occupy, the dragoons took up stations on either side of the door.

Hal suppressed a chuckle when he saw the annoyed look on Kay's face. She unlocked the door, went inside, and slammed it closed behind her.

The innkeeper didn't fail to notice what had happened.

"She somebody special?"

"Special to us," Hal said. "The dragoons take protecting her very seriously."

The innkeeper shrugged.

"She don't need no protecting here. It's not like anything exciting ever happens in this village. Suit yourselves, though. I'll be downstairs if you need anything. Dinner will be served in the tavern in about an hour. Breakfast is served an hour after sunup, with lunch at noon. The cook don't like it if you're late."

"I'll keep that in mind. Thank you."

The innkeeper went back down the stairs. Hal unlocked the door and entered his room. It was small, with a bed, a wooden chair, and a nightstand featuring a pitcher and a washbasin.

Hal decided to freshen up. He leaned his staff in the corner and, after pouring some of the water in the washbasin, rolled up his sleeves and splashed water on his face and arms to wash some of the road grime from himself.

There was no telling how long it would take Tildi to arrive or send word with further instructions. He might as well make himself comfortable while waiting. The work of learning the final school of magic would be here soon enough.

CHAPTER 30

TILDI ARRIVED THE NEXT MORNING. At least Hal thought it was morning. A glance out the window showed it to be still dark outside. She woke him with a knock on his door. She didn't wait for him to answer or even unlock the door. Before he could get out of bed, the door unlatched itself and the mage let herself in.

"Welcome to Garth, Hal. Hurry up and get dressed. We've got a lot of work to do and very little time in which to do it."

Hal pulled on his pants and grabbed his cloak from the peg on the wall.

"Has something else happened, Tildi?"

"The Emperor's forces have started to push back against the rebel army arrayed against them. They've managed to win several battles over the last few days. We are running out of time. Now let's go. You and I have to leave before anyone else wakes up."

Hal grabbed his staff and followed Tildi out the door. The two dragoon troopers lay slumped on the floor.

"Are they alright?"

"They're fine. I just put them to sleep for a while. They will have a bit of a headache when they wake up, but the two of them will be none the worse for wear."

Hal spared the soldiers one last glance and then followed Tildi down the stairs to the common room. She led him outside where two horses were tied up.

"Mount up," the mage said. "We have a long day's journey ahead of us."

"Why don't we just open a portal to travel where we're going, as you've done in the past?"

"Because the Emperor's pet mages have figured out a way to track the use of magic anywhere on the continent, especially portal magic because it's so powerful."

"That must be how they've been able to follow me as I went from place to place. I thought it was just coincidence."

"Ain't no such thing, boy. You should know better by now."

Hal started to mount his horse but stopped.

"I should leave a note or message for Kay to let her know where I've gone."

Tildi shook her head.

"No, you should not. Kay is safer without you nearby. She'll figure out where you've gone on her own, and we're not likely to be coming back this way. Don't worry; she's capable and resourceful. Now mount up. It's time to leave."

Hal pulled himself up on the horse and settled into the saddle. Grabbing the reins, he gave the horse a kick with his heels and trotted after Tildi into the darkness.

He followed her as she entered the dark forest on the outskirts of the village. It grew even darker under the thick leaves of the forest canopy above. On more than one occasion over the next several hours, Hal found himself ducking with barely a second's notice when tree limbs threatened to sweep him from the saddle in the dark.

By the time the sun arose, they were many miles away from Garth. The terrain climbed upward into the foothills of the nearby mountains. By mid-morning, they'd left the edge of the forest behind, traveling through several mountain passes that left Hal thoroughly confused as to how to get back the way he'd come.

They stopped around noon. Tildi set out a wedge of cheese, some roast beef, and a half-loaf of bread.

Hal tried to make conversation while he assembled his sandwich.

"Have you heard anything about Ragnar? I heard the mage hunters captured him after he sent me to Bronwynn. Is that true?"

"It is."

"Have you heard where they're keeping him?"

"No."

"Shouldn't we try and secure his escape? After all, he is one of our allies."

"No."

After the last question, Tildi excused herself and stepped away into a nearby stand of trees. Hal assumed she was relieving herself.

He finished making his lunch and began eating. He was disappointed. He'd hoped she might be more forthcoming with information or at least have a plan on how they might rescue Ragnar. Hal figured he'd need the help of all the mages when the time came to go and get his family back.

Thinking of his family's rescue turned his thoughts to Mona and how she was doing. He wished again he could come up with a way to send her word that he was planning to get them. Hal had no idea what the Emperor had told Mona about him or why she was here in Fantasma.

Hal was still brooding about his family when Tildi returned. She broke off a piece of cheese and a hunk of bread for herself before returning the food to her saddlebags.

"Let's mount up. I want to get where we're going before dark."

"Fine by me," Hal said, getting up. "It's not like I'm learning anything sitting here."

"Don't worry, Hal. Your lessons will start up again soon enough once it's safe to do so. We can't do that here, though."

Hal mounted and followed after Tildi. She rode along a winding trail up into the mountains. It was slow going for the horses because of the broken and challenging terrain. It was near dark when they entered a narrow canyon with a trickle of a stream running out of it.

After several hundred yards, the narrow canyon opened into what Hal could only describe as a gigantic bowl created by the surrounding cliffs. A small waterfall cascaded down on the opposite side of the vale, creating the stream that passed through the middle of the valley before disappearing down the center of the canyon through which they'd just ridden.

The waterfall, while beautiful, wasn't the most prominent feature of the tiny valley. That distinction went to the squat, stone tower that lay at its center. Just as Bronwynn's tower was tall and slender, like its mistress, Tildi's tower resembled her short stature. It was no less formidable. In fact, its isolated location in this canyon lent the tower its imposing nature.

Hal also noticed something else. Tildi was smiling. It was the first time he'd seen anything other than a scowl on her face since they'd left the village. The change had come over her as soon as they'd exited the narrow track through the mountains and entered this sanctuary.

"It's beautiful, Tildi. If this is your home, it must be wonderful to live here."

"I used to have several towers I stayed in at different times, depending on my mood or particular needs at the time. All the others have fallen into the Emperor's hands. This last place has not. That is due in part to its isolated location and to the peculiar nature of the surrounding cliffs. Notice the reddish hue to the rock?"

Hal nodded. He'd seen the tint of red in the cliffs and thought nothing of it. He wasn't a geologist after all.

"The rock around these parts is full of iron ore. It acts as a sort of shield, keeping the magical energies from being detected by those outside this tiny valley. At least that is my hope. We have much training to do with some powerful magics."

"I'm ready when you are, Tildi. I have to get my family back and I expect you to show me how."

"Ho, ho," Tildi chuckled. "You think so, do you? It's true I have many things to teach you, but I'm not sure I have any grand plan that might help you rescue your family. That, I'm afraid, will have to be up to you, Hal."

"When do we start?"

"At dawn," Tildi said as she dismounted. "You tend to the horses. There's a small barn around back. You see to that while I open the tower. You can meet me inside when you're done."

Hal leaned down and took the reins of Tildi's horse, leading it around the tower to the rear. Hal found a small stone barn built up against the wall of the tower. He unsaddled the horses and put them in their stalls for the night. He found a few bales of hay and broke them up before filling the feeding troughs.

Water for each was taken care of by a series of clay pipes leading up to the waterfall above. The pipes filled a small basin in each stall with a constant flow of fresh water. The overflow spilled out and down a gutter leading under the wall and back to the central stream.

By the time he was finished with the mounts, there was a golden glow of light coming from several of the tower's windows. Hal washed his hands in one of the basins, fetched his pack and Tildi's saddlebags, and headed into the tower via a door at the back of the barn.

He entered the kitchen and dining area of the first floor. There was a fire blazing in the hearth and a small roast turning on a spit in front of the glowing coals at the base of the blaze. The spit revolved using a series of cogs and shafts running to the outside wall. He realized it all moved thanks to a small water wheel he'd seen outside the tower.

"Hal," Tildi called down from the top of a spiral staircase in the far corner. "Finish getting dinner together. You'll find a bin with some potatoes and turnips next to the hearth. Wash a few of them and set them by the coals to bake."

"I'll see what I can do."

After putting his staff and the bags down, Hal searched until he found the vegetable bin in the corner. He rinsed off two potatoes and two turnips in the sink, with running water piped in using a similar arrangement as was used in the barn.

He set them down on the hearth close to the coals and snatched his hand back after placing each one. The heat was intense. It wouldn't take too long to roast them, given the fire's intensity and the heat radiating off the glowing coals at its base.

While he waited for the meal to finish cooking, Hal spent some time examining the contents of the first floor of Tildi's tower. In addition to a table and four chairs, there was a sink and counter for food preparation, plus several cabinets of dishes and bowls as well as other cooking utensils.

On the far side of the room was another door, presumably the one Tildi had entered when she came into the tower. To the right of the door, there was a bookshelf filled with leather-bound tomes of various sizes. Just to the left of the door was the spiral staircase leading upward. There didn't appear to be a basement.

Hal crossed to the bookshelf, pulled a few of the books out, and flipped through them. Most were in a language he didn't recognize. A few were written in Fantasma's common tongue. The book that caught his attention most of all was a thick one with English lettering on the spine.

Game Engineering and Computer Programming for Beginners was the last thing he expected to find in a fantasy mage's tower. Still, it made sense. She'd told him how she created the game to transport him to this world. He didn't think there was any technology involved. After all, creating a portal was something you did with magic, right?

"Ah, I see you found my secret stash."

Hal slapped the book shut and put it back on the shelf as quickly as he could. Tildi had come down the stairs behind him undetected.

"I'm sorry. I didn't mean to snoop, but the English title caught my attention. I have to say, I'm more than a little surprised to see it, having mastered some magic as I have. I don't see any way to combine it with something as technologically advanced as computer programming."

"You'd be surprised, Hal. There's a lot more in common between magic and computer technology than you might think. Both require logical thought processes to complete a task or create a spell. Both require energy of some sort to enable them to carry out their instructions. When you come right down to it, there's almost no difference between them at all. Once I realized that, the rest was just a series of increasingly difficult problems to solve to bring you here."

Hal scratched his head. A random thought nagged at him.

"How come we don't have magic on Earth?"

"For all I know, you may have at one time. It seems, though, technology and magic have a hard time existing at the same time and place. That was one of the hardest hurdles I had to overcome. In the end, I created a portal where magic existed on one side, but technology maintained it on the other, using a series of surprisingly simple segments of the computer code."

"So, technology kills magic?"

"Not so much kills as renders it unnecessary. I suspect the ability to use magic has been bred out of the people of your world. Only perhaps one person in a thousand possesses the innate ability to become a mage and harness the energies of magic. Of those, most would only be able to do the simplest of spells if they received any training. Without someone to train them, they never realize they have the spark of magic inside them. On the other hand, technology can be used by anyone without the need for a genetic spark. Once technology becomes ubiquitous, magic isn't needed anymore to accomplish great things. I fear the same may be happening here in Fantasma. The discovery of fire sand is one example of how technology can render a type of magic obsolete. Over time, other technologies will likely do the same to the other schools of magic here."

Tildi crossed to the hearth to check on the roast and vegetables.

"Dinner is almost ready, I think. Help me set the table. It will be good to sit down and eat in the civilized fashion for a change. Tomorrow, the final lessons begin."

CHAPTER 31

TILDI WOKE Hal early the next morning, urging him to get dressed so they could begin their training together. He grabbed some bread, sliced ham, and a small wedge of cheese for breakfast and made a quick sandwich to eat as he walked alongside Tildi. He listened while she described the basis of wind magic.

"There is no place in Fantasma untouched by the winds. The air around us fills every void, even dissolving in water, thus touching the bottom of the oceans themselves. For this reason, wind magic is considered by many the master of all magical forces. For most spell-casters, this is true."

"But not all?" Hal asked.

Tildi smiled and raised a finger.

"There is another school of magic. It is very rare to find a caster able to master it because they must have the unique ability to control more than one school of magic. In the past, this has been limited to those who could master two of the elemental schools. These are known as the arch mages. By mastering two schools, they could combine both magical sources into unusual and unique combinations."

"So you, Ragnar, Bronwynn, and Theran all have mastered two schools of magic?"

"Yes, in all our cases, we have mastered our primary school and one other. For myself, it was wind and earth. For each of the others, it was the school they taught you, with wind as a secondary form. There are also arch mages serving the Emperor. Most of them were our pupils or colleagues once upon a time. All are the same. They can control two schools of magic."

"What about me? I already have some mastery over three of the four primary schools."

"What about you, indeed." Tildi chuckled. "Now you see the reason why your ability is sought after by the Emperor. He seeks to understand how you have this expanded ability. He doesn't understand how the rules of the game in your world allow you to bend the rules of magic here in our world."

Tildi continued in silence for a few seconds, letting her words sink in as Hal walked beside her.

"You, Hal, possess the ability to master all four primary elements. I believe this will allow you to unlock a hidden ability, one I call spirit magic. This magic transcends other forms and will allow endless permutations of spells across what are impassable boundaries for the rest of us."

"And that spirit magic is how you expect me to defeat the Emperor?"

"Perhaps. To be honest, I only wanted to bring you here to disrupt things long enough to allow the rest of us who oppose Kang to organize ourselves against him. Your return this time, and the higher stakes you face regarding your family, adds a new wrinkle to my plans. I do not know if you will be the one to defeat him. I believe it depends on what you choose to do next."

"The only thing I'm focused on is rescuing my family and getting them away from that monster. I worry how he could be turning them against me."

"Then you must master wind magic and unlock the potential of the spirit element. Powerful spells ward the Emperor and his palace. Arch mages from all four major schools of magic created those barriers. The spell wards overlap and allow no magical penetration of the shield by anyone. Believe me, I've tried on numerous occasions to sense what is happening inside the palace. No matter what I try, I cannot get through."

"But I've already seen inside the palace."

"You have? When?" Tildi replied with a shocked look on her face.

Hal described the two occasions he used the crystal in his staff to travel with his mind to the palace. He also related how the Emperor was manipulating his wife and daughter in the palace.

"Hal, this is a major step. I had no idea the crystal possessed the power to penetrate the shields set by the Emperor's mages. It means you've already started to access the spirit energy within yourself."

Tildi stopped and stood still for a second, a frown darkening her face. The expression filled Hal with apprehension.

"I had hoped you would not develop this ability before you learned all four forms. There is a theoretical danger to what you can do with the spirit ability."

"The risk that I might kill myself in the process of using it? I think I've already figured that out. On two occasions, I've found I can tap into my in-game health levels to cast spells beyond the finite energy given to me by each elemental school. Does that sound like what you're talking about?"

"Yes," Tildi agreed. "I hadn't thought about it, but it is likely it would manifest in your game interface that way. It is very dangerous because, if you are not careful, you could drain all your life force and die when trying to use that power."

"I figured as much," Hal told the arch mage.

Tildi stopped at the edge of the canyon opening that led out to the rest of the mountains.

"Your training with the wind begins here. Feel the breeze here. It blows in a constant flow through this channel of rock. Once you sense it with your magical abilities, try to stop the wind. Succeed here in stopping the wind's progress and you will have demonstrated a capacity to learn the elemental school of wind."

Quest accepted: Learn to control wind magic.

Hal stood staring into the stiff breeze blowing up the canyon. He blinked his eyes against the grit carried by the wind. How could he stop the wind from flowing around and over him?

"Tildi, can you give me a hint at what to do to get started? This seems a lot more than a basic magical task."

When she didn't answer, he glanced behind to ask again, but the mage was gone. Only her footprints in the dirt remained to show she'd been here at all.

Hal turned back to the canyon. He'd mastered control over the cold, over earth, and over fire. He could do this, too. It was a matter of finding the handles that let you control something like the wind.

Raising his staff over his head with both hands, Hal called out for the wind to cease, directing all his will into the effort.

Nothing happened. If anything, the breeze increased in force and velocity.

He thought about the way he'd drawn on the water vapor with his ice magic and tried to use the same process to grab ahold of the air itself.

This time, he was sure. The breeze was no longer just a breeze; it had become a series of gusts of increasing force. The wind buffeted him, as if telling him to stop trying to control it.

When one gust hit him with enough force to knock him down to one knee, Hal's fury boiled up with all the frustration of weeks of not being with his family.

Screaming his rage against the howl of the gale-force winds now buffeting him in the mouth of the canyon, Hal pushed back with all his might and drew on every ounce of his will to remain standing and not be knocked down.

Burning pain flashed across all his exposed skin. The wind seemed to fight back, picking up more and more sand and grit, driving it into him like a million tiny needles. The wind-driven sand whipped at him again and again.

Health damage: Health -10
Health damage: Health -10
Health damage: Health -10

Covering his face with his hands to protect his eyes, Hal bellowed in defiance. He refused to be beaten by the wind.

Growling deep in his throat, Hal drew in all the magic he knew how to touch — earth, fire, and ice — until he could hold no more. He filled himself to bursting and still tried to hold more.

Then he saw it.

In his mind's eye, Hal sensed a gap, a place between the other magical forces where wind magic must fit if he could touch it. It had a distinct, multifaceted shape, like the shape of a diamond or other cut crystal.

Hal took the shape and imagined the wind as a force flowing through the crystalline form.

The force of the gale lessened.

Hal, seeing success just out of reach, attacked the wind with sheer willpower. He used the multifaceted shape to contain more of the swirling air around him. It whipped at him but folded into the polyhedron in his mind representing wind magic.

The gale lessened again. It became a stiff, gusting breeze.

Yelling at the top of his lungs, Hal pushed with every part of his being until he'd filled every nook and cranny of that polygonal shape with air.

And it was done.

The hurricane of buffeting gusts was gone, replaced by the gentle breeze he'd felt when he first arrived at the canyon's mouth.

Inside him, amidst all the swirling fury contained within that single multifaceted diamond box in his mind, Hal found he could push and pull at the breeze surrounding him now with all the finesse of a concert violinist playing the most delicate of songs.

Quest completed: Learn to control wind magic.

13,000 experience points awarded.

Hal leaned forward, his hands on his knees and his chest heaving from the exertion of holding on to the wind. The sudden sound of Tildi's voice next to him- made him jump.

"Now you know why wind magic is the master of all. You must contain the fury of the tornado and the hurricane to do the smallest of spells."

Hal shook his head, awe filling him.

"I would have told you that fire is the hardest to control because of the wild nature of a naked flame, but in the end, it's just controlling the presence or absence of heat, just like ice magic controls cold. With wind, it's like all of nature's most destructive forces are pent up in one aspect of magic."

"This is why only a few who try to become arch mages succeed in their quest. The wind kills most who seek to control it."

Hal shivered at the thought of dying that way. He knew it was possible, judging by the tiny dots of blood covering his exposed skin where the granules of sand had pelted him. He could have been flayed alive if it had continued increasing in intensity.

"Come," Tildi called over her shoulder. She was already walking back to the tower. "There is much we must do and learn to complete your training."

Hal reached out with his mind one last time. The breeze brushed against his raw skin, this time with the gentle caress of a lover. It seemed to bid him goodbye.

He smiled. "Until next time."

Hal turned and followed Tildi to the tower.

CHAPTER 32

FOR THE BETTER PART OF two weeks, Tildi drilled Hal in all the forms of wind magic. He began to gain more and more experience with each task she had him perform. He didn't just spend all of his time studying wind magic; he also spent time expanding his knowledge of the other schools of magic.

Now he'd gained some proficiency in all four of the elemental schools, Hal noticed that his character sheet had updated, finally identifying the unknown magical ability as the spirit elemental school. Hal hadn't learned any spells from this school yet, but he knew that it was vital if he stood any chance of rescuing Mona and Cari.

Name: *Hal Dix*
    Class: *Mage*
    Level: *11*

Attributes:
    Brawn: *26 — +9 defense*

Wisdom: 20 — +6 *defense*
Luck: 30 — +11 *to all saving throws (Max)*
Speed: 16 — +4 *defense*
Looks: 8
Health: 155/155

Character skills: Chakra regeneration — 3 (heal 18hp; 1/day)
    Mage experience: 166,425/250,000
    Ice elemental school:
    Resist cold, Ice shield, Ice armor, Ice darts, Ice lance, Wall of fog, Hail, Blizzard.
    Earth elemental school:
    Plant growth, Neutralize poison, Heal wounds, Deal wounds, Detect magic.
    Fire elemental school:
    Summon fire, Control fire, Fire spray, Fire resistance, Fireball, Wall of fire, Heat metal.
    Wind elemental school:
    Wall of force, Sandblaster, Vacuum voids.
    Spirit elemental school:
    Multi-elemental school:
    Lava flow, Ice boulder.

Warrior experience: 140,800/250,000
    Rogue experience: 146,100/250,000

During his training, Hal discovered he could make wind as hard as a pane of glass and use it to pick a lock. He found he could create pockets of vacuum in the distance, using them to move nearby objects as the air explosively filled the voids he'd made with soft pops of sound. All of this practice led to a gain of almost ten thousand experience points.

He continued to work on his skills until Tildi finally smiled and placed her hand on his shoulder.

"Enough, Hal, enough."

"But I have more to learn, more to do. I have to master this."

"You have gone beyond what I could have expected. You exceeded even my greatest pupil, Decimus, the man who now counts himself as the Emperor's closest advisor. The next task is one you must undertake alone. You must learn to combine all four forms until you have mastered the secrets of spirit magic. I cannot teach you this. No living person can, since no one has ever done it with all four primary schools before."

"Then how will I do it if no one can teach me?"

"You have the necessary skills; you must practice and learn. I believe, if you continue these things with all four schools together, you will find the method you must use to unlock the secret to spirit magic. You'll find it, I'm certain. Now I must teach you the final lesson of wind magic, how to open a portal to wherever you wish. While the other schools can open small, limited doors to other places, only wind magic masters can open portals sufficient to transport more than the casters themselves."

Hal listened with care, concentrating on Tildi's next words. He wanted to be able to return home with his family once he found them. Having the ability to open a portal would be the first step on the road to traveling from Fantasma back to Earth.

Tildi continued her instruction on portals, and Hal discovered he'd already started down the road to this sort of magic. The vacuum bubbles he'd played with were very similar to what Tildi showed him next, only on a larger scale. Rather than pumping the air from the void created, she removed everything from within the portal's boundaries and substituted the substance of wherever she wanted to go. In this case, she opened a doorway to the other side of the valley.

Once she demonstrated the technique, it only took Hal a few

tries to adapt the vacuum bubble method to creating a full portal. The first one he opened was more like a window than a door, but he was able to toss a rock through it and see the rock land from the other side a few hundred yards away.

Hal cheered, he could almost save his family, but he knew his ability to open and create portals still needed work.

With the ability to open portals, the bare roots of a plan tickled the back of his mind. He tried different ideas out in his head. In every version he could think of, the ability to open a portal without any delay or warning figured heavily. That required hard work and practice.

He spent the rest of the day and part of the next getting that practice. He opened portals over and over, around the canyon valley. Each time, Hal stepped through to the other side and then created another to come back. After twenty-five or thirty tries, he'd almost reached the level of skill he knew he required. He had to be able to open a portal anywhere, anytime, without having to expend conscious thought about the steps in the process.

The time working on it was paying off. Hal could step through to any location within view in a heartbeat. Of course, it would take more work to open a portal to a location he didn't know well, but the technique was the same in theory.

Hal prepared to open yet another practice portal when Tildi appeared next to him, stepping out of a short-range doorway of her own. He recognized now that was how she popped around and disappeared without a trace all the time. It had added to the mystery that followed her wherever she went, until you knew how she did it.

"Hey, Tildi, I'm just working on refining my technique. I think I've found a way to moderate the energy used to open and maintain the portal. Watch."

She held up a hand to forestall his spell.

"You're going to have to work on it somewhere else. I just received word from the east. Kay has rejoined the army east of Hyroth. She sent a message via Theran. The army is marching towards the imperial capital, despite my warnings to stay away until you were ready."

"Damn." Hal couldn't decide if he was glad to be moving or angry at being forced into action before he was ready. There was no reliable plan yet in his mind. Going in without a plan could get everyone, including Mona and Cari, killed. He pounded his fist into his hand in frustration.

"I have to join them. I need to find a way to break through the spell barriers and the only way I can do that is to see them myself."

"Remember, Hal, Kay and the others are being forced into action by the Emperor's plans. Don't fall into the mistake of reacting to him and not acting in your own interests."

"I'll try. Now I guess you should open a portal for me."

"Use what you've learned to join them, Hal. You don't need me to do this for you anymore. Think of where you wish to go or the person you want to see, and the magic will guide the opening of the portal for you."

Tildi held up a warning hand as he turned to leave.

"One thing to keep in mind, Hal. Outside of this shielded place, every portal is easily detected by any wind mage in the vicinity. The greater the distance of the jump, the more power used, and the farther away, the jump will be detectable. The mage hunters have refined their methods and will be tracking you every time you use that spell."

"I'll keep that in mind. That is why I've been trying to modulate the amount of energy I use to create the portal. Have you ever tried to mask the energy you use in some way, kind of like a stealth teleport?"

"I don't even know how that would work," Tildi replied, though Hal could see the wheels turning in her mind as she pondered the problem.

"It's gotta be something about the energy signature," Hal said, wondering aloud. "It would be a matter of gauging the amount of energy needed to open a portal precisely without any bleed of extra energy. It's that extra energy signature that signals where you are when you land. The energy to open the portal is all used up in the process. If you used just the energy you needed and no more, there'd be nothing to detect."

"It's an interesting problem. I'm not sure it's practical in process since you'd have to calculate carefully to find the exact energy needs. Usually, a portal is a spell of convenience or necessity. Unless you calculated the precise distance, elevation, and direction ahead of time, you'd be hard-pressed to do it all on the fly."

"I'm gonna work on it. There must be a way to fudge the system and make it work. Even dampening the energy down on a larger jump would hinder detection from a distance."

"It would be useful in many ways if you could manage that, Hal. Many of the safeguards used to create magical wards and barriers are based on detecting and interrupting the flow of magical energy before it can manifest in a completed spell. If you could use magical energy in a way that evaded detection, you might circumvent the wards."

Hal listened and nodded. It was a concept he planned to keep in mind and continue refining. In the meantime, it was time to leave.

He packed quickly. Hal didn't have many possessions to bring along, just a few changes of clothing along with his weapons and staff.

He arrived back at Tildi's side near the tower's entrance fifteen minutes later, with everything he owned in Fantasma either in his hands or on his back.

"Thank you, Tildi, for everything you've done to prepare me for what comes next. I think I'm going to need it all before this is done."

"I knew you were more than capable the first time I met you back at that flea market so long ago. Trust your instincts and you'll be fine."

Tildi held out a hand to clasp wrists with Hal, but he didn't think that was enough. The diminutive mage squawked in surprise when Hal pulled her into a brief embrace. He stepped back, leaving Tildi a little flustered, and thought about where Kay was. He pictured her in his mind's eye.

He cast the spell and opened the portal. A lush plain of waving, golden grain lay on the other side.

"Be well, Hal Dix. I will lend what aid I can when I can. Remember, though, only you have the power to complete the task at hand. Trust yourself."

Hal smiled at her and turned, then stepped through the gateway to the east, letting it blink shut behind him.

CHAPTER 33

SENTRIES ON HORSEBACK challenged Hal as soon as he appeared on the grassy plain far to the east of Tildi's secret canyon. The squad of armored lancers rode up and held him at bay with the tip of their lances, calling out to him to halt and identify himself.

Hal had no intention of going anywhere or doing anything that might get him spitted on the end of one of those lances. He smiled at the officer in charge of the troop when the man lifted his visor.

The boy leading this unit couldn't be older than eighteen. Hal realized he must be a junior nobleman from one of the western free cities.

"Who are you, vagabond? How did you get inside our ring of sentries undetected? I warn you, do not lie to me, or I'll order one of my men to run you through."

"Easy, lad," Hal replied, raising his hands to show he held nothing but his staff. "I need to speak with the leaders of your army. I have important information they must know before they launch their attack on the Crystal City."

"I am not in the habit of letting strange men, who infiltrate our lines, bother this army's leaders or even my senior officers. Tell me your name and why you are really here and perhaps I'll let you live."

Hal sighed. He'd hoped to avoid embarrassing the earnest lad.

"Son, I'm tired of playing games with you. I'm Hal Dix, once a general in command of this army, or at least part of it. Now take me to Her Highness Princess Kareena or General Otto. I must speak with them on an urgent matter."

"You are not General Dix, sir. General Dix is a great warrior of unsurpassed skill and knowledge. He is somewhere to the west, gathering more forces for our cause. You cannot be him."

The young officer dismissed Hal with a backhanded wave of his gauntleted hand.

"Kill him and leave the body for the carrion birds."

"That's it," Hal declared. "Don't say I didn't warn you."

Hal cast a wind spell, hardening the air around him. Several of the lancers charged forward, trying to be the first one to reach him and run him through, and promptly snapped their lances in half.

One of the men was unhorsed when his lance struck the invisible barrier, the force driving him backward and pitching the man from his saddle.

Having protected himself from the lancers, Hal turned to deal with the upstart young officer.

A quick shot of earth magic, and fast-growing vines grew up beneath the officer's horse, wrapped around the man's spurred boot, and pulled him from the saddle to crash in a heap on the ground beside his mount.

Shouts of "mage" and "wizard" sounded from the lancers. Two of them wheeled their mounts and bolted away towards the encampment Hal saw in the distance.

The remaining lancers lowered their weapons and moved their horses to stand between Hal and the camp.

Hal approached the officer struggling to rise. He rolled back and forth on his back like an upside-down turtle. Hal laughed aloud and extended his hand.

"Come on, kid. Get up before one of your superiors sees you and decides you don't belong in command of this unit of lancers."

The young soldier stopped trying to get up on his own and stared at Hal, realization dawning in his eyes.

"You're really him. Hal Dix — I mean, General Dix."

"I told you who I was. I'm not in the habit of lying to my troops. Now get up and take me to the command tent. I have news they must have before the assault on the capital begins."

The officer reached up and took Hal's hand. Hal pulled him to his feet with a grunt. The boy and his armor weighed a lot more than he'd expected. Once the youngster was back in an appropriate vertical position, the officer saluted as he snapped to attention.

"Lieutenant Alvarez, at your service, General."

"As you were, Lieutenant. Escort me to the camp so I may pass along my messages."

"Yes, sir."

By the time Hal and the cavalry escort reached the camp, word had begun to spread of his arrival. Soldiers from various towns and cities to the west stood and pointed at him. A few even cheered. Hal suspected those cheering and calling out greetings to him were members of his army of escaped slaves.

The command pavilion at the center of the camp was a bustle of activity, with runners and clerks coming and going in a constant stream. The sides of the massive tent had been rolled up, so the pavilion became a sort of awning erected to protect those inside from the sun and other elements. It still allowed a little breeze to pass through, which was a blessing in the dry heat of these eastern plains.

Hal strode past the guards without challenge and entered the covered area. Sergeant Madry and the familiar squad of dragoons had set up guard around the tent. Hal nodded a greeting as he passed by the guards. A large table was laid out in the center, covered with maps, charts, and other various documents. Around it, Kay, Anders, Otto, Rune, Junica, and even the goblin chieftain Churg stood looking over their situation.

He didn't fail to notice two more dragoon troopers standing to one side, keeping a watchful eye on Kay. He caught their eyes and smiled in approval. The two men grinned in response and returned his affirmation with subtle nods.

Kay and Otto spotted him first as he strode up to the table.

"Well, look what the cat dragged in," Otto quipped.

"It's good to see you, too, old friend."

"What's with the wise man outfit? Where's your armor and your sword? I thought you'd be coming to fight alongside us again."

"I'm here to help you, that much is true, but first you must call off this ill-advised attack. You'll never penetrate the magical wards, and if you managed to break through, you'd lose too many troops to have enough force to take the capital on the other side."

"I suppose you have an alternative?" Otto asked.

"Sure, sort of. It's going to take some time to pull it off, but yeah, I have an idea of what we have to do."

"Hal, it's good to see you," Kay added, "but do you really have a plan or is this another one of your 'make it up as you go' situations?"

"I have a plan, Kay, but it's not one I'll share here in front of everyone and any prying eyes and ears the Emperor has inside your camp. Clear the pavilion. I'll fill you in on what I plan to do once everyone is pulled back far enough to be out of earshot. I have to warn you all, though, you're not going to like it."

Otto gave Hal a fierce grin. "If memory serves me, no one likes your ideas at first, Hal. They do have a way of working out in the end, though."

The general called out to the men and women around the pavilion.

"All of you, clear out of here until you're called to return. Now. Go!"

Hal waited as the various clerks and messengers left the large tent. Even the two dragoon troopers were asked to move off to a distance until no one was close enough to hear what Hal said in the center of the tent. Eventually, he was alone with Kay, Otto, Rune, Junica, Anders, and Churg.

"Alright, Hal," Otto said. "We're alone now. What do you want us to do?"

"Hold on, Otto. There's one more precaution I need."

Hal spread out his magical senses and cast two spells, dropping two hardened domes of air over the pavilion, one inside the other, with a void of vacuum in between to insulate against any sound leaving the area. There would be a limited supply of oxygen inside the inner bubble, but he didn't plan on taking that long. He'd dispel the domes before anyone started suffocating.

Satisfied with the final precaution, Hal laid out his plan for his friends. He gave his reasons for the drastic nature of the initial parts of it, countering the numerous objections raised. In the end, Hal overcame all their concerns with a single sentence.

"This will end this war once and for all."

By the time the air started to get a bit stale inside the pavilion, everyone knew their part in Hal's elaborate plan and where they had to be at the appointed time. All seemed a bit uneasy, except for Rune, but he never looked flustered by anything. The eastern monk's outward demeanor remained impassive and neutral, which Hal took as a form of approval for the plan.

Hal lifted the barriers against eavesdroppers, letting fresh air flow into the tent.

"Remember, people. Keep this to yourselves. Secrecy is the most important part. Everything hinges on it."

"We know, Hal," Junica said. "Don't worry. We'll have your back when it matters most."

"Try not to blow me up this time, alright, Junica?"

The blonde archer shrugged. "You told me to fire those arrows no matter what, Hal. I follow orders. Besides, you're fine. How bad could it have been?"

Hal chuckled. "I was inside that explosion. Believe me, I thought I'd died, too, until Tildi woke me up and took me back home."

"I'll admit I was happy to find out I hadn't blown you up, too.

Next time, though, you'd better be ready to run. I'd do it all again if victory requires it."

"I'd expect nothing less, Junica."

Kay and Anders came to stand beside him as the messengers and clerks flooded back into the tent to continue running the camp and issue the new orders based on Hal's change of plans.

"Are you sure you want to do this, Hal?" Kay asked amidst the renewed hustle and bustle.

Anders stepped up to stand beside her and nodded.

"My beloved Kareena is correct, Hal. There are no guarantees the initial stages of your plan will be successful. What then?"

"If I fail, Anders, you can always go back and try your original plans. Besides, my plan has to succeed so the two of you can get married in the palace where you belong."

"I don't need to get married in any palace," Kay said. "That's not who I am anymore. That princess died alongside her parents a long time ago."

Hal knew the past still haunted Kay, but her lineage figured in his plans. Killing the Emperor was only the first part of it. This land would need a new ruler. He needed her prepared for what came next. He didn't want to have to return five years from now and do all this again with some new warlord who'd taken over.

"Where to now, Hal?" Anders asked.

"First, I want a hot meal and some time to rest for a solid night's sleep."

"And then?"

"Then, it's off to find some mage hunters and get captured."

CHAPTER 34

HAL AWOKE the next morning rested and well fed. Today was the day he kicked off everything. Months of preparation, training, and fighting had all led to this moment. If everything worked out, he'd free Mona and Cari within a few days.

After gearing up with everything he thought he'd need, Hal picked up his staff and stepped outside the tent provided for him last night. Kay and Anders were discussing something with a cavalry officer nearby. The woman saluted, mounted her horse, and raced off at a gallop.

"Everything alright?" Hal asked.

"That was the last of the orders for everything you asked for yesterday," Kay explained. "I hope you know what you're doing, Hal. This is a big risk you're taking. The Emperor could just have you killed on sight. He's tried before."

"I think not, Kay. There are questions he wants answered about me and how I do what I can do. If I can offer him those answers, he'd be a fool to kill me before he gets them out of me."

Anders clapped a gauntleted hand on Hal's shoulder.

"You're a brave man, Hal Dix. I don't know many who'd willingly offer themselves up for capture on the slim chance the Emperor might be reasonable that day. Besides, how do you even know they'll know where to come after you?"

"Ask Kay. They've been dogging my tail ever since I got here. At first, I thought the mage hunters were tracking the other arch mages. I was wrong. It's me they're after, and I think they'll want me alive once they hear what I have to say. I plan on obliging them."

"Hal, I know it seems like they've been following us. Even so, how do you know for sure they'll track you here or anywhere else?"

"It's hard to explain, Kay. Let's just say I've figured out how to use magic in a way that's less noisy than others. Usually, that lets me use spells in ways that can't be easily detected. However, the opposite is also true. I'm powerful enough that I can make more magical noise than usual if I want as well. I did that when I opened the portal and arrived yesterday outside this encampment."

Hal fixed them with a savage grin.

"I'm betting every imperial mage hunter for a hundred miles in all directions heard me when I stepped out of the portal here. By now they've arrived with their forces and are waiting to see what I do next. All I have to do is jump somewhere else and wait for them to follow. My hope is they mistake my noisy portal use as evidence of my inexperience and being a general noob at using magic. I'll sucker them in and they'll take me right to the Emperor and my family."

Kay didn't seem convinced and Hal explained again what he had to do.

Anders beamed with excitement as Hal described how he planned to get captured.

"It's a shame I cannot come with you to witness your capture. I suspect it will be a magnificent fight. You'll have to resist at first or they'll know something is amiss."

"You and Kay, just make sure the troops are ready when they get the signal. There will be a limited time frame in which to act. If you miss it, I'm gonna be all alone on my own in there."

"Don't worry about us, Hal," Kay assured him. "We won't let you down. When the signal comes, we'll all be ready to go."

"That's all I need. Here, take this and be ready to bring it with you." Hal handed his staff to Kay. "With a little luck, I'll see you both again in a few days."

"I'll take good care of it in the meantime, Hal."

Hal clasped wrists with Anders and Kay in turn. It was time to get moving. He didn't relish the next step. It was the first in a series of calculations he'd made based on limited knowledge. Those calculations were pretty much guesses. He had no way to ensure the hunters would do what he expected them to do.

He hoped he'd calculated right. He'd find out soon enough.

"I think it's time to go," Hal said.

Quest accepted: Lure mage hunters in and get captured.

"Godspeed, Hal," Kay said, stepping back to give him some room.

Drawing in wind magic, Hal opened a portal to a nearby village. Scouts had reported it abandoned, which meant there'd be no one caught in the crossfire when the spells started flying. As the doorway to another place opened before him, a familiar rattling sound began. The choice he'd made invoked that strange slot machine sound rolling in his head. His luck was in play.

It was time to see if it rolled his way once again.

Hal stepped forward, leaving the camp and the others behind him.

He now stood between a pair of humble, one-room dwellings. The huts had small gardens in front of them, now untended and overgrown. There was no sign of anyone nearby, and Hal heard no sounds but the chirp of birds and the buzz of insects.

He released his hold on the spell, and the portal closed behind him. Hal made sure to let plenty of excess magical energy bleed outward as he let go of the magic.

He smiled as his senses picked up the echoes of his spell

resonating outward. That should bring the mage hunters running. It would undoubtedly grab his own interest if he was tuned in and paying attention to such things.

That reminded him, it might be a good idea to tune his senses to magic in the vicinity. It would be good to know when his invited guests had arrived. He wanted to be prepared to give them the fight they expected before he let them capture him. It was imperative they think he was nearly spent and desperate when he surrendered to them. Hal ducked into a tool shed at the rear of one of the huts and crouched down to wait.

The first sign of pursuit happened almost ten minutes after Hal had arrived. A twinge in the magical sensor net he'd extended out from his hiding place alerted him to a portal opening nearby. A few seconds later, a second and then a third portal opened in different locations around the village.

Hal smiled. They had him surrounded. He had them just where he wanted. Waiting until he heard voices approaching, Hal gazed through a crack in the wooden door of the shed and spotted the first of the hunters. He drew in energy for his initial spell.

It was time to drop some magic on them. He was looking forward to getting some payback for their kidnapping his family.

Hal reached out to create a fine mist and spread it outward from the center of the village, using the community's central well as a moisture source. As the mist accumulated, it became a thick fog, filling the whole central square with the suspended water vapor. It would blind everyone in the village now. It would also do something else as the moisture penetrated the clothes and armor of his opponents.

Smiling, Hal tried something he had thought up during his training with Tildi. He decided to call it "crossing the streams."

Holding on to his ice magic flows creating the mist, Hal opened up a channel to fire magic. Intense heat flashed outward from Hal's location, super-heating the fog into steam in a heartbeat. Screams of pain sounded all around him as the scalding vapor burned everyone not inside some sort of shelter when the spell released.

2,400 experience points awarded.
 2,400 experience points awarded.
 3,000 experience points awarded.

The steam dissipated in an instant, using up the energy that created it. Looking out the door of the shed, Hal saw several bodies lying in the streets all around him. He heard other voices groaning in pain nearby. Now, he had to let them see him so they knew it wasn't just a trap and that the chase was on.

Darting from his hiding place, Hal readied a series of offensive and defensive spells all at once. His new and improved ice armor appeared, encasing his entire body in a sheath of resilient, yet flexible ice plates, harder than steel. He was ready.

Hal ran into the street, into the fight of his life with everything he held dear in the balance. In his mind, the slot machine rolled and rattled with fury. He hoped luck was on his side.

He was going to need it. The mist had all burned away when it flashed to steam. The hunters spotted Hal right away.

The first attack came from behind, knocking him to the ground when a crossbow bolt slammed into his back. It hurt like hell. The armor did its job, though, and the missile pinged away, ricocheting to the street beside him.

Health damage: Health -8

After pushing himself up to one knee, Hal turned and fired a spell at the crossbow-wielding hunter. The man, clad in black leather armor, fumbled to reload his crossbow.

He never got the chance as the ice lance took him in the chest, impaling him.

2,400 experience points awarded.

Shouts to Hal's left alerted him to an approaching group of mage hunters. He got up and ran to the nearest building, peering around the edge.

Chips of stone and stucco shredded off the corner of the cottage as a series of spells slammed into the wall next to Hal's vantage point.

Jerking his head back as more spells, including a fireball, slammed into the building, Hal turned, ran in the opposite direction, and circled the building.

The cottage he hid behind was now aflame. The thatched roof caught fire as soon as the fireball exploded. Hal continued circling the burning home. He hoped to surprise this new group of attackers from behind.

They anticipated his move, though. Four hunters waited for him on the adjacent street. Two had crossbows leveled at point-blank range; two launched spells in his direction as he ran around the corner into the open space between the buildings.

One of the crossbowmen called out. "Halt! In the name of Emperor Kang, you will surrender yourself to us."

"Fat chance," Hal replied and readied spells of his own.

Their spells landed first.

Vines grew up from the packed dirt of the street and clutched at his feet and lower legs. They had trouble finding purchase on the ice armor encasing his lower body, but some of the thorns struck home through the few gaps around his knees and ankles.

Health damage: Health -12

He struggled to pull free as the second spell struck home, wrapping him in straps of flaming iron, binding his arms to his side. Even with his fire resistance, the white-hot iron bands burned him, melting through his ice armor in places.

Health damage: Health -14

Hal created a sheath of dual hard-sided air bubbles around himself, with an insulating vacuum void between, and pressed outward, expanding the bubbles.

The increasing air pressure pushed the binding iron bands away from him until they fell to the ground.

He threw up a wall of ice across the street between himself and the attackers just as the crossbowmen fired at him.

The thin wall shattered from the missiles, but the bolts were spent on impact and fell to the dirt.

More shouts behind him told Hal additional hunters had circled around his position. He needed to move. He didn't want to let them catch him too quickly.

Another fireball sizzled at his back, exploding just behind him as he ran between two buildings. The blast threw Hal to the ground, and the wash of heat managed to melt the remaining ice armor on his legs, causing partial burns to the back of his thighs.

Health damage: Health -20

Hal struggled to get back to his feet and keep running. Two more crossbow bolts hit him from behind, shattering his back armor and knocking him down again.

Health damage: Health -8
  Health damage: Health -8

More vines grew up around him, threatening to pin him down to the dirt. Hal tried something new and fired discs of razor-sharp ice from his hands across the ground, slicing through the thorny vines. It worked.

He jumped up and limped on his burned legs.

Hal stopped in a nearby doorway, loosing a fireball behind him into the street as he ducked inside. Screams of alarm and agony sounded, telling him he'd caught a few more of the mage hunters in the blast.

2,400 experience points awarded.
  3,000 experience points awarded.
  3,000 experience points awarded.

Hal looked for another exit from the building he'd entered and saw none. He'd ducked inside a storehouse of some kind. Sacks of grain and farming tools lay scattered around the room. There was no sign of even a window to offer him a way to escape.

Turning, he ran back to the doorway and peeked outside. Three crossbow bolts slammed into the doorframe, and he yanked his head back. He'd seen enough.

Hal counted ten figures in the street outside the storehouse, covering the doorway with either crossbows or spells ready for release. They'd cornered him.

Scanning the room a final time for some way out so he could continue the fight a little longer, Hal noticed nothing.

A voice called from the street outside.

"Hal Dix! We know it's you in there. We have orders not to kill you."

"You have a strange way of showing that."

"We didn't know it was you at first. For that, we apologize. Surrender and we will tend to your wounds before taking you back to the Emperor. He extends an invitation to you."

"You expect me to believe I can just walk out of here and you will spare my life?"

"Mr. Dix, I'm one of the mages who has visited your world. I've seen where you come from. The Emperor knows you have no real connection to this world. He would like to talk with you about an alternative outcome to the current hostilities."

That mage out there had been to Earth. In all likelihood, that meant he'd been among the ones who'd entered his home and kidnapped his wife and child. Hal's fingernails dug into his palm, scraping painful gouges in the soft skin as he clenched his hands.

Hal had a score to settle with this one and any of the others who'd dared to lay hands on his wife and daughter. He longed to run outside and fire off every spell he had until they were all dead in the street.

He figured he had an even chance of succeeding. Except that wasn't success in this case.

Revenge would have to wait. Hal forced his hands to relax and released the spells he'd begun casting on reflex.

Keeping his eyes on the prize, Hal called out through the door. "And all he wants to do is talk? I'm not sure I can believe you."

"I cannot offer any assurances you'd find acceptable in this situation. I do not have to. Suffice it to say, I have enough magical firepower here to level this whole village if I order it. I have not given such an order because your death is not our desired outcome.

Surrender and come with us back to the Crystal City. You will see I tell the truth for yourself."

Hal knew this was what he wanted, but his slots still rolled in the back of his mind. The important decision he was due to make had not been made yet or that would have stopped.

"I'm coming out. Don't shoot."

Ping. The bell sounded as the slot machine ground to a halt. Whatever was going to happen was locked in now.

Hal kept his hands in view at his sides, away from the daggers on his belt, and stepped through the doorway.

The mage hunter was right. Hal saw at least a dozen mages and twice as many ordinary hunters and trackers. They'd come ready for a fight.

"Walk forward to the center of the street and stop there, Mr. Dix. Make no sudden moves or we'll be forced to defend ourselves."

Hal complied, stepping out until he stood between the buildings. Two hunters shouldered their crossbows and ran forward. They shackled his hands and feet. Runes covered the iron bands around his wrists and ankles. He suspected they would inhibit magic use if he tried to cast a spell now.

The mage in the blue robes stepped forward. He must have noticed Hal examining his bonds.

"Those are mage cuffs, Mr. Dix. They reflect spell energy back on the user. Anything you try to do to us will only hurt you at this point. I urge you not to try anything."

"I'll come along peacefully. I'm tired of this place. I just want to go home."

"My name is Decimus, Mr. Dix. I will vouch for your safety as long as you do not resist. Do you understand?"

Hal nodded and Decimus smiled.

"Excellent. Then let us return to the Crystal City. The Emperor will be most pleased to know you've decided to come and meet with him."

"It's not like I have much choice. You've been hounding me across the entire continent."

"Let's not dwell on past unpleasantries. I think you will find His Majesty fair in his judgment and disposition, given all you've done to thwart him here in Fantasma."

Decimus nodded, and one of the other mages opened a portal in the street, spanning the whole distance between the buildings. Hal was impressed. That was some gateway.

"Come, Mr. Dix. The Emperor awaits."

Quest completed: Lure mage hunters in and get captured.
  5,000 experience points awarded.

CHAPTER 35

THE PORTAL DEPOSITED Hal and Decimus outside enormous bronze gates, set in tall stone walls stretching in both directions as far as he could see. Hal craned his neck to look around his escort of mage hunters.

"Impressive, is it not?" Decimus said. "This is the great wall surrounding the Crystal City. Wards against all four elemental schools prevent us from opening portals inside this boundary. Do not worry. It is not a long walk to where I have carriages waiting."

A horn sounded in the distance, and a grinding thrum vibrated up through his feet. The great doors swung open in a slow, precise sweep. Inside, a thirty-foot tunnel extended through the wall. Daylight showed in an arched opening at the far side.

"Come. We mustn't keep the Emperor waiting. I have sent word of your capture. He will be pleased our endeavors to locate you finally succeeded. He was most displeased with our progress until now."

The hunters started forward, prodding Hal to keep up with Decimus.

"Sorry to disappoint you. I didn't want to be captured and thrown into a dungeon. Perhaps if you'd extended an invitation rather than having your thugs chase after me with magic and crossbow bolts..."

"An unfortunate misunderstanding. One I hope we might remedy moving forward."

"Hey," Hal said, holding up his shackled hands. "I'm the one in the chains here. It's not like I can do anything to change how we're getting along."

"Indeed. Well, perhaps that can be changed. First, we must make sure you understand the consequences if you attempt to escape or otherwise defy the Emperor's wishes. I believe we have certain leverage over you now, do we not?"

There it was, Hal thought. The implicit threat they'd injure his wife and daughter. Hal decided to bring the issue out into the light of day.

"Speaking of leverage, when will I be allowed to see my family?"

"Your wife and daughter have been treated with the utmost courtesy for the last several months, Mr. Dix. I assure you they are safe, for the time being at least. Ah, here we are. The carriages are waiting for us as I expected."

They exited the gate tunnel into the sunlight, within the walls of the Crystal City. The buildings inside looked much like all the buildings in this part of the world. Built of stone, covered with a stucco cement so they had smooth sides, those closest to the gate were two stories tall and contained shops and market stalls one might expect to see near the gates of a major city.

The people, however, were not. Their eyes shifted from side to side, as if watching constantly for a surprise attack. The pedestrians closest to Hal and the others shrank back, a combination of fear and awe showing on their faces.

Those who didn't move quickly enough for the hunter guards around Decimus and Hal were shoved backward amid shouts and threats of violence if they didn't comply. People, for the most part, didn't need to be told to stay back twice. They cowered and shrank back away from the group as Hal and the others approached a pair of carriages in the street.

A squad of four mounted knights accompanied each carriage. The mounted soldiers' polished, silvery chainmail armor shined in the sunlight, the spikes of their helmets peeking out from the center of the turbans wrapped around the metal headgear.

Decimus led Hal forward to the lead carriage. The footman opened the door and waited for Hal to climb aboard. The chains and shackles on his ankles prevented him from lifting his foot high enough to reach the step, and Hal fixed Decimus with a baleful stare.

"I can't get in with these on."

"Hunters, assist Mr. Dix in boarding the carriage if you will."

Three hunters stepped up, one on each side lifting Hal under his arms while the third pushed from behind. Hal stumbled and fell into the carriage, barely managing to land on one of the cushioned benches inside.

Decimus climbed in behind him and sat on the bench opposite Hal's. Two of the armed hunters boarded as well and sat on either side of Hal.

"We may go, Major," Decimus called out to the lead cavalry officer outside.

"Yes, sir."

The officer saluted and began barking orders. The carriage jolted to a start, the horses in their traces pulling them down the street at a trot. Outside, the mounted troops formed up with four in the lead clearing their path and the final four coming up behind them.

The streets seemed almost deserted compared to a similar street in Tandon or Hyroth at this time of day. There were only a few civilians in sight at any time as they passed onward towards the palace at the center of the city.

Decimus noticed Hal's interest in the city outside the carriage. "Impressive, is it not? This is the shining jewel of the entire Empire."

"I'm sure," Hal said, unconvinced. "It seems deserted. Where are all the people?"

"Unfortunately, a certain element of dissidence in the city has caused us to detain large numbers of the populace on suspicion of sedition. We are working our way through questioning them. Those who are found innocent are released back to their jobs and homes. It is tedious work, but the Emperor's safety is of paramount importance when compared to a few people's inconvenience."

"I'm sure those imprisoned for no reason would not consider it an inconvenience. They might call it oppression."

"Mr. Dix," Decimus cautioned, "I would recommend you not engage in such talk while in the palace, especially in front of the Emperor. He does not take disagreement lightly."

"I've heard about his disposition towards those who disagree with him. His reputation precedes him."

"Again, Mr. Dix, you would do well to remedy your defiant tone. I don't think it would please His Majesty, and since so much you hold dear depends on his benevolence, you should watch your words and tone in his presence."

Hal closed his mouth before another sharp comment popped out. He had to keep the purpose of his surrender firmly in his mind. He was here to free Mona and Cari. Deposing the Emperor could wait.

The carriages passed through another set of gates guarding a second wall halfway to the center of the vast imperial capital. Based on how Kay had described the city to him, this must be the entrance to the imperial compound.

They stopped moving soon after passing through the gates, and the footman opened the door. Decimus exited, followed by the two hunters. They caught Hal as he half-hopped, half-fell out of the carriage.

Holding him upright, they urged him forward and forced him to shuffle after Decimus towards a massive building with ornate, tiled mosaics across the high walls. The scenes depicted great battles and acts of heroism with a central, golden-armored figure at their center. Hal had an idea who that was supposed to be.

Entering a pair of golden doors, Hal noted his chains had stopped rattling against the paved ground. Now, they dragged across carpeted floors while he shuffled down a long hallway with many doors on either side.

One door opened, and a clerk in purple imperial robes exited with a pile of scrolls and papers in his hands. He nearly dropped them all after running into the leading hunter bracketing Hal's progress down the hallway.

As he passed the room, Hal saw a row of desks inside. Busy clerks hunched over their work without looking up at the prisoner in the corridor.

"Please endeavor to keep up, Mr. Dix," Decimus called over his shoulder. "It is not advisable to keep the Emperor waiting."

"I'll keep that in mind. Sorry if my chains are holding up your progress."

"Tone, Mr. Dix. Remember to watch your tone in the presence of His Majesty. I'd hate for anything untoward to happen to those you love."

Hal started to answer but bit his tongue, swallowing the words he wanted to say. His opportunity to have the last word would come soon enough.

The hallway ended in a set of double doors guarded by a quartet of armored knights. One of them pulled the right-hand door open and held it as they approached and passed through. Hal paid attention to the details of the palace and its defenses and staff. It might impact his plans to escape with Mona and Cari.

Soft music played on the far side of the doors as Hal entered a colossal audience chamber with a large dais at the opposite end. The source of the music was a small, sixteen-piece chamber orchestra situated off to one side.

Every ten feet along the walls, another armored knight stood at attention. They all followed Hal's progress with their eyes as if they expected him to attack at any moment. Hal smiled. None of the guards had any idea how right they were.

He'd learned in his management training program the cultural tone of an organization started with its leadership. In this case, it meant the Emperor feared him and what he could do. That could be used to work in his favor.

Hal got his first glimpse of the Emperor in person when they approached the dais. The circular stone platform sat on two stone steps extending all the way around the throne at the center. There were numerous male and female attendants standing around Kang, who was seated on the throne at the center.

The man himself didn't seem as fat as he had in Hal's visions through the crystal. He looked up and met Hal's gaze, and Hal saw a cruel smile creep across the Emperor's face. He waved off one attendant with a pile of papers in his arms and leaned forward to watch Hal's shuffling progress across the carpets arrayed atop the floor of the chamber.

Decimus stopped at the base of the stairs leading up to the dais. Hal shuffled up to stand next to the chief mage.

Decimus offered a deep bow, bending until his nose approached his knee. Hal decided to offer a similar show of respect. It was time to use a little flattery and a few compliments to show he wasn't the threat they all thought he was.

Rising from his bow to the Emperor, Hal stifled a gasp. He saw Mona in person for the first time. The reaction was not missed by His Majesty. A smirk crossed the Emperor's face. It irked Hal and he almost said something, but he couldn't take his eyes off Mona.

She'd dressed as the other imperial female attendants did, in diaphanous silk robes and a veil covering the lower half of her face. There was no mistaking those deep blue eyes. Hal knew them within the depths of his soul, and the way they looked at him drove a spike into that soul.

Mona was angry with him. He'd seen that look before but never with the intensity he saw now.

He was here. Didn't she know what he'd done to find her?

"Greetings, Hal Dix. I have longed to meet you since you first graced our world with your annoying presence. In the end, I was forced to find other ways to learn more about you."

The Emperor gestured to Mona, and she stepped up to stand next to the throne. Kang reached out and placed his hand on the small of her back. The move enraged Hal even though he knew it was a calculated ploy to get his goat.

"Your Majesty," Hal said, struggling to choose the correct words to say in this situation. His plan of swooping in and rescuing a grateful wife and daughter had been dashed by the reaction Mona gave him on arrival. "I surrendered willingly after I heard from your servant here you wished to converse with me and would grant me safe passage. I offer myself to that conversation at your convenience."

Hal added a small bow, unsure of the protocol when addressing the Emperor directly.

"You led my mage hunters on quite the chase these last few months. I hoped when I retrieved dear Mona and your daughter, you'd come directly to me to win their freedom. I told Mona as much, didn't I, my dear?"

"You did, Your Majesty. I was as surprised as you were when he didn't present himself here to retrieve us as soon as he arrived." Mona's voice was icy calm, which Hal knew belied the hot fury beneath.

What had happened to her since she'd been here in the palace? Had some spell been placed on her?

"I was detained by other matters that kept me from journeying here as quickly as I wanted. My apologies to you both."

Hal tried to catch Mona's eyes to convey how sorry he truly was, but she looked away, indifferent to his feelings.

"No doubt it was more interference from that infernal witch Tildi that put you on a different path to my door than the direct one. It is unfortunate you chose to heed her flawed council. I know it pained your family that your priorities shifted from what they expected. I spent long hours attempting to console dear Mona. She was quite distraught each time we heard of your further delays and adventures, weren't you, my dear?"

"I was shocked, to say the least, Your Majesty."

Kang pulled his hand away from Mona's back and returned it to the arm of his chair.

"I assure you, Hal...I hope it's alright if I call you Hal. I feel as if I know you well after all the hours I spent talking with Mona about you. Anyway, I want to offer assurances, I have been nothing but a true gentleman with regard to your wife and daughter. I hope that my more than generous treatment of your family demonstrates I'm not the monster others portray me to be, despite the rebellion you raised against me."

Kang paused, as if expecting an answer from Hal. The silence hung heavy in the massive room for longer than comfortable.

Hal wasn't sure what to say. His mind still swam with confusion over how Mona had turned against him. He struggled for the right words that might appease a man in Kang's position.

"I am, uh, I guess, pleasantly surprised to see they are well cared for, Your Majesty. Your reputation for ruthlessness is well documented in other parts of the Empire. I'm glad others' representations of you and your lack of benevolence were mistaken."

"Quite true, Hal. They are mistaken. Of course, some things happened when I took over rulership of a failed empire. Some expediencies had to occur, no matter how regretful they were. Since then, I've tried to change the existing cruel system from within. It is unfortunate the changes have not trickled down to the distant, provincial parts of the realm where things are more barbaric in general."

"Perhaps, then, Your Majesty, we could reset our bad start and try to build on this new beginning we have here."

"I would like to believe we can do that, Hal, but your actions leading up to and including your capture do not engender confidence in me. I don't believe you are trustworthy in any way."

Kang's hand returned to the small of Mona's back.

"You have much to prove to me and to others you have wronged before I'm willing to forget all you have done in the past. We will talk again after I have considered what I will do in this matter."

The Emperor turned away from Hal and waved a hand in the air. Guards grabbed Hal by his elbows and dragged him back from the dais towards a nearby door. Mona's eyes followed him out. For an instant, as the guards dragged him through the doorway and out of sight, Hal caught a hint of concern in her eyes. He wasn't sure if he saw it or dreamed it, and he replayed the tilt of her head, the set of her eyes, and the stony expression on her face over and over in his mind. The only answer he came up with gave him a bare glimmer of hope that she wasn't as set against him as it had first appeared. That brought a smile to his face, despite the way the guards manhandled him down the long flight of stairs to the dungeon cells below.

CHAPTER 36

HAL SHIELDED his eyes from the glaring lamplight when the cell's door creaked open. To go from two days in total darkness to even the dim light of an oil lantern in an instant nearly blinded him.

Hal squinted as his eyes adjusted to the new light. He made out the silhouettes of two figures in the doorway, backed by the flickering torchlight in the dungeon beyond them. The gruff voice of the guard broke the silence.

"You have ten minutes. No more. The orders from His Majesty were specific on that count. Make the best of it. The condemned do not get visitors once sentence is passed."

"Thank you. Please leave us so I may speak to my husband alone."

Hal shifted his still adjusting eyes to the slender figure on the right, realizing it was Mona. Somehow, she'd convinced the Emperor to allow her to come and see him.

Hal knew in the back of his mind it might be a trap. She could have been turned against him, and he replayed her imperceptible glance from the dais over again for the thousandth time since he was thrown in the cell two days ago.

He had to be sure. The time had come to play his hand, and his wife had to be a willing participant or the rescue would never work.

"Mona." Hal's voice cracked from disuse, and he tried to clear his parched throat before continuing. "I wasn't sure you ever wanted to see me again."

"I heard the Emperor planned to pass down his decision on what to do with you soon. I asked for the opportunity to speak with you and bring you over to our side."

Hal winced at the words "our side." He wondered again if he was wrong about what he remembered seeing. He needed to have a frank and private conversation with his wife, and there was no doubt this discussion had eavesdroppers. It was time to test a theory about the magical shackles binding his wrists and ankles. The runes inscribed on the metal were meant to inhibit the casting of magic.

By default, that included all four traditional schools of magic: ice, earth, fire, and wind.

Did it also include the mysterious school of spirit magic? He was about to find out.

"Please come in and sit." Hal lifted his shackled hands where they were chained to the wall. "Forgive me if I don't stand."

Mona moved closer and Hal's eyes adjusted to the light from the lantern she carried. She set the lantern down on the floor and sat on a stone bench jutting out from the wall. Hal closed his eyes and focused on the room and the doorway to the dungeon where the guard stood with his back to the door. Instead of drawing on one of the four basic magical elements, Hal instead reached out for the previously untapped spirit magic. He wasn't sure what he was doing, but he had to try something.

The magical energy met resistance, but Hal persisted and pushed at the tenuous barrier. An instant later, he was rewarded for his efforts as the barrier melted away, dispelled by his spirit magic. Hal's magic flowed outward without impediment, sealing the room in a bubble of silence. With the success of his spell, he saw several notifications flash across his vision.

Spell learned — Dispel magic.
   All five Elemental Schools have been mastered.
   Thief and Warrior skills reactivated.

Not only could Hal and Mona speak in peace without being over-heard, but now that his other abilities had returned to him, he was almost ready to set the rest of his plan in motion.

Mona noticed the sudden lack of sound coming from outside the cell. The bubble worked in both directions, and she looked at Hal, tilting her head in a quizzical expression.

"We can't hear anything outside this room, and no one can hear us from out there. I figure we only have a limited time before someone checks on why they can't hear us talking. Come over here and sit next to me. We have to make it look like we weren't talking on purpose."

"This is the first time we've been able to talk for months and you want me to cuddle you?"

"There's no time to argue, and I have to fill you in on the plan to get you and Cari out of here. Come here and make it look like we're embracing. That'll alleviate suspicion, at least for a little while."

Mona's eyes flashed with anger, but she got up and came over. Sitting on the bench next to where Hal was bound to the wall, she slipped a hand around his shoulders and leaned against him.

The fragrance of her hair and touch of her skin were too much for him. It was a moment of bliss in the midst of a horrible situation, and the flood of emotions caught Hal unprepared. Tears flowed down his face as he struggled to hold back sobs.

"How's Cari? I was able to scry into the palace twice and see you on two occasions, but I never saw her."

"She's well. The Emperor assigned me a nanny who keeps Cari away from me most of the time. I only get to see her in the evenings when I return to our bedchambers. It is his way of controlling me."

"So, you're not taking his side?" Hal blurted. "Thank God."

"Of course not. He's a monster. The things I've seen him do or order done are horrifying. But what else am I to do? He brought us here, tearing us out of our home and into this strange, distant land. Then he tells me you've been coming here for some time and never told me."

"It's a long story, Mona. I wasn't sure it was real at first, and the second time I came was on my trip to the leadership retreat. There was no time to tell you about it until I came home, and they'd kidnapped you before I could. Time works differently here, so weeks and months pass in Fantasma when only hours or days pass at home. I came after you as soon as I found out you were missing."

"But the Emperor said you've been here for over two months. Why has it taken you so long to come for us?"

"I had to level up before I was strong enough to confront him."

"Level up? Like in a game?" Mona's voice rose in anger. "This is real life, Hal, not one of your stupid computer games."

"Maybe it's sort of both. Have you noticed anything strange since you've been here? Seen or heard things or words that weren't there?"

Mona tilted her head to one side and nodded.

"I thought it had something to do with the magic they use here. It made me think I was going crazy at first. Now, I just ignore the notes and messages."

"The reason people from our world, Earth, can see and hear those things is because the interface between the two places is built upon the *Fantasma* game back home. A magic user named Tildi created it in hopes someone like me would come here and be some sort of mythical hero. You, and I suppose Cari, too, have the same abilities."

"This is crazy, Hal. You know that?"

"I know it took me a while to realize I wasn't inside my game and going insane. Once I realized this was all real, though, it began to make sense, sort of."

The guard at the door glanced over his shoulder and leered at the two of them. They didn't have much time.

"Mona, you have to listen to me. They're going to come and make you leave soon, and I have to tell you my plan to get us all out of here."

"How are you going to do that, Hal? You're shackled to the wall with iron chains."

"The same way I made the room silent. The same way I dispelled the magic on these shackles. I have abilities no one else has. I suspect you do as well if you start paying attention to the messages you've been ignoring. Now listen. The anniversary of the Emperor's coronation is in two days. The plan to rescue you hinges on that event. Knowing what I do about him, I suspect he's going to make a spectacle of my execution at that time and then keep you and Cari here to learn how to level up like I did. You need to be ready to get Cari and escape with my friends even if I don't survive."

"You're planning to die now, Hal? How is that going to help Cari and I get away?"

"Shhh. I'm not planning on dying, but I also don't know if I can do everything fast enough to avoid getting killed before help arrives. All I do know is when that help comes, find a woman named Kay. She'll be leading the charge. Find her. She'll protect you, take you both away from here, and try and get you home."

The guard turned again and started into the room. Hal let the silencing bubble of spirit magic dissipate as he entered the room and then leaned forward to kiss Mona.

"Alright, you two, enough of that. I let you have your fun, but now it's time to go."

The guard grabbed Mona by the arm and pulled her up and away from Hal.

"Mona, tell me you've got this."

She stared at him, her eyes boring into him. If they got out of this alive, he knew he was going to hear more about how she felt.

"Yeah, Hal, I've got this."

Mona wheeled around, pulling her arm free of the guard's grimy hand. She slipped him a coin of some sort, and he smiled and nodded. Then she was gone, and the door closed, encasing him in blackness again. He didn't need to sit in darkness anymore, though. Hal enabled his dark vision thief ability, so he could see the room, and began to plan for what was to come in two days.

CHAPTER 37

HAL SHUFFLED between two huge imperial guards in full armor, once again heading towards the dais in the Emperor's audience chamber. This time, it was to receive his sentence for rebellion against the Empire. The Emperor had decided he didn't need Hal, something for which Hal had planned. He had no doubts as to what that sentence was to be.

This was the moment of truth, Hal knew. This was going to decide not only if he survived to get out of here but if he could manage to free Mona and Cari from their captivity. He reviewed the things he had to do when the time came to act. He kept his head down and his hands clasped in front of him, trying to appear submissive as he walked the length of the audience hall.

Emperor Kang wanted a show. He'd ordered the audience hall filled with nobles, visiting dignitaries, and leading bureaucrats in the capital. Now they all watched as Hal Dix, the man who'd been stirring up all the trouble to the west, was brought before the Emperor to receive judgment for his crimes.

Given the number of people and guards in the room, Hal decided this was going to be a more significant challenge than he'd planned.

He thought it would be the empty room as before, with only about twenty guards and another ten sycophants clustered around the Emperor. This unexpected situation required some changes to adapt the plan to fit the circumstances.

Hal shifted his hands inside the metal cuffs on his wrists and tried to hide the rivets holding the shackles closed. If anyone inspected them closely, they'd see how they'd been cut almost all the way through as if by a blowtorch.

Once Hal had used his command of spirit magic to dispel the magic cast on his metal bonds, it had been easy to use a focused jet of high-intensity heated plasma from his forefinger to cut through the metal on each cuff.

He'd repeated the process on the shackles wrapped around his ankles. If he calculated correctly, Hal should be able to break free with only a sharp jerk against his bonds. All that depended on the condition of the shackles escaping notice from the guards.

He was almost to the dais when he raised his eyes and saw Mona standing there, holding Cari in her arms. The two-year-old looked older than the last time he'd seen her. Kids her age grew so fast, and two months could seem like forever.

Seeing his daughter for the first time since he'd come back to Fantasma brought tears to his eyes. Blinking them away sent a few streaming down his cheeks. This produced a snort of laughter from the Emperor. No doubt he thought Hal was crying out of fear. Hal wished he could wipe the damp trails of his tears from his face, but he couldn't lift his hands high enough, at least not yet.

One of the guards flanking him tugged on the chain attached to Hal's wrists, halting his forward movement. He was about ten feet from the Emperor, ten feet from Mona and Cari. That was a long way when bare seconds counted the distance between success and failure.

Hal tensed his forearms as he prepared to make his move. It was all about the timing for maximum effectiveness and surprise now.

"Greetings, Hal Dix." The Emperor announced his full name as if everyone in the chamber had no idea who His Majesty held captive before him.

Hal didn't bow this time. Instead, he held his head high and met Kang's gaze, matching him stare for stare.

"Hello to you, too."

"I trust you enjoyed your accommodations while staying here in the palace the last few days?"

The question brought titters and chuckles from the people assembled around the room. They all knew the Emperor had kept Hal in the dungeon's dank cells below the palace.

"They were adequate for what I needed to do."

Kang scowled. He didn't like that answer. It was clear Hal wasn't acting the way he was supposed to. He wasn't the cowed, condemned prisoner, waiting for his death sentence.

"Insolence at this time will not get you any leniency, you fool. Did you think you could stand here and defy me in my house?"

"It's not technically your house, now is it? I mean, you stole it from the previous owners. That makes you a thief and a murderer, not a king and an emperor."

Kang bolted to his feet, pushing two of his concubines away from where they sat at the base of the throne.

"How dare you! You think you can cast doubt on my claim to the throne here in the presence of my loyal subjects? Do you forget I hold your wife and daughter as my hostages?"

"No, I do not forget. They are the reason I came here, so I could stand before you and face you one on one. One of us is not going to survive the day."

"Now you threaten me, too." Kang laughed aloud. "I am tired of this false bravado, Hal Dix. Guards, make him kneel so I might pass down my verdict and sentence him for his crimes."

One of the guards kicked Hal's leg with a steel-toed boot, knocking him down to his knees. He almost fell over but managed to remain upright in the new position. Hal decided those two guards would be the first to go.

"Hal Dix, you have fomented rebellion across the western provinces, raised an army against my lawful rule, and assassinated the Wardens set to represent me around the Empire. For these crimes and more, you must die the death of a traitor. Know as well that I will use what I've learned about you and your origins to take power from your wife and child to use as my own. When I am finished, they will be empty, lifeless husks, and I will be the most powerful ruler Fantasma has ever seen."

As the Emperor spoke, two other guards stepped up behind Mona and grabbed her arms, securing her. Another snatched Cari from her arms, making Hal's daughter cry out and begin to sob while calling for her mother. Alarm and fear flashed in Mona's eyes, stoking Hal's anger to white-hot intensity.

"You're a fool, Kang," Hal hissed through gritted teeth. "Your arrogance leads to your downfall. I would have enjoyed killing you, but alas, I promised that task to another."

The slot machine in Hal's head clattered to life, its wheels spinning the chances of his luck. It was louder than ever before.

Time to press his luck one more time.

Kang's eyes widened, his mouth hanging open at Hal's brazenness in the face of his death sentence and all arrayed against him.

With the Emperor speechless, and stunned shock passing through the room at the condemned man's words, Hal decided it was time.

He closed his eyes and drew on all his magical energy, readying the spells he'd need to pull this off. A note of alarm sounded from a cluster of mages near the dais.

"Impossible, he's drawing in energy. He can access his magic. Stop him!"

Hal clenched his fists and snapped his forearms away from each other. The force broke the remaining metal holding his wrist shackles, dropping them to the floor.

Leaping to his feet, Hal kicked outward at the guard to his right, caught the man by surprise, and knocked him clattering to the floor.

The kick also served to snap the leg shackles off, freeing him completely to engage his enemies.

The imperial guard on his left drew his sword and prepared to hack the unarmed prisoner down.

He never got the chance.

Hal loosed a spell, and an ice dart drove up into the unarmored chin of the guard, stabbing into his brain. The man collapsed in a heap on the floor.

3,000 experience points awarded.

After scooping up the sword, Hal manifested his ice armor and shield and charged toward the throne in a feint. The guards there formed around the Emperor rather than coming to engage him, allowing Hal to shift his focus to the cluster of eight mages, including Decimus.

Each of the magic users had begun casting magic of their own. Hal had to act fast. He'd only used this spell once before, so he wasn't sure if it would work, but he didn't have time to think about it.

Using a variation of the dispel magic spell he'd used on the enchanted shackles, Hal cast an invisible, anti-magic bubble around the imperial spellcasters. *Nice of them to stay together in a group like that.*

Hal's spell was rewarded by the looks of consternation on their faces when all their magic failed simultaneously. He hoped it took them a while to figure out why their spells weren't working. The area of anti-magic was static in that location. All it would take would be for one of them to move out of the bubble.

Hal turned back toward the dais, pointed off to one side, and focused all his spirit energy, while casting the wind spell to open a portal. The plan had been to get inside the wards around the Crystal

City where they would be weaker. In theory, the spirit magic would pierce the outer barrier and allow one gigantic portal spell to work.

That was a lot of ifs.

A chime in his head alerted Hal the slot machine had stopped.

His luck held.

The portal opened wide to the left of the dais. Armed soldiers rushed through, led by Kay, Anders, and Otto. Rune and Junica charged out just behind them, then the rush of soldiers became a torrent.

Hal held the portal open, knowing he couldn't let it go until everyone was through, even though it left him defenseless.

"Kill him!" Kang shouted.

Three guards charged at Hal from where they stood along the walls. Others rushed to stem the tide of rebels flooding into the audience chamber.

Hal allowed himself a trickle of energy to beef up his ice armor, but that was all he could do to meet the coming attacks. He had to maintain his focus on the portal.

The first guard to reach him hammered at his back with his sword. The blow nearly took Hal down, but he somehow remained on his feet.

Health damage: Health -12

He steeled himself for the next blows to fall as the other two guards reached him and the first guard prepared to strike again. An arrow whizzed by Hal's face and took the first guard in the eye, pitching him over backward with the force of the recurve bow in Junica's hands.

A blurred form in yellow robes met the other two. Hardened hands and feet snapped out, first disarming and then disabling the two remaining guards coming at Hal.

The blur stopped moving, taking a guarding stance. Rune smiled at him while Hal shook his head. The bald, eastern monk wasn't even breathing hard after that display of martial prowess and explosive force.

Junica ran over to join Rune, taking up a station on Hal's opposite side, another arrow nocked as she prepared to defend him while he held the portal open.

Hal kept it in place for thirty seconds longer. Then the doorway snapped shut, the spell's energy spent. It cut off the flow of men and women from the rebel army outside the city's wards. It had been enough, though. Several hundred rebel knights and soldiers spread out, engaging the imperial forces charging forward to protect the Emperor.

Theran was there and fired off a series of fire spells at the open doors into the audience chamber. The explosions cut off more imperial reinforcements trying to enter the room.

A shout to his left drew Hal's attention. The Emperor, inside a ring of guards, was being hustled away toward a side door. The group dragged Mona and Cari along with them.

"Finish the mages," Hal told Rune and Junica, pointing to the cluster of magic users nearby. "The spell stopping their magic will fail soon."

Both turned to assault the imperial mages, joined by Theran and Otto. As he ran by, the fire mage tossed Hal his staff.

Hal grabbed the staff from the air then took off after the retreating Emperor. Kay and Anders also pursued the retreating cluster of guards. All would be lost if the Emperor managed to get away.

They almost caught up with Kang in time.

The Emperor and those holding Mona and Cari backed away and disappeared through a side door, leaving behind five of the imperial guards. All were highly trained and prepared to die to protect their ruler.

Hal pulled up short and leveled his staff. He fired a blast of hail at the nearest of the guards. Two of them went down as hardened, fist-sized ice balls slammed into their armored forms, leaving them in twin piles of dented, bloody metal on the floor.

3,000 experience points awarded.

3,000 experience points awarded.

Kay and Anders charged toward the other three guards. Hal ran in right behind them.

Hal used his ice shield to bash into his opponent, knocking the guard's shield to one side and stunning him. Spinning his staff one-handed over his head, Hal brought the enhanced wooden shaft down on the guard's helmet, denting in the cheek plate and eliciting a grunt of pain.

The guard countered with a slashing attack that chipped away at Hal's shoulder armor.

Health damage: Health -14

Hal didn't have time to deal with this guard. Kang was escaping with his wife and daughter. Growling deep in his throat, he released a series of vicious combined attacks on the guard, which utilized both his magic and weapons together.

Bringing his shield up to fend off the barrage of ice darts and fire jets, the guard blocked his vision enough to allow Hal a break in the follow-up attacks from the guard. Noting his opportunity, Hal swung the staff low, struck the guard in the ankles, and took his legs out from under him.

"Sweep the leg!" Hal shouted.

He spun the staff overhead once, twice, then brought it down, butt first into the guard's unprotected face. The crunch of his facial bones cracking like an egg reverberated up the staff. The supine guard spasmed one time and was still.

3,000 experience points awarded.

Kay finished her opponent, too. She turned to help Anders, who'd drawn the officer of the imperial guard as his opponent. They were soon all three tied up in a blazing duel of swordplay.

Kay spared a single glance Hal's way.

"Go! Get your family before it's too late."

Hal didn't have to be told twice. He reached down and scooped up the guard's sword, then dashed through the door and down the hallway on the other side, with his staff in one hand and the borrowed blade in the other.

The hallway ended in stairs heading up.

A voice echoed down from above, followed by a scream.

Hal took the stairs two at a time. In the back of his mind, he knew this exposed him to attack at every turn in the staircase.

He didn't care.

He had to reach Mona and Cari before it was too late.

The hair on the back of his neck stood on end. His battle prescience warrior ability gave him a warning. On pure instinct, Hal dove for the floor of the next landing as soon as he reached it. A double-bladed axe whistled past his head just before he hit the floor.

Diving to the landing drove the air from his lungs with a whoosh. Knowing he had to keep moving despite the pain of trying to draw in a breath with collapsed lungs, Hal rolled over to the left. The axe slammed down into his shoulder rather than his back. It didn't kill him, but it still hurt.

Health damage: Health -12

Gasping to catch his breath, Hal continued rolling onto his back and raised his staff to deflect the next blow from the axe.

The axe's blade skittered down the staff's shaft and hit the flagstone floor with a shower of sparks. Hal got his first look at the wielder. The wild, hairy, half-orc standing over him pulled the axe back up past his shoulder for another strike.

Hal raised his sword and lunged upward with all his strength.

The blade took the guard in the gut and slit it open sideways, spilling intestines out on the floor. The half-orc dropped the axe, clutched his opened belly, and slumped to the floor.

4,000 experience points awarded.

Hal jumped to his feet and started up the stairs again. The initial sprint and the fight on the landing had winded him, and he moved slower up the next flight of stairs while he tried to catch his breath.

That was when the glass ball rolled down the stone risers from above and broke open two steps above his.

The blast of the fiery explosion knocked him back down to the landing, wrapping him in flames.

Hal managed to cast his resist fire spell but not before he'd been burned across his face, chest, and arms.

Health damage: Health -25

A quick check of his health status showed him he was in bad shape.

Health: 22/155

Groaning at the agony of the burns on his face, and with the taste and smell of burned flesh in his nostrils, Hal rolled over and got back on his feet. The pain was so intense he couldn't concentrate on his chakra healing when he tried. In the end, he was only able to heal up nine points' worth that way.

Knowing he didn't have the time to cast any healing magic, Hal pushed through the pain and headed back up the steps. This time, he readied an ice shield spell that was large enough to block the stairs if another magic grenade came bouncing down at him.

He heard the glass globe before he saw it.

Hal cast the ice wall just before the globe burst. This time, the explosion splashed against the wall of ice. It melted about half of the frozen, foot-thick barrier before burning out. The ice melt helped to douse the flames.

Dispelling the ice into mist with a wave of his hand, Hal prepped a fireball to return the blast if he ever caught up with the mage dropping the strange spell grenades down on him.

After rounding the last bend in the staircase, Hal burst onto a flat roof surrounded by crenelated battlements looming up like teeth growing from the parapet.

He spotted Mona and the Emperor, who held Cari in his arms. At the same time, two crossbow bolts slammed into Hal's shoulder and chest. The bolt striking his chest shattered the remainder of his ice armor, and the strike to his shoulder pinned him back against the wooden door jamb as the missile traveled all the way through his arm into the wood behind him.

Health damage: Health -5
Health damage: Health -10

A warning message flashed up, showing his current health status in red.

Health: 16/155

Despite the pain, Hal pulled at his pinned shoulder and tried to dislodge himself from the wall. He had to get free. He had to get to Mona and Cari.

Kang's laughter filtered through Hal's pain and rage.

"Look at Tildi's mythical Opponent now. Not so dangerous, are you?"

"Let Hal go, Kang," Mona pleaded. "If you do, I'll agree to stay here with you. That is what you want, isn't it? You said you envied Hal's life, our life. You can have it if you want."

"My dear, you don't give your husband the credit he deserves. He would never settle for that. He would keep coming after you until he either succeeded or died. Tell her I'm right, Hal."

"I'm going to kill you, Kang. I once promised your life to someone else, but I think, under the circumstances, she'll understand."

"See, Mona, he will never stop coming after you or me."

The Emperor looked at the two remaining guardsmen and pointed to Hal. "Finish him."

Everything happened at once as Hal tugged at his trapped shoulder in a desperate attempt to free himself.

The two guards advanced on Hal with swords raised. The Emperor held Cari up, so she could see her father die. The toddler started crying, as did Mona.

Hal cringed as the two sword-wielding guards pulled back their blades for the killing thrusts at his chest.

It couldn't end this way. He had to free himself.

There had to be a way. There was no such thing as a no-win situation, no such thing as a true Kobayashi Maru scenario.

Then he saw it.

The swords swung forward, and Hal focused all his remaining magical energy, hoping his practice in Tildi's canyon paid off.

Kang's laugher choked off in a sputtering cry of agony.

The Emperor stared down at the two sword blades sticking out of his chest from behind, then at the small shimmering disc of a portal in front of Hal's chest.

The two guards stared at their swords where they disappeared into the portal. It took them a moment to realize their blades had thrust into their Emperor's chest rather than Hal's. They released their grips on the hilts at the same time the Emperor stumbled forward on the other side of the roof, yanking the blades from their grasp the rest of the way through the portal.

Hal let the portal snap shut and slumped against the wall, held up only by the crossbow bolt pinning him in place. The two guards forgot about him as they watched their lord and master's life slip away around their sword blades. They exchanged a glance and bolted for the stairs.

"Give me my baby, you monster," Mona screamed.

Hal opened his eyes long enough to see his wife snatch Cari from the Emperor's arms. Once she had the crying child, Mona leaned back and leveled a kick at Kang's stomach, knocking him backward, his arms windmilling for balance as he neared the edge of the parapet.

Kay and Anders burst from the stairs just in time to see Kang topple over the edge and fall screaming from the roof of the palace to the paved courtyard below.

Quest completed: Rescue Mona and Cari.

35,000 experience points awarded.

Hal's last memories of the palace roof included Anders wrenching the bolt free of his shoulder, liberating him from the wall, while Kay and Mona lowered him to the rooftop.

He smiled up at them, then drifted away as darkness closed in.

CHAPTER 38

"HOLD STILL, Hal. You need to look your best for the coronation."

Mona tugged at his white linen shirt where it peeked out from under his cloak and adjusted the ornate chain draped around his neck so it didn't pull at the sling securing his injured shoulder. At the end of the chain was a golden starburst medallion, the symbol of a prince of the realm.

"I always wanted to marry a prince," she said as she fussed over him. A tiara of her own sat perched in her blonde curls. "It turns out I was married to one all along and didn't know it."

"I'm still angry with Kay for making this her first official act as Empress upon her coronation. I don't want to be royalty; I just want to take you and Cari home."

"Tildi explained that to you, Hal. You have to rest before you can open a portal of that distance. Besides, I kind of like it here, for a little while at least. Let's enjoy our time here for a few days longer."

Mona smoothed the ornate silk dress she wore. It fit her well and he knew how much Mona liked her fancy clothes at home. This was no different.

"Plus, Hal. If you're declared a prince, that makes both Cari and me princesses, right?"

The maid sat on the floor playing with Cari, stacking blocks and watching the toddler knock them down. The two-year-old looked up at the mention of her name and smiled at her parents.

Hal wondered if she'd bear any memory of this place when she was grown or even be aware that somewhere, in another world, she was royalty.

Cari didn't seem to care either way. She returned her attention to the stack of blocks before her and swung an arm, knocking them down, giggling with glee as the wooden cubes fell to the carpeted floor.

"It must be nice to be a child without a care in the world; maybe we should bring her with us to the coronation?" Hal asked his wife.

"Nonsense. Marta has her. I'm looking forward to the whole affair, especially the ball afterward. Now, come on. We're going to be late if we don't hurry."

Hal spared one last glance at Cari and the maid, then followed his wife from their palace apartments.

Their escort waited for them outside, the guards falling in behind them as they walked towards the grand audience hall. It didn't take them long. Their apartments were close to Kay's in the royal wing of the palace.

The buzz of all the voices, along with the music from the orchestra, reached Hal's ears before they got to the double doors leading to the hall. After turning the corner with Mona on his arm, Hal waited for the chamberlain to announce them to the throngs of nobles and dignitaries attending the coronation of Empress Kareena I. Some were already calling her Kareena the Great for her exploits that had brought the throne back to her family.

The chamberlain stomped the butt of his staff of office on the marble floor, drawing all eyes in the room to the entrance.

"His Royal Highness, Protector of the Realm, Prince Hal Dix and his wife, Princess Mona."

A rousing cheer went up across the hall. The rush of warmth to Hal's face told him he was blushing. He didn't care. Mona was right.

He'd earned this. They all had. He let a big, toothy grin spread across his face as he led Mona down the broad aisle to their places of honor at the front of the room.

The ushers seated them next to Duke Korran and his wife. They both nodded their greetings, as did the three remaining arch mages, Theran, Bronwynn, and Tildi.

Sadly, Ragnar had been discovered in the palace dungeon, dead for several days from wounds suffered at the hands of the Emperor's jailers. Hal was still upset about it. He'd be unable to thank the ice mage for his help in completing his quest to save his family.

Chimes sounded from the back of the hall, drawing everyone's attention to the grand entrance. Hal saw Kay, dressed in regal robes of crimson and gold. Anders accompanied her, escorting his betrothed down the length of the grand hall until they reached the front and the altar erected there for the coronation.

An aged bishop stood waiting at the altar, flanked by several priests and a dozen of Kay's official bodyguards, the newly named Empress's Own Dragoons. Hal recognized several of the dragoon troopers, from their trip through the Vale of the Morning Sun, among the honor guard. He gave a quick nod to the newly promoted Commander Madry, who gave a salute in return.

Kay knelt on a red velvet cushion and bowed her head while the Bishop spoke words of prayer and encouragement for her to live long and rule well. He then lowered the jeweled crown of the Empire onto her head.

"Stand, Kareena the First, Empress of the Realm, Protector of the People, Defender of the Western Reaches."

Kay stood and turned in place, maids rushing forward to pull the train of her long coronation robe so it lay spread out behind her. The newly crowned Empress looked out over her subjects, and another cheer rose from those assembled, Hal included.

He couldn't believe this was the same young woman he'd first met in a jail cell all those long months ago, indeed years ago to the residents of this world. Now she turned out to be the ruler of everything.

The crazy events leading them here were almost too fantastic to be credible, if he hadn't lived it for himself.

Kay waited for the crowds' cheering to die down and raised a hand for silence.

"Prince Hal Dix, step forward."

Feeling nerves flutter up from his gut, Hal advanced to stand before his companion and comrade in arms. She had a beaming smile on her face.

"Prince Hal, you have demonstrated great loyalty to myself and to the Empire in its time of greatest need. For that reason, we bestow upon you and your family, in perpetuity, the title of Princes and Princesses of the Western Reaches and Champion of the Crown. These titles will rest with you and yours for all time. Do you accept this bequest?"

Hal cleared his throat after his first answer ended in a coughing croak rather than words.

"I do, Your Majesty, and on behalf of my family, we thank you for the honor."

"It is well deserved. Kneel so we may bestow the imperial blessing and crown that is now yours."

Hal dropped to his knees on the red velvet pillow placed in front of him for the purpose. Kay lowered a thin golden circlet on his head and laid a hand on it.

"I bestow the blessings of our throne on you, Hal Dix, knowing that, should I have need, you will be our champion as your office requires."

"I accept."

Hal's voice was loud and clear this time. As he spoke, the slots in his head rattled for a few seconds then chimed as his luck inexplicably engaged. He saw no manifestation of it and mentally shrugged. He never managed to master how his strange luck worked here in Fantasma. In the end, he'd found he made his own luck with quick wits and preparation.

He rose to his feet, bowed to the Empress, and then returned to his seat beside Mona. She took his hand and squeezed it. Next to Mona, out of the corner of his eye, Hal saw Tildi nodding, as if satisfied with everything. She'd set all this in motion, after all.

Hal wondered what his life would be like if he'd never met that strange little woman in the flea market stall. It all seemed so long ago, part of another life to which he wanted to return. Despite all the adventure and excitement, Hal longed for some parts of his normal life.

He was ready to go home.

CHAPTER 39

Two Fantasma years after the coronation ceremony, Hal stood in the private courtyard of the royal apartments. Mona was by his side, their daughter Cari standing at her mother's feet, swinging a child-sized practice blade in broad arcs. Kay, Anders, and Tildi stood across from them.

"Must you go back forever, Hal," Kay said. "You, Mona, and Cari have become like family to us."

"It's been wonderful to visit here every weekend for the last six months at home, but people are starting to notice back on Earth. Cari is the problem. She's only supposed to be two years old, but she is now almost four because of the time differential here in Fantasma. Mona's mother has started asking awkward questions about her granddaughter's amazing growth and maturity, along with how she talks about her imaginary friends. Mona and I think it's time for us to return for good."

"You could stay here permanently, Hal," Anders said. "Kareena could use your counsel. She is still trying to put the Empire back together and bring the few rebellious generals Kang left behind to heel."

Hal shook his head. "It's time for me to return, for all of us to go home for good, Kay. This is your world, not mine. The companions who remain will be good councilors to bolster your rule."

The Empress of Fantasma gave a rueful smile and nodded. Hal had already had this conversation with her several times over the last week. He'd told her he wouldn't change his mind.

"You and your family will always have a place here in Fantasma, Hal, should you ever find your way back."

"Thank you. If I return someday, I'll make sure to stop by and take you up on the offer of hospitality."

"If you don't, I'll put a warrant out for your arrest, Hal Dix."

Hal laughed. He knew she wasn't kidding.

Mona stepped up and hugged Kay. "Hal and I will be forever grateful for the way you've welcomed us into your home, Kay. We don't take our departure lightly. Hal has been asked to join the executive board of his company, a great honor. He will have to devote more time and energy to his career and won't have the time to come here on the weekends anymore."

"I understand the burden of commitment, Mona. It would still be nice to see you and Cari once in a while, though. It's like she's my own daughter."

Mona pointed to the rounded bulge of pregnancy showing through Kay's dress. "You'll have your own child soon enough."

"True, but my children could use a big sister and protector, too."

Mona shook her head.

"It is time for Cari to grow up without the confusion of having two worlds in which to live. We've decided she must forget about Fantasma for now."

"That makes me sad, Mona," Kay said. "I would like to think she'll have fond memories of her time here."

"Too many people don't understand why she talks the way she does. Soon, she'll pass the time where she should have imaginary friends and believe in magic and princesses. When that happens, people at home will not understand why she insists it is all real. It is better to make a clean break."

Kay nodded but didn't seem happy about it.

"Let's go home, Mona," Hal said. "I'm ready if you are."

Mona smiled and picked up Cari, still clutching the wooden practice sword to which she'd become attached.

"Me, too."

"Farewell, Hal Dix. Farewell, Mona," Kay called as Hal opened the portal back to Earth for the last time. Hal waved once and followed Mona and Cari through the gateway home.

Hal turned to call back through the portal in return, but as he stepped through, the magic doorway to Fantasma closed with a pop before he could get the words out. He swallowed his disappointment and turned back to Mona and Cari.

They'd returned home for the final time. Their fantastical times in Fantasma were over for good. Hal would miss his friends in Fantasma, but this was where he belonged. He'd had enough adventure for one lifetime. So had his wife and daughter. It was time to build on his successful life and apply the lessons learned in Fantasma to his time on Earth.

Level Up!

———

The portal closed, and Kay turned to Tildi.

"I really hoped they'd opt to remain here."

"He was never of this world, Your Majesty. That was the secret of his power and ability. In the end, he had to go back to his own place and time."

"But what if we have need of him again?" Anders asked.

"I have prepared for that eventuality. The prophecy does allow for the Opponent's return, at least it doesn't say he cannot come back to us."

Tildi pulled a small rectangular box from beneath her robes with both hands and handed it to the Empress.

Kay accepted the wooden box, covered in ornate carvings of mystical runes, inlaid with gold and mother-of-pearl. After releasing the latch, she opened the lid to reveal an ovoid object resting on black velvet inside. It was gray with a transparent layer stretched over the top of the base material. The top layer was made of a strange substance Kareena had never seen before. At one end of the object were two, rectangular buttons.

"This must only be invoked in your hour of greatest need, for it can only be used once."

"What does it do?"

"It will send a message across time and space, summoning the Opponent to return to Fantasma. I must warn you, it is not foolproof, and the magic to enable it is unstable at best. It is an artifact of great power, and even I am unsure of how it works in this instance. Only use it when you have no other option."

Kay picked up the object. It fit against her palm as if made to rest there, with her finger over the two buttons.

"What's it called?"

Tildi chuckled. "I have no idea why, but it is called a mouse."

The End

Continue the saga with the *Accidental Duelist*. Book 1 of the Accidental Champion trilogy.

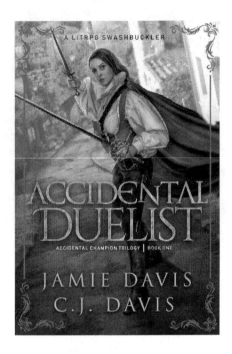

Blue and Gray Angel

—

The Broken Throne Series

The Charm Runner

Prophecy's Daughter

The Queen of Avalon

Stolen Destiny

The Mended Throne

—

Follow on Facebook for updates, news, and upcoming book excerpts

Facebook.com/jamiedavisbooks

—

To learn more about LitRPG and GameLit books and have discussions with other readers and authors, check out the RPG GameLit Society and GameLit Society Facebook groups.

We Need Your Help ...

Without reviews indie books like this one are almost impossible to market.

Leaving a review will only take a minute — it doesn't have to be long or involved, just a sentence or two that tells people what you liked about the book, to help other readers know why they might like it, too. It also helps us write more of what you love.

The truth is, VERY few readers leave reviews. Please help us out by being the exception.

Thank you in advance!

Jamie Davis
    C.J. Davis

ABOUT THE AUTHOR

Jamie Davis, RN, NRP, B.A., A.S., host of the MedicCast Podcast and Nursing Show (NursingShow.com) is a nationally recognized medical and nursing educator who began educating new emergency responders as a training officer for his local EMS program. His programs and resources have been downloaded over 6 million times by listeners and viewers.

Jamie lives and writes at his home in Maryland. He lives in the woods with his wife, three children, and a dog.

C.J. Davis is an IT professional, an avid gamer, and a collector of all things geeky. He lives and works in Maryland with his fiancé.

Follow Jamie Online
www.jamiedavisbooks.com